STEP BY STEP 聽懂CNN™

全新增修版

Master Listening with CNN News

STEP BY STEP 聽懂 CNN
Master Listening with CNN News
全新增修版

發 行 人	鄭俊琪
總 編 輯	陳豫弘．王琳詔
責任編輯	璩雅琪．林怡君．周盈秀
校　對	廖慧雯．張玉芬．卓君威
特約作者	Kate Weaver
英文編輯	Doug Nienhuis．Eric Hansen．Joseph Schier
英文錄音	Eric Hansen．Heather Brown
封面設計	李尚竹
美術編輯	郭丁元．李海瑄
特約美編	高文娟．李偉雅
技術總監	李志純
程式設計	李志純．郭曉琪
光碟製作	姜尹涵．李宛晏．翁子雲
出版發行	希伯崙股份有限公司
	105 台北市松山區八德路三段 32 號 12 樓
	劃撥：1939-5400
	電話：（02）2578-7838　傳真：（02）2578-5800
	電子郵件：Service@LiveABC.com
法律顧問	朋博法律事務所
印　刷	禹利電子分色有限公司
出版日期	民國 96 年 7 月　初版一刷
	民國 99 年 9 月　初版十一刷
	民國 100 年 5 月　再版一刷
	民國 101 年 7 月　再版四刷

STEP BY STEP 聽懂CNN™

全新增修版

Master Listening with CNN News

收聽國際英語新聞是與國際接軌、掌握時事脈動最好的方式之一，然而許多人對於收看英語新聞或收聽英語廣播視為畏途。事實上只要掌握一些聽力訣竅，要聽懂英語新聞就指日可待。本書藉由多元的 CNN（美國有線電視新聞網）新聞，告訴你如何克服聽懂英語新聞的障礙。

CNN 是最具國際知名度的新聞媒體之一，除了美國籍的新聞記者外，亦派駐許多當地的特派記者，雖然皆以英語來播報新聞，但各地不同的口音常讓許多母語不是英語的人更難以掌握新聞內容。不過在本書中則主要摘錄美語與英語口音播報的新聞，只要你掌握了聽懂 CNN 的訣竅，要進一步聽懂其他不同口音的新聞，也就會容易得多。

本書內容分為【聽力技巧篇】、【基礎訓練篇】以及【實戰應用篇】三個部分。【聽力技巧篇】中概略介紹了口說英語中常見的發音現象，包括：連音、同化音、省略音等，以及重讀、弱化音、美語和英語發音的差異等等。由於語言中的聽、說能力往往相輔相成，因此了解口說特色，除了能幫你提升口說能力，也有助於提升聽力理解力。無論是平常的英語會話，或是聆聽英語演講、收看英語新聞，這些特色與訣竅都能派得上用場。

接下來的【基礎訓練篇】則節錄了二十八篇 CNN 新聞，逐句說明所應用的發音規則，你可以依照我們所建議的步驟來做練習，藉由不斷反覆聆聽、驗證，熟悉英語的音調、節奏，並體會所謂的連音、同化音、省略音、重讀、弱化等各種發音技巧。

【實戰應用篇】分為 Part I、Part II 兩部分，共收錄三十二篇完整的 CNN 新聞，涵蓋政治、財經、科技、體育、生活、娛樂等題材，提供讀者多元的聽力素材。Part I 與 Part II 的差別在於前者的新聞主題普遍較不陌生，口音也較容易理解。事實上在所選錄的新聞當中，每個主播或特派員都各有其播報的風格，口音、腔調也有所差別，這些都可能是影響英文聽力的因素。不過只要循序漸進，反覆聽讀，自然就能掌握聽懂 CNN 新聞的技巧。另外，你也可利用書上所列的關鍵字彙、發音提示等作為聽力輔助工具，並試著作答書中所附的聽力測驗題目，來驗收自己聽力的成果，而新聞內容中所附的 Notes & Vocabulary 則能加強你的英文字詞能力。

本書內文採中英對照，方便讀者迅速掌握每則新聞的內容。另外，主播或特派員在播報新聞時可能會有口誤的情形發生，我們的更正方式為在錯誤字詞上加單槓刪除線，並在方括號中補註正確的用法，例如：~~have~~ [is] thought to have fallen . . .。至於播報時，若省略的字詞影響到對新聞的理解，我們會在原文後方加入方括號標示出省略掉的字詞，例如：French high school kids [are] learning about . . .。

本書中的單字拼法及音標是依照韋伯字典（Merriam-Webster's 11th Collegiate Dictionary）第十一版為準。以下為書中詞性的縮寫說明：

adj.	adjective	形容詞
adv.	adverb	副詞
conj.	conjunction	連接詞
n.	noun	名詞
phr.	phrase	片語
prep.	preposition	介系詞
v.	verb	動詞

兩個字以上的名詞片語，經韋伯字典收錄並列為名詞者，標示為 n.，未收錄者則標為 n. phr.。由動詞和介副詞所組成的片語動詞（如：get around），在本書中標為 v.，而其他作動詞用的片語（如：fall short of）則標為 v. phr.。

希望透過《Step by Step 聽懂 CNN》這本書，提供基礎的英語聽力技巧，作為引領你聽懂英語新聞的入門磚，假以時日，你的英語聽力能力一定能更上一層樓。

編輯室報告 004

如何使用光碟 009

聽力技巧篇 015

基礎訓練篇

Unit 1 舊金山大地震一百週年 028

Unit 2 視障者的另一雙眼睛——GPS 全球定位系統 030

Unit 3 這就是他們的童年——尼泊爾童奴 032

Unit 4 愛迪達收購銳跑 034

Unit 5 成就青藏鐵路　代價知多少？ 036

Unit 6 深入人體的醫生——超迷你手術機器人 038

Unit 7 諾基亞、西門子兩大通訊巨頭合併　預將裁員九千人 040

Unit 8 搶救北極熊 042

Unit 9 神舟六號任務成功　中國計劃五年內興建太空站 044

Unit 10 嘲諷回教先知漫畫風波延燒阿富汗 046

Unit 11 Wii 初期銷售狀況勝過 PS3 048

Unit 12 踏進植物天堂——伊甸植物園 050

Unit 13 沃爾瑪跨足銀行業引起反對聲浪 052

Unit 14 無所不用其極的商業間諜戰 054

Unit 15 電視族新主張　一機兩看新科技 056

Unit 16 「CSI 效應」發燒　正宗警探難為 058

Unit 17 英王室電話遭竊聽　安全漏洞再現 060

Unit 18 地球之肺在燃燒——亞馬遜雨林的危機 062

Unit 19 窮人銀行家尤努斯　九美元讓乞丐變商人 064

Unit 20 揭開性感女神夢露香消玉殞之謎 066

Unit 21　天塹變通途　焉知禍福？——三峽大壩工程的得與失 068
Unit 22　悠仁太子誕生　解除日本皇位繼承危機 070
Unit 23　資源回收與環境污染的矛盾 072
Unit 24　未來機器人讓你大開眼界 074
Unit 25　CNN 專訪亞洲巨星金城武 076
Unit 26　世界最高樓杜拜「哈利法塔」啟用 078
Unit 27　"unfriend" 獲選牛津字典年度辭彙 080
Unit 28　蘋果發表輕薄筆電 MacBook Air 082

實戰應用篇 Part I

Unit 1　速食咖啡挑戰咖啡龍頭 086
Unit 2　逛街購物新概念——觸控式櫥窗 092
Unit 3　小心！你的電子郵件裡寫什麼——老闆都知道 100
Unit 4　無後一身輕——美國社會吹起頂客風 106
Unit 5　誰是密碼真正的主人？ 112
Unit 6　走過四分之一世紀——個人電腦發展回顧 118
Unit 7　堅持與榮耀　阿格西揮別網壇 126
Unit 8　部落格——改變傳統媒體生態的新監督力量 134
Unit 9　活著，真好　巴格達前線美軍的一天 140
Unit 10　馬爾地夫將自地表消失？ 146
Unit 11　訂不到餐廳座位怎麼辦？ 152
Unit 12　誰才是我爸爸？　匿名捐精者子女上網覓手足 158
Unit 13　從「漢堡」大學看麥當勞的員工訓練哲學 166
Unit 14　電玩科技爭霸戰　Sony 又出新招 174
Unit 15　「性」趣缺缺的貓熊家族 182
Unit 16　環保就從選擇食材做起 190

實戰應用篇 Part II

Unit 1 天文大發現 火星・生命・水 200
Unit 2 古老印度瑜珈 現代人的解壓良方 206
Unit 3 颶風狂掃 爵士城一夕變色 212
Unit 4 與絕種命運賽跑的獵豹 218
Unit 5 網路犯罪的新剋星——網路駭客 224
Unit 6 我要活著回去——駐伊美軍每日面對的死亡威脅 232
Unit 7 Adobe 卯上微軟 軟體大戰開打 238
Unit 8 水都威尼斯的水患之苦 246
Unit 9 iPod 的市場壟斷策略 252
Unit 10 打造劇院魔力——安德魯・洛伊・韋伯談音樂劇 258
Unit 11 捍衛駕駛艙 民航機師帶槍飛行 266
Unit 12 歷史上難以抹滅的一頁——納粹集中營解放六十週年 274
Unit 13 揭開阿姆斯壯過人體能的秘密 282
Unit 14 3-D 動畫武林盟主 皮克斯的成功之路 288
Unit 15 英國朝野同心 面對反恐難題 296
Unit 16 到底誰抄誰？山寨平板電腦與 iPad 的羅生門 304

聽力測驗解答 313

➲ 系統建議需求

【硬體】
- 處理器 Pentium 4 以上（或相容 PC 個人電腦之處理器 AMD、Celeron）
- 512 MB 記憶體
- 全彩顯示卡 800*600 DPI（16K 色以上）
- 硬碟需求空間 200 MB
- 16 倍速光碟機以上
- 音效卡、喇叭及麥克風（內建或外接）

【軟體】
- Microsoft XP、VISTA、Win7 繁體中文版系統
- Microsoft Windows Media Player 9
- Adobe Flash Player 10

➲ 光碟安裝程序

步驟一：進入中文視窗。

步驟二：將光碟片放進光碟機。

步驟三：本產品備有 Auto Run 執行功能，如果您的電腦支援 Auto Run 光碟程式自動執行規格，則將自動顯現【CNN 互動英語雜誌——Step by Step 聽懂 CNN】之安裝畫面。

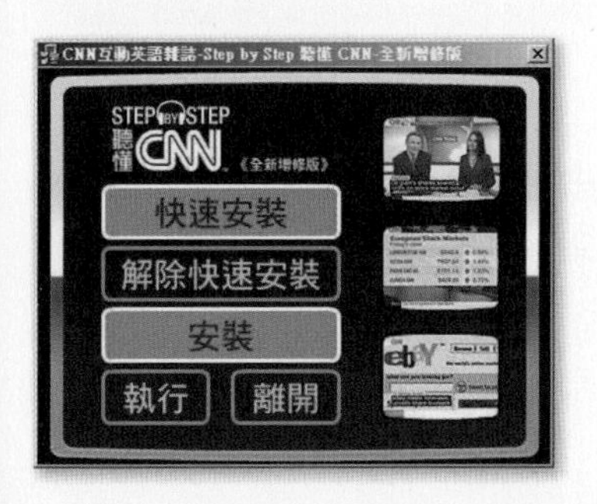

◆ 如果您的電腦已安裝過本公司產品，如【CNN 互動英語雜誌】或【ABC 互動英語雜誌】，您可以直接點選「快速安裝」圖示，進行快速安裝；否則，請點選「安裝」圖示，進行安裝。

◆ 如果您的電腦無法支援 Auto Run 光碟程式自動執行規格，請打開 Windows 檔案總管，點選光碟機代號，並執行光碟根目錄的 autorun.exe 程式。

◆ 如果執行 autorun.exe 尚無法安裝本光碟，請進入本光碟的 setup 資料夾，並執行 setup.exe 檔案，即可進行安裝程式。

◆ 如果您想要移除【CNN 互動英語雜誌——Step by Step 聽懂 CNN】，請點選「開始」，選擇「設定」，選擇「控制台」，選擇「新增／移除程式」，並於清單中點選「CNN 互動英語雜誌——Step by Step 聽懂 CNN」，並執行「新增／移除」功能即可。

◆ 當語音辨識系統或錄音功能失去作用，請檢查音效卡驅動程式是否正常，並確認硬碟空間是否足夠，且 Windows 錄音程式可以作用。

➲ 操作說明

點選 Play，即進入本光碟的教學課程。依序說明如下：

✻ 主畫面 ✻

說明：

1. 主畫面共有七個圖示，分別為：基礎訓練、實戰應用 I、實戰應用 II、索引、說明、LiveABC 及離開。
2. 點選任一類別（基礎訓練、實戰應用 I 或實戰應用 II），將於螢幕中列出所有課程，點選後可進入該課程的影片學習畫面。

✻ 影片學習 ✻

說明：

在主畫面中點選任一單元，即進入本學習畫面。

工具列說明：

1. 畫面右側由上至下依序為：自動播放、播放／暫停、停止、播下一句、播上一句、反覆播放本句、全螢幕播放、設定。
2. 點選「設定」圖示，即可設定「反覆朗讀」的播放次數及間隔的秒數；若您想恢復為一直播放的模式，只要將次數調回 0 即可。
3. 畫面左側由上至下依序為：目錄、上一篇、下一篇、單字解說、測驗、文字學習、回主畫面、離開。
4. 畫面下方的英文及中文字幕，經由選取字幕前的圖示，可選擇出現或隱藏字幕，以進行聽力練習。
5. 字幕下方有一影片播放點控制列，可決定影片播放起點。

✻ 文字學習 ✻

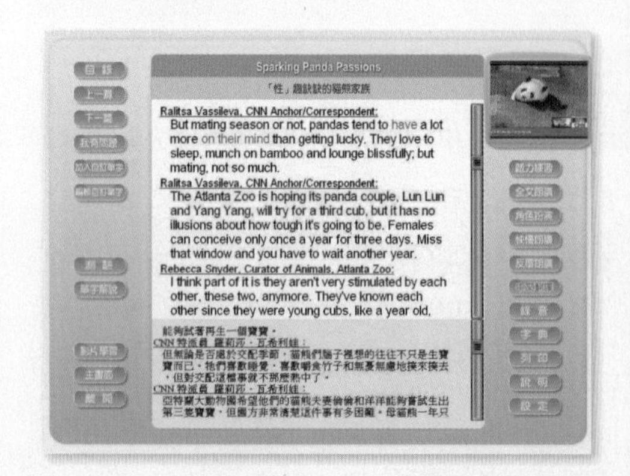

說明：

1. 在影片學習中，點選「文字學習」圖示，即進入本畫面。
2. 在畫面的右上方會有一影片視窗，在聲音播放的同時，您可以在此視窗看到該段聲音的影片。

工具列說明：

聽力練習 聽力練習
點選「聽力練習」圖示，螢幕中的課文內容將會消失，讀者只能過右上角的影片畫面進行聽力練習。

全文朗讀 全文朗讀
點選「全文朗讀」圖示，電腦會自動朗讀本段新聞的內容。

角色扮演 角色扮演
點選「角色扮演」圖示，則會在圖示左側出現人名。此時，您可選擇所欲扮演的角色，程式將關閉該角色的聲音，由您和電腦進行練習，當您的發音不正確時，則會出現一對話框，您可以選擇「再唸一次」、「略過」、或「唸給我聽」來完成或跳過該句對話；也可以調整語音辨識的靈敏度。若您的發音正確，則對話會一直進行下去。

快慢朗讀 快慢朗讀
當您覺得影片原音速度太快時，可以點選「快慢朗讀」圖示，再點選「全文朗讀」圖示或任一句子，可聽慢速朗讀。慢速朗讀時，為了讓您聽得更清楚，錄音老師將一句話斷成幾小段，逐句錄音。若您覺得速度太慢，想恢復一般速度，只要再次點選「快慢朗讀」圖示，即可恢復成一般速度。

反覆朗讀 反覆朗讀
點選「反覆朗讀」圖示後，再點選任一句，即反覆播放該句。您可以點選「設定」自行設定「反覆朗讀」的播放次數，若您想恢復為一直播放的模式，只要將次數調回 0 即可。

中文翻譯 中文翻譯
點選「中文翻譯」圖示後，畫面下方將出現中文翻譯框，您可在中文翻譯框內看到課文的中文翻譯。若您點選中文翻譯框中的某句中文，則會朗讀相對應的英文句子；同樣的，點選內文中的任一句子，也會朗讀該句英文，並標示出其中文翻譯。

錄 音 錄音
1. 點選「錄音」圖示後，開啟錄音視窗。

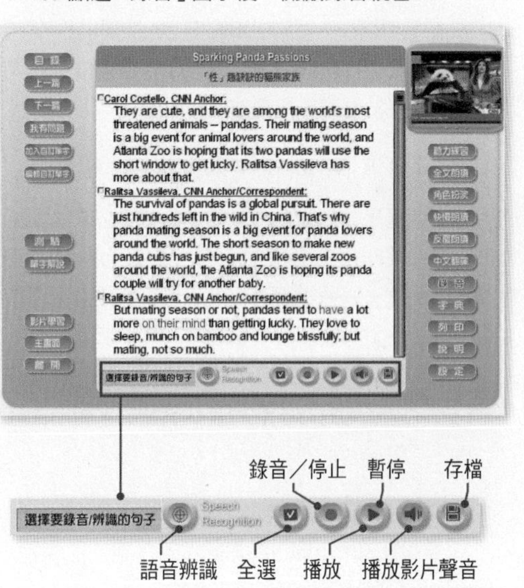

2. 按鍵功能由左至右為：全選、錄音／停止、播放／暫停、播放影片聲音及存檔。按最左方的「全選」圖示，會出現全部句子錄音；若您只想選擇某段內文，只要在該段前方的方框（□）點選一下即可。若您選取「播放影片聲音」圖示，則在您進行錄音或播放錄音前，都會將播放該段影片原音。

3. 錄音步驟如下：
   (1) 先點選您要進行錄音的句子，並選擇是否要在錄音前播放原音。
   (2) 點選「錄音」鍵。
   (3) 請在電腦「播放原音」後，對著麥克風唸出您所選取的句子。
   (4) 當您完成該句錄音後，請按鍵盤上的「空白鍵」(space bar)，結束錄音。
   (5) 點選「播放」鍵即可聽到你錄下的聲音。

4. 點選左方的「Speech Recognition」圖示，將啟動語音辨識功能，請依照以下步驟進行語音辨識：
   (1) 先選擇要練習發音的句子，並選擇是否要在語音辨識前播放原音。
   (2) 點選「Speech Recognition」圖示。
   (3) 當畫面出現「請錄音」時，您必須對麥克風唸出您選取的句子，如果您的發音正確，則將繼續進行下一句；如果發音不正確，則會出現一視窗，您可選擇「再唸一次」、「略過」或「唸給我聽」來完成或略過該句對話；也可在此調整語音辨識的靈敏度。
5. 當您要在中途結束錄音或語音辨識，請在任意處點選一下即可結束該功能。

字典

當您選取「字典」圖示後，在畫面下方將出現字典框，此時任意點選課文中的單字，字典框內會出現該單字的音標及中文翻譯，並唸出該字發音。

列印

當您選取「列印」圖示後，在畫面下方將出現列印控制鍵。您可選擇「全部列印」或「局部列印」；列印內容可選擇是否包括中文翻譯。此外，本光碟還提供儲存功能，您可以選擇全部儲存或局部儲存；並選擇是否儲存中文翻譯。

說明

當您選取「說明」圖示，即會進入輔助說明頁。您可藉此瞭解本光碟文字學習的操作說明及用法。

on their mind **學習重點**

當您在點選課文中藍色字體的學習重點，畫面下方會出現說明框，並有發音；若在開啟「中文翻譯」功能時點選，則朗讀您點選的句子。

Ralitsa Vassileva, CNN Anchor/Correspondent: **段落朗讀**

當您點選課文中的人名，程式將自動朗讀此人的該段話。若您是處於「慢速朗讀」模式，則播放該段話時，聲音及文字反白將以小段方式出現。

測驗

在文字學習畫面或影片學習畫面中，若想做測驗，可以點選「測驗」圖示，進入測驗介面。

加入及編輯自訂單字

點選加入自訂單字後，可以點選您要記錄的單字。

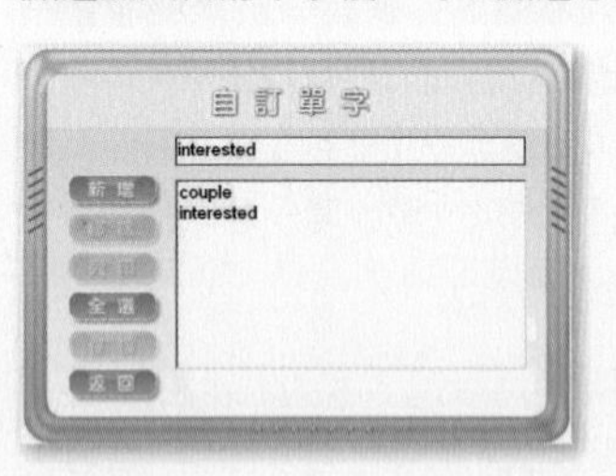

在此，您可以進行單字學習也可以移除或列印任一單字。

單字解說

列出本課之重點單字（詞性、音標、中文解釋），點選該單字會發聲。

✻ 測驗說明 ✻

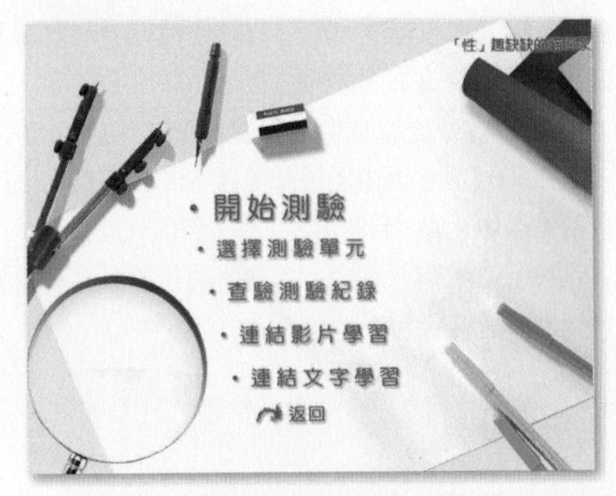

1. 依本書所分的基礎訓練、實戰應用 I、實戰應用 II 三部分課程，測驗的題型分別為——基礎訓練：是非題；實戰應用 I、II：是非題、選擇題、填空題。點選「開始測驗」後即可作答。

2. 實戰應用部分，當您覺得影片太難，無法理解大部分的意思時，您可以先點選左下方的「生字提示」圖示，我們有列出該文章中較難的單字及專有名詞，可以幫助您聽懂課文的意思。

3. 請點選影片右方 Play 圖示播放影片並作答，完成該題後，點選「下一題」圖示進行下一題，完成該測驗題型後，可繼續進行其他測驗，或可點選「離開」退出測驗介面。

✻ 題型說明如下 ✻

(1)是非題：

(2) 選擇題：

(3) 填空題：

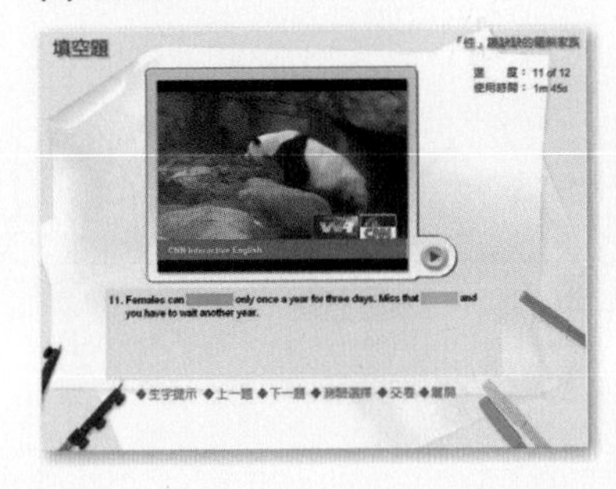

✻ 索引 ✻

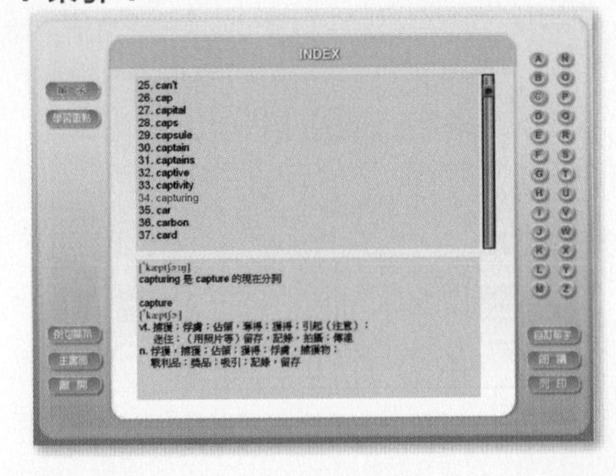

說明：

1. 在主畫面點選「索引」圖示，進入索引畫面，內含單字檢索及學習重點索引。

2. 單字檢索：

   (1) 在此將所有的單字依字母分類，點選單字會出現該單字的音標、中文翻譯及發音。

(2) 連續點選單字兩次或點選「例句顯示」圖示，即會顯現該單字的課文例句。

(3) 連續點選例句兩次或點選「連結課文」圖示，即跳至該例句的「文字學習」畫面。

(4) 點選「自訂單字」圖示，您可以在此看到您在課程學習加入的自訂單字。

(5) 點選「朗讀」，則會將所選字母的單字從頭到尾唸一次；點選「列印」，則將該字母的單字列印出來。

(6) 點選任一單字後，再點選「列印」圖示，可列印該單字的內容。

3. 學習重點：

(1) 在此列出本光碟所有課程的學習重點。游標點選任一學習重點，會自動朗讀。

(2) 連續點選兩次或點選「連結課文」圖示，即跳至該學習重點的「文字學習」畫面。

(3) 點選「返回」圖示則回到單字檢索畫面。

(4) 點選「朗讀」，則會將所有的詞語補充從頭到尾唸一次；點選「列印」，則將所有的學習重點列印出來。

✻ 說明 ✻

1. 在主畫面點選「說明」圖示，在此提供「操作說明」及「語音辨識設定說明」。
2. 您可藉此瞭解本光碟教學節目的各項操作說明、用法及語音辨識設定上的安裝說明。

✻ 網站 ✻

點選本圖示，將連結到 LiveABC 英文學習網站，您可以在網站上學習更多內容。

✻ 課文朗讀 MP3 ✻

DVD-ROM 中的「~MP3-1」資料夾中，含有基礎訓練篇的課文原音及慢速朗讀 MP3 的內容，而「~MP3-2」資料夾中則為實戰應用 I 與 II 的內容。您可以放在 MP3 播放器聆聽，也可以將光碟置於電腦中，從「我的電腦」點選您的光碟機，再從中選擇光碟資料裡 MP3 的檔案夾，使用播放軟體將檔案開啟聆聽 MP3 內容。

請注意！

在 Vista 系統中，安裝互動光碟如遇到以下問題：

- 出現【安裝字型錯誤】之訊息。
- 出現【無法安裝語音辨識】之訊息。

請執行以下步驟：

1. 移除該產品
2. 進入控制台
3. 點選「使用者帳戶」選項
4. 點選「開啟或關閉使用者帳戶控制」
5. 將「使用（使用者帳戶控制）UAC 來協助保護您的電腦」該項目取消勾選
6. 再次執行安裝光碟

在 Windows7 系統中，安裝互動光碟如遇上述問題，請執行以下步驟：

1. 進入控制台，開啟程式集，進入程式和功能，移除該產品
2. 進入控制台，點選「使用者帳戶和家庭安全」選項
3. 再點選「使用者帳戶」
4. 點選「變更使用者帳戶控制設定」
5. 將控制拉桿調整至最底端（不要通知的位置）
6. 按確定後，需重新啟動電腦
7. 再次執行安裝光碟

聽力技巧篇

Listening ability is important in learning a language because it influences every aspect of the learning process. It obviously aids learners' ability to understand, but it goes much deeper than this. It also helps develop proper pronunciation and speech cadence. Those who can hear and then mimic native speech not only develop a more natural accent, but also develop proper word choice and correct grammar patterns.

聽力是學習語言中重要的一環，因為聽力對學習過程中的每個環節都會造成影響。聽力好顯然對學習者的理解能力有所助益，但不只如此而已，聽力好也有助於培養正確的發音及說話時的抑揚頓挫。會聽母語者說話並加以模仿的學習者，不只口音較為自然，而且用字較為準確，文法句型也較為正確。

Proper word choice touches on two aspects of fluency: knowledge of how to apply individual words correctly, and knowledge of which words and phrases should be used in different situations. That is, through listening to native speakers, one develops natural understanding of the differences between similar, yet differently applied words, such as *wish* and *hope*. As well, one develops a natural understanding of how and when to use language according to whether it is formal or casual.

用字適當與否關係語言流暢度的兩個面向：知道如何正確應用每一個字，以及知道在不同場合如何用字譴詞。也就是說，透過聽母語人士說話，就能逐漸培養出了解用法相異的相似詞之間差別的能力，如 wish 及 hope。同樣地，你也會自然而然了解如何根據正式或非正式場合來適時地運用語言。

Good listening skills are imperative to understanding how grammar rules are applied in the spoken language. Take the sentence *I live in Tokyo*. Because of the liaison (sound linking) of the [v] in *live* and the [ɪ] in *in*, learners often believe they hear *I living Tokyo*. This is grammatically incorrect, and if learners hear and mimic it, they develop incorrect grammar patterns in their speech.

聽力好對於了解文法規則是怎麼在口語中應用有其必然關係。以 I live in Tokyo. 這個句子為例，因為 live 中的 [v] 與 in 中的 [ɪ] 連音，學習者常會覺得自己聽到的是 I living Tokyo.，這個句子不符合文法，如果學習者聽後便跟著學，那麼他們在交談時就會用到錯誤的文法。

With proper listening tools, learners can self-assess language improvement. You can feel proud when you hear *Tsup?* and realize that it is a contracted liaison of *What's up?* You'll become comfortable using *wanna* (elision) instead of *want to*. These steps help your ability to understand spoken English plus they help to make your own speaking style more natural and correct.

有了適宜的聽力方法，學習者便能自我評估語言的進步程度。當你聽到 Tsup? 知道是由 What's up? 連音縮寫而來，你一定會感到驕傲。你會慢慢習慣用 wanna（省略音），而不用 want to。這些過程都有助於你了解口說英文，此外，也會讓你說得更自然、且更精準。

To maintain your improvement, immerse yourself in English. Watch English-language movies and television sitcoms—of course without your native-language subtitles. Listen for the words of songs to make sure you're singing them correctly. Radio and news programs can be difficult, but you'll be surprised what you begin to understand by applying the listening tools provided in the following guidelines.

為了要不斷地進步，就把自己沉浸在英文的環境中。觀看英文電影及電視影集，當然不要有你的母語字幕。仔細聽你所喜愛的歌曲裡的歌詞以確保沒有唱錯。廣播和新聞性節目可能會很難，但藉由應用接下來所解說的聽力準則，你將會因為發現開始聽得懂而感到驚訝。

Guidelines: Facets of Listening to Spoken English
聽力準則：聽懂口說英文

1. Ease of Pronunciation 發音便利原則

In spoken English, pronunciation of words change in order to make speech smooth and easy. Some of the most common change effects are sound linking, elision, and assimilation.

口說英文中，為了讓說話更加流暢與容易，字的發音會隨著改變。最常見的一些變化為「連音」、「省略音」及「同化音」等現象。

1-1. Sound Linking 連音

Sound linking is the joining of words in spoken English. There are two basic types. One is liaison, or consonant sound linked to vowel sound. The other is the linking of the same or similar consonant sounds. As an example of liaison, take *fill up* for example. Separately, the words are [fɪl] and [ʌp]. When spoken together however, they become [fɪ·lʌp], the consonant [l] linking to the vowel [ʌ]. For same or similar consonant linking, consider *cut down*, which is spoken [kʌ·daʊn]. The consonants [t] and [d] are similar in sound, so the [t] in *cut* merges with the [d] in *down*. Same/similar consonant linking assures that an extra syllable doesn't occur between words.

連音是口說英文中字音的結合，有兩種基本類型：一是子音與母音的連結，這種連音又稱作 liaison。另一種是相同或類似子音的連結。以 fill up 這個例子來說，兩字分開時唸作 [fɪl] 及 [ʌp]，但一起唸時會變成 [fɪ·lʌp]，子音 [l] 與母音 [ʌ] 連結起來了。我們來看一下 cut down，發成 [kʌ·daʊn]，這是相同或類似子音的連音例子。子音 [t] 和 [d] 為類似的音，所以 cut 中的 [t] 與 down 中的 [d] 合在一起。相同或類似子音的結合是為了不讓字與字之間多出一個音節。

Listen to the following excerpt from the CNN report, *San Francisco Marks the Centennial of the Deadly 1906 Quake*.
請聽下面這一段節錄自 CNN 新聞的《舊金山大地震一百週年》。

Track 1

Looking at San Francisco, it is hard to believe that nearly 90 percent of it burned to[a] the ground a hundred years ago.[b]

看著舊金山市，實在很難相信這座城市在一百年前曾經有將近百分之九十的建築物盡數燒毀。

a. Listen for the same/similar consonant link in *burned to*. In the excerpt, these two words are pronounced [bɝn·tu]* because the [d] and [t] sounds merge.
請聽 burned to 中相同或類似子音的連結。在節錄的這段新聞中，這兩個字發為 [bɝn·tu]（註），因為 [d] 與 [t] 合併了。

* Note that past-tense *burned to* is pronounced just like present-tense *burn to*. Native speakers understand the tense from the context of the sentence.
註：請注意，過去式 burned to 的發音聽起來像是 burn to，母語人士可從前後文理解時態的不同。

b. Now listen for the liaison in the last two words in the excerpt, *years ago*. The final sound in *years*, the consonant [z], connects to the initial vowel sound in the word *ago* [əgo], creating [jɪr·zəgo].
請聽節錄的最後兩個字 years ago 的連音。years 中字尾子音 [z] 與 ago [əgo] 中字首母音結合後發成 [jɪr·zəgo]。（編註：本書為了讓讀者了解連音變化，特以 KK 音標來幫助說明，不過略去重音、次重音的標注，僅著重在字音變化。）

1-2. Elision 省略音

Elision is the omission of sounds, and it occurs when sound combinations are difficult to pronounce. This can occur when words are put together, as with the words *want to*, which are often pronounced *wanna* [wɑnə]. Some syllables are regularly omitted, such in as the word *comfortable*, which is usually pronounced [kʌmf·tə·bəl].

省略音是指一些音的省略，常發生在聲音組合不好發音的情況中。有些字放在一起時也會有音省略的現象，如 want to 通常會發成 wanna [wɑnə]。有些音節也經常會被省略，例如 comfortable 常發成 [kʌmf·tə·bəl]。

Elision also occurs with sounds in unstressed function words. For example, the function word *that* is so common that it is often unnecessary to be clear about its sound. If it begins a sentence, it can lose its [ð], becoming [æt] or [ət]. Function words that can be contracted, *would ('d)*, *will ('ll)*, *had ('d)*, etc., usually are contracted, even if the contraction isn't proper. For example, *Dan will bring the cake*. becomes *Dan'll bring the cake*.

省略音也常出現在非重音的功能詞上。例如，that 這個功能詞十分常用，通常不用特別唸得很清楚。如果出現在句首，[ð] 音可能會聽不見，變成 [æt] 或 [ət]。可以縮寫的功能詞，如 would ('d)、will ('ll)、had ('d) 等常會縮寫，即使有時這樣的縮寫並不是很恰當，例如：Dan will bring the cake. 變成 Dan'll bring the cake.。

Listen to the following excerpt from the CNN report, *Protecting Prince Charles' Private Lines.*
請聽下面這一段節錄自 CNN 新聞的《英王室電話遭竊聽 安全漏洞再現》。

Track 2

Antiterrorism officers are[a] leading this investigation. And this of course is not the first embarrassing security breach for the royal family.[b]

調查行動目前正由反恐官員負責進行。當然，英國王室已經不是第一次出現這種令人發窘的安全漏洞。

a. Listen to the words *officers are*. The word *are* is contracted with *officers*, making "officers're" [ɑfɪsɚzɚ], even though this isn't a proper contraction.
請聽 officers are 這兩個字，are 與 officers 縮寫成 officers're [ɑfɪsɚzɚ]，雖然這樣的縮寫不是很恰當。

b. Now listen to the pronunciation of the last word in the excerpt, *family*. This word is spoken with one syllable omitted, contracting from [fæməlɪ] to [fæmlɪ].
請聽節錄中的最後一個字 family。這個字省略了一個音節，從 [fæməlɪ] 簡化成 [fæmlɪ]。

1-3. Assimilation 同化音

Assimilation is the change of a sound to blend more easily with neighboring sounds. In the words *run back*, the [n] in *run* changes to [m] to blend more easily with the following [b] in *back*, making [rʌmbæk]. In the words *it is*, the unvoiced [t] changes to a voiced [d] to blend more easily with the (voiced) vowels surrounding it, becoming [ɪdɪz]. Some common assimilations are *doncha* [dontʃə] for *don't you*, and *didja* [dɪdʒə] for *did you*, and *gonna* [gənə] for the future-tense modifier *going to*.

同化音是為了與鄰近音更易結合所產生的聲音改變。在 run back 中，run 中的 [n] 為了與 back 中的 [b] 容易一起發音而變成 [m]，形成 [rʌmbæk]。在 it is 中，無聲子音 [t] 為了與前後的母音（有聲）較易一起發音而變成了有聲子音 [d]，形成 [ɪdɪz]。一些常見的同化音有：don't you 變成 doncha [dontʃə]、did you 變成 didja [dɪdʒə]，及表未來式的 going to 變成 gonna [gənə]。

Listen to the following excerpt from the CNN report, *TalkAsia Exclusive Interview with Taiwanese-Japanese Actor Takeshi Kaneshiro*.
請聽下面這一段節錄自 CNN 新聞的《CNN 專訪亞洲巨星金城武》。

Track 3

. . . there is very little chance, if you care anything at all[a] about Asian culture or film in general, that you're[b] going to[c] remain ignorant of him for very long.

……但如果你還算關心亞洲文化或電影相關事物的話，那你還能一直不知道這號人物的機會恐怕是微乎其微。

a. Listen to the pronunciation of *at all* in the excerpt. The [t] in *at* becomes a [d] in order to blend with the vowels that surround it, making [ædɑl].*
請聽節錄中 at all 的發音。at 中的 [t] 為了與前後的母音較易一起發音而變成了 [d]，形成 [ædɑl]（註）。

* Note that Taiwan's phonetics system (KK) denotes *all* as [ɔl], which is the British pronunciation of the word. Even though KK is supposed to represent American English pronunciation, it doesn't actually contain the pronunciation symbol for the American-English sound of the *a* in *all*. Listen for the difference between the KK [ɔl] and the way the American speaker pronounces *all*.
註：KK 音標系統把 all 標為 [ɔl]，這是英式發音的標示法。雖然 KK 音標是用來標示美語的發音，但它並沒有準確地把 all 這個字中的 a 的美語發音標出來。請注意聽 KK 音標的 [ɔl] 及美國人所發的 all 的差別。

b. Now listen to the words *that you're*. The *t* to *y* assimilation becomes [tʃ], making [ðætʃɚ].*
請聽 that you're 這兩個字。t 與 y 同化形成 [tʃ]，形成 [ðætʃɚ]（註）。

* This word combination ends in [ɚr] because *you're* and *your* are usually simplified to [jr]—more about this will be discussed in the following section, *Stress and Weakening*.
註：you're 和 your 常簡化成 [jr]，所以尾音為 [ɚr]，接下來的「重讀與弱化」部分會探討更多這種現象。

c. Now listen to the pronunciation of *going to*. The speaker pronounces this *gonna* [gənə], which is a common pronunciation of *going to* used as a verb modifier.* *Gonna* is both assimilation and elision in that sounds are assimilated and one syllable is omitted.
請聽 going to 的發音。說話者把它發成 gonna [gənə]，這是 going to 之後接動詞（註）時常見的唸法。gonna 既是同化情況也是省略的結果，因為有些音被同化且省略了一個音節。

* The simplified pronunciation *gonna* is used only when *going to* modifies a verb.
註：gonna 這種簡化的發音只用於 going to 之後接動詞的情況中。

I'm going to read a book. → I'm *gonna* read a book. 我要讀一本書。(✓)
I'm going to the store. → ~~I'm *gonna* the store~~. 我要去商店。(×)

Another common assimilation occurs with the *d*, *t* and *k* sounds. Native speakers often substitute them with a glottal stop to transition more easily between sounds. A glottal stop is made by constricting the throat to stop the breath, resulting in a brief pause. This can be observed in the pronunciation of *Britain*. In both British and American accents, instead of [brɪtən], the word often becomes [brɪʔən].

另一種常見的同化音出現在 d、t、k 等音中。英文母語人士常會用喉塞音來代替這些子音，讓音與音之間轉換得更順暢些。喉塞音是指發音時咽喉阻塞而造成氣流短暫停頓。我們可在 Britain 這個字的發音中聽到喉塞音。不論是英語還是美語的發音，這個字通常會發成 [brɪʔən]，而不會發成 [brɪtən]。（編註：[ʔ] 是表示喉塞音的符號，但不屬於 KK 的符號系統。）

Listen to the following excerpt from the CNN report, *Robo Surgeons: Tiny Mechanical Docs May Soon March through Your Insides*.
請聽下面這一段節錄自 CNN 新聞的《深入人體的醫生——超迷你手術機器人》。

Track 4

It[a] may seem like the preposterous vision of a mad scientist, but[b] there are those who say it[c] will happen.
這聽起來也許像是瘋狂科學家的癡心妄想，可是有些人卻說這樣的未來一定會實現。

a. Listen carefully to the way the *t* is pronounced in the words *It may*. There is a slight stop and release of breath that creates a pause before the [m] sound. The pause is not distinct or loud, but it replaces what would have been a [t] with a glottal stop. Glottal stops frequently occur at the end of words.
仔細聽 It may 中 t 發音的方式。[m] 音前有停頓，是因為氣息輕微停頓然後才釋放出來。這個停頓不是很明顯，也不是很大聲，但喉塞音取代了原來的 [t]。喉塞音的現象常發生在字尾。

b. Listen to how the speaker says *but* there. The *t* at the end of *but* is expressed as a glottal stop to ease transition to the following [ð] sound.
聽聽看這裡 but 的唸法。but 字尾的 t 變成了喉塞音，以便於轉換到之後的 [ð] 音會順暢些。

c. Listen to the pronunciation of *it*. The [t] is pronounced as a glottal stop even though there is a substantial pause before the next word is spoken. This glottal stop occurred in anticipation of the initial consonant sound of the following word.
請聽 it 的發音。[t] 在此為喉塞音，雖然發下個字之前有明顯的停頓。這裡出現喉塞音是因為預期下一個字字首為子音。

More than one of the above effects—sound linking, elision, and assimilation—can be combined (as in the above example of *going to*). Keep in mind that the purpose of these effects is to ease pronunciation.

上述這些發音現象——連音、省略音及同化音——都可能會同時發生（如上面 going to 的例子）。只要記住，這些發音現象都是為了方便發音。

2. Stress and Weakening 重讀與弱化

Stress and weakening of words indicate what it is the speaker wants to emphasize. Words that help deliver meaning are stressed. Function words are regularly weakened because they usually only provide the structure of the sentence. However, if function words help deliver meaning, they are stressed.

字的重讀及弱化可顯示出說話者想強調的是什麼。有助於傳遞意思的字會有強化重讀。功能詞經常會被弱化，因為功能詞通常只具有句子結構的功能。但是，如果功能詞有助於傳達意思，就會重讀。

Example:

I *found* my keys. = My keys are no longer lost.
我「找到」我的鑰匙了。（我的鑰匙「找到」了。）

I found my *keys*. = Something else is still missing.
我找到我的「鑰匙」了。（「其他東西」仍然未找到。）

I found my keys. = It was I who found my keys, not someone else.
「我」找到我的鑰匙了。（找到我的鑰匙的人是「我」，不是別人。）

I found *my** keys. = Someone else's keys are still missing.
我找到「我的」（註）鑰匙了。（「其他人的」鑰匙仍然未找到。）

* Notice that *my* is a function word, but it is stressed to deliver meaning.
註：請注意，my 是功能詞，這裡因為要傳達訊息所以重讀。

2-1. Stress 重讀

Stress can be done through volume, length, pitch, and clear pronunciation. That is, a stressed word or syllable might be said loudly, it might be lengthened, it might be said at a different pitch (higher or lower), and/or the full word might be pronounced clearly and completely.

重讀可藉由音量、音長、音高和清楚的發音來顯示。也就是說，重讀的字或音節可能會唸得很大聲、唸得很長、用不同的音高（較高或較低）來唸，以及／或者清楚且完整地唸出整個字。

Listen to the following excerpt from the CNN report, *Eden Project Spreads Natural Wonder and Inspiration*.
請聽下面這一段節錄自 CNN 新聞的《踏進植物天堂——伊甸植物園》。

Track 5

Eden is about reflection,[a] sustainability and[b] a global view.[c]
伊甸計畫的重點是省思、永續發展、還有全球觀。

a. Listen to the word *reflection* to hear the stress technique of the speaker. She speaks it loudly, she raises the pitch of her voice, and she lengthens the word. Also notice that the stressed syllable [flɛk] exhibits the most stress. The speaker uses the same pattern with the word *sustainability*, the stressed syllable [bɪl] exhibiting the most stress.
請聽 reflection 這個字以了解說話者使用的重讀技巧。她講得很大聲、提高音調，還有把這個字唸得比較長。同時請注意，重音節 [flɛk] 聽起來特別加強重音。她唸 sustainability 這個字時也用了同樣的方式，重音節 [bɪl] 聽起來有特別加強重音。

b. Now listen to the word *and*. Normally *and* is not stressed because it is a function word. In this case, the speaker stresses it to dramatically transition to the final words. She speaks it loudly, she raises the pitch of her voice, she lengthens the word, and most notably, she pronounces it clearly and completely. See the next section, *Weakening*, for the unstressed pronunciations of *and*.
請聽 and 這個字。一般來說 and 不會重讀，因為 and 是功能詞。在這個例子中，說話者在這個字上加了重音，形成與最後的字詞之間十分明顯的轉接過程。她唸得很大聲、提高音調，最明顯的是，她還把這個字唸得很清楚、完整。and 不加重音時的唸法請見下面「弱化」的介紹。

c. Now listen to the pronunciation of *global view*. Notice that the speaker brings it to a lower pitch, which is a common way to end a statement. She also lengthens the words and pronounces them clearly.
請聽 global view 的發音。請注意，說話者的音調降低，這是結束陳述時常見的唸法。另外，她把這兩個字唸得比較長，也唸得很清楚。

2-2. Weakening 弱化

Weakening is done by changing vowels to a schwa [ə] and omitting sounds. The word and has many weak forms. Its vowel can be changed to a schwa: [ənd], its *d* can be omitted: [æn], its vowel can be changed and its *d* omitted: [ən], its vowel can be omitted: [nd], and its vowel and *d* can be omitted: [n]. In the words *your* and *for*, the vowel is omitted, making [jr] and [fr]. The initial [h] is omitted in some unstressed function words, such as *he*, *him*, and *her*. For example, *gave him* would be pronounced [gevɪm] or [gevəm].

弱化可藉由把母音變成非重音的中性母音 [ə] 以及省略一些音來達成。and 這個字有許多弱化的形式，可以把母音變成非重音的母音：[ənd]、可以省略 d：[æn]、可以改變母音並省略 d：[ən]、可以省略母音：[nd]，還可以省略母音及 d：[n]。your 及 for 這兩個字則可省略母音，形成 [jr] 和 [fr]。字首的 [h] 音在一些非重音的功能詞中會省略掉，如 he、him、her。舉例來說，gave him 會發成 [gevɪm] 或 [gevəm]。

Weakening can also be accomplished by changing an unvoiced consonant to its voiced counterpart. For example, *to* may be pronounced [tə] or [də], the voiced counterpart of [t] being [d].

弱化也可藉由把無聲子音變成相對應的有聲子音來達成。例如，to 可發成 [tə] 或 [də]，與 [t] 相對的有聲子音為 [d]。

Listen to the following excerpt from the CNN report, *Cartoons Incite Afghan Student Protests.*
請聽下面這一段節錄自 CNN 新聞的《嘲諷回教先知漫畫風波延燒阿富汗》。

Track 6

Time, apologies and[a] calls for calm can't[b] seem to[c] stop the furor over newspaper cartoons depicting the Prophet Mohammed.
時間、道歉和呼籲冷靜，似乎都無法平息報紙漫畫描述先知穆罕莫德所引發的憤怒。

a. Listen to the pronunciation of *and* in the excerpt. Notice that it is linked to *apologies* and is pronounced in its weak form [ən]. The two words together become [əpɑlədʒizən].
請聽節錄中 and 與 apologies 形成連音，且發成弱音 [ən]。兩字連起來形成 [əpɑlədʒizən]。

b. Now listen to the word *can't*. Notice that it is pronounced [kæn]. In their weak forms, *can* is pronounced [kn] while *can't* is pronounced [kæn] (or [kɑn] in British pronunciation).
請聽 can't 這個字。請注意 can't 發成 [kæn]。can 這個音弱化時會發成 [kn]，而 can't 則發成 [kæn]（英式英語中則發為 [kɑn]）。

c. Now listen to the pronunciation of *to*. The speaker pronounces it in its weak form [tə].
請聽 to 的發音。說話者把 to 這個音弱化，發成 [tə]。

Common Simplifications 常見的簡化形式

If the following function words are unstressed, they will usually (but not always) be pronounced in simplified form.

若下列功能詞未強調，通常（但不一定）會以簡化的形式來發音。

- can = [kn]
- can't = [kæn] [kɑn]
- and = [ənd] [æn] [nd] [ən] [n]
- to = [də] [tə]
- your = [jr]
- for = [fr]
- function words that start with an "h"(he, his, her, him, etc.) = [h] omission
- have to = [hæftə]
- would've, could've, should've = [wʊdə] [kʊdə] [ʃʊdə]
- going to (as a verb modifier) = gonna [gənə]
- want to = wanna [wɑnə]

3. Accent 口音

Although there are many variations of both American and British accents, there are general tendencies of American and British pronunciation. The British language is non-rhotic, which means that the letter *r* is usually unspoken or reduced to a schwa [ə]. The American structure is rhotic, meaning a full [r] is pronounced. This means Brits would pronounce *bigger* as [bɪgə], *near* as [nɪə], and *artist* as [ɑtɪst], but Americans pronounce them [bɪgər], [nɪr], and [ɑrtɪst].

雖然美語口音及英語口音間有許多差異，但也有一些大致的方向可循。英語是去捲舌音的語言，意思就是 r 常常不會唸出來，或者是會減化成非重音的母音 [ə]。而美語是帶捲舌音的語言，即 [r] 音會完整唸出來。也就是說，英國人會把 bigger 唸成 [bɪgə]、near 唸成 [nɪə]、artist 唸成 [ɑtɪst]，而美國人則唸成 [bɪgər]、[nɪr] 及 [ɑrtɪst]。

Ending sounds are often different between the two accents, as in the case of words that end in *y*. The standard British pronunciation of an ending *y* is [ɪ], whereas the American pronunciation is [i]. For example, Britons would pronounce *quickly* as [kwɪklɪ] but Americans pronounce it [kwɪkli]. Note that the KK system uses the British pronunciation for *y* endings ([ɪ]) instead of the American pronunciation ([i]).

這兩種腔調的英語之間，字尾音常會發得不一樣，字尾為 y 的字就是一例。標準英語口音會把字尾 y 發成 [ɪ]，而美語口音則會發成 [i]。例如：英國人唸 quickly 會唸成 [kwɪklɪ]，但美國人唸成 [kwɪkli]。請注意 KK 音標系統標 y 字尾是用英式發音 [ɪ]，而不是美式發音 [i]。

Another pronunciation tendency between standard British and American accents regards the pronunciation of the *a* vowel. Often, where an American would use an [æ], a Brit would use an [ɔ] or [ɑ]. For example, Americans pronounce *can* as [kæn], whereas a Brit would pronounce it [kɑn]. This is not always the case, as in the word *pasta*; Americans say [pɑstə], while Britons say [pæstə].

標準英語口音與美語口音之間另一個傾向是母音 a 的發音差別。通常，美國人會發 [æ]，而英國人會發 [ɔ] 或 [ɑ]。例如，美國人把 can 唸成 [kæn]，而英國人唸成 [kɑn]。但也不是一向如此，例如 pasta 這個字，美國人唸 [pɑstə]，而英國人則唸 [pæstə]。

There are numerous differences like this—too many to name here. As well, there are many more accents of English than standard British and American. By using your listening skills, you'll be able to discover the differences on your own.

這類的例子不勝枚舉，無法在此一一列舉。同樣地，英文口音的種類也不只有標準英語及標準美語而已。利用自己的聽力技巧，你也能自行發現箇中的差異。

4. Formal and Casual Speech 正式與非正式的用語

There are some basic tendencies for pronunciation and word choice in relation to how formal or casual a situation is. In casual situations, you'll find more contractions, elision, and assimilation. Basic, simple words are preferred. In formal situations, speech pronunciation is more distinct and proper, meaning fewer contractions, elisions, and assimilations. What are commonly referred to as "big words", those that are technical and often three or more syllables, are used more often in formal situations.

發音、用字與場合是正式還是非正式之間的關係有一些基本的方向可循。在非正式的場合中，你會聽到比較多縮寫形式、省略音及同化音，也較常使用基本、簡單的字詞。在正式場合中，演說時發音會比較清楚且恰當，也就是說較少縮寫形式、省略音及同化音。那些艱澀冷僻的字眼、專門用語及三個以上音節的字則較常在正式場合中使用。

While these tendencies are not hard and fast rules, they are important to understand. For example, in a casual conversation, it would be strange to say, "I like how the leaves on the trees *transform* in the fall." *Transform* is a technical word associated with formal speech; *change* is the correct word choice for casual conversation. However, in a formal situation it would be a problem to say, "These new products're the coolest buncha things we ever made. You just gotta love 'em!" This much elision, simple wording, and grammar deviation is too casual. Again, these are tendencies and not hard and fast rules. Listening to native speakers will aid you in learning what is appropriate for formal and casual situations.

儘管這些並不是嚴格的規則，但對這些規則有所了解還是很重要。例如，在非正式場合中說「我喜歡秋天樹上葉子『改變（transform）』的樣子」就很奇怪。transform 是專業用字，而 change 才是非正式場合中會使用的字。然而，在正式場合中說「這些新產品ㄕ我們做過最酷的東西勒。你們一定會很哈的！」聽起來就是不對勁，使用這麼多省略音、簡單用字及偏差文法都顯得太隨便。老話一句，這些方向不是嚴格的規則。聽母語人士講英文能幫助你學會在正式和非正式場合中要怎麼使用才適當。

—by *Kate Weaver*

Kate Weaver 曾任 LiveABC 互動英語教學集團《biz 互動英語》及《ALL$^+$ 互動英語》雜誌的英文主編。曾經在國立台灣大學研究所學程的寫作研討會發表演說，亦曾受邀至中央研究院演講並擔任研究員發表英文期刊的寫作指導，目前正在修習大眾傳播的碩士學位。

基礎訓練篇

【基礎訓練篇】建議使用方法：

Step 1　播放 DVD-ROM 或課文原音 MP3

Step 2　瀏覽聽力解說

Step 3　再聽一次原音

Step 4　聽一次慢速朗讀

Step 5　閱讀原文、重要字彙及中譯

Step 6　再反覆多聽幾次

Lessons from the Ashes

San Francisco Marks the Centennial of the Deadly 1906 Quake

舊金山大地震一百週年

符號說明：

連音 ‿

省略音 。

喉塞音 •

弱化音 灰色字

補充說明：

1. ground 100 中的 100 在此讀作 a hundred，故 ground a 產生連音。

2. and 一般在口語中會發成 [ən]，在強調時才會唸成 [ænd]。

Looking at San Francisco, it is hard to believe that nearly 90 percent of it burned to the ground 100 years ago.

Hard to believe that neighborhoods like Telegraph Hill were blackened[3] and bare.[4]

That the domed[5] city hall collapsed[6] in just seconds.

That the city that called itself the Paris of the Pacific looked like it had been bombed and burned.

看著舊金山市，實在很難相信這座城市在一百年前曾經有將近百分之九十的建築物盡數燒毀。

也很難相信像電報山那附近一帶在當時竟然是一片焦黑的廢墟。

舊金山的圓頂市政廳竟然在短短幾秒內夷為平地，

而這個自詡「太平洋巴黎」的城市在當時看起來儼然遭到轟炸、焚燒的模樣，也一樣令人不敢置信。

Notes & Vocabulary

lessons from the ashes 灰燼換取教訓

ash 指的是「灰燼；廢墟」，標題中所說的 lessons from the ashes，指的是舊金山一九〇六年發生的七點八級大地震，幾乎把這個城市夷為平地，而當時政府的處理更是雪上加霜。不過這場大地震後，舊金山迅速重建，在一九一五年時承辦世界博覽會，如浴火鳳凰般重生，也就是英文中所說的 rise from the ashes，儘管目前仍未能預測地震的發生，但舊金山的居民都已做好準備面對未知的未來。

1. **mark** [mɑrk] *v.* 紀念
2. **centennial** [sɛn`tɛnɪəl] *n.* 一百週年紀念
3. **blackened** [`blækənd] *adj.* 被薰黑的；被弄黑的
4. **bare** [bɛr] *adj.* 光禿禿的
5. **domed** [domd] *adj.* 有圓頂的；半球形的
6. **collapse** [kə`læps] *v.* 倒塌；崩潰

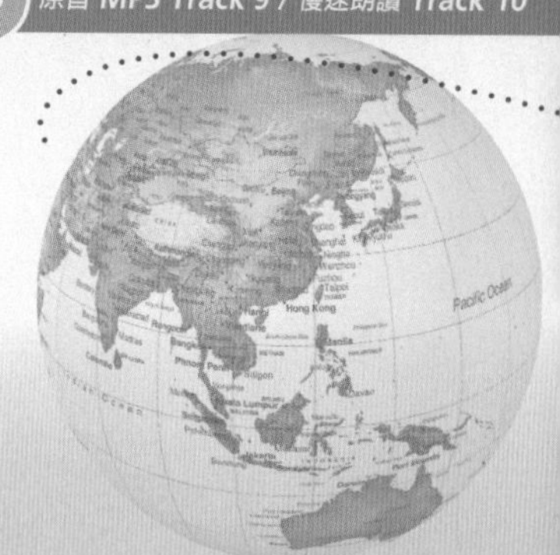

Eyes in the Sky

GPS System Offers Freedom and Mobility to the Blind

視障者的另一雙眼睛——GPS全球定位系統

符號說明：

連音 ‿
省略音 °
喉塞音 •
弱化音 灰色字

補充說明：

1. 在美式口語中，非強調或非重音時，your 會發成 [jr]。
2. 在非強調或非重音時，to 會發成 [tə]，而 and 會發成 [ən]。

Maybe you've got one that helps you get around[3] the roads, or you've got it programmed[4] into your cell phone.

These days though, specially designed GPS units are offering the blind a new way to get around without the aid of another human being.

CNN's Dan Lothian met a man who lost his sight[5] at the age of 11, and now that he's electronically[6] equipped,[7] he leads a more independent life.

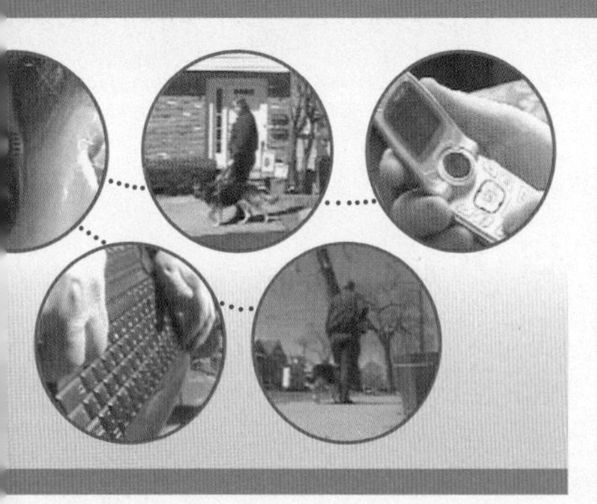

也許您也有一套能帶你到處趴趴走的全球定位系統，或者您的手機已經輸入了這套程式。

如今經過特殊設計的全球定位系統正提供盲人一種不需他人協助即可以自由走動的新方式。

本台記者丹・羅西恩訪問了一名十一歲時便失明的人，現在他在裝上了電子裝備後，已經過著更獨立的生活了。

Notes & Vocabulary

GPS 全球定位系統

Global Positioning System 是由美國軍方研發出的「衛星導向系統」（satellite navigation system），後來發展出廣泛的民間用途。其原理是以二十幾顆人造衛星向地面的接受器（receiver）發送無線電波，讓接受器判讀所在位置的經度（longitude）、緯度（latitude）和海拔高度（altitude）。

1. **eyes in the sky** *n. phr.* 人造衛星的別稱
2. **mobility** [mo`bɪlətɪ] *n.* 移動性；機動性
3. **get around** *v.* 行動；走動
4. **program** [`pro͵græm] *v.* 設定在……中
5. **lose one's sight** *v. phr.* 失明；失去視力
6. **electronically** [ɪ͵lɛk`tranɪklɪ] *adv.* 電子地
7. **equip** [ɪ`kwɪp] *v.* 裝備；配備

Cycle of Slavery

Impoverished Nepalese Parents Sell Children into Lives of Servitude

這就是他們的童年——尼泊爾童奴

符號說明：

連音 ‿

喉塞音 •

弱化音 灰色字

補充說明：

1. the 在子音前唸作 [ðə]，母音前 [ði]，若在標題、名字或強調獨一性時，則常唸 [ði]。此處另外有一個插入音 uh，口語中停頓時很常見。

2. million 中的 [l] 音是跟著第一音節，而非第二音節，所以應發為 [ˈmɪl · jən]。

3. 在非強調或非重音時，to 會發成 [tə]，而 and 會發成 [ən]。

In Nepal, the <uh> prevalence[4] of child slavery there is a major concern for child advocates[5] around the world.

Millions of children make up the nation's child labor force[6] and many of them are sold into virtual[7] slavery, sometimes by their own families.

Seth Doane met one child caught up in this practice[8] and learned what one organization is trying to do about it.

尼泊爾兒童奴役盛行的情況，引起世界各地兒童保護人士的嚴重關切。

尼泊爾有數百萬的童工，其中許多人是被賣去從事奴役工作，有時候還是被自己的家人賣掉的。

賽斯．多安和一名被賣身為奴的兒童見面，並得知有一個組織打算採取行動來改善這種情況。

Notes & Vocabulary

make up 形成；構成

make up 這個片語是用來表示某物組合而構成另一物的部分或整體，若用被動語態表示，後面須加上 of。主動的用法為 A make up B，而被動為 B is made up of A。

- Five players make up a team.
  五名球員組成一隊。
- The dish was made up of organic ingredients.
  這道菜是有機食材做的。

其他 make up 常用的意思有：

編造故事、藉口

- Tim made up a story about losing his homework.
  提姆為自己弄丟功課編了一個故事。

和好

- The couple made up after their argument.
  那對情侶吵過後就和好了。

彌補（+ for . . .）

- The company quickly made up for losses in the first quarter.
  這家公司很快就彌補今年第一季的損失。

1. slavery [ˋslevərɪ] *n.* 蓄奴；奴役
2. impoverished [ɪmˋpɑvrɪʃt] *adj.* 窮困的
3. servitude [ˋsɜvəˏtud] *n.* 奴役；束縛
4. prevalence [ˋprɛvələns] *n.* 廣泛；盛行
5. advocate [ˋædvəkət] *n.* 提倡者；擁護者
6. labor force [ˋlebɚ] [fɔrs] *n.* 勞工
7. virtual [ˋvɜtʃuəl] *adj.* 事實上；實際上的
8. practice [ˋpræktəs] *n.* 習慣；常規

Adidas Fires Shot in Shoe Wars

愛迪達收購銳跑

符號說明：

連音 ‿

省略音 ◦

喉塞音 •

弱化音 灰色字

補充說明：

1. billion 中的 [l] 音是跟著第一音節，而非第二音節，所以應發為 [ˋbɪl · jən]。

2. 在非強調或非重音時，to 會發成 [tə]，而 and 會發成 [ən]。

Adidas-Salomon is buying U.S. rival[1] Reebok for $3.8 <eight> billion.

Now the move is an attempt to challenge Nike's long-running[2] industry dominance.[3]

Adidas, the number-two sporting goods maker behind Nike, has been unable to crack[4] their urban[5] market in the United States.

The group says the acquisition[6] of Reebok will more than double its North American sales and boost[7] its basketball business.

愛迪達所羅門公司出價三十八億美元買下美國競爭對手銳跑公司。

該公司企圖以此舉挑戰耐吉長期以來在運動用品業的優勢地位。

在運動用品業排行第二名、僅次於耐吉的愛迪達公司，一直無法打入美國的都會市場。

該集團表示，收購銳跑公司將能讓他們在北美洲的營收倍增，並且提高籃球商品的業績。

Notes & Vocabulary

double 雙倍

double 在這裡作動詞用，指「雙倍」，在英文中三倍（triple）、四倍（quadruple）、五倍（quintuple）都還算常用，若六倍以上就多半直接用 times 來表示，如八倍可說 eight times。

- The company's workforce is eight times what it was ten years ago.
  這間公司的員工人數是十年前的八倍。

除了 times，我們也可以用百分比的概念來表示倍數，如上述例句也可寫成：

- The company's workforce has increased 800 percent in the past ten years.
  這間公司的員工數在過去十年增加了百分之八百。

1. **rival** [ˋraɪvl̩] *n.* 競爭對手
2. **long-running** [ˋlɔŋˋrʌnɪŋ] *adj.* 持續長時間的
3. **dominance** [ˋdɑmənəns] *n.* 優勢；支配地位；領導地位
4. **crack** [kræk] *v.* 強行進入；砰的一聲打開
5. **urban** [ˋɝbən] *adj.* 城市的
6. **acquisition** [ˏækwəˋzɪʃən] *n.* 取得；獲得
7. **boost** [bust] *v.* 增加；增大

The End of the Line for Tibet?

Beijing Rail Link Threatens Region's Unique Culture and Environment

成就青藏鐵路 代價知多少？

符號說明：

連音 ‿

喉塞音 •

弱化音 灰色字

補充說明：

在非強調或非重音時，and 會發成 [ən]。

Well, the new trains connecting Tibet to China's interior[4] are being hailed as a great advancement,[5] driving China's transportation[6] network forward, and opening new economic opportunities.

Though, not everyone's celebrating.

Some are voicing[7] concerns about the environmental and cultural impact, as Dan Rivers reports, it's not just animals and their habitat[8] that are said to be at risk, but also humans and a way of life.

連接西藏與中國內陸的新鐵路號稱是一大躍進，不但推動中國運輸網的發展，也開展了新的經濟機會。

不過，並不是所有人都對此額手稱慶。

有些人擔心青藏鐵路會對環境與文化造成衝擊。丹．里維斯的報導告訴我們，不只動物及其棲所面臨危機，當地居民及其生活方式也可能面臨危機。

Notes & Vocabulary

the end of the line for Tibet
青藏鐵路的終點站

標題中的 the end of the line 除了字面上的意思外，同時也暗指這條鐵路是否為西藏珍貴傳統資產的末日。因為鐵路帶來大量的觀光客，對原有的景觀與文化會造成多大的破壞，令許多學者十分憂心。

hail as 譽為……
hail 有「向……歡呼；招呼；承認……為」的意思，be hailed as 為被動式，as 後通常接身份或拿來比喻的事物。

- The new drug has been hailed as a cure for several deadly diseases.
  這種新的藥物號稱可以治療許多致命的疾病。

1. **Tibet** [tə`bɛt] *n.* 西藏
2. **threaten** [`θrɛtn̩] *v.* 威脅
3. **unique** [ju`nik] *adj.* 獨特的
4. **interior** [ɪn`tɪrɪɚ] *n.* 內陸；內地
5. **advancement** [əd`vænsmənt] *n.* 進展；進步
6. **transportation** [ˌtrænspɚ`teʃən] *n.* 運輸；運輸工具
7. **voice** [vɔɪs] *v.* 表達；說出
8. **habitat** [`hæbəˌtæt] *n.* 棲息地

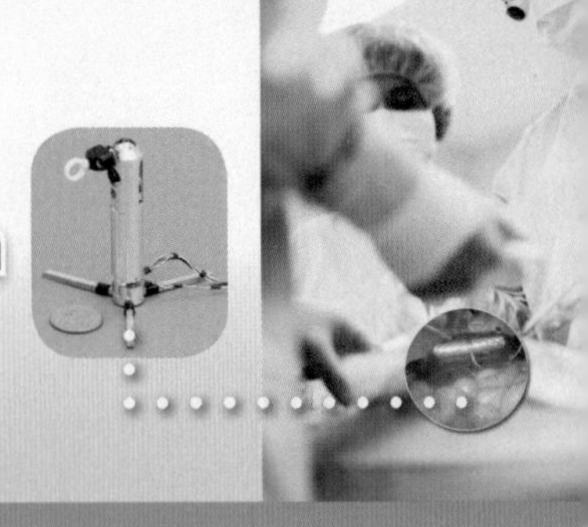

Robo Surgeons
Tiny Mechanical Docs May Soon March through Your Insides
深入人體的醫生——超迷你手術機器人

符號說明：
連音 ‿
喉塞音 •
弱化音 灰色

補充說明：
英式英語中的 [r] 音常省略，如 swarm、here、heart、there。

What if you could swallow a swarm[3] of microscopic robots[4] that would roll through the passageways[5] of your body sorting out any medical needs you may have?

A gallbladder[6] removal here, perhaps a heart bypass[7] there.

All without any skin being broken, and so all with a minimum[8] of recovery[9] time.

It may seem like the preposterous[10] vision of a mad scientist, but there are those who say it will happen.

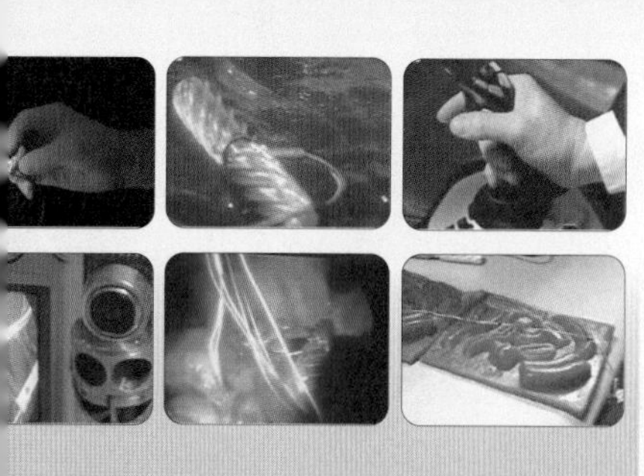

如果你吞下一群微型機器人，讓它們從人體通道滑進體內解決各種身體健康上的問題，結果會怎麼樣呢？

它們也許會幫你切除膽囊，或者做個心臟繞道手術，

不但不需要割開皮膚，而且復原時間短之又短。

這聽起來也許像是瘋狂科學家的癡心妄想，可是有些人卻說這樣的未來一定會實現。

Notes & Vocabulary

sort out 解決；整理

此慣用語泛指藉由「整理」、「區分」來挑選、整頓或解決問題，可以是實質的人事物，也可能是抽象的思想或情勢、狀態，是個用途廣泛的片語。其意義和用法主要可區分為以下幾種：

sort sb out 解決……的問題；教訓某人；修理某人

- The repairman sorted out the computer problem.
  維修人員解決了電腦的問題。

sort (sth) out 解決問題；將……處理妥當；恢復正常；整頓；釐清；分類

- Don't worry, these things will sort themselves out in the end.
  別擔心，船到橋頭自然直。

1. **surgeon** [ˋsɝdʒən] *n.* 外科醫生
2. **insides** [ɪnˋsaɪdz] *n.* 內臟
3. **swarm** [swɔrm] *n.* 群；一群；一大批
4. **microscopic robot** [ˏmaɪkrəˋskɑpɪk] [ˋroˏbɑt] *n. phr.* 顯微機器人
5. **passageway** [ˋpæsɪdʒˏwe] *n.* 通道
6. **gallbladder** [ˋgɔlˏblædɚ] *n.* 膽囊
7. **heart bypass** [hɑrt] [ˋbaɪˏpæs] *n.* 心臟繞道手術
8. **minimum** [ˋmɪnəməm] *n.* 最小值
9. **recovery** [rɪˋkʌvərɪ] *n.* 復元；恢復
10. **preposterous** [prɪˋpɑstrəs] *adj.* 十分荒謬的；可笑的

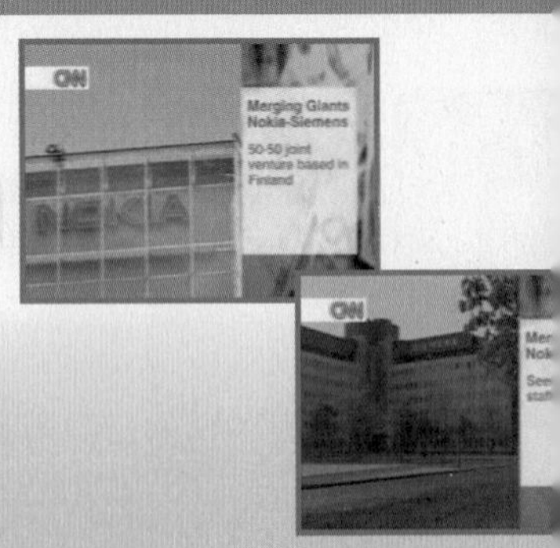

Telecom Giants Join Forces, Cut Staff

諾基亞、西門子兩大通訊巨頭合併　預將裁員九千人

聽力解說

符號說明：

連音 ‿

省略音 。

喉塞音 ·

弱化音 灰色字

補充說明：

1. 在非強調或非重音時，to 會發成 [tə]，而 and 會發成 [ən]。
2. 母語人士常會把句首的功能詞 the 省略或唸得很輕。
3. will 當助動詞時，常會與主詞合併，如文中的 it'll，這時的發音比較像是 [ˈɪdl̩]。

Nokia and Siemens have announced plans to combine their telephone equipment units to save money and share know-how.[3]

The resulting[4] company, Nokia-Siemens Networks, will have annual sales ~~of~~ almost $20 billion.

It'll be run as a 50-50 joint venture.

Although the CEO comes from Nokia, headquarters'll[5] be in Nokia's homeland, Finland.

The deal is expected to be completed by January of 2007.

The merged[6] company will look to cut up to 9,000 staff over the next four years, 15 percent of its workforce.[7]

諾基亞與西門子宣布將合併兩家公司的電話設備部門，以節省開支並分享技術。

合併後的新公司：諾基亞西門子網路，年營收將逼近兩百億美元。

雙方將以各持股百分之五十的方式合資經營該新公司。

新公司的執行長將由諾基亞指派，總部將設在諾基亞公司的母國芬蘭。

該項交易預計將在二〇〇七年一月之前完成。

合併後的新公司計畫在未來四年內至多裁汰九千名員工，占其目前員工總數的百分之十五。

Notes & Vocabulary

joint venture 合資事業

joint venture 簡稱 JV。兩個企業或組織互相結合，雙方都投入資產（equity），並分享營收（revenue）、花費成本（expense）和該企業或組織的掌控權（control）。相對於這種實際資產上的結合，另一種不牽涉資產的聯合是 strategic alliance（策略聯盟、策略結盟），兩個獨立的公司或組織為達成特定目標而合作結盟。

1. **telecom** [ˋtɛlə͵kɑm] *n.* 電信公司；電信業者（為 **telecommunication** 的簡寫）
2. **cut staff** [kʌt] [stæf] *v. phr.* 裁員
3. **know-how** [ˋno͵haʊ] *n.* 技術；專業知識；竅門
4. **resulting** [͵rɪˋzʌltɪŋ] *adj.* 形成……結果的（較口語、非正式的用法，是動詞 **result** 的變體）
5. **headquarters** [ˋhɛd͵kwɔrtɚz] *n.* 總部；總公司
6. **merge** [mɝdʒ] *v.* 合併
7. **workforce** [ˋwɝk͵fɔrs] *n.* 工作人員；勞動力

Keeping Their Heads Above Water

Drowning Polar Bears Signal Deeper Problems in Arctic North

搶救北極熊

符號說明：

連音 ‿

省略音 。

喉塞音 •

弱化音 灰色字

補充說明：

在非強調或非重音時，to 會發成 [tə]，而 and 會發成 [ən]。其中在第一句後面的 and drowned bears 裡的 and 則是因強調而發成 [ænd]。

The disappearance[2] of the sea ice off the north coast of Alaska was reported at the end of last year by the U.S. Minerals Management Service, which matched it up with[3] a sharp rise in sightings[4] of swimming and drowned bears.

They're drowning because they're apparently[5] trying to swim to shore, as much as 80 miles, in a desperate attempt to find the food that was once readily available[6] on the ice.

Harry Reynolds has been studying bears his whole life and he had never heard of a polar bear drowning until recently.

美國礦物管理局在去年底通報指出，阿拉斯加北岸的海冰逐漸消融。就在同一段時期，目擊北極熊在水裡游泳或者溺水的案件數目也急遽升高。

北極熊之所以溺水，是因為冰上本來豐富的食物來源已經消失，所以牠們只好游過長達八十英里的海面到岸上覓食。

哈利．雷諾茲畢生研究熊類，以前卻從來沒有聽過北極熊溺水的情況。

Notes & Vocabulary

desperate attempt
孤注一擲；非常手段

人在窮途末路或狀況危急時，往往會被逼到顧不得風險，而必須「孤注一擲」或「狗急跳牆」以求絕處逢生，這種「非常手段」英文可以說 desperate attempt/effort/measures。

- William made a desperate attempt to save the stranded cat.
  威廉拚了命去救那隻受困的貓咪。

desperate 的字義很多，包括：絕望的、危急的、鋌而走險的、拚命的、孤注一擲的、極度渴望的。影集 *Desperate Housewives* 台灣翻成《慾望師奶》，其實大陸譯名《絕望的主婦》應較貼近其原意。

1. arctic [ˋɑrktɪk] *adj.* 北極圈的
2. disappearance [͵dɪsəˋpɪrəns] *n.* 消失
3. match up with *v.* 使相配
4. sighting [ˋsaɪtɪŋ] *n.* 目擊；發現
5. apparently [əˋpɛrəntlɪ] *adv.* 明顯地
6. readily available [ˋrɛdəlɪ] [əˋveləbl̩] *phr.* 易於取得

Successful End to China's Space Flight

神舟六號任務成功 中國計劃五年內興建太空站

符號說明：

連音 ‿

省略音 ∘

喉塞音 ・

弱化音 灰色字

補充說明：

1. 母語人士常會把句首的功能詞 the 省略或唸得很輕。

2. 在非強調或非重音時，to 會發成 [tə]，而 and 會發成 [ən]。

Now, China is celebrating the safe return of two of its astronauts[1] from space.

Emerging from the space capsule,[2] the two air force[3] pilots[4] received a hero's welcome.

The men spent five days in space in China's second manned[5] space mission.

And China plans to perform a spacewalk[6] the next time it sends men to space.

Officials say they hope to build a Chinese space station in five years and eventually put men on the moon.

China's only the third country to achieve manned space exploration.[7]

中國正在慶祝兩名太空人安全自太空中返回地球。

兩位從太空艙中現身的空軍飛行員受到英雄式的歡迎。

這兩人在中國第二趟載人太空任務中，在太空中度過五天的時間。

而中國計劃在下一次載人太空計劃中進行太空漫步。

官員表示，中國希望五年內建造一座中國的太空站，最終能把人送上月球。

中國是第三個完成載送人類到太空探險的國家。

Notes & Vocabulary

the third country 第三個國家

中國是繼美國、俄國後，成為第三個載送人類上太空的國家。美俄之間著名的太空競賽（space race）是從一九五七年俄國成功發射首顆人造衛星（artificial satellite）。中國的太空事業於五〇年代末期起步，一九七〇年成功發射自製的人造衛星，到二〇〇三年才成功載送首位太空人（astronaut）上太空，此次是中國第二次成功載送太空人上太空，並打算在接下來的「嫦娥工程」中將人送上月球。

1. **astronaut** [ˋæstrəˏnɔt] *n.* 太空人
2. **capsule** [ˋkæpsəl] *n.* 太空艙；膠囊
3. **air force** [ɛr] [fɔrs] *n.* 空軍
4. **pilot** [ˋpaɪlət] *n.* 領航員；飛行員
5. **manned** [mænd] *adj.* 載人的
6. **spacewalk** [ˋspesˏwɔk] *n.* 太空漫步
7. **exploration** [ˏɛkspləˋreʃən] *n.* 探險

Cartoons Incite Afghan Student Protests

嘲諷回教先知漫畫風波延燒阿富汗

符號說明：

連音 ‿

喉塞音 •

弱化音 灰色字

補充說明：

1. 這裡的 can't 也是英式口音很明顯的特色，發作 [kɑnt]，而不是美式的 [kænt]。
2. 在非強調或非重音時，to 會發成 [tə]，而 for 會發成 [fr]。其中，and 在此發成 [æn]，為英式口音常見唸法。
3. 英式英語常不發 [r] 音，如 over、newspaper、cartoons、particularly、minister。

Time, apologies and calls for calm can't seem to stop the furor[2] over newspaper cartoons depicting[3] the Prophet[4] Mohammed.

Some 2,000 Afghan students burned U.S. and Danish flags and threatened to join al-Qaeda during a protest on Monday in Jalalabad.

Students also protested outside the Danish embassy[5] in Tehran.

The demonstrations[6] followed a particularly violent weekend—28 people were killed in riots[7] in two Nigerian states.

Iran's foreign minister, though, is calling for an end to all the protests.

時間、道歉和呼籲冷靜，似乎都無法平息報紙漫畫描述先知穆罕莫德所引發的憤怒。

週一在賈拉巴德舉行的一場抗議活動中，約有兩千名阿富汗學生焚燒美國及丹麥國旗，並威脅要加入蓋達組織。

學生們也在德黑蘭的丹麥大使館外群集抗議。

在此之前則是一個暴力充斥的週末，共有二十八人在奈及利亞兩個省份發生的暴亂事件中喪生，

伊朗外長因此呼籲結束所有抗議活動。

Notes & Vocabulary

call for 呼籲；求助

call for 在本文出現兩次，第一次是當名詞用，for 後面接受詞，第二次出現則是當動詞用，均作「呼籲」的意思。

- The union leaders called for a general strike.
  工會領袖呼籲發起一場全面性的罷工。

call for 也可作「尋求協助」的意思。

- The nurse couldn't help the injured man, so she called for the doctor.
  那位護士幫不了那位傷患，所以她找醫生來幫忙。

1. incite [ɪnˋsaɪt] *v.* 激起；煽動
2. furor [ˋfjʊrˏɔr] *n.* 狂怒；喧鬧
3. depict [dɪˋpɪkt] *v.* 描畫；描述；描寫
4. prophet [ˋprɑfət] *n.* 先知
5. embassy [ˋɛmbəsɪ] *n.* 大使館
6. demonstration [ˏdɛmənˋstreʃən] *n.* 遊行
7. riot [ˋraɪət] *n.* 暴動

Wii Beats Out PS3 in Early Sales

Wii 初期銷售狀況勝過 PS3

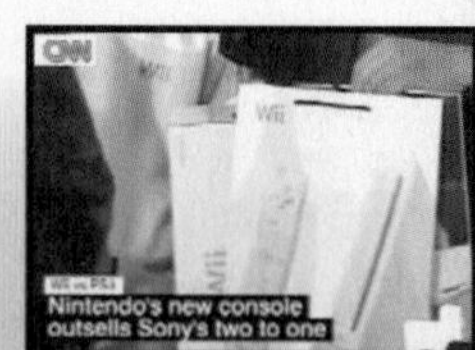

聽力解說

符號說明：

連音 ‿
省略音 。
喉塞音 •
弱化音 灰色字

補充說明：

1. 476,000 of 中為 thousand 與 of 連音。
2. 英式英語常不發 [r] 音，如：November、number、research、short、four、year。
3. is that 發生同化現象，發成 [ɪzæt]。
4. 在非強調或非重音時，for 會發成 [fr]。

Nintendo sold 476,000 of its Wii games consoles[2] in the U.S. this November. So, why is that interesting?

Well, it's because it's more than twice the number of Sony PlayStation 3s sold in the same period.

Well, those latest sales numbers from the research group MVP have fueled[3] speculation[4] that Sony's crown may indeed be slipping.

The firm had said it would ship 400,000 PS3s to the U.S. for its launch[5] but ~~have~~ [is] thought to have fallen short of[6] that.

Nintendo says it expects to ship four million Wiis worldwide by the end of this year.

任天堂十一月在美國賣出了四十七萬六千台 Wii 遊戲機。這有什麼值得注意的呢？

因為這個數字比索尼在同一時間的 PS3 銷售量高出了一倍以上。

研究組織 MVP 所發布的這些最新銷售數字，引發眾人臆測索尼的霸主地位已然滑落。

索尼當初聲稱 PS3 一旦在美國上市，將有四十萬台機器運抵當地以供銷售，但一般認為並未達到預期數量。

任天堂表示，Wii 的全球供貨量預計在年底前達到四百萬部。

Notes & Vocabulary

one's crown is slipping
失去寶座；失去優勢

crown 意為「王冠」，王冠象徵第一或唯一的榮耀，動詞 slip 是「滑落；滑掉」，所以 one's crown is slipping 在文中隱喻索尼公司銷售量總是位居第一的寶座即將被取代。

- The championship team has been losing the whole season. People are starting to think its crown is slipping.
  這支冠軍隊伍在整個球季裡一直輸球，人們開始認為他們的王座不保了。

crown 還可以作動詞，指「加冠；加冕；立……為王」。

- Louis XV was crowned at Reims.
  路易十五在雷姆斯宮加冕為法蘭西國王。

1. **beat out** *v.* 擊敗；戰勝
2. **console** [ˋkɑn͵sol] *n.* 主機
3. **fuel** [ˋfjuəl] *v.* 激起；引起
4. **speculation** [͵spɛkjəˋleʃən] *n.* 臆測；推測
5. **launch** [lɔntʃ] *n.* 發行；發射
6. **fall short of** *v. phr.* 低於預料或預期

Spheres of Influence

Eden Project Spreads Natural Wonder and Inspiration

踏進植物天堂——伊甸植物園

聽力解說

符號說明：

連音 ‿

喉塞音 •

弱化音 灰色字

補充說明：

1. 英式英語常不發 [r] 音，如：modern、theater、delivers、visitors、year、more、park、ordered。
2. 在非強調或非重音時，to 會發成 [tə]，而 and 在此發成 [æn]，為英式口音常見唸法。
3. around 的 [d] 音與 you 的 [j] 音發生同化現象，形成類似 [dʒ] 的音。

Housed[2] in Britain's best loved modern building, the Eden Project bills itself as a living theater of plants, people and possibilities.

What it delivers is a challenge to each of the 1.2 million visitors a year: Think more about the world around you.

This is no green theme park.[3]

No rows of neatly ordered blooms[4] to be glanced[5] at and just as quickly forgotten.

Eden is about reflection,[6] sustainability[7] and a global view.

伊甸計畫設置在這座英國最受喜愛的現代建築裡，號稱為植物、人類與無限可能性齊聚一處的劇場。

這項計畫對於每年前來參觀的一百二十萬名遊客提出這項挑戰：多想想自己週遭的世界。

這裡不是綠色主題樂園，

沒有一排排栽種整齊、讓人看過就忘的美麗花朵。

伊甸計畫的重點是省思、永續發展、還有全球觀。

Notes & Vocabulary

sphere of influence 勢力範圍

標題中的 sphere of influence 原為政治用語，指一國的政經勢力所能影響的範圍，現在也用在政治以外的地方。

- China's sphere of influence extends throughout Asia.
  中國的影響範圍遍及亞洲。

sphere 是指「球體；球形；星球」，可用來表示 Eden Project 裡許多的大型「球形」溫室，而那其中包羅了全世界不同氣候區的植物，又有如一個小型的「地球」。sphere 還有「範圍；領域；區域」的意思，Eden Project 這個「區域」發揮著正面的影響，標題以「勢力範圍」一語的字面意義，表示出 Eden Project 這個地方是個「帶來影響的球形世界」。

bill . . . as 將……標榜為

bill 作名詞有「海報、傳單」之意，而當動詞時則可表示「貼海報宣佈」，引申為「標榜宣傳」的意思。用法為 bill A as B「以 B 為標榜來宣傳 A」。

- The film is billed as the big hit of the summer.
  這部電影被視為暑期強片來進行宣傳。

1. **inspiration** [ˌɪnspə`reʃən] *n.* 靈感
2. **house** [haʊz] *v.* 存放有……；收藏了……
3. **theme park** [θim] [pɑrk] *n.* 主題公園
4. **bloom** [blum] *n.* 盛開的花
5. **glance** [glæns] *v.* 一瞥；瞥過；瞄一眼
6. **reflection** [rɪ`flɛkʃən] *n.* 深思；反省
7. **sustainability** [səˌstenə`bɪlətɪ] *n.* 持續性

Critics Line Up against Wal-Mart Banking Plan

沃爾瑪跨足銀行業引起反對聲浪

符號說明：

連音 ‿

喉塞音 •

弱化音 灰色字

補充說明：

在非強調或非重音時，to 會發成 [tə]，而 and 會發成 [æn]。

Wal-Mart is in focus[2] today.

Its decision to break into the banking business is drawing some sharp criticism.

Labor unions, consumer groups and bankers are set to make their case[3] at a hearing today for preventing the world's largest retailer from operating an in-house[4] bank.

They will argue the chain is already too big since it already makes up a significant part of the retail market, and that a Wal-Mart bank would unfairly concentrate power over retail and small business lending.

But supporters say the move would benefit consumers by lowering prices in an industry with little competition.

Wal-Mart shares are down more than half a percent.

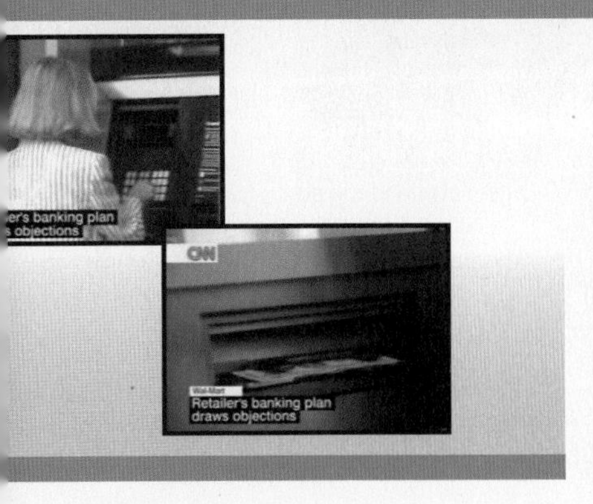

沃爾瑪是今天的焦點。

沃爾瑪決定進軍銀行業，引來一些尖銳的批評。

工會、消費者團體和銀行業者準備好要在今天的聽證會中作證，以防止這家全球最大的零售業者在內部成立銀行。

這些人將力陳這家連鎖百貨規模已經太大，因為沃爾瑪已經是零售市場的龍頭老大，而沃爾瑪銀行一旦設立，會造成對零售業及小型企業放款能力過度集中於該家銀行的不公平狀況。

但支持者表示，此舉將壓低此產業中原本欠缺競爭的價格，進而嘉惠消費者。

沃爾瑪目前股價下跌超過百分之零點五。

Notes & Vocabulary

retailer 零售業者；流通業者

零售業者是商品供應鏈（supply chain）的最末端，以商店據點等交易形式，將貨品販賣給末端消費者（end-user consumer）的業者，為商品通路（channel）的一種，屬於流通業的一環。

傳統的流通業包含所有從事財貨流通買賣的業者，如貨物的供應商（supplier）、盤商或批發商（wholesaler）與零售商等。台灣近年來，大賣場（hyper market）和連鎖便利商店等新興的大型零售經營模式蔚為主流，他們直接向供應商採購的模式逐漸取代了傳統的層層遞銷關係，因此越來越多人以流通業者來加以稱呼，以別於過去的零售商。

1. line up against *v.* 群起反對；一致反對
2. in focus *phr.* 成為焦點
3. make one's case *v. phr.* 表達論點；說明理由
4. in-house [ˋɪnˏhaʊs] *adj.* 內部附屬的；機構內的

Shady Business
Corporate Spies Keep an Eye on the Competition
無所不用其極的商業間諜戰

符號說明：
連音 ︶
省略音 。
喉塞音 ・

補充說明：
在非強調或非重音時，to 會發成 [tə]，而本文中的 and 發得較重，發成 [ænd]。

How common is corporate spying?

An Ethics Resource Center survey found one of every 25 employees has seen misuse[3] of confidential[4] competitive information.

But one of the fiercest[5] competitions in American business, Pepsi versus[6] Coke, had an entirely different outcome.[7]

This summer, a Coke employee tried to sell company secrets to Pepsico.

But they didn't take the bait.[8]

Pepsico executives[9] did the right thing and immediately told Coke.

The result, criminal charges against three people, following a sting operation in which corporate competitors cooperated[10] with each other.

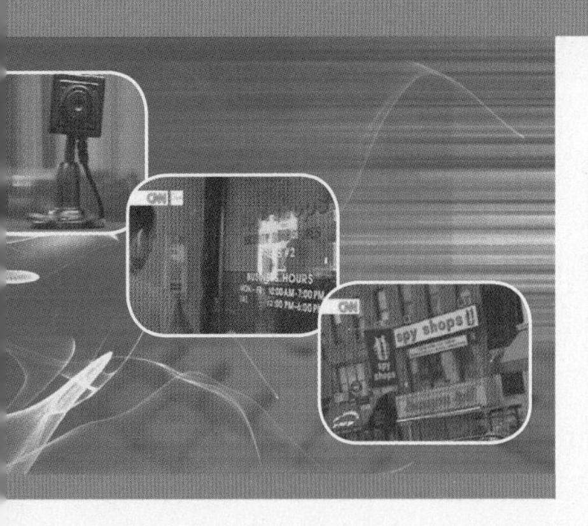

企業間諜行為有多麼普遍？

道德資源中心的一項調查發現，每二十五名員工就有一人目睹過濫用機密競爭資訊的情形。

不過，美國商業界競爭最激烈之一的百事可樂和可口可樂，卻做出了完全不同的選擇。

今年夏天，可口可樂一名員工企圖把公司機密賣給百事可樂，

他們卻沒有因此見獵心喜。

百事可樂的主管為所當為，立即通知了可口可樂，

於是原本的競爭對手合作進行誘捕行動，讓三個人受到刑事起訴。

Notes & Vocabulary

sting operation　偵查犯罪的誘捕行動

sting 在這裡指的是「精心設計的詐騙」的意思，sting operation 是指在安排設計一項誘捕計畫，為的是要逮捕涉嫌詐欺（deception）犯罪行為的人。

1. **shady** [ˋʃedɪ] *adj.* 聲名狼藉的；不名譽的
2. **corporate** [ˋkɔrprət] *adj.* 公司的；全體的
3. **misuse** [mɪsˋjus] *n.* 誤用；濫用
4. **confidential** [ˏkɑnfəˋdɛnʃəl] *adj.* 機密的
5. **fierce** [fɪrs] *adj.* 猛烈的
6. **versus** [ˋvɝsəs] *prep.* 對；對抗
7. **outcome** [ˋaʊtˏkʌm] *n.* 結果
8. **bait** [bet] *n.* 圈套；誘餌
9. **executive** [ɪgˋzɛkjətɪv] *n.* 主管
10. **cooperate** [koˋɑpəˏret] *v.* 合作

Double Vision

TV for Two May End War for the Remote

電視族新主張 一機兩看新科技

聽力解說

符號說明：

連音 ‿

省略音 ˚

喉塞音 •

弱化音 灰色字

補充說明：

1. as the 發生同化現象，聽起來像 [æsɪ]。

2. top 中的 p 發音時原本應該使氣流從雙唇噴出，但在此並未如此，但仍在 p 發音完結時緊閉雙唇。

Football on television at the same time as the evening sitcoms?[2]

No problem. Sharp has developed a liquid crystal display[3] panel that allows viewers on the right and left side of a sofa to watch different TV programs staring at the same screen.

Earphones are still required, but the Japanese firm, the world's top maker of LCD sets, says directional[4] sound would be examined.

In the interim, couch potatoes[5] now have a dual[6]-view display that means fewer battles for control of the zapper,[7] and indeed a TV for two.

橄欖球比賽轉播和夜間連續劇節目時間相衝？

沒問題。夏普已研發出一種液晶顯示螢幕，可讓電視觀眾坐在沙發左右兩側在同個螢幕上同時觀看不同的電視節目。

目前還是必須使用耳機，但是日本這家世界頂尖的液晶電視製造商表示他們將研究導向式擴音系統。

電視懶骨頭族目前有雙視顯示器可用，這表示以後不用再為了搶奪遙控器而爭吵不休，而且這也確實是為兩人設計的電視機。

Notes & Vocabulary

double vision 雙重影像；複視

標題中的 vision 意指「電視影像」，而 double vision 一詞在醫學上指的是「複視現象」，也就是雙眼視焦沒對好，看東西會出現「分身」的情形，這個用語也可以衍生用來表示「眼花；眼冒金星」。

- Alex thought he had double vision when he saw the twins.
  艾力克斯看到那對雙胞胎時還以為自己眼花了。

in the interim 在此期間；同時

interim [ˋɪntərɪm] 這個字當作形容詞使用時表示「過渡期間的、臨時的」。而 interim 當名詞時，則指「間隔時段」或「過渡時期」，慣用語為 in the interim，即「在兩件事銜接的過渡期間」的意思。另外也可以用拉丁文片語 ad interim 表示。

- In the interim between writing books, Helen often paints.
  海倫在寫書的空檔期常會畫點畫。

1. **remote** [rɪˋmot] *n.* 遙控器（= remote control）
2. **sitcom** [ˋsɪtˏkɑm] *n.* 情境喜劇（= situation comedy）
3. **liquid crystal display** [ˋlɪkwəd] [ˋkrɪstl̩] [dɪˋsple] *n.* 液晶顯示（常縮寫為 LCD）
4. **directional** [dəˋrɛkʃənl̩] *adj.* 指向性的；方向的
5. **couch potato** [kaʊtʃ] [pəˋteto] *n.* 懶惰、缺乏活動力的人；成天躺（坐）在沙發上看電視的人
6. **dual** [ˋduəl] *adj.* 兩的；雙位的
7. **zapper** [ˋzæpɚ] *n.* （俚）電視或錄影機的遙控器

Real Life Detectives Fight the CSI Effect

「CSI 效應」發燒 正宗警探難為

符號說明：

連音 ‿

省略音 ∘

喉塞音 •

弱化音 灰色字

補充說明：

1. 在非強調或重音時，to 會發成 [tə]。
2. help 中的 p 發音時原本應該使氣流從雙唇噴出，但在此並未如此，但仍在 p 發音完結時緊閉雙唇。
3. happened the 發生同化現象，聽起來有點像 [hæpənə]。
4. would 原唸作 [wʊd]，但常減縮成 'd，唸作 [d]，或弱化成 [ʊd] 或 [əd]，文中的 would 為弱化形 [ʊd]。

It's a murder with no witnesses.

Miami city homicide detective Freddy Ponce and Sergeant[3] Moses Velasquez head up[4] the investigation and immediately call in[5] a team of CSI technicians.

They spend the next 10 hours processing[6] the crime scene, finding clues to help detectives piece together[7] what happened the night 60-year-old Thomas Clark was killed.

On television's *CSI: Miami*, the case would be solved within the hour.

In the real world, prosecutors[8] are starting to complain that juries[9] expect too much.

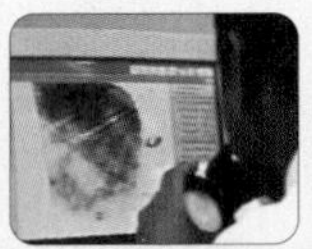

這是一樁沒有目擊證人的謀殺案。

邁阿密的兇殺組警探佛雷迪・龐斯和莫西斯・維拉史奎茲巡佐負責調查此案，並立刻召集了一組犯罪現場鑑識人員。

他們接下來的十個鐘頭都在犯罪現場採證，找尋能協助警探拼湊出六十歲的湯瑪士・克拉克遇害當晚情況的線索。

在《CSI：邁阿密》的電視影集中，案子不到一個小時就可以解決。

真實世界中的情況則是已經開始有檢察官們抱怨陪審團期望太高了。

Notes & Vocabulary

homicide & murder 殺人與謀殺

homicide [ˋhɑməˏsaɪd] 和 murder [ˋmɝdɚ] 這兩個字雖然都是殺人，意義卻不同：

homicide 泛指「殺人行為；殺人（罪）」，包括自衛殺人在內。在法律上，自衛殺人就稱為 lawful killing 或是 justifiable homicide（正當殺人）。

- The detectives investigated a double homicide.
  警探們調查一宗雙屍命案。

murder 則是指「謀殺」，亦即沒有正當理由、刻意並且有預謀的殺人。所以，命案發生時，警官們首先要釐清這是 homicide（他殺）還是 suicide（自殺），然後再調查這到底是意外殺人、自衛殺人，還是一宗 murder case（謀殺案）。

- The suspect was charged with murder.
  這名嫌犯以謀殺罪遭到起訴。

1. **detective** [dɪˋtɛktɪv] *n.* 警探；偵探
2. **CSI** *n.* 犯罪現場調查（= crime scene investigation）
3. **sergeant** [ˋsɑrdʒənt] *n.* 警官；警察小隊長
4. **head up** *v.* 領導；帶頭
5. **call in** *v.* 召集協助人馬
6. **process** [ˋprɑˏsɛs] *v.* 處理
7. **piece together** [pis] [təˋgɛðɚ] *v.* 拼湊
8. **prosecutor** [ˋprɑsɪˏkjutɚ] *n.* 檢察官（亦稱為 prosecuting attorney）
9. **jury** [ˋdʒʊrɪ] *n.* 陪審團

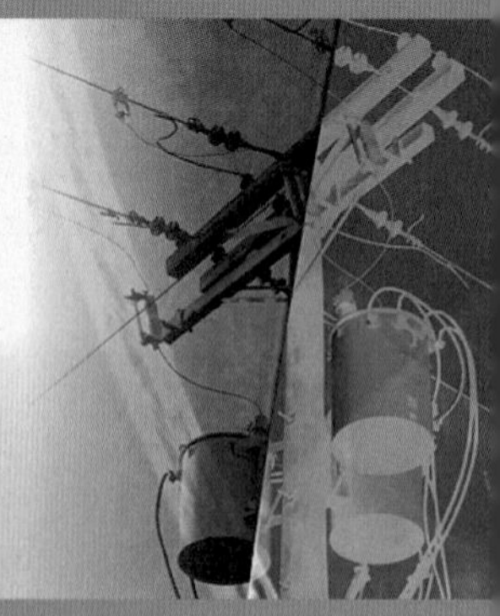

Protecting Prince Charles' Private Lines

英王室電話遭竊聽 安全漏洞再現

聽力解說

符號說明：

連音 ‿
省略音 。
喉塞音 •
弱化音 灰色字

補充說明：

1. 在非強調或非重音時，for 會發成 [fr]，而本文中的三處 and 發得較弱，發成 [æn]。

2. are 在口語中常減縮成 're，唸作 [ɚ]。

Well, it appears there has been a break-in[1] at the official residence[2] of Britain's Prince Charles, this one happening on the telephone lines.

Three men have been arrested[3] for wiretapping[4] the Clarence House residence.

One of the suspects[5] is the royal correspondent[6] for the *News of the World* newspaper.

Antiterrorism officers are leading this investigation.

And this of course is not the first embarrassing security breach[7] for the royal family.

A phone call between Prince Charles and his current wife Camilla, was recorded back in 1989.

They were caught having a sexually explicit[8] conversation—and this all happening while Charles was still married to Princess Diana.

And in 2003, a *Daily Mirror* reporter was hired as a royal footman[9] at Buckingham Palace, just before a visit from the U.S. president.

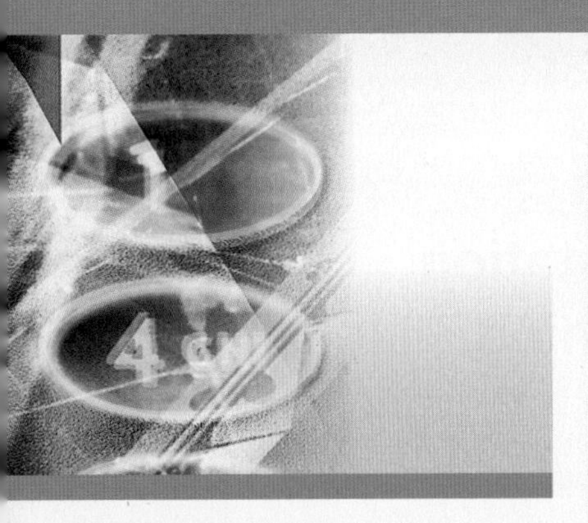

英國王儲查爾斯的官邸似乎遭到入侵，不過這回是電話線路。

三名男子因為竊聽克拉倫斯宮的電話遭到逮捕。

其中一名嫌犯為《世界新聞報》的王室新聞線記者。

調查行動目前正由反恐官員負責進行。

當然，英國王室已經不是第一次出現這種令人發窘的安全漏洞。

早在一九八九年，查爾斯王子和現任妻子卡蜜拉就曾有一通電話遭到盜錄，

對話中滿是露骨的淫褻話語，而且當時查爾斯與黛安娜王妃還維持婚姻關係。

此外，二○○三年在美國總統訪問英國前夕，《每日鏡報》一名記者被雇為王室侍者，順利混進白金漢宮。

Notes & Vocabulary

antiterrorism 反恐

anti- 這個字首是表示「反……；抗…… 」的意思，有兩種唸法：[ˋænti] 或 [ˋænˏtaɪ]，除了 antiterrorism「反恐」外，其他帶此字首常見的字有：

antiabortion 反墮胎的

antiaging 抗老的

antihero 非正統派主角

antinuclear 反核的

antiracist 反種族主義者(的)

antisocial 反社會的

antivirus 防毒的

1. **break-in** [ˋbrekˏɪn] *n.* 非法入侵
2. **residence** [ˋrɛzədəns] *n.* 住宅；官邸
3. **arrest** [əˋrɛst] *v.* 逮捕
4. **wiretap** [ˋwaɪrˏtæp] *v.* 竊聽
5. **suspect** [ˋsʌsˏpɛkt] *n.* 嫌犯
6. **correspondent** [ˏkɔrɪˋspɑndənt] *n.* 特派員；通訊記者
7. **breach** [britʃ] *n.* 漏洞；裂隙
8. **explicit** [ɪkˋsplɪsət] *adj.* 赤裸裸的；露骨的
9. **footman** [ˋfʊtmən] *n.* 侍僕

Burning Amazonia

A Closer Look at the Deforestation Contributing to Global Warming

地球之肺在燃燒──亞馬遜雨林的危機

符號說明：

連音 ‿
省略音 ∘
喉塞音 •
弱化音 灰色字

補充說明：

1. 英文口語中，which 通常會唸成 [wɪtʃ]，而不是 [hwɪtʃ]，此處更是完全沒發 [w] 音，形成 [ɪtʃ]。

2. 在非強調或重音時，to 會發成 [tə]。

We start with the Amazon, which is home to the largest rain forest and river basin[5] on earth.

It spans[6] more than 40 percent of South America and 60 percent of Brazil.

Because of all the oxygen[7] it produces, many describe it as the lungs of our planet.

But according to environmentalists, this vital[8] organ is one of the world's biggest environmental disasters, and has been for decades.

Last month at a U.N.-sponsored[9] environmental conference[10] in Brazil, Greenpeace stated less than 10 percent of the world's forest remain intact.[11]

Scientists say deforestation, logging,[12] burning and climate change are at the roots of the problem.

我們從亞馬遜地區開始，這裡有全球最大的雨林和河川流域，

面積佔南美洲的百分之四十以上，巴西的百分之六十。

這裡產生的氧氣非常多，因此有人稱之為地球之肺。

不過，環保人士指出，這個重要器官現在正陷於全世界最嚴重的環境浩劫當中，而且這情況已有數十年前之久。

上個月，在一場由聯合國贊助在巴西召開的環境會議上，綠色和平組織表示，全球仍然保存完好的雨林只剩下不到百分之十。

科學家表示，森林銳減、伐木、焚林以及氣候變化就是問題根源所在。

Notes & Vocabulary

deforestation 砍伐森林

deforestation 這個字的字首 de- 是表示「相反；減少；去除」的意思，通常用在動詞或名詞前面，常見帶有此字首的字有 debug（移去電腦程式中的錯誤）、decaffeinate（去咖啡因）、decode（解碼）、dehydration（脫水）等。

1. **Amazonia** [ˌæməˋzonɪə] *n.* 亞馬遜河流域
2. **deforestation** [diˌfɔrəˋsteʃən] *n.* 砍伐森林
3. **contribute** [kənˋtrɪbjut] *v.* 貢獻；導致
4. **global warming** [ˋglobḷ] [ˋwɔrmɪŋ] *n.* 全球暖化
5. **basin** [ˋbesn̩] *n.*（河川的）流域
6. **span** [spæn] *v.* 延伸；持續
7. **oxygen** [ˋɑksɪdʒən] *n.* 氧氣
8. **vital** [ˋvaɪtḷ] *adj.* 極其重要的；不可或缺的
9. **sponsor** [ˋspɑnsɚ] *v.* 贊助
10. **conference** [ˋkɑnfrəns] *n.* 會議；大會
11. **intact** [ɪnˋtækt] *adj.* 完整的；未受損傷的
12. **logging** [ˋlɔgɪŋ] *n.* 砍伐原木

Micro-finance Magician

Nobel Laureate Muhammad Yunus Turns Tiny Loans into Big Opportunities

窮人銀行家尤努斯 九美元讓乞丐變商人

符號說明：

連音 ‿

省略音 。

弱化音 灰色字

補充說明：

在非強調或非重音時，to 會發成 [də]。

To make money you have to have something to make money with.

You have to start with something.

Millions of people are trapped in poverty[2] because they don't have even the smallest something.

For more than 30 years, Muhammad Yunus and the Grameen Bank he founded have been lending money to clients[3] no conventional[4] banker would want, in amounts so small no conventional banker would bother.

Gram means village, and Grameen bankers go to rural[5] villages to offer loans from a few dollars to a few hundred dollars to start a small business.

As each borrower pays it back, the money is loaned out to others.

想要賺錢，就必須有賺錢的工具。

你總得要先有些資本才能起頭。

數百萬的人受困於貧窮，就是因為他們連最基本的資本都沒有。

三十多年來，穆罕默德．尤努斯和他所創立的鄉村銀行一直借貸給一般銀行不願往來的客戶，而且借貸款項常常是一般銀行不屑一顧的金額。

Gram 意指鄉村，鄉村銀行的行員會到村莊鄉里，提供村民幾美元乃至數百美元的貸款，好讓他們做點小生意。

只要借貸人償還款項，這些錢就可以再貸給別人。

Notes & Vocabulary

micro-finance 微型金融

micro- 原指「十的負六次方（10^{-6}）」，引申表示「十分微小的；微觀的」，相反詞是 macro-，表示「大量的；很長的；宏觀的」。常見的相關字有 microchip（微晶片）、micromanage（微觀管理）、microwave（微波爐）。

1. **laureate** [ˋlɔrɪət] *n.* 獲得殊榮者
2. **poverty** [ˋpɑvətɪ] *n.* 貧窮；窮困
3. **client** [ˋklaɪənt] *n.* 客戶
4. **conventional** [kənˋvɛnʃənl] *adj.* 傳統的；一般的
5. **rural** [ˋrʊrəl] *adj.* 農村的；田園的

Marilyn: In Her Own Words

Tapes Reveal the Final Days of the Troubled Screen Siren

揭開性感女神夢露香消玉殞之謎

From the mind of Hollywood's ultimate[2] starlet,[3] intimate[4] details about Marilyn Monroe's personal life—transcripts[5] of audio tapes the actress recorded for her psychiatrist[6] shortly before her death.

The transcripts come from former L.A. county prosecutor John Miner, who investigated[7] Monroe's death.

The psychiatrist has since died and the tapes are believed to have been destroyed.

Monroe's body was discovered on August 5, 1962.

The coroner[8] said she died of barbiturate[9] poisoning and the death was ruled[10] a probable[11] suicide.[12]

But Miner has always believed otherwise.

聽力解說

符號說明：

連音 ‿

省略音 ∘

喉塞音 •

補充說明：

1. 在非強調或非重音時，and 發得較輕，發成 [æn]。
2. barbiturate 這個字的最後兩個音節 turate，大部分的人都會發成 [tʃuwət]。

這位好萊塢最具代表性女星的心思揭露了她本身的私人生活——這是瑪麗蓮·夢露的心理醫師在她死前不久所錄下的錄音帶的文字抄本。

這份抄本來自於前洛杉磯檢察官約翰·麥納，他曾經調查過夢露的死因。

那名心理醫師後來也已過世，且一般人相信錄音帶已遭到銷毀。

夢露的遺體在一九六二年八月五日被人發現。

驗屍官表示她死於巴比妥酸鹽中毒，並判定她可能是自殺死亡。

不過，麥納卻持不同的看法。(註)

(註)一九六二年，夢露被發現陳屍在自家中，手中還握著電話筒，調查結果認為自殺可能性最大，但因外界廣為傳聞夢露與當時總統 John Kennedy(約翰·甘迺迪)及其弟 Bobby Kennedy(巴比·甘迺迪)有曖昧關係，因此盛傳她的死因可能並非自殺而另有隱情。

Notes & Vocabulary

troubled 憂慮的；不安的

troubled 是 trouble 的過去分詞作形容詞用，但不是解作「惹上麻煩的」，troubled 是指情緒上或行為上出現問題，有時 troubled 也指「憂鬱的」，可以用 depressed、disturbed 代換。

- Children who are raised by one parent are often troubled.
  單親父母撫養長大的孩子通常會有情緒上的問題。

1. **siren** [ˋsaɪrən] *n.* 迷人的女人；豔婦
2. **ultimate** [ˋʌltəmət] *adj.* 最終的
3. **starlet** [ˋstɑrlət] *n.* 剛展露頭角的年輕女演員；小女明星
4. **intimate** [ˋɪntəmət] *adj.* 親密的；私密的
5. **transcript** [ˋtrænˏskrɪpt] *n.* 手抄本
6. **psychiatrist** [saɪˋkaɪətrɪst] *n.* 心理醫師；心理學家；精神病醫師
7. **investigate** [ɪnˋvɛstəˏget] *v.* 調查
8. **coroner** [ˋkɔrənɚ] *n.* 驗屍官
9. **barbiturate** [bɑrˋbɪtʃərət] *n.* 巴比妥酸鹽(一種安眠藥)
10. **rule** [rul] *v.* 裁定
11. **probable** [ˋprɑbəbl̩] *adj.* 可能的；合乎情理的
12. **suicide** [ˋsuəˏsaɪd] *n.* 自殺

Rising Waters
Three Gorges Dam Project Fraught with Human Costs
天塹變通途 焉知禍福？——三峽大壩工程的得與失

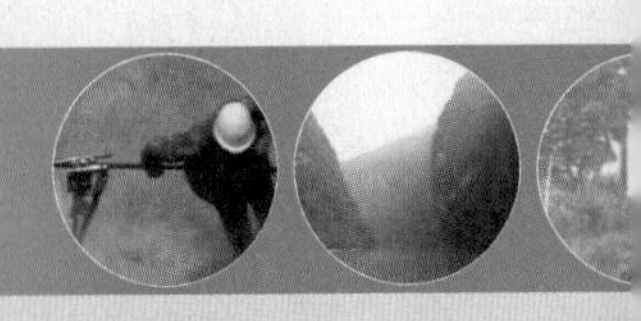

符號說明：
連音 ‿
喉塞音 ·

補充說明：
1. 英式英語中的 [r] 音常省略，如：greater、or、more、ever、nuclear、power、river、dollar。
2. 在非強調或非重音時，to 會發成 [tə]，for 會發成 [fr]，而 and 會發成 [ən]，此處更簡化到只發 [n]。

When it comes to global challenges, few are greater or more controversial[4] than the construction of the massive[5] Three Gorges Dam in central China.

It is the biggest dam, the largest hydroelectric[6] scheme[7] the world has ever seen.

When it is finished, it will generate[8] enough energy to equal 15 nuclear power plants.

But for all[9] the benefits, there's also a human cost.

Hundreds of towns and villages along the Yangtze River will be consigned to history, swallowed up[10] one by one by the rising waters.

For a country that says it is committed[11] to clean energy and sustainable[12] development, this is a high-profile[13] and multibillion-dollar gamble.

談到全球性挑戰，沒有幾件事會比在中國華中地區興建三峽大壩更惹人爭議。

三峽大壩是全球最大的水壩，也是有史以來最大的水力發電計畫。

一旦竣工後，三峽大壩將可產生相當於十五座核能發電廠所產生的電力。

但人類也得為這種種利益而付出代價。

長江沿岸數以百計的城鎮和村落將淹沒在歷史洪流中，它們將因為水位上升而逐一遭到吞滅。

對一個表示決心使用乾淨能源及達到永續發展的國家而言，這是一場萬眾矚目且金額達數十億美元的賭局。

Notes & Vocabulary

be consigned to history 走入歷史

我們常常用「走入歷史」這句話來表示事物已消逝或結束，英文中就是用 sth be consigned to history。consign [kən`saɪn] 在此意指「移走、處置」，是較正式的用語。

- If everything goes according to plan, fox hunting will soon be consigned to history.
  如果一切照計劃走，獵狐很快就會成為歷史名詞了。

1. **Three Gorges** [`gɔrdʒɪz] *n.* 長江三峽
2. **dam** [dæm] *n.* 水壩；水堤
3. **fraught with** [frɔt] *adj.* 充滿……的；伴隨……的
4. **controversial** [͵kɑntrə`vɝʃəl] *adj.* 倍受爭議的
5. **massive** [`mæsɪv] *adj.* 巨大的；大規模的
6. **hydroelectric** [͵haɪdroɪ`lɛktrɪk] *adj.* 水力發電的
7. **scheme** [skim] *n.* 計畫；方案
8. **generate** [`dʒɛnə͵ret] *v.* 生產（電、能量等）
9. **for all** *phr.* 儘管
10. **swallow up** [`swɑlo] *v.* 淹沒；吞沒；吞併
11. **commit** [kəm`mɪt] *v.* 做出擔保
12. **sustainable** [sə`stenəbl̩] *adj.* 能保持的；能維持的
13. **high-profile** [`haɪ`pro͵faɪl] *adj.* 倍受矚目的；高姿態的

The Rising Sun's New Imperial Son

悠仁太子誕生 解除日本皇位繼承危機

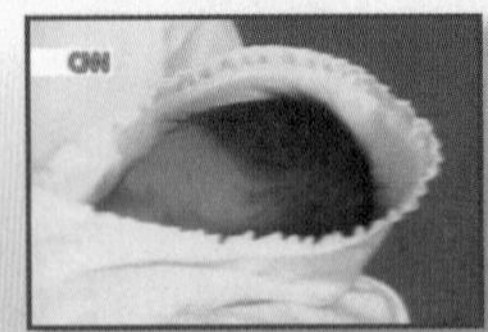

符號說明：

連音 ‿

省略音 °

弱化音 灰色字

補充說明：

1. 英文中有一些單字裡的字母不發音，如 wrap 中因為 w 與 r 不易一起發音，故 w 不發音。而 heir 中的 h 不發音則是源自羅馬時代，類似的字還有 honest、hour、honor 等。

2. 在非強調或非重音時，而 and 會發成 [æn]，此處發得更加省略，只發了 [æ]。

Japan's Prince Hisahito made his first public appearance just nine days after his birth, wrapped in his mother's arms, little more than a headful of dark hair peeking out.

Proud parents Princess Kiko and Prince Akishino unveiled[2] their son to the public as they returned home from the hospital after his delivery.[3]

They named their son Hisahito—"hisa" meaning "eternal[4] serenity"[5] and "hito" meaning "person of the highest moral standard."

Hisahito's birth on September 6 was celebrated across Japan.

He is the first male heir[6] born to the imperial family in more than four decades, averting[7] a succession[8] crisis.

日本皇子悠仁在出生僅九天後便初次亮相。悠仁在母親的懷抱中，只露出一頭黑髮。

得意的父母親紀子妃及皇子秋篠文仁，是在生產後從醫院返家時，首度讓他們的兒子曝光。

他們將孩子取名為悠仁，「悠」意指「永恆的寧靜」，「仁」意指「道德標準最高的人」。

悠仁九月六日誕生，日本舉國上下都為此慶祝。

悠仁是日本皇室四十多年來誕生的第一位男性繼承人，因此解除了日本皇位繼承的危機。

Notes & Vocabulary

the Rising Sun 日本的別稱

「日本」在英文中用的是 Japan 這個字，但其實日本人是以 Nippon 或 Nihon 自稱。Nippon 常用在較正式的場合，如貨幣、郵票或大型比賽，或者是作為官方用語，如日本銀行稱為 Nippon Ginko（日語讀音）。而 Nihon 則是一般人、較現代的用語。至於為何會有 the Rising Sun 之稱呢？原來「日本」字面上意思就是「太陽之本」，也就是太陽升起的地方，所以日本有時也被稱為「太陽之國」（the Land of the Rising Sun）。

1. **imperial** [ɪm`pɪrɪəl] *adj.* 皇帝的；帝國的
2. **unveil** [ˏʌn`vel] *v.* 使曝光；揭露
3. **delivery** [dɪ`lɪvərɪ] *n.* 誕生；分娩
4. **eternal** [ɪ`tɜnl̩] *adj.* 永恆的；不朽的
5. **serenity** [sə`rɛnətɪ] *n.* 寧靜；平靜
6. **heir** [ɛr] *n.* 繼承人
7. **avert** [ə`vɜt] *v.* 防止；避免
8. **succession** [sək`sɛʃən] *n.* 繼承

Recycling City
Chinese Municipality Feels the Effects of Being the World's Dumpster
資源回收與環境污染的矛盾

聽力解說

符號說明：
連音 ‿
省略音 。
喉塞音 •
弱化音 灰色字

補充說明：
1. 在非強調或非重音時，your 會發成 [jr]，而本文中的兩處 and 發得較輕，發成 [æn]。
2. in the 中的 [n] 與 [ð] 因發音位置接近樣而發生同化現象。

Welcome to "Recycling City," where you'll find mountains of cereal[3] boxes, frozen dinner containers,[4] even old American flags.

All of it is thrown out by environmentally conscious[5] people as far away as the U.S. and Britain.

And it turns up here, in the town of Lian Jiao, halfway around the world.

So after you've neatly separated all your recycled goods, much of it ends up in warehouses[6] such as this with the plastic bottles, the crushed cans, even the plastic[7] bags from the retailers[8] such as Sears, Target and Wal-Mart.

About a third of household plastics recycled in the U.S. are shipped to China.

Many factories here are paying higher prices for recycled products as China's demand for raw[9] materials grows.

歡迎來到「資源回收大本營」，這裡有堆積如山的早餐麥片紙盒、冷凍餐點的包裝容器、甚至老舊的美國國旗。

這些都是有環保意識的人丟棄的垃圾，他們的居住地可能遠在美國與英國。

但是這些垃圾卻繞過了半個地球，出現在這個稱為聯滘的小鎮。

所以，你把所有資源垃圾仔細分類後，其中許多垃圾就會集中到像這樣的倉庫，裡面可能堆滿了塑膠瓶、壓扁了的鐵罐、甚至是來自希爾思、塔吉特及沃爾瑪這類零售商的塑膠袋。

美國回收的家庭塑膠垃圾，約有三分之一都運到中國。

隨著中國對原物料的需求增加，這裡許多工廠也都必須以更高的價格購買回收產品。

Notes & Vocabulary

end up 結果為；以……為結果

end 為動詞「結束」，end up 在這裡則有「最後成為……」的意思。通常 end up 後面接 V-ing 表示「最後有什麼樣結果」。

- Because she was sick, Maggie ended up staying at home during the holiday.
  瑪姬因為生病，所以最後整個假期都待在家裡。

另一個類似的用法是：

wind up [waɪnd] 最後結果是……

- Many investors wound up broke after the stock market crash.
  在股市崩盤後，許多投資者都破產了。

1. **municipality** [mjuˏnɪsəˋpælətɪ] *n.* 自治市
2. **dumpster** [ˋdʌmpstɚ] *n.* 大型垃圾箱
3. **cereal** [ˋsɪrɪəl] *n.* 穀片；麥片類早餐
4. **container** [kənˋtenɚ] *n.* 容器（如箱、盒、罐等）
5. **conscious** [ˋkɑnʃəs] *adj.* 有意識的；特別注意的；故意的
6. **warehouse** [ˋwɛrˏhaʊs] *n.* 倉庫
7. **plastic** [ˋplæstɪk] *adj., n.* 塑膠（的）
8. **retailer** [ˋriˏtelɚ] *n.* 零售商
9. **raw** [rɔ] *adj.* 未加工的；未經處理的

Robots Strut Their Stuff at Japan Expo

未來機器人讓你大開眼界

符號說明：

連音 ‿
喉塞音 •
弱化音 灰色字

補充說明：

1. 在非強調或非重音時，to 會發成 [tə] 或 [də]。
2. 當 [t] 遇到 [ð]，通常會因為發音位置相近而同化成 [ð]，如文中的 at the 與 that they。

The robots at the 2005 World Expo in Japan have something to prove—that they can be human too.

Sort of.

Toyota's brass band[2] of swinging[3] robots features[4] humanlike manual[5] dexterity[6] and an eerie[7] coordinated[8] dance step.

So what's the fascination[9] with making robots more human?

What better way to find out about robots than to ask a robot?

Meet Kokoro, the Expo's android[10] receptionist.

She speaks four different languages and is designed to look as human as possible.

Visitors seem to like her, even if she can't give a straight answer.

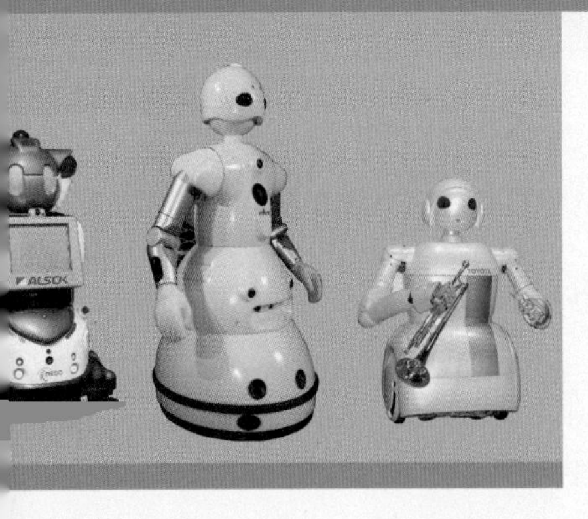

在日本的二〇〇五年世界博覽會上展出的機器人證明一件事——它們也可以跟真人一樣。

就某個程度上來說是如此。

豐田推出的機器人管樂隊擺動著身體，具有像人一樣的靈活度，舞步的協調性也足以讓人毛骨悚然。

把機器人做得更接近真人，究竟有什麼引人著迷之處？

要了解機器人，有什麼方法比直接問一個機器人更好呢？

來見過「心」，博覽會場的迎賓機器人。

她會說四種不同語言，而且外觀設計以極力逼近真人為能事。

遊客似乎都非常喜歡她，即使她會答非所問。

Notes & Vocabulary

strut one's stuff 大顯身手

標題中有一個慣用語 strut one's stuff，stuff 在這裡是表示一個人的能力、本事，而 strut [strʌt] 的原始字義為「神氣地走來走去」，引申為「賣弄、炫耀」的意思。而這個片語原先是用來表示「進入舞池一展身手」，後來擴大適用到所有「炫耀自己所有或所能」的情況。

- Tom struts his stuff on the dance floor.
  湯姆在舞池中大秀舞技。

1. **expo** [ˋɛkspo] *n.* 博覽會（= exposition）
2. **brass band** [bræs] [bænd] *n.* 管樂隊
3. **swing** [swɪŋ] *v.* 搖動；擺動
4. **feature** [ˋfitʃɚ] *v.* 以……為特色；以……作為號召
5. **manual** [ˋmænjuəl] *adj.* 手的；用手操作的
6. **dexterity** [dɛkˋstɛrətɪ] *n.* 靈巧；熟練；敏捷
7. **eerie** [ˋɪrɪ] *adj.* 神祕怪異而令人毛骨悚然的
8. **coordinated** [koˋɔrdəˌnetɪd] *adj.* 動作協調的
9. **fascination** [ˌfæsəˋneʃən] *n.* 魅力；著迷
10. **android** [ˋænˌdrɔɪd] *n.* 做得很像真人的機器人

Cinematic Chameleon

TalkAsia Exclusive Interview with Taiwanese-Japanese Actor Takeshi Kaneshiro

CNN 專訪亞洲巨星金城武

聽力解說

符號說明：

連音 ‿

省略音 。

喉塞音 ・

補充說明：

1. haven't 中的 t 常會省略不發。
2. 英式英語中的 [r] 音常省略，如：heard、star、versatility、after、daggers、perhaps。
3. that you're 發生同化現象，形成 [ðætʃə]；而 in the 形成 [ɪnə]。
4. 在非強調或非重音時，and 一般會發成 [ən]，文中較特別的是，主播以一拍的停頓代表 and，幾乎聽不到 and 的聲音。

Welcome to *TalkAsia*.

Now there is a chance you haven't yet heard of Takeshi Kaneshiro, but there is very little chance, if you care anything at all about Asian culture or film in general, that you're going to remain ignorant[4] of him for very long.

He's a pop star, he's an actor of considerable[5] versatility,[6] and now he's a model.

After hit TV shows and 29 films, *Time* magazine has described him as a chameleon, the Johnny Depp, no less, of the Asian film industry.

He was an hero in the ravishing[7] movie *The House of Flying Daggers*.[8]

But his latest film, consistent with[9] his professional restlessness,[10] is a big budget musical—*Perhaps Love*.

歡迎收看《亞洲名人聊天室》。

你有可能還沒聽過金城武，但如果你還算關心亞洲文化或電影相關事物的話，那你還能一直不知道這號人物的機會恐怕是微乎其微。

他是個偶像，是個多才多藝的演員，現在又成了模特兒。

他拍過紅極一時的電視劇和二十九部電影，《時代》雜誌形容他為變色龍，稱他是亞洲電影界的強尼．戴普毫不為過。

他是《十面埋伏》這部絕美的電影中的武打英雄，

但他最新的電影作品，則是一部大成本音樂劇《如果．愛》，延續了他在專業上變化多端的一貫作風。

Notes & Vocabulary

no less (than) 正是；多達

no less than 連用時字面意思為「不少於⋯⋯」，是英語句型中一種加強語氣的用法，表示「多達；有⋯⋯之多」，作用類似於 as much as。

- His novel has been translated into no less than 30 languages.
  他的小說已被譯成不下於三十種語言的版本。

而除了強調數量之多，no less 亦可用來強調所談及的人或物的重要性，即「正是、恰是」之意。例如本文中出現的 the Johnny Depp, no less, of the Asian film industry，這句暗示主播認為強尼．戴普在電影圈具有指標性的地位。

- The building was opened by Jack Welch, no less.
  為大樓主持揭幕典禮的人正是傑克．威爾許本人。

1. cinematic [ˌsɪnəˋmætɪk] *adj.* 電影的
2. chameleon [kəˋmiljən] *n.* 變色龍；善變的人
3. exclusive [ɪksˋklusɪv] *adj.* 獨家的；排外的
4. ignorant [ˋɪgnərənt] *adj.* 不知道的；無知的
5. considerable [kənˋsɪdərəbəl] *adj.* 相當大的；相當可觀的
6. versatility [ˌvɝsəˋtɪlətɪ] *n.* 多才多藝
7. ravishing [ˋrævɪʃɪŋ] *adj.* 令人陶醉的；迷人的
8. dagger [ˋdægɚ] *n.* 匕首；短劍
9. consistent with [kənˋsɪstənt] *phr.* 與⋯⋯一致
10. restlessness [ˋrɛstləsnəs] *n.* 待不住；求變化

World's Tallest Building Opening Soon

世界最高樓杜拜「哈利法塔」啟用

聽力解說

符號說明：

連音 ‿

省略音 ∘

喉塞音 •

補充說明：

1. 在非強調或非重音時，to 會發成 [tə]，for 會發成 [fr]。而 and 在此發成 [ən]。
2. 此處的 than [ðæn] 發成 [ðən]。

Preparations are underway for the inauguration of the world's tallest building.

Just hours from now, the 160-story Burj Dubai will open its doors to much fanfare.[1]

It contains the world's tallest outdoor observation deck[2] and an elevator with the longest travel distance in the world.

It contains more than a thousand residential[3] units, 160 hotel rooms and 37 floors for corporate offices.

世界最高樓落成典禮的準備工作正在進行中。

幾個小時後，一百六十層樓高的杜拜塔（編註：已改名「哈利法塔」）將敞開大門迎接風光的慶祝活動。

該大樓有世界最高的戶外觀景台和世界搭乘距離最長的電梯。

還有超過一千個住宅單位、一百六十個旅館房間和三十七層供作企業辦公室的樓層。

Notes & Vocabulary

inauguration 落成典禮；開幕式；就職

inauguration 的動詞形式為 inaugurate，除了指「落成典禮；開幕式」之外，亦可指人員的「就職；就任」。

- The next president will be inaugurated in late May, 2012.
  下一任總統將於二〇一二年五月底上任。

1. fanfare [ˋfænˏfɛr] *n.*
   （典禮前）號角齊鳴；慶賀活動；喧譁誇耀
2. observation deck [ˏɑbzəˋveʃən][dɛk]
   觀景台；瞭望台
3. residential [ˏrɛzəˋdɛnʃəl] *adj.* 住宅的；居住的

2009 Word of the Year: "Unfriend"

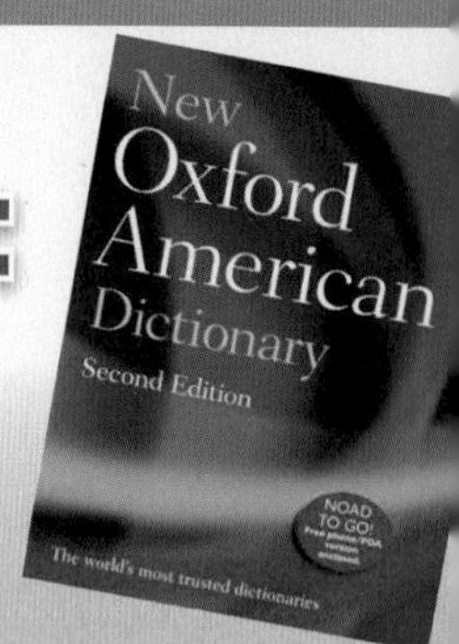

"unfriend" 獲選牛津字典年度辭彙

符號說明：

連音 ‿
省略音 ∘
喉塞音 •

補充說明：

在非強調或非重音時，to 會發成 [tə]，而 and 會發成 [ən]。

Well, on this program we often talk about the peaks[1] and the troughs[2] of the commodities[3] market, but as the writer Christopher Morley once said, "Words are a commodity in which there's never any slump.[4]"

So, without any further ado,[5] the 2009 word of the year as chosen by the New Oxford American Dictionary—"unfriend."

Now, the verb means to remove someone as a "friend" on a social networking site, such as Facebook. An example: "I decided to unfriend Maggie after we fought over the last crumpet[6] at the board meeting."

我們經常在節目上談到商品市場的起起伏伏，但是作家克里斯多福．莫勒曾經說過：「語言是種從未不跌價的商品。」

所以，話不多說，新牛津美語字典已經選出了二〇〇九年的年度單字——「刪除好友」。

這個動詞意思是「把像 Facebook 這類社交網站中某位名列『好友』的人移除。」例句：「我和梅姬在董事會議為了最後一塊烤餅起爭執，之後就決定要把她刪除好友了。」

Notes & Vocabulary

unfriend 刪除好友

知名社交網站 facebook 的用語 unfriend 被《新牛津美語大辭典》選為二〇〇九年度代表字，而 twitter 也被「全球語言觀察中心」（Global Language Monitor）選為二〇〇九年最熱門字彙。以下是其他網路科技新字彙：

twitter 推特（知名微網誌，也可作動詞用，同 tweet「發表推文」）

netiquette 網路禮節

netizen 網路公民；鄉民

vlog 影音部落格

webisode 網路影片；網路影片的一集

1. **peak** [pik] *n.* 高峰；尖頂
2. **trough** [trɔf] *n.* 低潮；低谷；蕭條階段
3. **commodity** [kə`mɑdətɪ] *n.* 商品；貨物
4. **slump** [slʌmp] *n.*（價值、數量等）猛跌；驟降
5. **ado** [ə`du] *n.*（無謂的）紛擾；麻煩
6. **crumpet** [`krʌmpət] *n.* 小圓烤餅

Apple Releases Smaller MacBook

蘋果發表輕薄筆電 MacBook Air

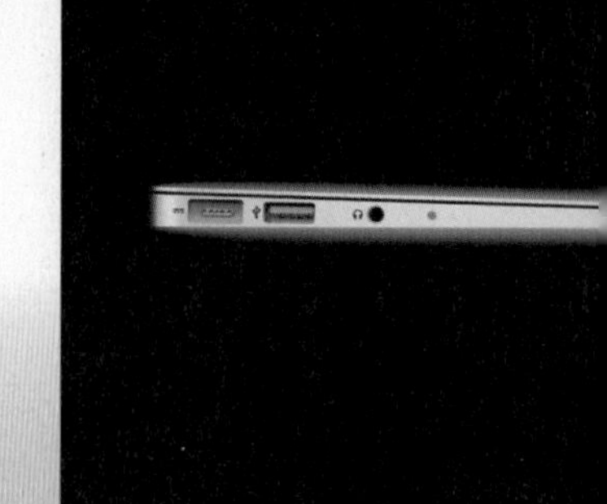

聽力解說

符號說明：

連音 ‿

省略音 。

喉塞音 ‧

弱化音 灰色字

補充說明：

1. the 在子音前唸作 [ðə]，母音前 [ði]，若在標題、名字或強調獨一性時，則常唸 [ði]。此處另外有一個插入音 uh，口語中停頓時很常見。

2. 在非強調或非重音時，can 會發成 [kn]。

This is the<uh> new device,[1] the new notebook that Apple released today.

This is the 11-inch MacBook Air. This is on my left. On my right, this is the traditional 13-inch MacBook. You can see the difference in size here, but also a huge difference in weight.

This new MacBook Air is incredibly[2] light. It's got a full-size keyboard and weighs just a little more than two pounds, and as we said, the full-size keyboard.

It's got 256 gigs[3] of flash memory. [It] does not have a typical[4] hard drive.

So you might call this a little bit of a game on between the new MacBook Air and the traditional iPad, but Apple clearly wants to play this game because they come out[5] the winners either way.

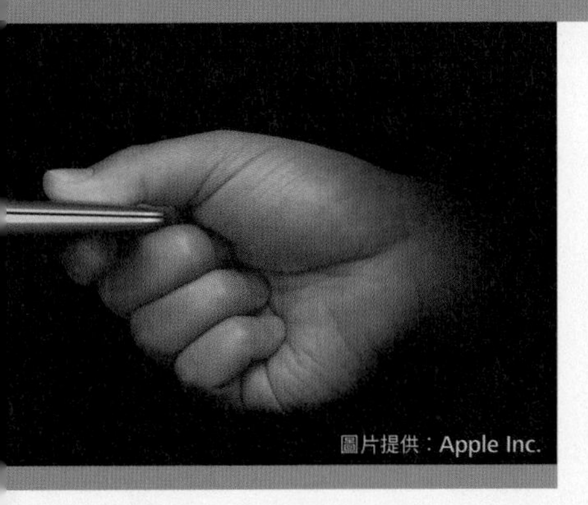
圖片提供：Apple Inc.

這是新機種，是蘋果今天推出的新筆電。

這是十一吋大的 MacBook Air，就是在我左手邊這一台。我右邊這台是標準的十三吋 MacBook。你可以看出大小的差異，而且重量也相差很大。

新推出的 MacBook Air 輕盈得令人難以置信，雖然配置了全尺寸鍵盤，重量卻只有兩磅多一點。我們剛剛提過，鍵盤是全尺寸鍵盤。

還有兩百五十六 GB 的快閃記憶體。這部筆電沒有一般的硬碟。

所以也許可以說新推出的 MacBook Air 和先前的 iPad 之間對戰。可是蘋果顯然願意進行這場競爭；因為無論如何他們最後都是贏家。

Notes & Vocabulary

game on 開打；對戰

原本是指「遊戲或比賽開始」，例如電玩的格鬥、比賽類型的遊戲開始和電腦或對手對戰，所以 game on 就表示「開打；對戰」。

- Jeff announced that it was game on after his sister played several pranks on him.
  杰夫被姊姊惡作劇好幾次之後，他宣佈要開戰了。

1. **device** [dɪˋvaɪs] *n.* 儀器；設備
2. **incredibly** [ɪnˋkrɛdəblɪ] *adv.* 不可思議地
3. **gig** [gɪg] *n.* 十億位元組（= gigabyte）
4. **typical** [ˋtɪpɪkəl] *adj.* 平常的；典型的
5. **come out** [kʌm][aut] *v.* 結果是

NOTES

實戰應用篇 Part I

McCoffee vs. Starbucks

Fast Food Giant Brews a Challenge to the Caffeine Kings

速食咖啡挑戰咖啡龍頭

如果你是使用 MP3 ，請聽 MP3 Track 63；如果你使用電腦互動光碟，請點選 DVD-ROM【實戰應用篇—Part I: Unit 1】，試試看是否聽懂新聞內容。

請瀏覽下列關鍵字彙，再仔細聽一次。

brew 煮（咖啡）	upmarket 高價位的
cognoscente 行家	premium 頂級的
gourmet 精緻美食的	last resort 不得已的選擇
dead heat 難分高下	

如果你還不是聽的很懂的話，請參考下列發音提示，再仔細聽一次。

連音	McDonald's as、smooth or bold、have eyes、gave folks
省略音	natural、going to
弱化音	have eyes
同化音	going to

試著作答下列聽力測驗題目。

True or False 是非題

____ 1. McDonald's is going to start using a better brand of coffee.

____ 2. The survey was done by professionals for CNN.

____ 3. Gaviña and Sons has been around for more than a hundred years.

____ 4. The Frenchwoman was happy to find out that she picked the McDonald's coffee.

____ 5. McDonald's coffee will be more expensive than Starbucks'.

Multiple Choice 選擇題

____ 1. Where did CNN go to conduct its survey?

a. France b. New York
c. California d. New Orleans

____ 2. What supplier will McDonald's be getting its new coffee from?

a. Starbucks b. the French
c. Gaviña and Sons d. Dunkin' Donuts

____ 3. According to the survey, which coffee did people like best?

a. McDonald's b. Starbucks
c. Dunkin' Donut's d. there was no clear winner

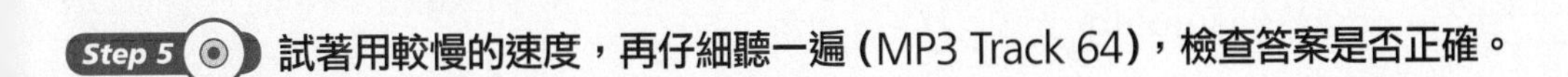

Step 5 試著用較慢的速度，再仔細聽一遍（MP3 Track 64），檢查答案是否正確。

Step 6 對答案、驗收成果，並詳讀原文，若仍有不懂的地方，可反覆多聽幾次。

（答案請見 p. 313）

CNN Anchor

Fast food chain McDonald's is going upmarket.[3] Its latest ploy[4] is to try to appeal to[5] the coffee cognoscente.[6] McDonald's says it's upgrading the beans it uses to a premium[7] blend[8] roasted in California. CNN's Jeanne Moos went to see if caffeine-crazy New Yorkers can tell their coffee from their McCoffee.

Jeanne Moos, CNN Correspondent

Imagine instead of ordering a Big Mac, walking into McDonald's and asking for a smooth or bold, move over[9] Starbucks, here comes gourmet[10] McCoffee.

Pedestrian 1

That's good. I like that.

Jeanne Moos, CNN Correspondent

McDonald's.

Pedestrian 1

Are you serious?

Jeanne Moos, CNN Correspondent

In an unscientific, totally amateur[11] taste test, we gave folks three kinds of coffee without telling them what was going down the hatch.

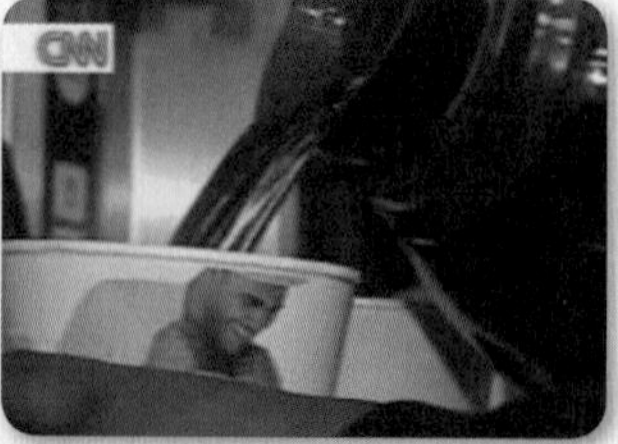

Pedestrian 2

I prefer this one.

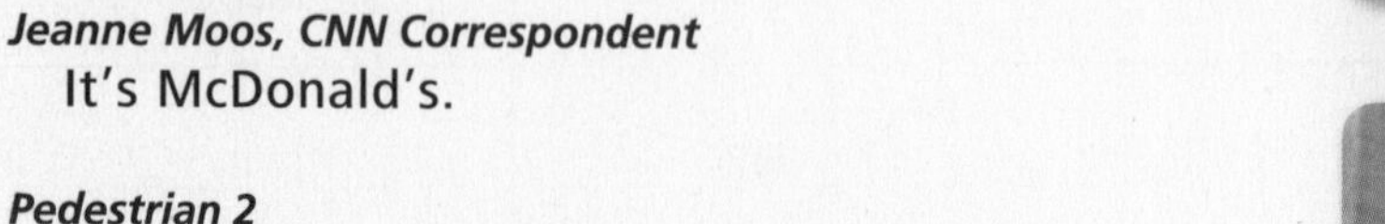

Jeanne Moos, CNN Correspondent

It's McDonald's.

Pedestrian 2

Really? Aw.

Jeanne Moos, CNN Correspondent

It fooled even the fussy[12] French.

CNN 主播

速食連鎖業者麥當勞現在有意走精緻路線。他們最新的策略是吸引咖啡達人。麥當勞表示他們已改用一種在加州烘烤的頂級咖啡豆。本台記者吉妮．莫斯要看看酷愛咖啡的紐約客是否能分出一般咖啡與「麥當勞咖啡」的區別。

CNN 特派員 吉妮．莫斯

試想你進入一家麥當勞，點的卻不是大麥克漢堡，而是「中等或重口味」的咖啡。閃一邊去吧！星巴克，麥當勞的精品咖啡要登場了！

路人甲

這杯味道好，我喜歡。

CNN 特派員 吉妮．莫斯

這杯是麥當勞咖啡。

路人甲

妳在開玩笑吧？

CNN 特派員 吉妮．莫斯

我們進行了一項不合乎科學方法、毫不專業的市場口味測試，讓民眾在不知道品牌的情況下，品嚐三種不同的咖啡。

路人乙

我喜歡這種口味。

CNN 特派員 吉妮．莫斯

這是麥當勞咖啡。

路人乙

真的嗎？哇咧！

CNN 特派員 吉妮．莫斯

連愛挑剔的法國人都被唬住了。

Notes & Vocabulary

smooth or bold 咖啡口感的分類

影響咖啡口感的因素很多，包括酸度（acidity）、稠度（body）與香氣（flavor）等。各家廠牌對於咖啡口感的分類方式不盡相同，但大致而言可分為 mild、smooth 與 bold 三種。其中 mild（柔和類）嚐起來最清淡，如哥斯大黎加（Costa Rica）、墨西哥（Mexico）咖啡等。smooth（滑順類）味道稍重，以濃縮烘焙（Espresso Roast）咖啡為代表；bold（濃郁類）的口感最為豐厚，蘇門答臘（Sumatra）與肯亞（Kenya）咖啡均屬此類。

down the hatch 大快朵頤

hatch 原指交通工具上供人員逃生或貨品搬運用的「小孔」，但在口語中則引申為「嘴巴」。英文中常用祈使句 Down the hatch! 來表示「盡情吃喝吧！大快朵頤吧！」或「乾杯！飲落去！」的意思，意同於 drink up。

1. **brew** [bru] *v.* 泡（茶）；煮（咖啡）；調製（飲料）
2. **caffeine** [kæˋfin] *n.* 咖啡因
3. **upmarket** [ˋʌpˋmɑrkət] *adj.* 高價位的；高消費的
4. **ploy** [plɔɪ] *n.* 計謀；策略
5. **appeal to** [əˋpil] *v.* 吸引；取得……的喜愛
6. **cognoscente** [ˏkɑnjəˋʃɛnti] *n.*【義】行家
7. **premium** [ˋprimɪəm] *adj.* 頂級的
8. **blend** [blɛnd] *n.* 混合物
9. **move over** *v.* 閃一邊；讓位
10. **gourmet** [ˋgʊrˏme] *adj.* 精緻美食的；老饕的
11. **amateur** [ˋæməˏtʃʊr] *adj.* 業餘的
12. **fussy** [ˋfʌsɪ] *adj.* 好挑剔的；難伺候的

Pedestrian 3
This one would be, maybe, the better one.

Jeanne Moos, CNN Correspondent
McDonald's.

Pedestrian 3
McDonald's. Sad.

Jeanne Moos, CNN Correspondent
It's natural to think of McDonald's as the coffee of last resort.[13] But now, they've got a new gourmet supplier—"Gaviña and Sons" has been around for over a century.

Pedestrian 4
I think this one's the best. That's a second and that's the worst.

Jeanne Moos, CNN Correspondent
You like McDonald's coffee better than Starbucks.

Our survey ended in a dead heat of the 30 or so people who swigged[14] sample after sample. A third preferred Dunkin' Donuts. A third preferred Starbucks and a third preferred McDonald's. McDonald's will still be the cheapest of the three.

Pedestrian 5
Are they going to add trans fats[15] to that like they do with their french fries?[16]

Jeanne Moos, CNN Correspondent
Who needs trans fats when you only have eyes for[17] caffeine.

Is that what happens when you get caffeinated?[18]

路人丙

這一杯應該比較好。

CNN 特派員 吉妮．莫斯

這杯是麥當勞咖啡。

路人丙

麥當勞。真可悲啊！

CNN 特派員 吉妮．莫斯

人們總認為只有在別無選擇下才會去買麥當勞咖啡，但如今麥當勞已經換了一家高級的咖啡供應商。「高維納父子」這家老字號已經有一百多年的歷史。

路人丁

我認為這一種最棒，那種其次，另外那種最差。

CNN 特派員 吉妮．莫斯

妳對麥當勞咖啡的評價比對星巴克的高呢！

約有三十位民眾參與評選，他們灌下了一杯杯的咖啡，結果三家廠牌的得票數難分軒輊。三分之一的人偏好 Dunkin' Donuts，三分之一的人選擇星巴克，另有三分之一的人喜歡麥當勞。相較之下，麥當勞咖啡的價位是最便宜的。

路人戊

他們會不會在咖啡裡頭加反式脂肪？就像他們在薯條裡加的一樣？

CNN 特派員 吉妮．莫斯

當你只注意到咖啡因的時候，誰還會去管反式脂肪呢？

你喝了咖啡之後都會像這樣嗎？

Notes & Vocabulary

dead heat 難分高下；平手

此詞出自十八世紀英國賽馬（horse race）術語，代表競爭者的成績「旗鼓相當；難分勝負」。heat 在此並非作「熱」解釋，而是指競賽中的「一輪賽事」。意義相近的片語還包括：

- photo finish
  指賽馬幾乎同時抵達終點，得看照片才能判定勝負
- stalemate
  下西洋棋雙方無子可動的狀況，比喻平手或形成僵局
- drawn battle/contest
  未分勝負的一戰

13. **last resort** [rɪˋzɔrt] *n. phr.*
    最後手段；不得已的**選擇**
14. **swig** [swɪg] *v.* 大口地喝；牛飲
15. **trans fat** [trænz] [fæt] *n.* 反式脂肪
    （包含 trans-fatty acids「反式脂肪酸」的脂肪，攝取過量易增加罹患心血管疾病的風險）
16. **french fries** [frɛntʃ] *n.*
    薯條（常用複數，且 french 首字常會大寫）
17. **only have eyes for** *v. phr.*
    只顧著……（而無視於其他事物）
18. **caffeinated** [ˋkæfəˏnetəd] *adj.* 含咖啡因的

Window Shopping

The Store's Always Open with Touch Screen Displays

逛街購物新概念——觸控式櫥窗

Step 1 如果你是使用 MP3 ，請聽 MP3 Track 65；如果你使用電腦互動光碟，請點選 DVD-ROM【實戰應用篇—Part I: Unit 2】，試試看是否聽懂新聞內容。

Step 2 請瀏覽下列關鍵字彙，再仔細聽一次。

touch screen　觸碰式螢幕	display　陳列；展出
merchandise　商品	gimmick　祕密裝置；竅門
embed　埋置；把……嵌入	transmit　傳送
interactive　互動的	

Step 3 如果你還不是聽的很懂的話，請參考下列發音提示，再仔細聽一次。

連音	a way of fighting、choose a color、enough for
同化音	let your、touch screen
去捲舌音	buyers、doors
省略音	it will

試著作答下列聽力測驗題目。

True or False 是非題

____ 1. Window shopping used to help people avoid the urge to spend.

____ 2. Passersby at New York's Ralph Lauren store are encouraged to touch the glass.

____ 3. The touch screen service is only available during normal store hours.

____ 4. Purchases are mailed to shoppers.

____ 5. Shoppers can make purchases from any department in the store.

Multiple Choice 選擇題

____ 1. What science fiction movie inspired Ralph Lauren's son, David?

a. *Blade Runner* b. *Minority Report*
c. *The Matrix* d. *I, Robot*

____ 2. What transmits the shopper's touch on the glass?

a. tiny wires b. lasers
c. a special liquid d. all of the above

____ 3. What do shoppers pay with?

a. cash b. check
c. credit card d. bank transfer

試著用較慢的速度，再仔細聽一遍（MP3 Track 66），檢查答案是否正確。

對答案、驗收成果，並詳讀原文，若仍有不懂的地方，可反覆多聽幾次。

（答案請見 p. 313）

CNN Anchor

Look, but don't buy. Window shopping is meant to be a way of fighting the urge[3] to spend, but that is all changing.

CNN Anchor

Absolutely. The fashion retailer[4] Ralph Lauren is at the pointy end of all of this, and is setting a trap[5] for impulse buyers. As Jeanne Moos reports, the shop may close its doors but its window is always open.

Jeanne Moos, CNN Correspondent

Let your fingers do the walking when you're window shopping? The guys who wash the windows aren't going to like this. Passersby[6] are encouraged to smudge[7] up the glass at Ralph Lauren on Madison Avenue.

You can touch it.

Pedestrian 1

Oh, how fabulous.[8]

Jeanne Moos, CNN Correspondent

Day or night, store open or closed, if that polo shirt on the mannequin[9] appeals to you, just touch. You can shop various departments, choose a color, choose a size, proceed to checkout,[10] type in your address to have the merchandise[11] mailed to you, then swipe[12] your credit card.

Pedestrian 2

I think it's a gimmick,[13] and I think it will work because everyone wants to try it one time. One time.

CNN 主播

看就好，不要買。純粹逛街，看看櫥窗裡的商品本來應該是一種抗拒購買慾的方式，可是這種現象已經開始改變了。

CNN 主播

確實如此。時尚零售商勞夫．羅倫走在時代尖端，為個性衝動的買家設下了陷阱。吉妮．莫斯的報導告訴我們，這家品牌的商店雖然會打烊，但是櫥窗永遠在營業中。

CNN 特派員 吉妮．莫斯

逛街的時候讓你的手指游走在櫥窗上？洗窗工人可不會喜歡這件事。麥迪遜大道上的勞夫．羅倫歡迎路人儘量觸摸他們的櫥窗玻璃。

你可以用手摸。

路人甲

真好。

CNN 特派員 吉妮．莫斯

不論白天還是夜晚，不論店門開著還是關著，只要模特兒身上的那件馬球衫吸引你，伸手觸碰就行了。你可以去逛不同的部門，選擇顏色，選擇尺寸，再到付帳，輸入商品寄送地址，然後刷卡。

路人乙

我覺得這是一種行銷手法，而且應該會有效，因為每個人都會想要試一次看看。就那麼一次。

Notes & Vocabulary

at the pointy end 在尖端

pointy 原意是「尖的」，end 在此是指物體的「一端」。「尖的那一端」通常是前端攻擊、戳刺用的部分，所以這個片語就是指身處「尖端」、在前頭的意思。

- This company's products are at the pointy end of high tech.
  這間公司的產品走在高科技最前端。

impulse buyers 一時衝動的買家

impulse 原為名詞，意思是「衝動」，在此為複合詞用法，例如 impulse buying 或 impulse purchase 就是指「衝動性購買」。

- Stores put small items next to their registers for impulse buyers.
  店家在收銀機旁放一些小東西吸引衝動型買家。

1. **touch screen** [tʌtʃ] [skrin] *n.* 觸碰式螢幕
2. **display** [dɪˋsple] *n.* 陳列；展出
3. **urge** [ɝdʒ] *n.* 衝動
4. **retailer** [ˋri͵telɚ] *n.* 零售商
5. **trap** [træp] *n.* 陷阱
6. **passerby** [͵pæsɚˋbaɪ] *n.* 路人（複數形為 passersby）
7. **smudge** [smʌdʒ] *v.* 弄髒
8. **fabulous** [ˋfæbjələs] *adj.* 驚人的；極好的
9. **mannequin** [ˋmænɪkən] *n.* 模特兒模型
10. **checkout** [ˋtʃɛk͵aut] *n.* 結帳
11. **merchandise** [ˋmɝtʃən͵daɪz] *n.* 商品
12. **swipe** [swaɪp] *v.* 刷（卡）；擦過
13. **gimmick** [ˋgɪmɪk] *n.* 竅門；廣告噱頭

Jeanne Moos, CNN Correspondent

It was Ralph Lauren's son, David, who dreamed this up, inspired[14] by Tom Cruise waving his hands around like a conductor[15] in *Minority Report*. Tiny wires embedded[16] in the glass transmit[17] your touch.

You haven't seen Tom Cruise here, have you?

Paul Zaengl, VP, Interactive Technologies

No, Tom hasn't been here that we know of.

Tom Cruise, Actor

Look at this kid.

Jeanne Moos, CNN Correspondent

Look at this kid. You know how to work a computer, right?

Unidentified Female Voice

Sure.

Little Girl's Father

She can buy anything if you give her the credit card.

Jeanne Moos, CNN Correspondent

Do you have your own credit card yet?

Little Girl

I—what?

Little Girl's Father

Do you have your own credit card?

Jeanne Moos, CNN Correspondent

Here. OK.

CNN 特派員 吉妮・莫斯

想出這個點子的人，是勞夫・羅倫的兒子大衛。他看到《關鍵報告》裡的湯姆・克魯斯像指揮家一樣揮舞雙手，結果得到了這個靈感。嵌在玻璃裡的細微電線會把你的觸摸轉換為訊號。

你還沒在這裡看過湯姆・克魯斯吧，有嗎？

互動科技副總裁 保羅・曾果

沒有。就我們所知，湯姆還沒有來過這裡。

演員 湯姆・克魯斯

看這個小孩。

CNN 特派員 吉妮・莫斯

看這個小孩。妳懂得怎麼操作電腦，對不對？

身份不名女性語音

當然。

小女孩的父親

妳只要給她一張信用卡，她什麼都會買。

CNN 特派員 吉妮・莫斯

妳有自己的信用卡嗎？

小女孩

我——什麼？

小女孩的父親

妳有自己的信用卡嗎？

CNN 特派員 吉妮・莫斯

來，給妳。

Notes & Vocabulary

dream up 想出；憑空想出

dream 當動詞是「作夢」的意思，常與 of 連用，在此與 up 連用，有「想出點子、主意」的意思。

- Steve dreamed up another one of his get-rich-quick ideas.
  史提夫又想出一個快速致富的主意。

與 dream 相關辭彙：

pipe dream 空想；妄想

- Bill wants to become a rock star, but it's a pipe dream.
  比爾想成為一名搖滾巨星，但只是空想而已。

dream team 夢幻隊

- The company put together a dream team of business leaders.
  這家公司將一群頂尖的商業領導人聚集在一塊。

14. **inspire** [ɪn`spaɪr] *v.* 激勵；激發
15. **conductor** [kən`dʌktɚ] *n.* 指揮家；領導者
16. **embed** [ɪm`bɛd] *v.* 埋置；把……嵌入
17. **transmit** [træns`mɪt] *v.* 傳送

Little Girl's Father

Thanks a lot.

Jeanne Moos, CNN Correspondent

By the time she's old enough for her own credit card, interactive[18] window shopping may be an everyday thing. Even a dog could score.

Owner of "Boccie" the Dog

Boccie, it's a visor[19] just for you! I think this would look wonderful on you, sweet pea. Can you jump up and touch it? Come on, jump up and you touch it! Good girl!

Jeanne Moos, CNN Correspondent

Next thing you know she'll be emptying[20] the ATM.[21]

小女孩的父親

多謝妳啊。

CNN 特派員 吉妮．莫斯

等她年紀夠大，能夠有自己的信用卡之後，互動式櫥窗購物可能早就已經普及了。連狗也可以購物。

狗兒「柏琦」的主人

柏琦，這個面罩剛好適合妳！小甜心，妳戴這個一定很好看。妳能不能跳起來碰這個地方？來嘛，跳！這樣就碰到了，乖女孩！

CNN 特派員 吉妮．莫斯

接下來她就會把你戶頭的錢全部花光了。

Notes & Vocabulary

even a dog could score 很簡單，連狗都會

用來表示某件事很簡單。score 原有「得分」之意，連狗都可以得分，就表示一件事情真的很容易，大家都會的意思。

- The test was so easy that even a dog could score.
  這個測驗太簡單了，就連狗都會做。

sweet pea 甜心

sweat pea 原指一種甜豌豆，在這裡是一種親密的稱呼，「甜心」的意思。常見的親暱稱呼有 dear、sweetie、honey、honey bunch、pumpkin 等，近來還流行一種新稱法 boo。

18. **interactive** [ˏɪntɚˋæktɪv] *adj.* 互動的
19. **visor** [ˋvaɪzɚ] *n.* 面罩；眼罩；高爾夫球帽
20. **empty** [ˋɛmptɪ] *v.* 使……成為空的；倒空
21. **ATM** *n.* 自動提款機
    （automated teller machine 的縮寫）

For Your Eyes Only?
More Employers Scrutinize Office E-mail and Instant Messaging
小心！你的電子郵件裡寫什麼——老闆都知道

Step 1 如果你是使用 MP3 ，請聽 MP3 Track 67；如果你使用電腦互動光碟，請點選 DVD-ROM【實戰應用篇—Part I：Unit 3】，試試看是否聽懂新聞內容。

Step 2 請瀏覽下列關鍵字彙，再仔細聽一次。

scrutinize 詳細檢查	monitor 監視
impulsive 衝動的	pompous 愛炫耀的
derogatory 貶低的	raise a red flag 發出警訊

Step 3 如果你還不是聽的很懂的話，請參考下列發音提示，再仔細聽一次。

連音	friend or、this official、asked that、what this、would do、tend to、right to、as standing
同化音	Internet

 試著作答下列聽力測驗題目。

True or False 是非題

____ 1. Laura knew her e-mail was being monitored.

____ 2. An official from Laura's company said the e-mail was one of many reasons she was fired.

____ 3. In the U.S., employers do not have the right to monitor employees' e-mail.

____ 4. Companies often use computer programs to monitor employees' e-mail.

____ 5. Laura is still afraid she will get fired from her new job.

Multiple Choice 選擇題

____ 1. How long after Laura sent her e-mail was she fired?

a. within an hour　　b. within a day
c. within a week　　d. within a month

____ 2. What did Laura say about her boss in her e-mail?

a. He was going to fire her.
b. He was acting arrogant and pompous.
c. He was monitoring her e-mail.
d. He was very weak with her.

____ 3. Why is e-mail different than gossip around the water cooler?

a. E-mail come back to you.
b. Everybody is aware of e-mail.
c. There is a written record.
d. It makes people angry and frustrated.

 試著用較慢的速度，再仔細聽一遍 (MP3 Track 68)，檢查答案是否正確。

 對答案、驗收成果，並詳讀原文，若仍有不懂的地方，可反覆多聽幾次。

(答案請見 p. 313)

Daniel Sieberg, NEXT@CNN Host

Now, the story of a woman who says she was fired after her employers monitored[2] her e-mail, and didn't like what they saw. The take-home lesson here: don't call your boss a jerk;[3] at least not in cyberspace.[4]

Laura, Fired Office Employee

I had written an e-mail to a coworker complaining about my boss, complaining about his behavior. And within a week of that e-mail, I was fired.

Daniel Sieberg, NEXT@CNN Host

This woman asked that we only identify[5] her as Laura. She's afraid of what this impulsive[6] e-mail would do to future employment prospects.[7]

Laura, Fired Office Employee

I had said that the boss was a jerk. He had been acting a bit arrogant[8] and pompous[9] with me all week.

Daniel Sieberg, NEXT@CNN Host

An official with her former employer says Laura was let go for a number of personnel[10] reasons. And that the derogatory[11] comments in her e-mail were a factor. This official also says the company informs all employees that their e-mail is monitored.

Did you know that your e-mail was being monitored?

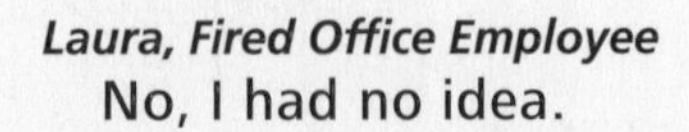

Laura, Fired Office Employee

No, I had no idea.

《CNN 科技新世代》主持人 丹尼爾．席柏格

接下來的報導有關一位女士，她說她的電子郵件受到雇主監控，結果因為信件內容引起他們不滿而遭到解雇。這故事給我們的啟示：不要罵老闆豬頭；至少別在網路上罵。

遭解雇的員工 蘿拉

我寫了一封電子郵件向同事抱怨我上司的行為，結果不到一星期我就被炒魷魚了。

《CNN 科技新世代》主持人 丹尼爾．席柏格

這位女士要求我們稱她為蘿拉就好。她擔心這封一時衝動所寫出的郵件，會對她未來求職造成影響。

遭解雇的員工 蘿拉

我在信裡說我老闆是個混蛋。他那整個星期對我都是一副自以為是的倨傲模樣。

《CNN 科技新世代》主持人 丹尼爾．席柏格

她前公司的一名主管表示，蘿拉是因為若干個人因素才遭到解雇。她在電子郵件裡的謾罵言詞只是其中一項因素。這名主管還說公司原本就有告知員工，他們的電子郵件全都受監控。

妳知道妳的電子郵件受到監控嗎？

遭解雇的員工 蘿拉

我根本不知道。

Notes & Vocabulary

let go 解僱；放手

let go 亦可指「放手；捨棄」。「解僱」比較常見的正式說法是 laid off、fire。其他的說法有下列幾種：

a. get the axe

- Brian knew his company was having problems, so he was ready when he got the axe.
  布萊恩知道公司有點問題，所以他被解僱時已有心裡準備。

b. pink-slip（名詞為 pink slip 指「解僱通知書」）

- I can't believe the boss pink-slipped you right before Christmas.
  我真不敢相信你老闆在聖誕節前夕炒你魷魚。

c. get canned

- The boss warned Harry about being late, but he was still surprised when he got canned.
  老闆已對哈利遲到一事下了警告令，但他被炒魷魚時還是很驚訝。

d. show sb the door

- After Mack got into a fight with a customer, the boss had no choice but to show him the door.
  麥克與客戶吵架，老闆不得不請他走路。

1. **scrutinize** [ˋskrutə͵naɪz] *v.* 詳細檢查；詳閱
2. **monitor** [ˋmɑnətɚ] *v.* 監視；監督；監看
3. **jerk** [dʒɝk] *n.* 蠢蛋；笨蛋；怪人
4. **cyberspace** [ˋsaɪbɚ͵spes] *n.* 網際空間；網際網路
5. **identify** [aɪˋdɛntə͵faɪ] *v.* 識別；確認
6. **impulsive** [ɪmˋpʌlsɪv] *adj.* 衝動的；由衝動造成的
7. **prospect** [ˋprɑ͵spɛkt] *n.* 前途；視野
8. **arrogant** [ˋærəgənt] *adj.* 傲慢的；自大的
9. **pompous** [ˋpɑmpəs] *adj.* 自負的；愛炫耀的；浮誇的
10. **personnel** [͵pɝsəˋnɛl] *n.* 員工；人事
11. **derogatory** [dɪˋrɑgə͵torɪ] *adj.* 貶低的；難聽的；負面的

Nancy Flynn, ePolicy Institute

Most employees tend to think, 'My e-mail is my business. My employer has no right to read my e-mail messages,' particularly if it's a message to a friend or a family member. But in reality, here in the U.S. the federal government gives employers the right to monitor all employee e-mail, instant messaging and Internet activity.

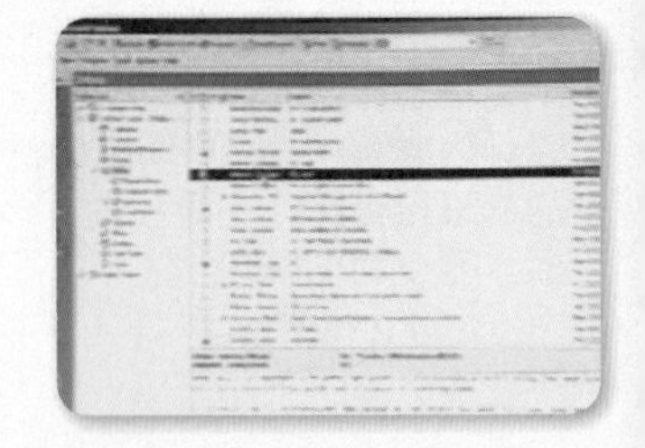

Daniel Sieberg, NEXT@CNN Host

Thousands of e-mail messages fly in and out of companies all day long. And while it's impossible for the boss to literally[12] look over your shoulder, businesses are turning to[13] technology—computers that can read every word of every e-mail and raise red flags.

Nancy Flynn, ePolicy Institute

What everybody needs to be aware of is that e-mail and instant messaging create written records. It's not the same as standing around the water cooler gossiping[14] about somebody. You gossip about somebody via e-mail, there's a written record of it. And it could come back to haunt[15] you and your employer.

Laura, Fired Office Employee

They still fear for their jobs a bit.

Daniel Sieberg, NEXT@CNN Host

For Laura the experience left her angry and frustrated. But right now, at least she doesn't have to worry about her e-mail. She's currently self-employed.[16]

電子政策學會 南西・佛蘭

大多數員工都認為：「我的電子郵件是我自己的事。雇主沒有權利讀取我的電子郵件」，尤其是寄給自己朋友或者親人的信件。但實際上，美國聯邦政府卻授權雇主得以監控員工所有的電子郵件、即時通訊以及網路活動。

《CNN 科技新世代》主持人 丹尼爾・席柏格

公司整天都有數以千計的電子郵件進進出出。雖然老闆不可能真的從你背後偷看你的信，但企業現在都轉而求助於科技——利用電腦讀取每封電子郵件的每一個字，並適時提出警告。

電子政策學會 南西・佛蘭

大家必須注意到，電子郵件與即時通訊會留下書面紀錄。這跟站在茶水間談論八卦是不一樣的。你在電子郵件裡講人家的八卦，就會留下書面紀錄。以後這項紀錄就可能會對你和你的雇主造成困擾。

遭解雇的員工 蘿拉

他們還是有點擔心會丟掉工作。

《CNN 科技新世代》主持人 丹尼爾・席柏格

這次經驗讓蘿拉既憤怒又沮喪。不過，現在她至少暫時不用擔心電子郵件的問題了——她現在成了一名自雇工作者了。

Notes & Vocabulary

look over sb's shoulder
窺探他人；小心提防

一個人的視線越過別人的肩膀去看別人正在做些什麼，是指「窺探別人」。那麼 look over one's shoulder，則是看看自己背後是否有異樣，即小心提防身邊的人事物，以防不利的意思，類似 to watch one's back。

- Susan finds it difficult to work with her boss always looking over her shoulder.
  蘇珊上班時老闆總是在旁邊東看西看，讓她感到難以工作。
- After receiving mysterious telephone threats, Josh was always looking over his shoulder.
  自從接到詭異的電話威脅後，喬許總是小心翼翼，提防有事發生。

raise a red flag 發出警訊；引起注意

a red flag（紅旗）是發出警示的標幟，也可表示引起注意並促人採取反應或行動的事物，通常會用在具負面意含的事物上。而升起紅旗、發出警訊這個動作就是 raise a red flag。

- Craig's sudden spending spree raised a red flag with his employer.
  克瑞格突如其來的瘋狂花費行為已經引起老闆的注意。

instant messaging 即時通訊

instant messaging（即時通訊功能）或 instant message(s)（所傳送的訊息）現在全世界都超流行，所以英語國家的人士為了方便，乾脆簡稱 IM，不只是指這個界面或功能，連傳即時訊息的動作也可以這麼說。下次再看到 IM 這個縮寫，您就不會一頭霧水了！

12. **literally** [ˋlɪtərəlɪ] *adv.* 不誇張地；實在地；逐字地
13. **turn to** *v.* 求助於
14. **gossip** [ˋgɑsəp] *v.* 講閒話；講八卦
15. **haunt** [hɔnt] *v.* 困擾；如鬼魂般纏住（某人）
16. **self-employed** [ˏsɛlfɪmˋplɔɪd] *adj.* 自己經營的；自雇的

Childless by Choice

More Couples Today Opt Out of Procreation

無後一身輕——美國社會吹起頂客風

Step 1 如果你是使用 MP3 ，請聽 MP3 Track 69；如果你使用電腦互動光碟，請點選 DVD-ROM【實戰應用篇—Part I：Unit 4】，試試看是否聽懂新聞內容。

Step 2 請瀏覽下列關鍵字彙，再仔細聽一次。

birthrate 出生率	all-time low 歷史新低
extol 頌揚	virtue 優點
on board 在行列中	nonbreeder 不生育者
pamper 嬌慣	

Step 3 如果你還不是聽的很懂的話，請參考下列發音提示，再仔細聽一次。

連音	old age、ruled out、today's society、expect to、one-third do、latest census
省略音	latest census

試著作答下列聽力測驗題目。

True or False 是非題

____ 1. The nation's birthrate is at an all-time high.

____ 2. Jennifer Shawne's book talks about the virtues of not having children.

____ 3. San Francisco is one of the top cities for child-free couples.

____ 4. Over the last 10 years the number of childless couples has decreased.

____ 5. Shawne says she might change her mind about not having kids.

Multiple Choice 選擇題

____ 1. What is the average number of babies born per 1,000 Americans?

a. 140 b. 100
c. 14 d. 104

____ 2. What are childless couples sometimes referred to?

a. DINKS b. KINKS
c. TWINKS d. PINKS

____ 3. What percentage of households had children in the 1800s?

a. 100 percent b. 20 percent
c. 80 percent d. 90 percent

試著用較慢的速度，再仔細聽一遍（MP3 Track 70），檢查答案是否正確。

對答案、驗收成果，並詳讀原文，若仍有不懂的地方，可反覆多聽幾次。

（答案請見 p. 313）

CNN Anchor

The nation's birthrate[4] is at an all-time low. The CDC[5] says just 14 babies born to every 1,000 Americans. It's not a new trend and it's often used as an argument in the debate over career and motherhood[6] in today's society. But guess what, this is not just a woman thing. It's also a couples thing. Sometimes they are called DINKS, sometimes worse. Selfish or sensible?[7] Randi Kaye talks to the childless by choice.

Randi Kaye, CNN Correspondent

They are a family of two, Jennifer Shawne and Allan Rapp, married five years and child-free.

Jennifer published this book, "Baby Not on Board,"[8] extolling[9] the virtues[10] of life as a nonbreeder.[11] Instead of late-night feedings, Jennifer and her husband go to late-night parties. Instead of spending weekends on the soccer fields and the playgrounds, they sleep late and do yoga. Instead of traveling to Grandma's, they travel the world. And instead of kids, they have cats.

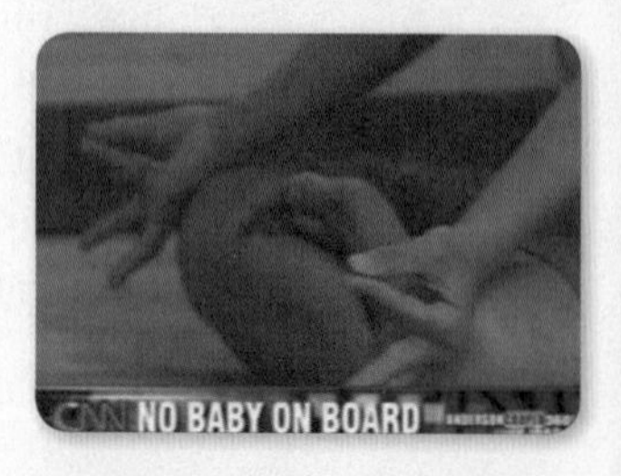

Some people might hear that and say that sounds really selfish of them.

Jennifer Shawne, Author, "Baby Not on Board"

You can turn the tables and say, gosh, isn't it selfish that you've had children that you expect to take care of you when you're old? Isn't it selfish that you want a replica[12] of yourself?

Randi Kaye, CNN Correspondent

Allan and Jennifer are not alone. According to the National Marriage Institute,[13] back in the 1800s about 80 percent of all households[14] had children. Today, less than one-third do.

CNN 主播

美國的生育率創歷史新低。美國疾病防治中心表示，目前每一千名美國人中只有十四名嬰兒出生。這是另一股新趨勢，在現今社會中經常成為拼事業與當母親孰輕孰重的一個辯論點。但現在這不只是女人的事，而是夫妻兩人的事。有時候他們被稱為頂客族，有時候則更難聽。究竟是自私還是有道理？藍蒂・凱伊採訪了幾對選擇不生孩子的夫妻。

CNN 特派員 藍蒂・凱伊

他們是一個兩人的家庭，珍妮佛・邵恩和艾倫・瑞普，兩人結婚五年，沒有小孩。

珍妮佛出版了一本名為《無後一身輕》的書，書中對於無須承擔養育責任的人生大加稱頌。珍妮佛和丈夫兩人在半夜時不需要起來餵奶，而是去參加派對。週末他們不需要把時間耗在足球場和兒童遊樂區，而是睡到日上三竿，還可以做瑜珈。他們不需要長途跋涉到祖母家，而是去環遊世界。他們不養孩子，而是養貓。

有些人聽到這些可能會覺得他們真的很自私。

《無後一身輕》作者 珍妮佛・邵恩

你可以反過來質疑：老天，你生孩子是為了指望你年邁時，能有人照顧你，這樣難道不自私嗎？你想要有個自己的複製品，這樣難道不自私嗎？

CNN 特派員 藍蒂・凱伊

有這種想法的不只有艾倫和珍妮佛，根據國家婚姻協會的統計，一八〇〇年代時，約有百分之八十的家庭都有小孩。如今，有小孩的家庭卻不到三分之一。

Notes & Vocabulary

all-time low 歷史新低

all-time 這個形容詞表示「所有時間的」、「創紀錄的；前所未有的」。要表達某項數值「達到歷史新高／新低」時，常見的說法為 at/reach/hit + an all-time + high/low。

- The president's approval ratings slid to an all-time low.
  總統的民調支持率跌落到歷史新低點。

turn the tables 扭轉局勢；反敗為勝

這個成語的起源有許多版本，其中最可信的理論與西洋雙陸棋（backgammon）有關。雙陸棋是一種古老而複雜的遊戲，雙方各持十五子，擲骰子來決定棋子移動的步數；十七世紀時人們習慣將其暱稱為 tables。這種遊戲中常會出現原本屈居劣勢的玩家因一步棋而乾坤大逆轉，突然反敗為勝的狀況，turn the tables 一語就這麼產生了。

- The schoolgirl turned the tables on the fraudster by tricking him into revealing his identity online.
  那名女學生對詐騙者反將一軍，誘使他在網上自曝身分。

1. **by choice** *phr.* 自己選擇的；自願的
2. **opt out of** *v.* 決定不參與；選擇退出
3. **procreation** [ˏprokriˋeʃən] *n.* 生產；生殖
4. **birthrate** [ˋbɝθˏret] *n.* 出生率
5. **CDC** *n.* 美國疾病防治中心（= Centers for Disease Control and Prevention）
6. **motherhood** [ˋmʌðɚˏhud] *n.* 母親的身分；母性
7. **sensible** [ˋsɛnsəbḷ] *adj.* 明智的；合情理的
8. **on board** [bɔrd] *phr.* 在船／飛機／車上；在行列中
9. **extol** [ɪkˋstol] *v.* 讚美；頌揚
10. **virtue** [ˋvɝtʃu] *n.* 優點；長處
11. **nonbreeder** [ˏnɑnˋbridɚ] *n.* 不生育者
12. **replica** [ˋrɛplɪkə] *n.* 複製品；複寫
13. **institute** [ˋɪnstəˏtut] *n.* 協會；研究所
14. **household** [ˋhaʊsˏhold] *n.* 家庭；一家人

And there is a slow but not so silent movement under way[15] by those who say "I do" to marriage, but "I don't" to kids.

We came here to San Francisco for our story because it's one of the top cities in America for child-free couples. There are fewer children here than almost every other city in the United States. And the trend is catching on.[16] The latest census[17] data shows that married couples without children grew by 11 percent over 10 years. We wanted to know why so many couples are trading family for freedom.[18]

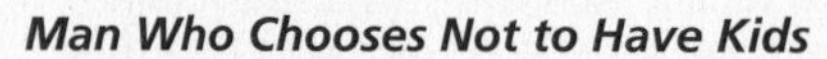

Man Who Chooses Not to Have Kids

You don't have to have kids, you don't have to, you know, produce. And produce children that consume[19] a lot of the resources. So, I don't really feel like I've been missing out.

Randi Kaye, CNN Correspondent

Do you ever worry that one day you might regret not having kids?

Man Who Chooses Not to Have Kids

I've got nieces and nephews. I'm going to pamper[20] them enough so that they'll take care of me in my old age.

Randi Kaye, CNN Correspondent

As for our nonbreeder author and her husband, they're good to their nieces and nephews, too. And after a little prodding,[21] turns out, they haven't completely ruled out[22] kids yet.

Jennifer Shawne, Author, "Baby Not on Board"

I like to tell people, I can still change my mind, which, if I had children, I could not say.

現在願意結婚，但不願意生小孩的人口正在緩慢增加中，並且還勇於表達這種想法。

我們來到舊金山採訪，因為舊金山是美國無子夫妻比例最高的城市之一，這裡的孩童人口幾乎在美國所有城市中殿後，而且這股風潮正持續發燒。最新的人口統計資料顯示，在過去十年間，舊金山市結了婚但不生小孩的夫妻增加了百分之十一。我們想知道為何有這麼多夫妻要犧牲家庭來換取自由。

選擇不生孩子的男子

你不需要生孩子，你不需要繁衍後代的。繁衍子孫會消耗大量資源，所以我不覺得自己錯過了什麼。

CNN 特派員 藍蒂・凱伊

你曾擔心過將來哪天可能會後悔沒有生孩子嗎？

選擇不生孩子的男子

我有侄子和姪女。我會很寵他們，等我老的時候他們就會照顧我。

CNN 特派員 藍蒂・凱伊

至於我們這位選擇不承擔養育責任的作者和她的丈夫，兩人對他們的侄子、侄女也都很好。經過一番追問，結果是他倆並未完全排除生孩子的可能。

《無後一身輕》作者 珍妮佛・邵恩

我喜歡跟別人說，我還可以改變心意，但是萬一我已經有了孩子，我就不能這樣說了。

Notes & Vocabulary

miss out 錯失；遺漏

這個片語係指「錯過大好機會」，與 miss the boat 意義相近，例如要向人推薦好康的活動時，就可以對他說 don't miss out（可別錯過）。若要更進一步指明所錯失的事物為何，則須在其後加上介系詞 on，例如：miss out on life（失去享受生活的機會）、miss out on getting a promotion（未能獲得升遷）等。

- Many investors missed out on the high-tech boom of the nineties.
  許多投資人錯過了九〇年代科技的飛躍期。

15. **under way** *adv.* 在進行中地
16. **catch on** *v.* 流行
17. **census** [ˋsɛnsəs] *n.* 人口普查；調查
18. **trade (A) for (B)** *v.* 拿 A 換取 B
19. **consume** [kənˋsum] *v.* 消耗；花費
20. **pamper** [ˋpæmpɚ] *v.* 寵溺；嬌慣
21. **prod** [prɑd] *v.* 敦促；刺激
22. **rule out** *v.* 排除；拒絕考慮

The Da Vinci Code on Trial

Author Dan Brown Defends Hit Novel from Charges of Plagiarism

誰是密碼真正的主人？

Step 1 如果你是使用 MP3 ，請聽 MP3 Track 71；如果你使用電腦互動光碟，請點選 DVD-ROM【實戰應用篇—Part I：Unit 5】，試試看是否聽懂新聞內容。

Step 2 請瀏覽下列關鍵字彙，再仔細聽一次。

plagiarism 剽竊；抄襲	refute 反駁
slate 預定	absurd 荒謬的
consult 查閱	originality 原創性
copyright 著作權	

Step 3 如果你還不是聽的很懂的話，請參考下列發音提示，再仔細聽一次。

連音	be found in、not to mention
同化音	takes the stand

試著作答下列聽力測驗題目。

True or False 是非題

____ 1. *The Da Vinci Code* was written in 1982.

____ 2. At the time of the trial, the movie had already been finished.

____ 3. Dan Brown said that he stole his ideas from *The Holy Blood and the Holy Grail.*

____ 4. Dan Brown did all of his research himself.

____ 5. Brown's lawyers say the ideas in *The Holy Blood and the Holy Grail* were very original.

Multiple Choice 選擇題

____ 1. Where is the trial being held?

a. New York City　　b. Italy
c. Los Angeles　　d. London

____ 2. What do Brown's lawyers say cannot be protected by copyright?

a. titles　　b. names
c. ideas　　d. books

____ 3. What's at stake in this trial?

a. Dan Brown's reputation
b. money from book sales
c. money from the movie
d. all of the above

Step 5 試著用較慢的速度，再仔細聽一遍 (MP3 Track 72)，檢查答案是否正確。

Step 6 對答案、驗收成果，並詳讀原文，若仍有不懂的地方，可反覆多聽幾次。

(答案請見 p. 313)

CNN Anchor

The author of the best-selling book *The Da Vinci Code* took the stand in a London courtroom on Tuesday. Dan Brown is seeking to refute[6] charges that he copied ideas for his hit novel from a 1982 book. Mallika Kapur brings us this report.

Mallika Kapur, CNN Correspondent

The movie is already in the can, slated[7] for release[8] in May. In the meantime, the little matter of just who came up with[9] the big ideas that have made *The Da Vinci Code* a global best seller.[10] The book makes a case[11] that Jesus married Mary Magdalene and had a family, the clues, according to the book, to be found in the paintings of Leonardo da Vinci. So author Dan Brown takes the stand at London's High Court this week to defend charges he stole his ideas from a book published 24 years ago called *The Holy Blood and the Holy Grail*.

Brown says, "It's absurd[12] to suggest that I have organized and presented my novel in accordance with[13] the same general principles[14] as that book." He told the court that much of the research for his work was done by his wife, and that neither he nor his wife consulted[15] *The Holy Blood and the Holy Grail* until *The Da Vinci Code*'s storyline was well developed.

CNN 主播

暢銷書《達文西密碼》的作者，星期二在倫敦的一處法庭出庭應訊。丹．布朗欲藉此駁斥外界指控他那本暢銷小說的構想是抄襲自一本一九八二年出版的書。瑪莉卡．卡波的報導。

CNN 特派員 馬莉卡．卡波

電影已經拍攝完畢，並排定五月上映。同時，究竟是誰想出如此了不起的點子讓《達文西密碼》能成為一本全球暢銷書，相形之下反而不是那麼重要。這本書認為耶穌娶了抹大拉的瑪麗亞，組了一個家庭，至於線索則是在達文西的畫中發現的。所以作者丹．布朗本週在倫敦高等法院出庭，針對外界指控他的點子是剽竊自二十四年前出版的《聖血與聖杯》一書為自己提出辯護。

布朗說：「說我是依照那本書的大綱來組織和呈現我的小說，實在是件荒謬的事」。他告訴法庭，他的作品大部分的研究工作是由他的妻子負責，他和他的妻子在完成《達文西密碼》的主要情節前，都不曾參考《聖血與聖杯》一書。

Notes & Vocabulary

take the stand 出庭應訊

法庭上受訊問的證人必須坐在「證人席」(the witness stand)上。所以 take the stand 表示在法庭上「接受訊問、提供證詞」之意，意同於動詞 testify。而 take a/one's stand 則是指「表明支持某種立場」。

- Ron took a stand to protect the environment.
  羅朗表明他支持環境保護的立場。

in the can 已完成

拍攝電影時使用的電影軟片(motion picture)，是以金屬或塑膠的有蓋盒子來包裝的。拍攝完成後，攝影師會將拍好的底片再收回盒中保存。所以若說 a movie is in the can，就表示這部電影已殺青而且製作完成準備上映了。由此典故引申來表示事物「已經完成」準備。

- After months of shooting, the film was finally in the can.
  在經過幾個月的拍攝後，該片的製作終於完成。

1. **trial** [traɪl] *n.* 審問；審判
2. **defend** [dɪ`fɛnd] *v.* 答辯；為……進行辯護
3. **hit** [hɪt] *n.* 熱門暢銷品
4. **charge** [tʃɑrdʒ] *n.* 指控
5. **plagiarism** [`pledʒəˏrɪzəm] *n.* 剽竊；抄襲
6. **refute** [rɪ`fjut] *v.* 反駁；駁斥
7. **slate** [slet] *v.* 選定……；預定……
8. **release** [rɪ`lis] *n.* 發行；推出
9. **come up with** *v.* 想出……；提供……
10. **best seller** [bɛst] [`sɛlɚ] *n.* 暢銷書
11. **make a case** *v. phr.* 提出論點
12. **absurd** [əb`sɝd] *adj.* 荒謬的；愚蠢的；可笑的
13. **in accordance with** [ə`kɔrdəns] *phr.* 按照……；與……一致
14. **principle** [`prɪnspəl] *n.* 原則
15. **consult** [kən`sʌlt] *v.* 查閱(參考書、詞典等)

Peter Knight, Copyright Lawyer

I think the key points will be bringing out[16] at what stage in the process he was aware of the Leigh and Baigent book and trying to make it clear that he was aware of that at a very early stage, and then, casting[17] doubt as to whether, in fact, he can really remember exactly what from that he took and what he didn't take from that.

Mallika Kapur, CNN Correspondent

Brown's lawyers question the originality[18] of *The Holy Blood and the Holy Grail*, saying the authors are not alone in suggesting Jesus had a family with a bloodline[19] that continues to this day. They argue the ideas cannot be protected by copyright.[20] Certainly plenty is at stake in this case, not just Brown's reputation,[21] but millions of dollars in future book sales, not to mention revenues[22] from the film.

著作權法律師 彼得．奈特

我認為關鍵點會是在找出他何時注意到雷伊和拜根寫的那本書，並設法確認他很早就已經注意到了那本書，然後去質疑他是否記得自己究竟從那本書中擷取了哪些內容，以及哪些內容不是取自於那本書。

CNN 特派員 馬莉卡．卡波

布朗的律師質疑《聖血與聖杯》一書的原創性，並表示不只該書作者說過耶穌曾組織過一個家庭，而這個家庭的血脈仍延續至今。他們認為這個構想並不能受到著作權法的保護。這件案子牽涉到很多利害關係，不僅是布朗的聲譽，還包括未來數百萬美元的賣書收入，其電影的營收更是不在話下了。

Notes & Vocabulary

at stake 瀕臨危險；存亡攸關

stake可指「賭注；賭金」。賭金隨著賭局變化，隨時可能被輸掉，因此片語 at stake 常見的意思是形容「處在緊要關頭、在危急存亡之秋」。與其意義、用法相同的片語包括：at risk、in jeopardy、on the line 等。

- Both teams played hard because the championship was at stake.
  兩支隊伍都打得很賣力，因為冠軍隨時會拱手讓人。

16. **bring out** *v.* 了解到（真相、祕密）；闡明
17. **cast** [kæst] *v.* 把……加於
18. **originality** [əˌrɪdʒəˋnælətɪ] *n.* 原創性；獨創性
19. **bloodline** [ˋblʌdˌlaɪn] *n.* 血脈
20. **copyright** [ˋkɑpɪˌraɪt] *n.* 著作權；版權
21. **reputation** [ˌrɛpjəˋteʃən] *n.* 名聲
22. **revenue** [ˋrɛvəˌnu] *n.* 總收入；稅收

The PC Turns 25

The Now-Ubiquitous Device Defined the Late 20th Century

走過四分之一世紀——個人電腦發展回顧

Step 1 如果你是使用 MP3 ，請聽 MP3 Track 73；如果你使用電腦互動光碟，請點選 DVD-ROM【實戰應用篇—Part I：Unit 6】，試試看是否聽懂新聞內容。

Step 2 請瀏覽下列關鍵字彙，再仔細聽一次。

ubiquitous 普遍存在的	revolutionize 徹底改革
debut 首次露面	unveil 揭露
sit up and notice 感到驚艷	graphic 圖解的
interface 介面	muscle in 硬闖入

Step 3 如果你還不是聽的很懂的話，請參考下列發音提示，再仔細聽一次。

連音	look at it、full of、changed along the way、wearable even、muscled in
弱化音	changed along the way
省略音	personal、memory
同化音	craze for cubes、interface、Internet

試著作答下列聽力測驗題目。

True or False 是非題

____ 1. IBM's personal computer was the first computer ever sold.

____ 2. The IBM 5150 was the first computer that was popular with businessmen.

____ 3. The PC was named "Machine of the Year" by *Newsweek*.

____ 4. Early on, people bought PCs to use spreadsheet and word processing programs.

____ 5. The iPod Nano has the same amount of memory as the first PC.

Multiple Choice 選擇題

____ 1. What was the number of computers expected to be sold in the year the report was broadcast?

a. 96 billion　　b. one million
c. 16,000　　d. 196 million

____ 2. What did the Apple Macintosh have that made it easier to use?

a. the Internet
b. a mouse and a graphic user interface
c. 16K of memory
d. spreadsheets and word processing

____ 3. What year was the World Wide Web introduced?

a. 1990　　b. 1985
c. 1981　　d. 1996

試著用較慢的速度，再仔細聽一遍（MP3 Track 74），檢查答案是否正確。

對答案、驗收成果，並詳讀原文，若仍有不懂的地方，可反覆多聽幾次。

（答案請見 p. 313）

CNN Anchor

It wasn't the first machine on the market. To some people, it's now just part of office furniture.

CNN Anchor

But whichever way you look at it, IBM's personal computer has completely revolutionized[3] the way we live, work and play, and a quarter of a century after its debut,[4] its power has radically[5] increased in more ways than one.

Christie Lu Stout, CNN Correspondent

A craze for cubes,[6] a White House full of jelly beans,[7] and one long walk down the aisle[8]—it was 1981, also the year IBM unveiled[9] the 5150, the world's first personal computer for the mainstream[10] consumer. Now, with just 16 kilobytes of memory, the IBM 5150 was obviously limited. Some critics said it wasn't nearly as good as other computers on the market, but the 5150 triggered[11] a wave of[12] excitement. It made the business world sit up and notice that the PC was not just for geeks.

CNN 主播

它並非市場上的第一部機器。對某些人而言，現在它是辦公室中不可或缺的器具。

CNN 主播

但無論您用什麼角度看它，IBM（國際商業機器）的個人電腦已經徹底改變了我們的生活、工作和遊戲方式。在個人電腦問世四分之一個世紀後，它的影響力已經以多種方式迅速提升。

CNN 特派員 克莉絲蒂・陸・史道

一股魔術方塊熱，白宮到處可見豆豆糖的蹤影，還有沿著長廊向前走去（指英國皇室的世紀婚禮），當時是一九八一年，也是 IBM 為主流消費者生產全球第一部個人電腦 5150 問世的那一年。5150 的記憶體容量只有十六千位元組，功能明顯受限。有些評論家說，5150 和當時市面上的其他電腦還差得遠，但 5150 卻讓商業界很感興趣，並且注意到個人電腦不只是電腦技客才會用的東西。

Notes & Vocabulary

a craze for （一時的）狂熱；大流行

craze 較強調「一時的風潮、流行」。相似詞為 fad「流行一時的狂熱、風尚（略帶負面意味）」、rage「風行一時的潮流」。

- The popular singer sparked a craze for big hats.
  這位紅歌星掀起了一股大帽子熱潮。

sit up and notice 感到驚艷

一般用法可寫作 sit up and take notice。

- The singer's first single made record execs sit up and take notice.
  這位歌手的首支單曲讓唱片公司高層為之驚艷。

geeks 怪胎；書呆子；電腦技客

geek 一字源於馬戲團做穿插表演或餘興節目（sideshow）的馬戲團雜耍員（circus geek），表演項目通常是生吃動物或者是咬掉雞頭等奇怪的演出。傳統上帶有貶義，不過現在 geek 則指「對電腦有異常熱情、用電腦成痴的人」（一般翻作「技客」、「極客」、「奇客」等）。

1. **ubiquitous** [juˋbɪkwətəs] *adj.* 普遍存在的
2. **define** [dɪˋfaɪn] *v.* 給……下定義；為……的特色
3. **revolutionize** [ˏrɛvəˋluʃəˏnaɪz] *v.* 徹底改革
4. **debut** [ˋdeˏbju] *n.* 首次露面；初次登台
5. **radically** [ˋrædɪklɪ] *adv.* 徹底地；根本地；極端地
6. **cube** [kjub] *n.* 益智方塊
7. **jelly bean** [ˋdʒɛlɪ] [bin] *n.* 豆豆糖（或稱雷根糖）
8. **aisle** [aɪl] *n.* 走道；通道
9. **unveil** [ˏʌnˋvel] *v.* 揭露；使公諸於世
10. **mainstream** [ˋmenˏstrim] *n.* 主流
11. **trigger** [ˋtrɪgɚ] *v.* 觸發；引起
12. **a wave of** *phr.* 一陣

Time magazine named the PC "Machine of the Year," and an industry was born—IBM built the boxes, Intel wired the chips and Microsoft made the software. A young Bill Gates called the project "super exciting."

IBM sold nearly one million personal computers by 1985, but Compaq and others quickly worked out how to make cheaper versions.

In 1984, Apple computer launched its PC alternative.[13] The Macintosh was the first successful mouse-driven computer with a graphic[14] user interface,[15] which made computing a whole lot easier.

Spreadsheets[16] and word processing powered[17] early PC sales, but it was the Internet that further pushed demand.

In 1990, Tim Berners-Lee launched the World Wide Web, a multimedia[18] branch of the Internet. And browsers like Mosaic, and later Netscape Navigator would help popularize the Web and let a billion Web sites bloom, like Hotmail, Amazon, Google, Skype and eBay—the place to buy stuff you never touch from people you would never see—all that from the clunky[19] box on your desk.

《時代》雜誌稱個人電腦為「年度機器」，一項產業於焉誕生。IBM 負責製造電腦機殼，英特爾安裝晶片，微軟則生產軟體，年輕的比爾．蓋茲稱這項計畫「超級刺激」。

到了一九八五年時，IBM 一共賣出一百萬台個人電腦，但不久之後康柏和其他電腦公司就研究出如何製造出更便宜的個人電腦。

一九八四年，蘋果電腦提供消費者另一項選擇，進而推出該公司的個人電腦。麥金塔電腦是第一台可以成功使用滑鼠操作，並輔之以圖像式使用者介面的電腦，運用電腦從此變得容易許多。

試算表和文書處理帶動了早期的個人電腦銷售，但網際網路進一步提升對個人電腦的需求。

一九九〇年，提姆．伯納斯李將全球資訊網帶入市場，也就是多媒體版的網際網路。如 Mosaic 和後來推出的網景 Navigator 等瀏覽器，協助將網際網路普及化，十億多個網站如雨後春筍般冒出，例如 Hotmail、亞馬遜、Google、Skype 和 eBay 等，在這裡你可以向素未謀面的人購買到從未觸摸過的商品，而這一切靠的都是您書桌上那笨重的盒子。

Notes & Vocabulary

let a billion Web sites bloom
如雨後春筍般冒出

這一句是從毛澤東 Let a hundred flowers bloom; let a hundred schools of thought contend.（百花齊放，百家齊鳴）轉變而來的。在一九五六至一九五七年之間，毛澤東提出了 Hundred Flowers Movement，原意是要讓不同的觀點盡情發聲，但是後來和毛氏唱反調的人都沒有好下場。

bloom 在此當動詞用，有「蓬勃發展；大量出現」的意思。

- Hundreds of coffee shops bloomed across the country.
  全國各地出現了數百家的咖啡廳。

13. alternative [ɔlˋtɜnətɪv] *n.* 供選擇的東西
14. graphic [ˋgræfɪk] *adj.* 圖像的
15. interface [ˋɪntəˏfes] *n.* 界面；介面
16. spreadsheet [ˋsprɛdˏʃit] *n.*（電腦）試算表
17. power [ˋpaʊə] *v.* 給……提供動力
18. multimedia [ˏmʌltɪˋmidɪə] *n.* 多媒體
19. clunky [ˋklʌŋkɪ] *adj.* 笨重的

The hardware also changed along the way. The PC got smaller, faster, wearable[20] even, though I don't think this getup[21] really made it past the convention door.

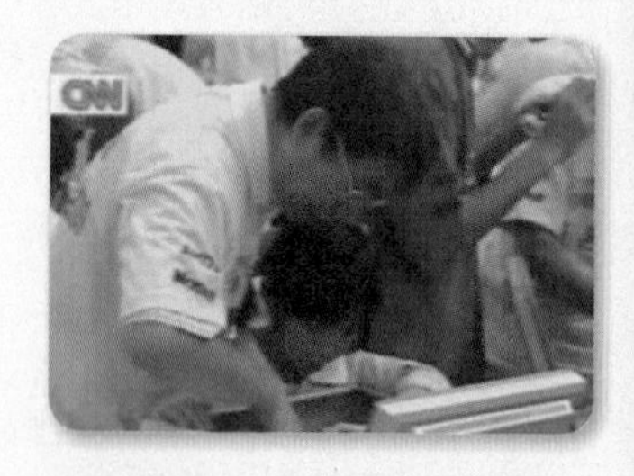

But the more typical models are still selling well. In fact, global personal computer sales are set to hit 196 million this year—that's a record high. But these days the PC is no longer master of the universe. Mobile devices like BlackBerry, the cell phone and the PDA have all muscled in.

CNN Anchor

Now 25 years on, it's clear that personal computing is taking a lot less space. The iPod Nano has 4 gigabytes of memory—that's roughly 4 million kilobytes. Now compare that to the first PC. And yes we've come a long way since 16K.

硬體部分也一直在改變。個人電腦變得更小、更快速、甚至可以穿戴在身上，不過我不認為這身打扮能進得了展場大門。

但是基本款的個人電腦如今仍有不錯的銷路。事實上，今年全球個人電腦的銷售額將創下一億九千六百萬台的歷史紀錄。但現在個人電腦已經不再佔有絕對優勢了。像黑莓機、行動電話和個人行動秘書等這類行動工具，已經強勢攻佔市場。

CNN 主播

二十五年以來，個人電腦佔用的空間明顯變小。iPod Nano 的記憶體容量便高達四個十億位元組，約相當於四百萬個千位元組。拿它來和第一台個人電腦相比，從 16K 記憶體發展至今，個人電腦的進展實在太大了。

Notes & Vocabulary

master of the universe
主宰；龍頭；佔有絕對優勢的人（事、物）

這個片語是用來表達在某個領域裡的「主宰；龍頭」，或是「佔有絕對優勢的人、事、物」。

- The chess player felt like the master of the universe, often winning the championship.
  這位棋手經常贏得冠軍，自覺天下無敵。

muscle in 強勢侵入；硬闖入

muscle in 的相似詞有 intrude [ɪn`trud]、encroach [ɪn`krotʃ]、butt in。

- The new computer start-up muscled in on the competition.
  這個新型的電腦來勢洶洶加入競爭。

come a long way 有長足的進步

come a long way 表示「有長足的進步」，a long way 在此取其抽象意義，表示「進步很多」。這個用法在六〇至七〇年代因為香煙 Virginia Slims 的廣告詞 You've come a long way, baby. 而大為流行，這句廣告詞在當時也有女權進步的意義。

- Medical science has come a long way since the 19th century.
  醫學科技從十九世紀以來已經有了長足的進步。

20. **wearable** [`wɛrəbəl] *adj.* 可以穿戴的
21. **getup** [`gɛt͵ʌp] *n.* 裝束；裝扮

Game, Set and Good-bye

Tennis Legend Andre Agassi Bids a Tearful Farewell

堅持與榮耀 阿格西揮別網壇

Step 1 如果你是使用 MP3 ，請聽 MP3 Track 75；如果你使用電腦互動光碟，請點選 DVD-ROM【實戰應用篇—Part I：Unit 7】，試試看是否聽懂新聞內容。

Step 2 請瀏覽下列關鍵字彙，再仔細聽一次。

bid farewell 道別	impact 影響
crossover 交叉；跨越	gratitude 感激之情
reclaim 取回	dropout 中輟生

Step 3 如果你還不是聽的很懂的話，請參考下列發音提示，再仔細聽一次。

連音	walks away、this as well、lies ahead
弱化音	blame him
省略音	probably

試著作答下列聽力測驗題目。

True or False 是非題

____ 1. Andre Agassi won his final match at the U.S. Open.

____ 2. Agassi was one of five men to complete a career grand slam.

____ 3. At one point, Agassi dropped off the Top 100 list of tennis players.

____ 4. Agassi graduated from college before becoming a professional tennis player.

____ 5. Agassi became the number-one ranked tennis player for the first time in 1999.

Multiple Choice 選擇題

____ 1. How many tennis majors did Agassi win during his career?

a. five
b. eight
c. twenty
d. zero

____ 2. Why do tennis players owe a debt of gratitude to Agassi?

a. Agassi said image is everything.
b. Agassi started a charter school.
c. Agassi helped make tennis popular.
d. Agassi retired from playing tennis.

____ 3. What plans does Agassi have now that he has retired?

a. He doesn't have any plans.
b. He plans on getting his high school diploma.
c. He plans to found a charter school in his home town.
d. He plans on marrying Steffi Graf.

試著用較慢的速度，再仔細聽一遍 (MP3 Track 76)，檢查答案是否正確。

對答案、驗收成果，並詳讀原文，若仍有不懂的地方，可反覆多聽幾次。

(答案請見 p. 313)

CNN Anchor

Well, he ended as a tearful loser. And who could blame him? It was so emotional,[3] but he will always be remembered as a winner. Andre Agassi bid tennis a fond[4] farewell on Sunday. Larry Smith has more now on the impact[5] made by one of the game's all-time greats.

Larry Smith, CNN Correspondent

A gimpy[6] Andre Agassi tearfully succumbed to[7] Father Time on Sunday, losing his third-round match at the U.S. Open to a 25-year-old opponent[8] who idolized[9] him as a child and then joined the legion[10] of Agassi fans to say good-bye.

Andre Agassi, Tennis Legend

I'm overwhelmed[11] with how they embraced me at the end and, you know, they saw me through my career and they've seen me through this as well.

CNN 主播

他以淚流滿面的敗軍之姿結束了自己的網球生涯，但誰會怪他呢？當時的場面如此令人感動，後人記憶中的他將永遠是個贏家。安德烈・阿格西在週日依依不捨地向網球告別。賴瑞・史密斯要告訴我們這位網球場上的偉大選手造成了什麼樣的影響。

CNN 特派員 賴瑞・史密斯

星期日，阿格西帶著蹣跚的腳步與滿面的淚痕屈服於無情的歲月。他在美國公開賽的第三回合輸給了二十五歲的對手。這位與他對打的選手從小就把阿格西當成偶像，賽後也加入其他球迷的行列，一起向阿格西道別。

網球傳奇選手 阿格西

他們在最後如此熱情地擁抱我，實在令我感動不已。他們陪我度過我的網球生涯，也陪著我走到最後。

Notes & Vocabulary

game, set and good-bye 揮別網壇

標題中的 game, set and good-bye 是從 game, set and match 衍生而來，game 在網球比賽中指的是「局」，裁判在每一局結束，都會宣佈誰贏了這一局，例如阿格西贏了，裁判就會說 Game, Agassi.。set 則是「盤」，而 match 則是整個比賽。後來有人用 game, set and match 形容「完全勝利」，本課標題是配合阿格西而設計，表示他光榮結束網球生涯，揮別網壇。

all-time greats 空前的偉大事物

all-time 指的是「空前的」。這裡的 great 當名詞，指的是「偉大的人或事物」。常見組合用法有 all-time record、all-time leaders、all-time coaches 。

- The driver set an all-time speed record.
  這位車手創了空前的車速紀錄。

Father Time 時間老人

此為時間的擬人化說法，其形象為手持鐮刀（scythe）與沙漏（hourglass）的老人。其他相似用法有 Father Christmas / Santa Claus（聖誕老人）、Mother Earth（大地、后土）、Mother Nature（大自然）。

1. **bid farewell** [bɪd] [ˋfɛrˋwɛl] *v. phr.* 道別
2. **tearful** [ˋtɪrfəl] *adj.* 含淚的
3. **emotional** [ɪˋmoʃənl̩] *adj.* 感情豐富的；情緒化的
4. **fond** [fɑnd] *adj.* 喜愛的
5. **impact** [ˋɪmˏpækt] *n.* 影響
6. **gimpy** [ˋgɪmpɪ] *adj.* 跛腳的
7. **succumb to** [səˋkʌm] *v.* 壓垮；屈服
8. **opponent** [əˋponənt] *n.* 敵手
9. **idolize** [ˋaɪdəˏlaɪz] *v.* 崇拜偶像；把……當偶像崇拜
10. **legion** [ˋlidʒən] *n.* 眾多；大量
11. **overwhelmed** [ˏovɚˋhwɛlmd] *adj.* 被壓倒的；承受不住的

Larry Smith, CNN Correspondent

Agassi walks away a legend, not just an eight-time major winner and one of only five men to complete the career grand slam,[12] but someone who morphed into[13] a sports icon[14] along the way. He was once a precocious[15] phenom,[16] who blazed a trail through the game to the tune of "image is everything."

Andy Roddick, Tennis Player

I think what makes him so different is just his crossover[17] appeal. He was able to take tennis to a totally different demographic,[18] create interest in tennis at all times.

James Blake, Tennis Player

We all owe a little debt of gratitude[19] for what he's done for the sport because he's transcended[20] the sport to become an international superstar, more so than any other tennis player of the last 20 years probably.

Larry Smith, CNN Correspondent

Later, Agassi discovered that substance is better. He rebounded[21] from dropping out of the top 100 and from his divorce from his first wife, actress Brooke Shields, to reclaim[22] the number-one ranking in 1999, later becoming the only man to hold the top ranking in three different decades.

CNN 特派員 賴瑞‧史密斯

阿格西以傳奇的身影走下球場。他不僅有八座大滿貫冠軍獎盃，並且是網球史上完成大滿貫的唯五之一，他更在這段過程中蛻變成為體育界的偶像人物。他曾是早熟的天才選手，以「形象就是一切」的姿態橫掃網球場。

網球選手 安迪‧羅迪克

我認為他與眾不同之處，就在於他能夠吸引各種不同的人。他把網球帶進了完全不同的族群當中，隨時都讓大眾對網球充滿興趣。

網球選手 詹姆斯‧布雷克

我們所有人都必須感謝他對網球的貢獻，因為他超越了網球這項運動，而成為國際性的超級巨星。過去二十年來的其他網球選手恐怕都無法望其項背。

CNN 特派員 賴瑞‧史密斯

後來，阿格西發現實力比較重要。他揮別了世界排名跌落一百名以外的低潮，以及與第一任妻子，演員布魯克‧雪德絲離婚的陰霾，而在一九九九年重新登上世界排名第一的王位，後來更成為唯一在三個不同年代都得以排名世界第一的網球選手。

Notes & Vocabulary

blaze a trail 做開路先鋒

blaze 在此為動詞，是指「火焰熊熊燃燒」的意思，trail 則是「小道；痕跡；足跡」，燒出一條小路表示拓荒，也就是做開路先鋒、成為典範的意思。

- Tiger Woods blazed a trail for other young golfers.
  老虎‧伍茲替年輕的高爾夫球員們樹立了一個典範。

其他相關的用法有：

trailblazing 有開拓性的；具新意的

trailblazer 拓荒者

- The trailblazing photographer was the center of several controversies.
  這位創新的攝影師是許多爭議的焦點。

12. grand slam [grænd] [slæm] *n.* 大滿貫
13. morph into [mɔrf] *v.* 蛻變成
14. icon [`aɪˏkɑn] *n.* 偶像；崇拜的對象
15. precocious [prɪ`koʃəs] *adj.* 早熟的
16. phenom [`fiˏnɑm] *n.*（口）特別優秀的人或物
17. crossover [`krɔsˏovɚ] *n.* 交叉；跨越
18. demographic [ˏdɛmə`græfɪk] *n.* 人口統計時認定的人口族群
19. gratitude [`grætəˏtud] *n.* 感激之情；感恩
20. transcend [træn`sɛnd] *v.* 超越；優於
21. rebound [rɪ`baʊnd] *v.* 重新振作；彈回
22. reclaim [rɪ`klem] *v.* 取回

Off the court,[23] the eighth-grade dropout[24] received his high school diploma[25] through correspondence courses.[26] His foundation has started a charter school in his hometown of Las Vegas.

Chris Evert, Former Tennis Player

He got older, and he started using his head out there on the tennis court and started really training harder, married Steffi Graf. You know, he has two kids now and he has a great foundation. He really gives back a lot to society.

Andy Roddick, Tennis Player

I don't think we've seen his greatest accomplishment[27] yet, and that's a big statement, considering what he's accomplished already.

Larry Smith, CNN Correspondent

And that may have little to do with tennis. A good-bye to his playing days, Agassi says "hello" to tomorrow, and whatever lies ahead.

Andre Agassi, Tennis Legend

I'm going to wake up tomorrow, and start with not caring how I feel. That's going to feel great. And then, I'm imagining for a long time, anytime somebody asks me to do something, I'm going to go, "sure, why not?"

網球場外，這位在八年級輟學的中輟生藉由函授課程取得高中學歷。他的基金會在家鄉拉斯維加斯成立了一所特許學校。

前網球選手 克莉絲．艾芙特

他年紀漸長，在網球場上開始用心思考，而且更加努力訓練，後來又娶了史黛菲．葛拉芙。你也知道，他現在有兩個小孩，還有一個很了不起的基金會。他確實回饋了很多給社會。

網球選手 安迪．羅迪克

我認為我們還沒看到他最偉大的成就。以他早已達成的成就來看，這句話的口氣其實是很大的。

CNN 特派員 賴瑞．史密斯

而他未來的成就很可能與網球無關。阿格西告別了打球的時光，同時也全心迎接未來的日子，不論未來會帶來些什麼。

網球傳奇選手 阿格西

我明天起床後開始不再在乎自己的感覺。這樣一定很棒。接著，我想再來會有很長一段時間，只要有人問我想不想做些什麼，我就會說：「好啊，來吧！」

Notes & Vocabulary

charter school 特許學校

charter 是指設立公司、大學等的「特別許可」或「特許狀」，charter school 通常是私人或公司設立的，不屬於公立學校體制（public school system）及地方規範約束，但會受到州教育局的監督。特許學校設立的目的是在鼓勵創新教學，教學上會比一般公立學校來得有創意。

- Robert's children attend a charter school.
  羅伯的小孩上的是特許學校。

23. **off the court** *phr.* 場外；場下
24. **dropout** [ˋdrɑpˏaʊt] *n.* 中輟生
25. **diploma** [dəˋplomə] *n.* 文憑
26. **correspondence course** [ˏkɔrəˋspɑndəns] [kɔrs] *n.* 函授課程
27. **accomplishment** [əˋkʌmplɪʃmənt] *n.* 成就

Blogs Take On Traditional Media

部落格——改變傳統媒體生態的新監督力量

如果你是使用 MP3 ，請聽 MP3 Track 77；如果你使用電腦互動光碟，請點選 DVD-ROM【實戰應用篇—Part I：Unit 8】，試試看是否聽懂新聞內容。

Step 2 請瀏覽下列關鍵字彙，再仔細聽一次。

journal 日誌	peanut gallery 無足輕重的小人物
unaccountable 無責任的	mainstream 主流
campaign 競選活動	allege（無充份證據而）宣稱
press corps 記者團	

如果你還不是聽的很懂的話，請參考下列發音提示，再仔細聽一次。

連音	fifth estate、anonymous source
去捲舌音	blogsphere、personal、service、perspectives、target、favors

試著作答下列聽力測驗題目。

True or False 是非題

____ 1. Blogs and bloggers have already had an effect on American politics.

____ 2. Most bloggers agree with traditional journalists.

____ 3. After the U.S. political conventions, many bloggers bought watchdogs.

____ 4. CBS defended its story for ten days before saying it was a mistake.

____ 5. A softball question is a question about baseball.

Multiple Choice 選擇題

____ 1. To the nearest second, how often are weblogs being created?

a. five seconds
b. six seconds
c. eight seconds
d. forty seconds

____ 2. What did Dan Rather do that made him a target for bloggers?

a. called someone Buckhead
b. challenged traditional media sources
c. told a story about George W. Bush
d. wrote a blog

____ 3. What happened to Jeff Gannon after the press conference?

a. He resigned.
b. He joined the White House staff.
c. He was fired.
d. He divorced himself from reality.

試著用較慢的速度，再仔細聽一遍（MP3 Track 78），檢查答案是否正確。

對答案、驗收成果，並詳讀原文，若仍有不懂的地方，可反覆多聽幾次。

（答案請見 p. 313）

Michael Holmes, CNN Correspondent

Hello, I'm Michael Holmes with a special report on blogging. Well, how many people have even heard of blogging or blogs, or the blogosphere? Well, if you haven't, you should. It's here, it's growing and it's having an influence in your world. Recently, I hosted a lively[2] panel[3] discussion on the issue of blogging and the fifth estate; its impact and its future. Here now, a look at how blogs have influenced some big issues in the United States.

Somewhere around the world, a weblog is created every 5.8 seconds—part personal Web journal,[4] part Internet wire service[5] and very often, critic[6] of traditional journalists.

Kurt Anderson, Media Columnist

At their best, bloggers are, you know, truth tellers, fact-checkers, you know, the peanut gallery throwing spitballs[7] at the, until recently fairly unaccountable[8] pooh-bahs[9] of the mainstream[10] media.

Michael Holmes, CNN Correspondent

Take last year's U.S. political conventions[11] when the media concluded there was no real news there, it was the sometimes unusual perspectives[12] of the bloggers that made them the big story.

Blogger

We can't get much blogging done because all the journalists want to talk to us and ask us what kind of blogging we're doing.

Michael Holmes, CNN Correspondent

With the end of the campaign,[13] blogs took on a new role—media watchdog.[14] Their first target—broadcast news icon Dan Rather.

CNN 特派員 麥可・霍姆斯

大家好，我是麥可・霍姆斯，為各位帶來一則有關部落格的特別報導。到底有多少人曾聽過「部落格」或者「部落圈」呢？如果您沒聽過的話，那您應該要知道。部落格就存在我們目前的社會當中，不但日益壯大，而且對您的世界也有所影響。我最近主持了一場氣氛熱烈的專題討論，主題是部落格與第五權，其所造成的衝擊，以及其未來的發展。現在，我們來看看部落格對美國若干重大議題所造成的影響。

現在，每五點八秒，世界上的某處就有一則網路日誌誕生——部分屬於個人網誌，部分屬於網路新聞報導，而且通常是對傳統新聞的批判。

媒體專欄作家 科特・安德森

部落客都是竭盡全力揭發真相、探求事實的人，也都是向主流媒體中那些向來說話不必負責的大人物吐槽的老百姓。

CNN 特派員 麥可・霍姆斯

以去年美國的政黨代表大會為例，當時媒體認為那些大會沒什麼新聞可報；有時候就是因為部落客的獨特觀點，才把這些事件變成大新聞。

部落客

我們沒什麼時間寫網誌，因為有一大堆記者想要採訪我們，問我們都寫些什麼網誌。

CNN 特派員 麥可・霍姆斯

在大選接近尾聲之際，部落格又扮演了一個新角色——媒體監督者。他們的第一個目標是電視新聞代表性人物丹・拉瑟。

Notes & Vocabulary

the fifth estate 第五權（第五階級）

將記者或媒體（the press）稱作「第四權」的說法在國內很普遍，不過事實上英文中係稱其為 the fourth estate，原意應為「第四階級」，這種說法始自十九世紀，至於第一到第三階級指的是封建時代社會的教士（clergy）、貴族（nobility）及平民（commoners）三個社會階層。the fifth estate 是從第四權衍生出的新詞，意指監督並制衡第四權的力量。

peanut gallery 無足輕重的小人物

美國俚語，本義是「劇場中票價最低的最高樓座」。據說十九世紀時美國戲院的票價是按座位距離舞台的遠近而定，後排的座位（gallery）價位最低，為平民百姓聚集之處。坐在 gallery 看表演的觀眾，若覺得演出水準不夠，常索性把手邊正在嗑的花生等零食往台上扔去，擾亂演員的注意力（本句後半的 throw spitballs at ... 也是類似的情境，只是把花生米換成了小紙團），故後排座位就有 peanut gallery 這樣的別稱，坐在那兒朝台上丟花生的人則被認為是「愛吵鬧的下層民眾」（rowdy rabble）；後來引申指「烏合之眾」或「不值得重視的小人物」。

1. **take on** *v.* 開始和……較量、爭鬥
2. **lively** [ˋlaɪvlɪ] *adj.* 熱烈的；活潑的
3. **panel** [ˋpænl̩] *n.* 專門小組；專題討論小組
4. **journal** [ˋdʒɜnl̩] *n.* 日記；日誌
5. **wire service** [waɪr] [ˋsɜvəs] *n.* 新聞通訊社
6. **critic** [ˋkrɪtɪk] *n.* 評論家；批評家
7. **spitball** [ˋspɪt͵bɔl] *n.* 紙團
8. **unaccountable** [͵ʌnəˋkaʊntəbl̩] *adj.* 無責任的
9. **pooh-bah** [ˋpu͵bɑ] *n.* 顯要；自命不凡的人
10. **mainstream** [ˋmen͵strim] *n.* 主流；主要趨勢
11. **convention** [kənˋvɛnʃən] *n.* 會議；大會
12. **perspective** [pɚˋspɛktɪv] *n.* 觀點
13. **campaign** [kæmˋpen] *n.* 競選活動
14. **watchdog** [ˋwɑtʃ͵dɔg] *n.* 監督者；看門狗

When Rather's *60 Minutes* story alleged[15] that George W. Bush received special favors[16] during his Air National Guard service, it wasn't traditional media sources that challenged the story, but an Internet post[17] by an anonymous source named Buckhead. For 12 days, CBS defended its story, then this:

Dan Rather, CBS News Anchor

It was a mistake. CBS News deeply regrets it. Also, I want to say personally and directly, I'm sorry.

Michael Holmes, CNN Correspondent

It wasn't long before the bloggers took on one of their own. Jeff Gannon, a White House correspondent for the little-known[18] *Talon News Service*, lobbed[19] so-called softball questions during West Wing briefings;[20] easy questions. Few in the press corps[21] complained. But then in early 2005, Gannon was called on[22] by President Bush during a live televised[23] news conference.

Jeff Gannon, Discredited Talon Reporter

Harry Reid was talking about soup lines and Hillary Clinton was talking about the economy being on the verge of[24] collapse.[25] How are you going to work with people who seem to have divorced themselves from reality?[26]

Michael Holmes, CNN Correspondent

The blogs pounced,[27] accusing him via the Internet of everything from political bias[28] to using a false name with the knowledge of the White House to being a gay escort.[29] Ten days later Gannon resigned.

拉瑟在《六十分鐘》節目中的報導指稱小布希在國民兵航空隊服役期間利用特權享受優待；結果質疑這則新聞的力量不是傳統媒體，而是網路上一則作者署名「鹿頭」的匿名留言。往後的十二天內，CBS（哥倫比亞廣播公司）全力為其報導辯護，但接下來的發展卻是這樣的：

CBS 新聞主播 丹・拉瑟

該項報導是個錯誤。CBS 新聞對此深感遺憾。此外，我也要親自而且直截了當地說：我很抱歉。

CNN 特派員 麥可・霍姆斯

不久之後，部落客也揪出了一個自己人。傑夫・甘農（註 1）是名不見經傳的《利爪新聞服務社》派駐白宮的特派員。他在白宮西翼簡報當中一再提出所謂的「軟球」問題，也就是輕鬆易答的問題。記者團裡也沒什麼人抱怨。但在二〇〇五年初，甘農卻在一場電視直播的記者會上受到布希總統點名。

身分遭揭穿的利爪記者 傑夫・甘農

哈里・瑞德（註 2）提到民眾排隊領湯的狀況，希拉蕊・柯林頓則談到經濟已瀕臨崩潰。你要怎麼和這些似乎已和現實脫節的人一起合作呢？

CNN 特派員 麥可・霍姆斯

部落格群起抨擊，透過網路指控他種種罪名，包括政治偏見、在白宮知情的狀況下冒用假名，甚至曾任同性戀伴遊。十天後，甘農就辭職了。

註 1：本名 James Guckert，於二〇〇三至二〇〇五年間擔任白宮特派員時化名 Jeff Gannon，擔任同志伴遊時暱稱則為 Bulldog。與白宮及共和黨關係良好。

註 2：內華達州參議員，參議院民主黨黨鞭。

Notes & Vocabulary

softball questions 不痛不癢的問題

softball 原意為「壘球」，相對於棒球而言，球較大較軟，球速也比較慢，自然較容易打擊。英文中常以 softball 來比喻容易做到的事物，例如本文中的 softball question 就是一個相當常見的固定用法，指「使對方能夠輕鬆回答、無關痛癢的問題」。至於前面的動詞，除了 ask 之外，還可以用其他表示「投球」動作的字，如：lob、loft、toss 等。

- The reporter did nothing but lob softball questions during the interview.
  那記者在訪談中盡是問些無關痛癢的問題。

15. **allege** [əˋlɛdʒ] *v.* （無充分證據而）宣稱
16. **favor** [ˋfevɚ] *n.* 偏袒；優待
17. **post** [post] *n.* （在網路上發佈的）留言；信息
18. **little-known** [ˋlɪtl̩ˋnon] *adj.* 鮮為人知的；沒聽過的
19. **lob** [lɑb] *v.* 緩慢地擲出；提出問題
20. **briefing** [ˋbrifɪŋ] *n.* 簡報
21. **press corps** [prɛs] [kɔr] *n. phr.* 記者團
22. **call on** *v.* 請求；號召
23. **televise** [ˏtɛləˋvaɪz] *v.* 電視播送；電視拍攝
24. **on the verge of** *phr.* 瀕於；即將
25. **collapse** [kəˋlæps] *n.* 倒場；崩潰
26. **divorce from reality** *v. phr.* 脫離現實
27. **pounce** [paʊns] *v.* 猛撲；發現錯誤並立即批評
28. **bias** [ˋbaɪəs] *n.* 偏見；成見；偏心
29. **gay escort** [ge] [ˋɛsˏkɔrt] *n. phr.* 男同性戀伴遊

On the Front Lines

Weary Soldiers Face Dirt and Danger outside of Baghdad

活著，真好 巴格達前線美軍的一天

Step 1 如果你是使用 MP3 ，請聽 MP3 Track 79；如果你使用電腦互動光碟，請點選 DVD-ROM【實戰應用篇—Part I: Unit 9】，試試看是否聽懂新聞內容。

Step 2 請瀏覽下列關鍵字彙，再仔細聽一次。

front line 前線	firsthand 第一手的
significance 重大意義	insurgent 叛亂份子
trigger 引爆	canal 河渠
patrol 巡邏	vital 極重要的

Step 3 如果你還不是聽的很懂的話，請參考下列發音提示，再仔細聽一次。

連音	sleep on、doles out、feels safe

試著作答下列聽力測驗題目。

True or False 是非題

____ 1. The soldiers were sleeping on the roof of a building.

____ 2. The soldiers think it is too dangerous to help the crying child.

____ 3. Baghdad is very comfortable and luxurious compared to this area.

____ 4. The soldiers think Americans back home know exactly what they're going through.

____ 5. Operating in this area is not very important.

Multiple Choice 選擇題

____ 1. How many times a day do these soldiers get to take showers?

a. once　　b. twice
c. four　　d. none

____ 2. How far is this area from Baghdad?

a. 4 miles　　b. 14 miles
c. 40 miles　　d. 140 miles

____ 3. Why don't the soldiers take the roads?

a. to make the farmers puzzled
b. because insurgents put bombs on the roads
c. because it makes them stronger
d. so they can look for wires

試著用較慢的速度，再仔細聽一遍（MP3 Track 80），檢查答案是否正確。

對答案、驗收成果，並詳讀原文，若仍有不懂的地方，可反覆多聽幾次。

（答案請見 p. 313）

CNN Anchor

So, what is it like out on the front lines, especially outside of Baghdad?

CNN Anchor

Arwa Damon gives us a firsthand[2] look at the dangerous, often dirty job facing coalition troops.[3]

Arwa Damon, CNN Correspondent

The morning wake-up call comes early at this house. But who really needs a wake-up call when you sleep on the roof? There are no showers here, just whatever fits in your backpack, whatever you can do to soothe[4] feet that will be pounded[5] all day. It's a far cry from the relative luxury of Baghdad, just 14 miles away. These soldiers are well past[6] being used to the sounds of war. This explosion, at least, was controlled.

A strange sound, a toddler[7] crying, his legs weak from a calcium[8] deficiency.[9] The troops don't have much, but the company[10] medic[11] doles out what he can. This simple scene actually carries great significance[12] for these troops. This man feels safe enough to come to the Americans for help, even though he risks being seen by insurgents.[13] It's one more Iraqi who may carry back the message that these men are here to help, and here to stay for a while.

These soldiers from the 10th Mountain Division[14] believe people back home have no idea what they go through. While America sleeps, they drag ditches,[15] looking for wires that could trigger[16] homemade bombs.

CNN 主播

前線的生活究竟是何等景況？尤其巴格達城郊又是如何呢？

CNN 主播

阿瓦．戴蒙帶我們直擊聯軍所面對危險、往往是令人討厭的工作。

CNN 特派員 阿瓦．戴蒙

這戶人家的起床號很早便響起。但如果你是睡在屋頂上，還會需要別人叫你起床嗎？這裡沒有淋浴設施，一切必需品都裝在背包中，只要能讓被折磨了一整天的雙腳感到舒服的東西都行。這裡和相對奢華的巴格達市相去甚遠，而巴格達市距此不過十四英里遠而已。這些士兵早已經習慣戰爭中發出的種種聲響。至少這次爆炸是在控制之中。

有一陣奇怪的聲音，是幼兒的哭泣聲，他的腿因為缺乏鈣質而虛弱無力。這支部隊的物資並不多，但連上的醫務兵仍盡可能地進行分配。對這支部隊而言，這個單調的場景其實相當重要。這名男子覺得前來向美軍求援應無安全上的顧慮，但他還是得冒著被叛軍看見的危險。又多了一個可能會回去傳達這則訊息的伊拉克人：這些人是來這裡幫忙，而且會待上一陣子。

這些隸屬於第十山地師的士兵們認為家鄉的民眾並不了解他們所經歷的一切。當美國人入睡時，他們是在溝渠中打撈，尋找可能引爆土製炸彈的引信。

Notes & Vocabulary

a far cry from 截然不同；大不相同

far cry 是指對很遠的地方大聲呼叫，表示距離相隔很遠，後來用來比喻差異很大，類似中文說的「相差十萬八千里」。

- The writer's latest novel is a far cry from his previous work.
  那位作家最新的作品與他之前的作品大相逕庭。

dole out （少量）發放物資；施捨

指以有限的數量來做少量分配，通常用在施捨、救濟的情況，例如發放金錢、食物等救濟物資。

- The aid workers doled out water and food to the refugees.
  救災人員發放水和食物給難民。

另外，dole 也可以當名詞，指「失業救濟」。

- Greg went on the dole after losing his job.
  葛瑞格失業後開始領失業救濟金。

1. **front line** [frʌnt] [laɪn] *n.* 前線
2. **firsthand** [ˋfɝstˋhænd] *adj.* 第一手的；直接取得的
3. **coalition troop** [ˏkoəˋlɪʃən] [trup] *n. phr.* 聯合部隊
4. **soothe** [suð] *v.* 舒緩；撫慰
5. **pound** [paʊnd] *v.* 腳步沈重地行走
6. **well past** *phr.* 遠越過
7. **toddler** [ˋtɑdlɚ] *n.* 學步的幼兒
8. **calcium** [ˋkælsiəm] *n.* 鈣質
9. **deficiency** [dɪˋfɪʃənsɪ] *n.* 不足；缺乏
10. **company** [ˋkʌmpənɪ] *n.* （軍）連；連隊
11. **medic** [ˋmɛdɪk] *n.* 軍醫；戰地醫療人員
12. **significance** [sɪgˋnɪfɪkəns] *n.* 重要性；重大意義
13. **insurgent** [ɪnˋsɝdʒənt] *n.* 叛亂份子
14. **division** [dəˋvɪʒən] *n.* 師（軍隊編制單位）
15. **ditch** [dɪtʃ] *n.* 壕溝；溝渠
16. **trigger** [ˋtrɪgɚ] *v.* 引爆；引發

Staff Sergeant, Andrew Wallace, U.S. Army

They have these canals[17] that run across. And an area like this right here would be great for concealment[18] for a command wire.[19] It's real thin wire and if they run it through right here, they could place a bomb on this road right here.

Arwa Damon, CNN Correspondent

Travel would be a lot quicker if the company could take the roads, but the insurgents routinely put bombs there, so the troops take to the stinking[20] canals instead. Before they arrived two weeks ago, U.S. commanders[21] say this area was a sanctuary for well-financed insurgents and al-Qaeda in Iraq.

This farmer says security[22] is better since they got here, though he's puzzled[23] why U.S. troops would try to jump a ditch when the dry road is only a few steps away. After patrolling[24] for four hours, jumping across canals, walking through mud and now soaking wet, these troops are not even going to get a shower when they return back to their base.

Operating out here is tough, but, say commanders, vital,[25] because denying[26] easy insurgent movement in this area helps protect Baghdad. It's hard to keep a smile when you smell like a toilet, but for these troops it's all just part of the mission. Out here, success sometimes means taking the slippery slope.

美國陸軍中士 安德魯．華勒士

伊拉克有一些穿梭其間的運河。像這樣的地方很適合用來藏匿炸彈的引信。那種引信很細小，如果他們在這裡安裝了引信，就能在這條路上放置一枚炸彈。

CNN 特派員 阿瓦．戴蒙

如果連隊移動時能走馬路，速度上會快很多，但是叛軍經常在馬路上放置炸彈，於是部隊選擇走髒臭的水溝。兩週前在他們抵達之前，美軍指揮官說這裡是資金充沛的叛軍和伊拉克境內蓋達組織的天下。

這名農夫說，自從他們抵達之後，這裡就變得比較安全了，但他對於為何馬路就在幾步之遙，美軍卻要選擇走水溝感到不解。在經過四個小時的巡邏、跨越水溝、走過泥濘、且現在已渾身溼透後，這些部隊連回到基地後都無法沖個澡。

在這裡進行軍事行動相當困難，但指揮官說這麼做很重要，因為不讓這裡的叛軍輕易行動才能協防巴格達。當你全身聞起來像廁所時，你很難保持笑臉，但對這些部隊來說，這不過是任務的一部分。在這裡，成功有時意味著你必須要走滑溜的陡坡。

Notes & Vocabulary

a sanctuary for ……的庇護所、天堂

sanctuary [ˋsæŋktʃʊˏɛrɪ] 原本是指寺廟、教堂、寺院等各種宗教的「聖堂」，也可表示弱者的「避難所；庇護處」或得到的「庇護」，用來比喻任何提供保護、安全無虞的地方，後面用 for 接得到保護的對象。

- The park is a sanctuary for endangered species.
  那座公園是瀕臨絕種物種的保護區。

well-financed 資金充裕的

well- 是狀態良好的意思，可作為字首，finance 當動詞指「提供資金；籌措資金」，所以 well-financed 是用來形容得到充分的資金。

以 well- 為字首的複合形容詞很多，例如：

well-educated 受過良好教育的

well-paid 薪水優渥的

the slippery slope 不利的情況

slippery 是「滑的」，slope 是「坡；斜面」。這個慣用語字面上是指「很滑的斜坡」，比喻情況不利、後續發展將會下滑，也對應了文中軍人捨道路而走溼滑的斜坡泥路的狀況。

- Once a public official takes an inappropriate gift, he is on a slippery slope that leads to corruption.
  公務員一旦接受不適當的禮物，情況就不妙了，會構成貪污。

17. **canal** [kəˋnæl] *n.* 河渠；水道
18. **concealment** [kənˋsilmənt] *n.* 隱藏；藏匿
19. **command wire** [kəˋmænd] [waɪr] *n. phr.* 引信
20. **stinking** [ˋstɪŋkɪŋ] *adj.* 發出惡臭的
21. **commander** [kəˋmændɚ] *n.* 司令官；指揮官
22. **security** [sɪˋkjʊrətɪ] *n.* 安全；防備
23. **puzzled** [ˋpʌzl̩d] *adj.* 感到困惑的
24. **patrol** [pəˋtrol] *v.* 巡邏；偵查
25. **vital** [ˋvaɪtl̩] *adj.* 極重要的；不可少的
26. **deny** [dɪˋnaɪ] *v.* 阻止；拒絕不給

That Sinking Feeling

Global Warming May Spell Doom for Island Nation

馬爾地夫將自地表消失？

Step 1 如果你是使用 MP3 ，請聽 MP3 Track 81；如果你使用電腦互動光碟，請點選 DVD-ROM【實戰應用篇—Part I：Unit 10】，試試看是否聽懂新聞內容。

Step 2 請瀏覽下列關鍵字彙，再仔細聽一次。

refugee 難民	perch on 座落於
bleach 漂白	organism 生物
resilient 堅韌的	acknowledge 承認
inundate 泛濫	vacate 撤退

Step 3 如果你還不是聽的很懂的話，請參考下列發音提示，再仔細聽一次。

連音	perched on、projects sea levels
同化音	temperatures here
省略音	temperature

 試著作答下列聽力測驗題目。

True or False 是非題

____ 1. The Maldives are small islands made out of coral.

____ 2. The Maldives' biggest industry is the production of coral.

____ 3. Rising ocean water will soon be a problem for the Maldives.

____ 4. Global warming isn't a big priority for the president of the Maldives.

____ 5. Some people are afraid that if the oceans rise, the Maldives will go underwater.

Multiple Choice 選擇題

____ 1. Where are the Maldives located?

a. in the Pacific Ocean　　b. in the Arctic Ocean
c. in the Atlantic Ocean　　d. in the Indian Ocean

____ 2. How much are sea levels expected to rise by the end of the century?

a. eight centimeters　　b. two meters
c. 88 centimeters　　d. 88 meters

____ 3. What do experts think might cause sea levels to rise?

a. polar ice caps melting
b. the threat of global warming
c. El Niño weather conditions
d. the end of the century

Step 5 試著用較慢的速度，再仔細聽一遍 (MP3 Track 82)，檢查答案是否正確。

Step 6 對答案、驗收成果，並詳讀原文，若仍有不懂的地方，可反覆多聽幾次。

(答案請見 p. 313)

CNN Anchor

With global warming apparently on the rise, the country of the Maldives worries its people could become climate change refugees.[3]

CNN Anchor

The Maldives, nearly 1,200 coral islands, sit only a few feet above sea level in the Indian Ocean, and as Seth Doane reports, they're in danger of disappearing.

Seth Doane, CNN Correspondent

Shaahina, a scuba[4] instructor,[5] worries her son Nick won't ever see the coral reefs the same way she has. The Maldives is a nation of nearly 1,200 islands perched on coral reefs[6] off the southern tip of India. The reefs attract divers and play a key role in the nation's two biggest industries[7]—tourism and fishing. But some fear they are in danger . . .

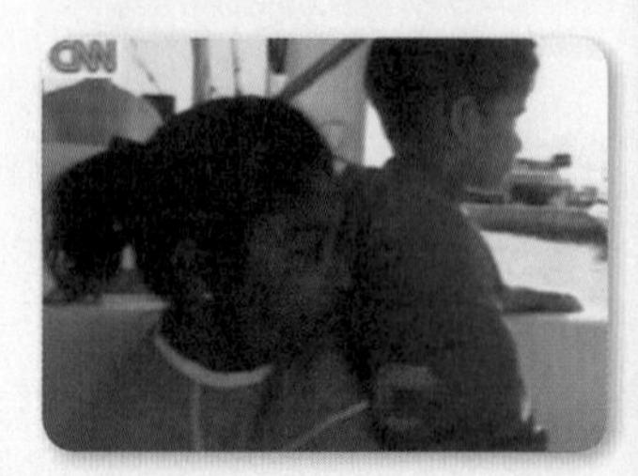

Shaahina Ali, Dive Instructor

Normally when we were children, without diving you could just snorkel[8] and see a lot of stuff—live coral, huge table coral—huge, massive[9]—a lot of fish. But now, to swim on a reef-top you don't see that much.

Seth Doane, CNN Correspondent

Coral is a living organism.[10] While it's resilient,[11] it thrives[12] in certain temperatures.[13] When El Niño weather conditions brought warmer water temperatures here a few years ago, many coral reefs were bleached.[14] Some worry that global warming will have a much greater impact. These pictures from our dive show bleached coral on what once was a thriving reef. If the water stays warm, the bleached coral may die.

CNN 主播

全球暖化現象明顯愈來愈嚴重，馬爾地夫因此擔心其國民將淪為氣候變化的難民。

CNN 主播

馬爾地夫由將近一千兩百個珊瑚礁島組成，位於印度洋中，只比海平面高了幾呎而已。根據賽斯．多安的報導，這個國家恐將面臨消失的命運。

CNN 特派員 賽斯．多安

莎赫娜是一名潛水教練，她擔心自己的兒子尼克以後再也看不到她所見過的珊瑚礁。馬爾地夫這個國家擁有近一千兩百個小島，全都立基於珊瑚礁上，散布在印度南端外海。這些珊瑚礁吸引許多潛水人士來到此地，在該國的兩大產業裡——觀光業和漁業——也扮演了關鍵性的角色。不過，有些人擔心珊瑚礁已經面臨危機……

潛水教練 莎赫娜．阿里

我們小時候，不必潛入水中，只要浮潛就可以看到很多東西——活珊瑚、巨大無比的桌面珊瑚，還有許多魚。現在就算游在珊瑚礁上方，也看不到那麼多東西。

CNN 特派員 賽斯．多安

珊瑚是一種活的有機體，雖然頗具韌性，卻只能存活在特定溫度之下。聖嬰現象在幾年前導致這裡的海水溫度升高，許多珊瑚礁都因此白化。有些人擔心全球暖化現象還會造成更大的衝擊。從我們潛水所拍到的這些畫面，可以看到原本生氣蓬勃的珊瑚礁上的珊瑚都已經白化了。水溫如果持續居高不下，這些白化的珊瑚就可能會死亡。

Notes & Vocabulary

on the rise 持續增加

rise 在此作名詞，是指數量或程度的「上升；增加」。

- The number of tourists traveling to Europe is on the rise this year.
  今年至歐洲旅遊的觀光人數持續增加中。

in danger of 處於……的危險之中

這個片語也可以說 at risk of。

- Tracy is at great risk of losing her job because she always shows up late.
  崔西老是遲到，所以她的工作可能不保。

be perched on 座落於……

perch 原本是鳥類「棲息；蹲踞」在樹上的意思，引申為「座落；位於……」，尤指位在高處，經常用被動。

- The monastery is perched on a cliff.
  那間修道院座落在懸崖邊上。

1. **spell** [spɛl] *v.* 招致；帶來
2. **doom** [dum] *n.* 世界末日；厄運
3. **refugee** [ˌrɛfjʊˋdʒi] *n.* 難民
4. **scuba** [ˋskubə] *n.* 自攜式水中呼吸器；氧氣瓶
5. **instructor** [ɪnˋstrʌktɚ] *n.* 教練；指導者
6. **coral reef** [ˋkɔrəl] [rif] *n.* 珊瑚礁
7. **industry** [ˋɪndəstrɪ] *n.* 產業
8. **snorkel** [ˋsnɔrkəl] *v.* 浮潛
9. **massive** [ˋmæsɪv] *adj.* 巨大的；大量的
10. **organism** [ˋɔrgəˌnɪzəm] *n.* 生物；有機體
11. **resilient** [rɪˋzɪljənt] *adj.* 堅韌的；適應力強的
12. **thrive** [θraɪv] *v.* 茁壯成長；茂盛生長
13. **temperature** [ˋtɛmprətʃɚ] *n.* 溫度
14. **bleach** [blitʃ] *v.* 漂白

Global climate change seems like such an abstract[15] concept until you're down there diving, seeing the bleached coral firsthand, imagining that impact multiplied[16] many times around the world and potentially[17] imagining it getting much worse. Saving the coral and acknowledging[18] the threat of global warming is a priority[19] for the president of the Maldives and his cabinet.[20]

The concern is that as polar ice caps melt, sea levels rise and threaten low-lying areas. The intergovernmental[21] panel[22] on climate change projects[23] sea levels could rise up to 88 centimeters by the end of this century. For Maldivians, that's a frightening figure, as most of this country is not even two meters above sea level. And it may be the coral—natural rings of defense that is being damaged first.

Mohamad Hussain Shareef, Chief Government Spokesman

The long-term scenario[24] or long-term fear is that the Maldives could very well be inundated[25] completely and that we, as a people, may have to actually vacate[26] these islands—this country—and move and hence, be termed "the world's first environmental refugees."

Seth Doane, CNN Correspondent

While the effects of global climate change are gradual, this nation may be among the first that is forced to deal with them.

全球氣候變化聽起來只是個抽象概念，但當你潛入水中，親眼目睹這些白化的珊瑚，然後想像更巨大的影響發生在全球各地，而且可能愈來愈嚴重，你就能了解全球氣候變化是多麼真實的現象。拯救珊瑚以及承認全球暖化威脅的存在，是馬爾地夫總統及其內閣的首要任務。

他們擔心極地冰帽一旦溶解，海平面即會上升，而對地勢低窪的區域造成威脅。各國政府組成的氣候變化小組預測，海平面在本世紀末將可能升高達八十八公分。對馬爾地夫的人民而言，這個數據實在令人恐慌，因為馬爾地夫大部分的國土都只比海平面高不到兩公尺。最先受害的可能會是珊瑚這種自然的防衛圈。

政府首要發言人 默罕瑪德．胡森．沙里夫

我們長期的預測，或者說長期的擔憂，便是馬爾地夫可能會完全遭到海水淹沒。如此一來，全國人民就真的必須撤離這些島嶼，撤離我們的家園，而成為所謂的「世界上首批環境難民」。

CNN 特派員 賽斯．多安

全球氣候變化的影響雖然是漸進的，馬爾地夫卻可能是全球最早被迫必須面對這個問題的國家。

Notes & Vocabulary

term 期間；稱作

term 在本文出現兩次，第一次作名詞用（與 long 構成複合形容詞 long-term），意指「期間」，term 作名詞，還可以指「學期；任期；術語」。

- The president serves a term of four years.
  總統任期四年。

term 第二次出現是作動詞用，意思是「被稱作」。

- Pluto has been termed a dwarf planet.
  冥王星已被稱作矮行星。

15. abstract [ˋæb͵strækt] *adj.* 抽象的
16. multiply [ˋmʌltə͵plaɪ] *v.* 以倍數成長、增加
17. potentially [pəˋtɛnʃəlɪ] *adv.* 潛在地；可能地
18. acknowledge [əkˋnɑlɪdʒ] *v.* 承認
19. priority [praɪˋɔrətɪ] *n.* 優先考慮的事
20. cabinet [ˋkæbnɪt] *n.* 內閣；全體閣員
21. intergovernmental [͵ɪntɚ͵gʌvɚˋmɛntl̩] *adj.* 政府與政府之間的
22. panel [ˋpænl̩] *n.* 專門小組
23. project [prəˋdʒɛkt] *v.* 預計；推斷
24. scenario [səˋnɛrɪ͵o] *n.* 情節；局面；事態
25. inundate [ˋɪnən͵det] *v.* 浸水；泛濫
26. vacate [ˋve͵ket] *v.* 撤退

原音 MP3 Track 83 / 慢速朗讀 Track 84

Seated in Style

The Fine Art of Wangling a Table in the Hottest Eateries

訂不到餐廳座位怎麼辦？

Step 1 如果你是使用 MP3 ，請聽 MP3 Track 83；如果你使用電腦互動光碟，請點選 DVD-ROM【實戰應用篇—Part I: Unit 11】，試試看是否聽懂新聞內容。

Step 2 請瀏覽下列關鍵字彙，再仔細聽一次。

wangle 用計獲得	eatery 飯館
culinary 烹飪的	socialite 社交名人
maitre d' 餐廳領班	clientele 顧客群

Step 3 如果你還不是聽的很懂的話，請參考下列發音提示，再仔細聽一次。

連音	table in、capital last year
同化音	seat yourself
去捲舌音	popular、partygoer、rarely、answer、director、diner、charm
省略音	restaurant

試著作答下列聽力測驗題目。

True or False 是非題

____ 1. Nicky Haslam is a socialist and politician.

____ 2. No restaurant manager wants to turn away customers.

____ 3. It's easy for business travelers to get tables at the hottest restaurants.

____ 4. Most people find it easy to just turn up at restaurants without a booking.

____ 5. The key to getting a table is using contacts and charm.

Multiple Choice 選擇題

____ 1. How many new restaurants opened in London last year?

a. about nine
b. nineteen
c. around ninety
d. one hundred and nine

____ 2. According to Dominic Corolleur, what is the secret of getting a table?

a. having a private line
b. being a regular customer
c. boasting about celebrity clientele
d. waiting two months

____ 3. How long can the waiting list at Gordon Ramsay be?

a. two hours
b. two days
c. two weeks
d. two months

試著用較慢的速度，再仔細聽一遍 (MP3 Track 84)，檢查答案是否正確。

對答案、驗收成果，並詳讀原文，若仍有不懂的地方，可反覆多聽幾次。

(答案請見 p. 313)

Richard Quest, CNN Business Traveler

Brasserie Georges is the oldest restaurant in Lyon. And, not surprisingly, it's very popular. Getting a table can be difficult—unless, of course, you know the right way to go about[3] it.

Ah! This seems to have worked out[4] rather nicely, doesn't it? I've wangled myself the best table in the room. So, now here's the CNN Business Traveler top tips[5] for how you, too, can seat yourself in style.

Shantelle Stein, CNN Correspondent

Around 90 new restaurants opened in the British capital last year. ~~Culinary~~[6] [Culinarily] speaking, London is swinging[7] again. And one man who's definitely not lost his mojo[8] is the socialite[9] and partygoer[10] Nicky Haslam. He says charm, contacts and tipping well are the key to getting a table and he rarely takes no for an answer.

Nicky Haslam, Interior Designer

It's not that hard really. I mean nobody wants to turn customers away.[11] They're all out to make money. And [with] some, you just have to be charming and make it work. It's not impossible to be charming.

Shantelle Stein, CNN Correspondent

But it's not so easy for a newly arrived business traveler who's hoping for a table at one of the hottest restaurants in town.

《CNN 商務旅行錦囊》理察・奎斯特

Brasserie Georges 是里昂最古老的餐廳。大家都知道它經常座無虛席。要訂到一張桌子可沒那麼容易，除非你知道正確的門路。

哈！這招似乎還蠻有效的，不是嗎？我好不容易掙到位置最棒的一張桌子，以下是《CNN 商務旅行錦囊》教你如何風光入座的祕訣。

CNN 特派員 珊泰兒・史坦

去年在英國首都開了近九十家新餐廳。就美食的觀點而言，倫敦再度復活了。此人肯定沒有失去他的魔力，他就是社交名流兼派對愛好者的尼克・哈士蘭。他說取得座位的關鍵在於魅力、人脈以及豐厚的小費，而他也幾乎從未失敗過。

室內設計師 尼克・哈士蘭

其實真的不難。沒有人會想要將顧客拒於門外，大家都想拼命賺錢。對付某些人，你得耍一點魅力才能成功，施展魅力並不是一件做不到的事。

CNN 特派員 珊泰兒・史坦

但是對一位初來乍到的商務旅客而言，想在城裡生意最好的餐廳弄到一張桌子可沒那麼簡單。

Notes & Vocabulary

in style 流行的；瀟灑地；盛大地

in style 當形容詞時，意指「流行的；時髦的」，和 in vogue、in fashion 意思相同。

- Fads come and go, but denim jeans seem to always be in style.
  時尚風潮來來去去，但丹寧褲似乎總是不褪流行。

in style 作副詞時，代表「（某事）做得漂亮」，往往隱含「令人心生敬佩」之意。

- Maddux won this game in fine style, giving up only three hits over seven scoreless innings.
  麥達斯這場比賽贏得漂亮，主投七局只被擊出三支安打，毫無失分。

另外，作副詞的 in style 亦可作「盛大、豪華」解釋，與 grandly、luxuriously 意義相近。

- Fans celebrated in style after the Red Sox won their first World Series title in 86 years.
  紅襪隊贏得睽違八十六年的世界大賽冠軍時，球迷盛大慶祝。

1. **wangle** [ˋwæŋgəl] *v.* 以計謀得到；巧妙取得
2. **eatery** [ˋitərɪ] *n.* 飯館；餐廳
3. **go about** *v.* 處理；開始進行
4. **work out** *v.* 事情發展得順利、有結果
5. **tip** [tɪp] *n., v.* 撇步；妙招；（給）小費
6. **culinary** [ˋkjuləˏnɛrɪ] *adj.* 烹飪、廚藝的
7. **swing** [swɪŋ] *v.* 變得精彩、熱鬧
8. **mojo** [ˋmodʒo] *n.* 魔力
9. **socialite** [ˋsoʃəˏlaɪt] *n.* 社交名人
10. **partygoer** [ˋpɑrtɪˏgoɚ] *n.* 社交聚會、派對常客
11. **turn away** *v.* 拒於門外

Russel Norman, Manager, Zuma

Another way, and this is very nerve-wracking[12] for a lot of people, is just to turn up.[13] You know I find myself, from my experience, when I go to other restaurants that if I turn up without a booking, and you're well-dressed, and you're polite, and explain that you haven't made a booking but you're prepared to wait, I can't think of any professional receptionist,[14] restaurant manager or maitre d'[15] that would turn you away.

Shantelle Stein, CNN Correspondent

Over in Mayfair, the Gordon Ramsay restaurant at Claridge's Hotel boasts[16] a celebrity clientele[17] as well as a two-month waiting list. According to Dominic Corolleur, the restaurant's director, the secret of getting a table is to become a regular diner.[18]

Dominic Corolleur, Manager, Gordon Ramsay at Claridge's

Most of our regulars don't actually call our reservation department. They actually call me direct because I do have a card with my private line on it, which not always people know, so I do give it to a few people obviously which are able to call me direct and I'll take care of their bookings, and I'll try to fit them in.

Shantelle Stein, CNN Correspondent

But for those of us who lack the charm or the contacts of a Nicky Haslam what's the answer?

Nicky Haslam, Interior Designer

You can say, "I'm a friend of Mick Jagger." See if you get in.

Zuma 餐廳經理 羅素・諾曼

另一種讓很多人感到神經緊繃的方法就是現場待位。依我個人的經驗來說，如果我去其他餐廳沒有先預約，但你穿著體面，態度客氣，並解釋雖然你沒有訂位但是你願意等候，我想沒有任何專業的領檯或餐廳經理會拒絕你。

CNN 特派員 珊泰兒・史坦

在倫敦梅菲爾區頗負盛名的克拉瑞奇酒店中的戈登蘭西餐廳擁有一群名人顧客及一張候位顧客已排到兩個月之長的名單。根據該餐廳負責人多米尼克・科瑞利爾的說法，要得到位子的祕訣就是成為常客。

克拉瑞奇酒店戈登蘭西餐廳經理 多米尼克・科瑞利爾

其實我們的常客多半不會打電話來預約，而是直接打電話給我，因為我有一張名片，上面有我的私人電話號碼，不見得所有人都知道，我會把這張名片給少數人，他們就可以直接打給我，我會處理他們的訂位，設法幫他們安排。

CNN 特派員 珊泰兒・史坦

但是對於我們這種沒有尼克・哈士蘭那般魅力或人脈的人，那又該怎麼辦呢？

室內設計師 尼克・哈士蘭

你可以說：「我是米克・傑格(註)的朋友」，看看人家會不會讓你進去。

註：米克・傑格是英國滾石合唱團的主唱。

Notes & Vocabulary

make a booking 訂位

booking 在此作名詞用，book 當動詞時指「預訂；預約（位子、房間、表演活動等）」。make a booking 也可以說 make a reservation。

- Kevin booked a table at a nice restaurant for his wife's birthday.
  凱文為了慶祝老婆生日，在一間很棒的餐廳訂了位。
- Joan made a reservation at the Brown Derby for Friday.
  瓊安已經訂了星期五，在布朗德比飯店。

12. **nerve-wracking** [ˋnɝv͵rækɪŋ] *adj.* 令人緊張、焦慮的
13. **turn up** *v.* (突然)出現
14. **receptionist** [rɪˋsɛpʃənɪst] *n.* 接待人員
15. **maitre d'** [ˋmetrəˋdi] *n.* 餐廳領班；飯店總管 (= maitre d'hotel)
16. **boast** [bost] *v.* 以擁有……而自豪
17. **clientele** [͵klaɪənˋtɛl] *n.* 顧客群
18. **diner** [ˋdaɪnɚ] *n.* 餐廳顧客；小餐館

Who's Your Daddy

Sperm Donor Offspring Search for Family and Identity

誰才是我爸爸？ 匿名捐精者子女上網覓手足

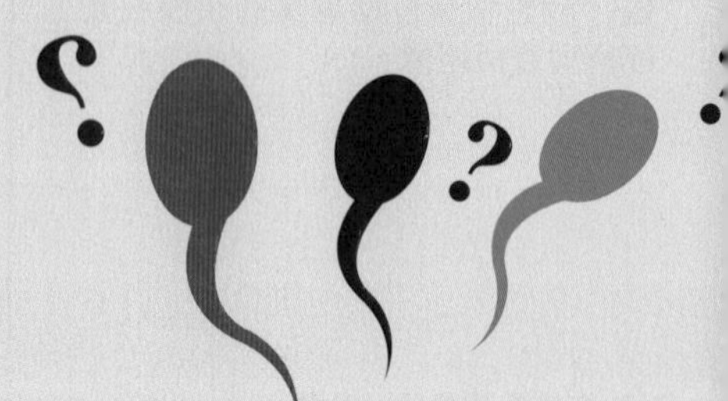

Step 1 如果你是使用 MP3 ，請聽 MP3 Track 85；如果你使用電腦互動光碟，請點選 DVD-ROM【實戰應用篇—Part I：Unit 12】，試試看是否聽懂新聞內容。

Step 2 請瀏覽下列關鍵字彙，再仔細聽一次。

sperm 精子	donor 捐贈者
offspring 子女；後代	anonymity 匿名
conceive 懷孕	genetic 基因的
potential 可能的	swab 擦；刮

Step 3 如果你還不是聽的很懂的話，請參考下列發音提示，再仔細聽一次。

連音	this summer、this site、surgical assistant、remain anonymous
省略音	sophomore

試著作答下列聽力測驗題目。

True or False 是非題

____ 1. Donating sperm is a very unusual practice.

____ 2. In some countries, sperm donors are no longer anonymous.

____ 3. Sperm banks are required to keep track of the number of children from each donor.

____ 4. It is getting harder and harder for children to find their genetic parents.

____ 5. Genetic fathers have legal and financial responsibilities to their children.

Multiple Choice 選擇題

____ 1. What job did "donor 66" have when he donated his sperm?

a. doctor　　b. dentist
c. surgical assistant　　d. student

____ 2. How many matches has DonorSiblingRegistry.com made?

a. 1,000　　b. 2,000
c. 10,000　　d. none

____ 3. Why is Ryan looking for his real father?

a. to get money
b. to have a relationship
c. to answer a few questions
d. all of the above

試著用較慢的速度，再仔細聽一遍（MP3 Track 86），檢查答案是否正確。

對答案、驗收成果，並詳讀原文，若仍有不懂的地方，可反覆多聽幾次。

（答案請見 p. 313）

Jonathan Mann, Insight

Hello and welcome. There are a lot of men out there and even more of their children who don't know their closest relatives. And that's no accident. Sperm donation is a common practice[4] and so is the presumption[5] that the donors remain anonymous.[6] Their identities are secret and if they have more than one offspring each would find the others out of reach[7] as a result. In a number of European countries—the United Kingdom, Sweden, Norway and the Netherlands, among them—the legal promise of anonymity[8] has been ended, but even in places where the law still promises anonymity, new technology is chipping away at it. On our program today—finding family trees. CNN's Deborah Feyerick has this story.

Deborah Feyerick, CNN Correspondent

They laugh and joke as if they've known each other forever. Five brothers and sisters, half siblings,[9] who share a father they have never met. In fact, they only met within the last year.

You guys are really the first generation,[10] on some levels, to be searching for one another. Why?

《CNN 新聞透視》強納森．曼恩

大家好，歡迎收看本節目。目前社會上有許多男人都不認識自己最親近的親人，甚至還有這些男人的眾多子女也都是如此。這不是意外。精子捐贈不但司空見慣，捐贈者應該匿名的觀念也早已深入人心。捐贈者的身分都是被保密的，因此一位捐贈者如果有許多子女，他們也都無法知道彼此的存在。在若干歐洲國家裡，包括英國、瑞典、挪威、以及荷蘭，有關匿名的法律規定已經被廢除。不過，就算在法律仍舊規定捐贈者必須匿名的地區，新科技也逐漸削弱了這種規定的效力。今天節目的主題就是──尋找家族系譜。本台記者黛博拉．費瑞克帶來這則報導。

CNN 特派員 黛博拉．費瑞克

他們開懷談笑，看起來像老朋友一樣。五名兄弟姐妹，全是同父異母的手足，而且也都沒有看過他們共同的父親。實際上，他們互相認識只不過是過去一年來的事情而已。

你們的確是第一代互相設法找尋對方的兄弟姐妹。為什麼呢？

Notes & Vocabulary

chip away at sth 逐漸削弱

chip 作動詞使用時有「使東西稍有破損、弄缺」的意思。片語 chip away at sth 原指用工具將東西表面上堅硬的覆蓋物一點一點地清除、鏟去，引申使事物逐漸受到無形損害的意思。

- The lawyer chipped away at the witness's credibility.
  這名律師一步步削弱了證人供詞的可信度。

1. **sperm** [spɝm] *n.* 精子；精蟲；精液
2. **donor** [ˋdonɚ] *n.* 提供者；捐贈者
3. **offspring** [ˋɔfˏsprɪŋ] *n.* 子女；子孫；後代
4. **common practice** [ˋkɑmən] [ˋpræktəs] *n. phr.* 慣例；習慣作法
5. **presumption** [prɪˋzʌmpʃən] *n.* 設想；推定
6. **anonymous** [əˋnɑnəməs] *adj.* 匿名的；來源不明的
7. **out of reach** *phr.* 無法觸及；不可企及
8. **anonymity** [ˏænəˋnɪmətɪ] *n.* 匿名
9. **half sibling** [hæf] [ˋsɪblɪŋ] *n.* 同父異母或同母異父的兄弟姊妹
10. **generation** [ˏdʒɛnəˋreʃən] *n.* 世代

Justin Senk, Child of Sperm Donor

It's like finding long lost siblings you never had. I mean how many chances . . . what are the odds that that's going to happen?

Deborah Feyerick, CNN Correspondent

More surprising for 15-year-old Justin, an only child. Unlike the others here, he only found out this summer he was conceived[11] using donor sperm. Immediately curious, he went online, and that's where he found the twins Erin and Rebecca, and siblings Tyler and McKenzie. All from the same donor—donor 66. All live in Denver area within an hour's drive ~~from~~ [of] each other.

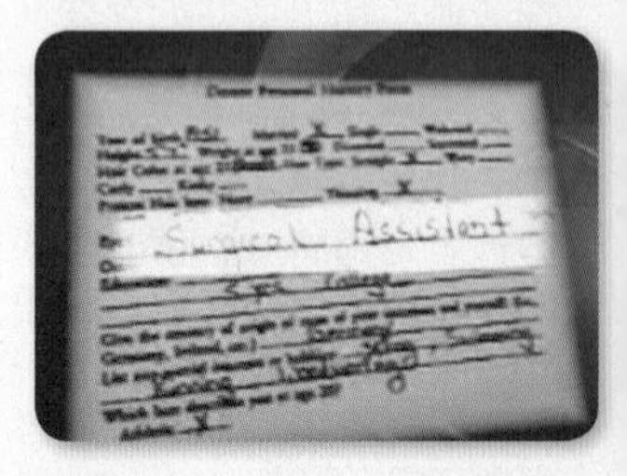

The one they haven't met is their genetic[12] father. But from his written profile,[13] which most potential[14] mothers get, they know donor 66 was a surgical[15] assistant. His sperm went to three mothers treated by the same doctor in the Denver area. Wendy Kramer brought the teens together through her Web site, DonorSiblingRegistry.com. She created it with her son Ryan to help him find his own donor dad. So far this site has made 1,000 matches between donor siblings or between donors and their children.

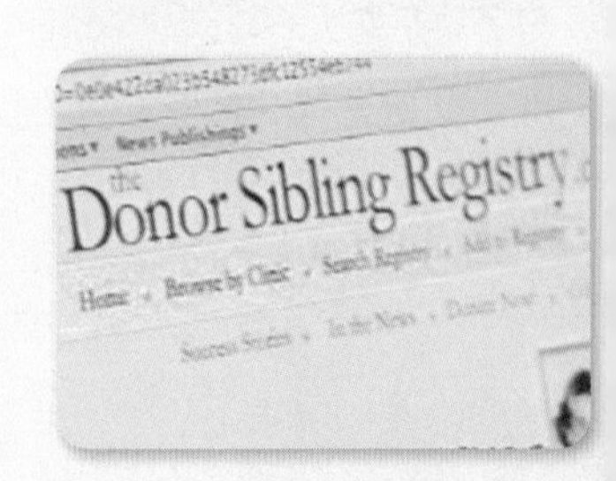

Sperm banks are not required to track the number of children born from any one donor. There may be two or 200. Since a donor may donate multiple[16] times, there's just no way to know for sure.

精子捐贈者之子 賈斯汀．山克

這就像是找到自己從來不曾有過的兄弟姐妹。我是說，一個人碰到這種情況的機會能有多少呢？

CNN 特派員 黛博拉．費瑞克

對於現年十五歲，身為獨子的賈斯汀，這種情況更是出乎意料。他和其他人不同，直到今年夏天才發現自己是捐贈精子受孕而來。在好奇心的驅使下，他立即上網查詢，結果找到了艾琳與蕾貝卡這對雙胞胎，還有泰勒與麥肯錫這對兄弟。他們全都來自於同一位捐贈者：六十六號。他們全住在丹佛地區，各自的住處都相距不遠，開車不必一個小時即可到達。

他們唯一還沒見過面的親人，就是他們的生父。不過，由受孕婦女所拿到的捐贈者檔案上，可知道六十六號是一位外科助手。他的精子受到三名婦女採用，這三名婦女都由丹佛地區同一位醫生診治。溫蒂．克雷墨透過她的「捐精手足登錄網站」讓這群兄弟姐妹得以團聚。這個網站是她和兒子萊恩一同設立的，目的是為了幫他找尋他自己的捐精父親。至今為止，這個網站已經完成一千筆比對，包括接受捐贈手足之間的比對，還有捐贈者與子女相認。

精子銀行沒有義務記錄捐贈者的子女人數。一名捐贈者的子女可能只有兩名，也可能多達兩百名。由於同一名捐贈者可能會多次捐贈，所以根本無法確知。

Notes & Vocabulary

odds 機會；機率

odds 這個名詞在英語中出現頻率相當高，固定以複數形式出現，分別包含以下幾種意義：

a. 事物發生的機會或可能性

the odds are (that) 可能會

- The odds are that Jimmy's team will win.
  吉米的隊伍大概會贏。

odds against（負面）機會

- The odds against winning the lottery are astounding.
  買樂透槓龜的機會高得驚人。

b. 困難

against all odds 儘管困難重重

- Against all odds, the mayor was reelected.
  儘管受到許多阻礙，那位市長還是順利連任了。

c. 不合；不一致

be at odds 爭吵；相矛盾

- Tom's parents are at odds over whether he should study in Canada.
  湯姆的爸媽對於是否該讓他到加拿大唸書的問題意見不合。

11. **conceive** [kən`siv] *v.* 懷胎；懷孕
12. **genetic** [dʒə`nɛtɪk] *adj.* 基因的；遺傳學的
13. **profile** [`pro͵faɪl] *n.* 人物簡介；概況
14. **potential** [pə`tɛnʃəl] *adj.* 潛在的；可能的
15. **surgical** [`sɝdʒɪkəl] *adj.* 外科的
16. **multiple** [`mʌltəpəl] *adj.* 多的；多種的

Wendy's son, Ryan, has never met any of them. He's 15 and by all accounts a genius. We met him at the University of Colorado, where he will soon be a sophomore[17] majoring in aerospace[18] engineering. He easily answers calculus and physics questions. But questions about his own biological dad are much, much tougher.

Ryan Kramer, Child of Sperm Donor

Parts about my face, you know, there ~~are~~ [is] my brow or teeth or my nose or certain things just, you know, clearly don't come from my mother. And to see those in somebody else, would just answer a world of questions for me.

Deborah Feyerick, CNN Correspondent

Most potential mothers sign contracts agreeing to respect a donor's privacy. Wendy says she never did.

It may not matter. Testing DNA is as easy as swabbing[19] your cheek, and the growth of genetic databases could make it all but[20] impossible for donors to remain anonymous. One teenager recently used a saliva[21] sample, had his DNA analyzed, and found his genetic father through a DNA database.

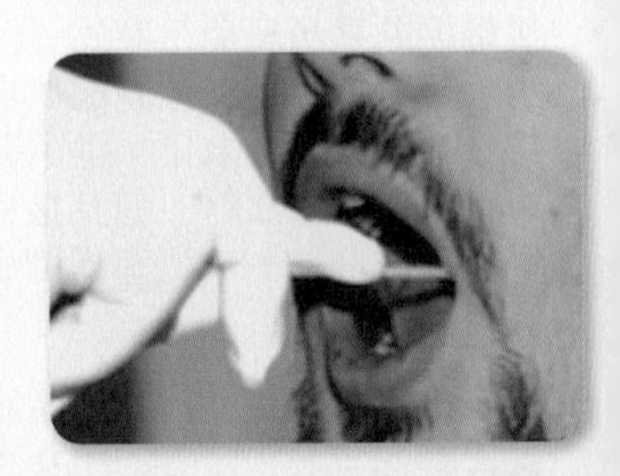

Donor dads have absolutely no legal or financial responsibility to their genetic offspring. So then, what is it children like Ryan really want?

Ryan Kramer, Child of Sperm Donor

Really, all I'm looking for from the donor is just to answer a few of those questions I have. You know, I'm not looking for a relationship or money or anything that, you know, a lot of people assume that donor kids want to know about them. Really, it's just a curiosity about who he is and, you know, where I came from.

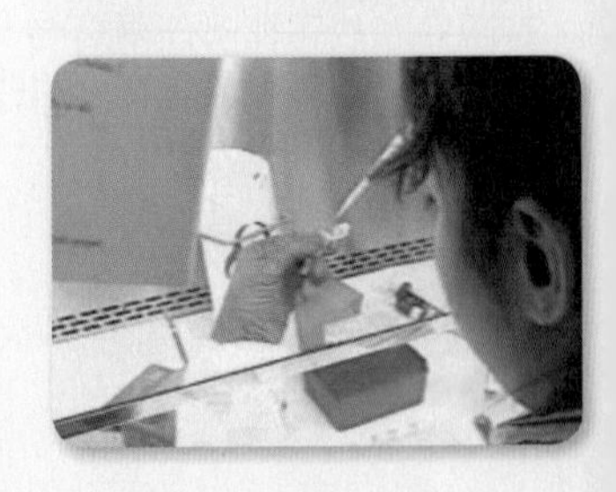

溫蒂的兒子萊恩從來不曾見過其他的兄弟姐妹。他今年才十五歲，大家都說他是個天才。我們在科羅拉多大學和他見面，他不久就要升上大二，主修航太工程學。他回答微積分和物理的問題都輕而易舉，但是回答有關自己生父的問題卻是困難得多。

精子捐贈者之子 萊恩・克雷墨

我臉上有些部位，你看，譬如我的眉毛、牙齒、鼻子，或者其他有些地方，一看就知道不是我媽媽遺傳給我的。如果能夠在別人身上看到這些特徵，一定能夠解答我心裡一大串的疑問。

CNN 特派員 黛博拉・費瑞克

接受精子捐贈的婦女，大多數都會簽約同意尊重捐贈者的隱私權。溫蒂說她從來沒有簽過這樣的文件。

這可能也不重要。DNA 檢測非常簡單，只要刮一下口腔內側即可，而且隨著基因資料庫愈來愈大，捐贈者可能再也無法保持匿名身分。不久之前，一名少年利用唾液樣本分析了自己的 DNA，結果透過一個 DNA 資料庫找到了生父。

捐精父親對子女完全不負法律或者經濟上的義務。那麼，像萊恩這樣的孩子究竟想要追尋什麼呢？

精子捐贈者之子 萊恩・克雷墨

事實上，我只想要捐贈者回答一些我心裡的問題。我要的不是父子關係，也不是錢，也不是一般人認為捐精子女想要知道的事情。真的，我只是好奇，想要知道他是什麼人，還有我究竟從哪裡來。

Notes & Vocabulary

by all accounts 人人都說……

account 作名詞時有「敘述、描寫」的意義，例如「目擊者的說法」是 eyewitness account。by/from all accounts 這個片語字面意為「根據所有敘述」，可用來表達「大家都說……」、「公認的……」。

- By all accounts, Rob is the best candidate for the job.
  大家都認為羅伯是這個職位的不二人選。

a world of 許許多多

world 常見的意思是「世界」，這裡指的是「大量；無數」。

- When we are young, we have a world of possibilities ahead of us.
  我們年輕的時候，前方擁有無數大好機會。

類似的計量詞還有：

a ton of

a mess of

a boatload of

a slew of

- Tina has a mess of work to finish before she goes home.
  蒂娜回家前有很多工作要完成。
- After the success of the movie, there were a slew of imitators.
  繼那部電影大賣後，一大卡車的模仿品出現。

17. **sophomore** [ˋsɑfˏmɔr] *n.* （大學、高中的）二年級學生
18. **aerospace** [ˏɛrəˋspes] *n.* 航空太空學
19. **swab** [swɑb] *v.* 擦拭；塗抹
20. **all but** *phr.* 幾乎
21. **saliva** [səˋlaɪvə] *n.* 唾液

Hamburgerology 101

McDonald's University Trains the Next Crop of Big Mac Managers

從「漢堡」大學看麥當勞的員工訓練哲學

Step 1 如果你是使用 MP3 ，請聽 MP3 Track 87；如果你使用電腦互動光碟，請點選 DVD-ROM【實戰應用篇—Part I：Unit 13】，試試看是否聽懂新聞內容。

Step 2 請瀏覽下列關鍵字彙，再仔細聽一次。

hum 繁忙；活躍	chaotic 混亂的
groom 培養；訓練	apply 應用
simulation 模擬	credit 學分；認可
flustered 慌張的	

Step 3 如果你還不是聽的很懂的話，請參考下列發音提示，再仔細聽一次。

連音	heard of、McDonald's says、flip burgers
同化音	would you、which has been、might not have
省略音	don't learn、flip burgers、restaurant、first simulation、designed to test、test the limits、just happened

試著作答下列聽力測驗題目。

True or False 是非題

____ 1. Hamburger University teaches people how to cook hamburgers.

____ 2. The course at Hamburger University is five days long.

____ 3. The people attending Hamburger University hope to be managers and owners.

____ 4. So far, fourteen people have graduated from Hamburger University.

____ 5. Some people who graduate from Hamburger University can get college credit.

Multiple Choice 選擇題

____ 1. Where is Hamburger University located?

a. Shanghai   b. McDonald's
c. Ohio   d. Chicago

____ 2. What kind of employees go to Hamburger University?

a. employees who get complaints
b. employees with a lot of potential
c. employees that are too slow
d. the sons and daughters of owners

____ 3. What kind of situations do students learn to deal with?

a. fires and emergencies
b. low wages and long hours
c. competing with Target and Wal-Mart
d. long lines and complicated orders

試著用較慢的速度，再仔細聽一遍（MP3 Track 88），檢查答案是否正確。

對答案、驗收成果，並詳讀原文，若仍有不懂的地方，可反覆多聽幾次。

（答案請見 p. 313）

Andrew Stevens, CNN Anchor

Now, to a university that's turning out some of the world's top hamburger experts. You might not have heard of the ~~Ohio~~ [Illinois] campus, but you'll recognize its logo in a flash. CNNMoney reporter Poppy Harlow gives us an exclusive look at the crash course[2] which has been producing Big Mac management professionals for more than half a century.

Poppy Harlow, CNNMONEY

Well, from Shanghai to Brazil to Chicago, more than a quarter million people have graduated from McDonald's Hamburger University. It is McDonald's training ground for their high-potential employees, and they graduate with a degree in hamburgerology, as you can see. We took a visit for ourselves.

McDonald's serves 60 million people a day, but here at Hamburger U, students don't learn how to flip burgers. The food is actually fake. These students are learning the management skills to make a restaurant hum[3] in a five-day course, grooming[4] them to be owners.

In the first simulation[5], long lines, frustrated customers and flustered[6] managers, then the orders get more complicated, designed to test the limits of the operation.

Female Hamburger University Instructor

How do you think this is impacting your customers?

Female Student

Everybody is getting upset. All you see is the manager running back and forth and not really helping. It's more chaotic[7] than anything else.

CNN 主播 安德魯‧史帝芬斯

現在，來看一所培育出一些世界頂尖的漢堡專家的大學。你可能沒聽過伊利諾校區，但是你馬上就能認出它的商標。《CNN 錢線》記者琶比‧哈洛帶我們一探究竟，看看這個速成課程，在超過半世紀以來，培育了許多大麥克的管理專業人才。

《CNN 錢線》琶比‧哈洛

從上海、巴西到芝加哥，超過二十五萬人已從麥當勞漢堡大學畢業。這是用來磨練高潛質員工的訓練基地，他們畢業會有漢堡學的學位，就像你看到的。我們親自走訪一趟。

麥當勞一天服務六千萬名顧客，但是在漢堡大學這裡，學生並不會學如何給漢堡翻面。這兒的食物事實上都是假的。這裡的學生正在上一個為期五天的課程，學習如何讓餐廳忙碌運作，磨練他們當老闆。

在第一場模擬實境中，到處大排長龍，失望的顧客和慌慌張張的經理，接著點餐將變得更加複雜，目的是要測試點餐櫃台運作的極限。

漢堡大學女性講師

你想這會如何影響你的顧客？

女學生

每個人都很不高興。你只看到經理跑來跑去，但卻沒幫到忙。這比其他任何場面都還要混亂。

Notes & Vocabulary

Hamburgerology 101 漢堡學入門

標題中，字尾 -ology 是「學科」的意思，所以 hamburgerology 就是「漢堡學」，一般是指麥當勞的員工訓練課程，101 則是美國大多數一年級入門課程的編號，所以就泛指「入門；基礎；導讀」的意思。

turn out 訓練出；生產出

turn out 的意思有很多，最常見的用法是「結果變成……」，但在此處指的是「產出；生產」。

- The business school turns out some of the world's top CEOs and leaders of industry.
  那間商業學校培養出一些全球頂尖的執行長與企業界的龍頭。

in a flash 瞬間；迅速地

flash 是「閃光；一閃；閃現」，是很短暫的時間，故 in a flash 就表示「瞬間；立即；迅速」。

- The chef had the order prepared in a flash.
  那位主廚一下子就把點菜做好了。

back and forth 來來回回

back and forth 是指在兩地之間「往返地；來回地」，即等於 to and fro、backward(s) and forward(s)。

- The ants marched back and forth from their nest to the food source.
  螞蟻在蟻窩與食物來源之間來來回回地走著。

1. crop [krɑp] *n.*（同時做某事的）一批人
2. crash course [kræʃ][kɔrs] *n.* 速成課程
3. hum [hʌm] *v.* 繁忙；活躍
4. groom [grum] *v.* 培養；訓練；做好準備
5. simulation [ˏsɪmjəˋleʃən] *n.* 模擬
6. flustered [ˋflʌstɚd] *adj.* 慌張的；激動不安的
7. chaotic [keˋɑtɪk] *adj.* 混亂的；雜亂的

Poppy Harlow, CNNMONEY
So, back to class.

Female Hamburger University Instructor
All right, my teams. Should we talk about what just happened?

Male Student
They were friendly. I just wasn't getting my food very quickly.

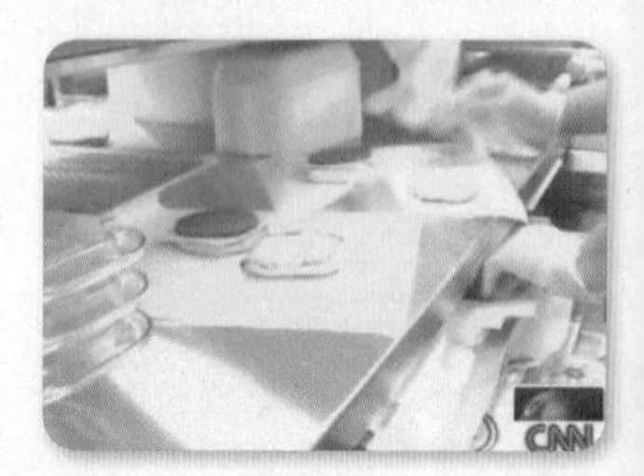

Female Student
It was just really busy. It kept holding, so she kept sending everybody on break.

Poppy Harlow, CNNMONEY
So they try again, this time, applying[8] the lessons of the classroom to cut the chaos in the kitchen.

Okay, here we go.

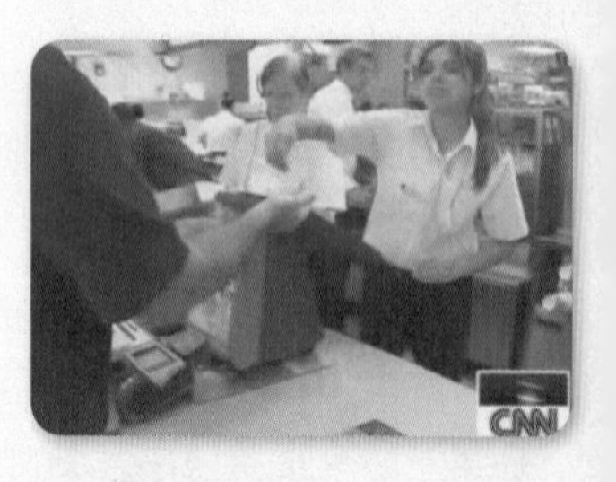

Female Hamburger University Instructor
Hi, would you like to try an iced mocha today?

Poppy Harlow, CNNMONEY
I would like Cinnamon[9] Melts; a bacon, egg and cheese bagel; a sausage egg McMuffin, and a hash brown.[10] I'm just really in a rush.

Pretty fast so far. Let's see if they get the order right.

Male Student
We have a bacon, egg and cheese bagel; we have a Cinnamon Melts and we have one hash brown.

《CNN 錢線》琶比．哈洛

回到課堂上。

漢堡大學女性講師

好，我的團隊們。我們可以談談剛剛發生了什麼事嗎？

男學生

他們態度很親切，但我無法很快拿到我的餐點。

女學生

實在是真的很忙。流程老是堵塞，所以她就一直叫每個人暫離崗位去幫忙。

《CNN 錢線》琶比．哈洛

所以他們再試一次，這次他們將應用課堂所學，減少廚房的混亂。

好了，我們走吧。

漢堡大學女性講師

你好，請問你今天想嚐嚐冰摩卡嗎？

《CNN 錢線》琶比．哈洛

我想要糖漿肉桂卷、培根蛋起司培果、豬肉蛋滿福堡和一份薯餅。我真的在趕時間。

到目前為止都相當快速。來看看他們有沒有正確備餐。

男學生

一個培根蛋起司培果、一個糖漿肉桂卷和一份薯餅。

Notes & Vocabulary

in a rush 瞬間；迅速地

rush 指的是「匆忙」。in a rush 是口語用法，表「急急忙忙地」，與 in a hurry 意思相似。而 in a big rush 表「非常匆忙」；there's no rush 則表「不急」。

- Carla was in a rush to finish her homework.
  卡拉趕著要完成她的功課。

8. **apply** [ə`plaɪ] *v.* 應用；套用
9. **cinnamon** [`sɪnəmən] *n.* 肉桂
10. **hash brown** [hæʃ][braʊn] *n.* 薯餅

Poppy Harlow, CNNMONEY
And what about the sausage McMuffin?

Male Student
Sausage egg muffin?

Poppy Harlow, CNNMONEY
C'mon, guys. They said it was in a rush. Let's go.

Male Student
And I got it for you.

Poppy Harlow, CNNMONEY
That was a minute and 30 seconds.

And Hamburger University isn't a new thing. It was founded all the way back in 1961 in the basement of an ~~Ohio~~ [Illinois] McDonald's with just 14 people, as I said, about a quarter of a million have graduated since then. And this is no joke, McDonald's says Hamburger University is the key to its success over the years. Major companies like Target and Wal-Mart have sent their executives in to see just how McDonald's trains its employees and some colleges even give credit[11] to students who attend Hamburger U. What this shows us is there's a lot more behind those golden arches than we knew before.

《CNN 錢線》琶比・哈洛
豬肉蛋滿福堡呢？

男學生
豬肉蛋福堡？

《CNN 錢線》琶比・哈洛
大家加油。他們說趕時間。動作快。

男學生
我幫你拿來了。

《CNN 錢線》琶比・哈洛
總共花了一分三十秒。

漢堡大學不是新成立的機構。它早在一九六一年就成立於伊利諾州的一家麥當勞地下室，剛開始只有十四個人。如同我先前說的，從那時候開始，大約有二十五萬人從這畢業。這可不是開玩笑的，麥當勞表示漢堡大學是這些年來的成功關鍵。許多大公司如塔吉特、沃爾瑪都曾派主管人員來觀摩麥當勞是如何訓練員工，有些學院甚至承認漢堡大學學生的學分。這告訴了我們，在麥當勞的金色拱門裡還有許多我們以前不知道的事。

Notes & Vocabulary

no joke 不是開玩笑；正經的

joke 是指「玩笑；笑話」，口語中常說 it is no joke 加上 that 子句，表示「某事不是開玩笑的；是認真嚴肅的」，no joke 也可換成 not a joke。

- It's no joke that most life-threatening accidents happen in the home.
  說真的，大部分威脅生命的意外都發生在家裡。

the key to success 成功的要訣

key「鑰匙」引申有「關鍵；要訣」的意思，後面用介系詞 to 加上事物。

- For Jeff, persistence has been the key to success.
  對傑夫來說，勤奮不懈就是成功的要訣。

11. credit [ˋkrɛdɪt] *n.* 學分；認可

Sony's Next Move

PlayStation 3 Takes a Stab at Motion Sensor1 Gaming

電玩科技爭霸戰 Sony 又出新招

Step 1 如果你是使用 MP3 ，請聽 MP3 Track 89；如果你使用電腦互動光碟，請點選 DVD-ROM【實戰應用篇—Part I：Unit 14】，試試看是否聽懂新聞內容。

Step 2 請瀏覽下列關鍵字彙，再仔細聽一次。

trail 落後；失利	virtual 模擬的
whopping 巨大的	augment 增加；提高；擴大
precise 準確的	accuracy 準確性
responsive 反應敏捷的	

Step 3 如果你還不是聽的很懂的話，請參考下列發音提示，再仔細聽一次。

連音	just unveiled、claims it's an、improvement on、find out、combines our units sold、new way、great time
同化音	have to
弱化音	up to do
省略音	sold just、used to、just see、different

試著作答下列聽力測驗題目。

True or False 是非題

____ 1. The Wii is popular with serious gamers but less popular with families.

____ 2. The success of the Wii is largely due to its wireless controllers.

____ 3. Sony is targeting the PlayStation Move mainly at serious gamers.

____ 4. The Sony PlayStation Move can insert video of the player into the game.

____ 5. One disadvantage of the PlayStation Move is that it is less responsive.

Multiple Choice 選擇題

____ 1. What is new about the Sony PlayStation Move?

a. its console　　b. its controller
c. its cheaper price　　d. its buttons

____ 2. Which company sold the least number of game consoles worldwide?

a. Microsoft
b. Nintendo
c. Sony
d. none of the above

____ 3. What does the game Start the Party do very well?

a. It has lots of difficulty levels.
b. It lets lots of people play at once.
c. It plays music very well.
d. It uses virtual objects very well.

試著用較慢的速度，再仔細聽一遍（MP3 Track 90），檢查答案是否正確。

對答案、驗收成果，並詳讀原文，若仍有不懂的地方，可反覆多聽幾次。

（答案請見 p. 313）

Andrew Stevens, CNN Anchor

Sony has just unveiled its latest weapon in the closely fought console war with Nintendo and Microsoft. It's called the Move controller, and Sony claims it's an improvement on the technology in Nintendo's Wii, which allows you to play games using the controller's own sensors to track your own movements. Now, Sony has some catching up to do.

As of the end of June, Sony had sold just over 38 million PlayStation 3s worldwide. That's still behind, but closing the gap on Microsoft's Xbox 360, which has global sales of almost 42 million, and the Xbox has appealed to the hard-core[2] gaming community. But both trail[3] far behind the Wii, with a whopping[4] 71 million units sold since its debut in 2006, largely due to the success of those wireless controllers, which have made the Wii popular with families, although perhaps less popular with serious gamers. Well, our Colleen McEdwards went to find out how the new Move actually works.

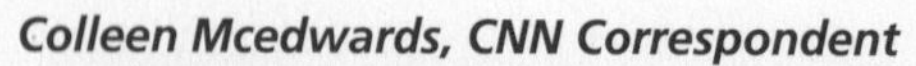

Colleen Mcedwards, CNN Correspondent

Joining me now is Richard Marks with Sony to explain what this and all of this actually does. Come on in here. Tell us about PlayStation Move.

Richard Marks, SONY R&D Manager

This is our new controller for PlayStation 3. It combines our PlayStation Eye camera and internal[5] sensors in our controller to give a new way to play PlayStation 3.

Colleen Mcedwards, CNN Correspondent

Now how . . . who are you targeting with this new product?

CNN 主播　安德魯．史帝芬斯

在與任天堂及微軟間競爭激烈的遊戲機大戰中，索尼剛推出最新武器一較高下，新武器稱作 Move 控制器。索尼宣稱這是任天堂 Wii 的技術再升級，讓你可以藉由控制器裡的感應器追蹤動作來玩遊戲。現在，索尼得要加緊腳步了。

截至六月底為止，索尼在全球已經售出三千八百萬台 PlayStation 3 遊戲機。雖然這個數字仍然落後微軟 Xbox 360 全球近四千兩百萬台的銷售量，但差距已經縮小，Xbox 則是成功吸引了中堅遊戲族群。然而這兩種遊戲機的銷量卻仍遠遠落後 Wii。自從 Wii 二〇〇六年問世以來一共賣出驚人的七千一百萬台；這主要要歸功於 Wii 的無線控制器，讓 Wii 受到家庭的歡迎，但卻可能比較不受高階玩家的青睞。本台記者科琳．麥克愛德華茲帶你看看新的 Move 究竟如何運作。

CNN 特派員　科琳．麥克愛德華茲

即將到來的是索尼公司的理查．馬克斯，他要說明這個和這些東西究竟有何功用。過來這裡吧，和我們講解一下 PlayStation Move。

索尼公司研發部經理　理查．馬克斯

這是我們為 PlayStation 3 新推出的控制器。它結合了我們的 PlayStation Eye 攝影機，以及控制器中內建的感應器，提供 PlayStation 3 一種新玩法。

CNN 特派員　科琳．麥克愛德華茲

那這怎麼……貴公司這款新商品鎖定的對象是誰？

Notes & Vocabulary

take a stab at　嘗試一下

標題中，stab 原指「刺；戳；捅」，在此指「嘗試；企圖」，take a stab 表示「嘗試一下」，後面用 at 加上嘗試做的事物。

- Jake took a stab at the *New York Times* crossword puzzle while he finished his coffee.
  傑克在喝咖啡的時候玩了一下《紐約時報》的填字遊戲。

close the gap　縮小差距

gap 是指「差距；隔閡」，close the gap 表示「縮小差距；減少隔閡」，後面用 on 加上拉近距離的對象。

- The mobile phone maker closed the gap on its closest competitor by lowering prices.
  那家手機製造商藉由降價拉近與最接近的對手的差距。

1. **sensor** [ˋsɛnsɚ] *n.*（探測光、熱、壓力等的）感應器
2. **hard-core** [ˏhɑrdˋkɔr] *adj.* 中堅的；死忠的
3. **trail** [trel] *v.* 落後；失利
4. **whopping** [ˋwɑpɪŋ] *adj.* 巨大的；很大的
5. **internal** [ɪnˋtɝnəl] *adj.* 內部的；內建的

Richard Marks, SONY R&D Manager

Actually, we're targeting everybody. We have very casual experiences for people who have never played games, but because it's so precise[6] and responsive,[7] we also have games that would appeal to people who are really good at games—core[8] players.

Colleen Mcedwards, CNN Correspondent

Ok, I have a seven-year-old. We have a Wii. We play it as a family. We love it, but show me what this can do. I'm curious to see. Let's have a look.

Richard Marks, SONY R&D Manager

OK, maybe the first thing you see right away is that we use our camera, so we can actually take video of the player and use the controller [to] insert[9] virtual[10] objects right into the video. One of our games called Start the Party actually does this very well where you can switch between lots of different objects, do different things. Things are flying at you. You have to hit them with a stick or you . . .

Colleen Mcedwards, CNN Correspondent

I'm still getting used to myself standing here with this giant sword.

Richard Marks, SONY R&D Manager

Yeah, this is called augmented[11] reality. You see yourself and you also see virtual objects rendered in with us. So I can switch between . . . if you push the big middle button, the Move button there, you can switch between many different objects.

Colleen Mcedwards, CNN Correspondent

You see, my seven-year-old would have this figured out already. Ah!

索尼公司研發部經理　理查．馬克斯

其實我們鎖定的是每一個人。針對從未玩過遊戲機的人，我們有提供非常輕鬆的遊戲體驗，但是因為它既精確且反應靈敏，我們也有吸引那些相當擅長打遊戲機的人，也就是核心玩家的遊戲。

CNN 特派員　科琳．麥克愛德華茲

我有個七歲的孩子，我們家有一台 Wii。我們全家都會玩，也很喜歡。讓我看看這台遊戲機有些什麼能耐。我很想要看看。咱們來瞧瞧吧。

索尼公司研發部經理　理查．馬克斯

也許你馬上會看到的是我們使用我們家的攝影機，所以我們可以把玩家的影像拍攝下來，再用控制器將虛擬物件放進影片中。我們有一個叫《派對總動員》的遊戲在這方面做得很棒，你可以更換很多不同的物件，做不同的事。東西會朝你飛過來，你必須用棍子去打它們，否則你就會……

CNN 特派員　科琳．麥克愛德華茲

我還在試著習慣自己手拿這把巨劍站在這裡。

索尼公司研發部經理　理查．馬克斯

對，這叫做擴充實境。你會看到你自己，也會看到虛擬物件跟我們一起呈現出來。所以我可以切換……如果你按中間那顆大按鈕，那個 Move 按鈕，你就可以在很多不同的物件之間切換。

CNN 特派員　科琳．麥克愛德華茲

你瞧，我那七歲的孩子早就搞懂怎麼操作了，唉！

Notes & Vocabulary

render in　呈現

render 的意思有很多，除了可指「以圖像或繪畫表現；以文字形式表現」之外，亦可指「呈遞；提出」或「翻譯」。

- Many of the creatures in the movie were rendered in high-definition computer graphics.
  這部電影裡的許多生物都是以高解析度的電腦繪圖來呈現。

6. **precise** [prɪˋsaɪs] *adj.* 準確的；精確的
7. **responsive** [rɪˋspɑnsɪv] *adj.* 反應敏捷的
8. **core** [kɔr] *n.* 核心；最重要的部分
9. **insert** [ɪnˋsɝt] *v.* 插入；嵌入
10. **virtual** [ˋvɝtʃuəl] *adj.* 模擬的；虛擬的
11. **augment** [ˋɔgmənt] *v.* 增加；提高；擴大

Richard Marks, SONY R&D Manager

It could be sports games; it could be a fighting game. You can do all sorts of different things. Of course, we wouldn't have to see video of ourselves. We could switch it to more of a normal virtual experience where you just see the object that you're holding, but the video really shows you how well it's tracking. It's rendering it right over the top of the controller perfectly.

Colleen Mcedwards, CNN Correspondent

So you think the hard-core gamer is gonna see a difference between this and what you would get in a Wii with your controller playing tennis or, you know, lightsaber duels, or whatever you're doing?

Richard Marks, SONY R&D Manager

Definitely, the accuracy[12] and the responsiveness ~~is~~ [are] very different.

Colleen Mcedwards, CNN Correspondent

So why is Sony coming out with this now? It's such a difficult economy. How concerned are you about that?

Richard Marks, SONY R&D Manager

We decided to make PlayStation Move when we could make the kind of experience we wanted to for both our casual and core players. But also I think now is a great time for our PlayStation 3. It's a great value for families. It does so many different things for a really good price point.

索尼公司研發部經理 理查・馬克斯

它可以是運動遊戲，可以是格鬥遊戲。你可以做各式各樣不同的事。當然，我們不一定要看自己的影像。我們可以將它轉換成一般的虛擬體驗，你只會看到你手上握的東西，但是從影像上你可以看得出來它追蹤得好不好。它把東西準確地放到控制器的正上方。

CNN 特派員 科琳・麥克愛德華茲

所以你覺得核心玩家會看得出來，用這台遊戲機的控制器來打網球，或玩光劍對決，或者不管做任何事，都和你從 Wii 中體驗到的有所不同？

索尼公司研發部經理 理查・馬克斯

那是一定的。兩者之間的精確性和反應天差地別。

CNN 特派員 科琳・麥克愛德華茲

為何索尼要選現在推出這台遊戲機？經濟景氣那麼差，你們會很擔心這點嗎？

索尼公司研發部經理 理查・馬克斯

當我們可以為一般玩家和核心玩家做出我們想要帶給他們的體驗時，我們就決定要生產 PlayStation Move 了。我也認為現在是我們推出 PlayStation 3 的大好時機。它對一般家庭而言價值極高。它的功能如此之多，以它的價位來看太划算了。

Notes & Vocabulary

(be) more of a/an + N.
很……的；很像……的

在此句型中，of 之後接名詞，二者合起來作為形容詞片語使用，表示「具有……性質、特徵的」。通常也會在 of 之前加上 much 或 less 等來修飾，以表示程度。

- I'm more of a personal assistant.
  我比較像是個人助理。

12. **accuracy** [ˋækjərəsɪ] *n.* 準確性；精確

Sparking Panda Passions

It's Breeding Season for the Animal Kingdom's Reluctant Romantics

「性」趣缺缺的貓熊家族

Step 1 如果你是使用 MP3 ，請聽 MP3 Track 91；如果你使用電腦互動光碟，請點選 DVD-ROM【實戰應用篇—Part I: Unit 15】，試試看是否聽懂新聞內容。

Step 2 請瀏覽下列關鍵字彙，再仔細聽一次。

reluctant 不情願的	artificial 人工的
mate 交配	replicate 複製
lounge 懶洋洋地站（或坐、躺）著	diminished 減少的
blissfully 幸福地；快樂地	

Step 3 如果你還不是聽的很懂的話，請參考下列發音提示，再仔細聽一次。

連音	animal lovers、put that around、who's cycling、there's some
去捲舌音	another year
省略音	just begun、didn't do

試著作答下列聽力測驗題目。

True or False 是非題

____ 1. The pandas at the Atlanta Zoo have already had two cubs.

____ 2. Among other things, pandas love to run around and swim.

____ 3. Female pandas can get pregnant for only three days a year.

____ 4. The two pandas at the Atlanta Zoo have known each other for one year.

____ 5. The Atlanta Zoo tried spreading male urine around the panda enclosure.

Multiple Choice 選擇題

____ 1. Why is getting pandas to mate such an important issue?

a. Pandas are very popular in zoos.
b. Pandas are very expensive animals.
c. Pandas are at risk of going extinct.
d. Pandas can only have one cub per decade.

____ 2. How do pandas in the wild mate?

a. Male pandas bring food to females.
b. Female pandas look for male pandas.
c. Female pandas get together in groups.
d. Male pandas compete with each other.

____ 3. Where are most of the pandas in the wild?

a. in Sichuan province
b. in northern Vietnam
c. in Myanmar
d. in eastern China

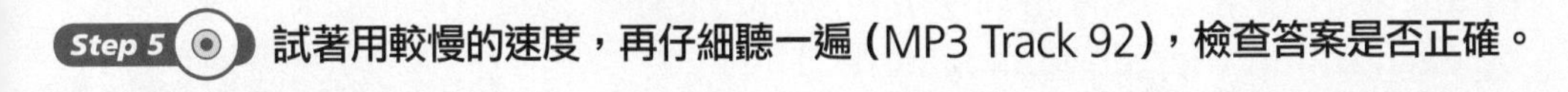

Step 5 試著用較慢的速度，再仔細聽一遍（MP3 Track 92），檢查答案是否正確。

Step 6 對答案、驗收成果，並詳讀原文，若仍有不懂的地方，可反覆多聽幾次。

（答案請見 p. 313）

Carol Costello, CNN Anchor

They are cute, and they are among the world's most threatened animals—pandas. Their mating[2] season is a big event for animal lovers around the world, and Atlanta Zoo is hoping that its two pandas will use the short window[3] to get lucky. Ralitsa Vassileva has more about that.

Ralitsa Vassileva, CNN Correspondent

The survival of pandas is a global pursuit. There are just hundreds left in the wild in China. That's why panda mating season is a big event for panda lovers around the world. The short season to make new panda cubs[4] has just begun, and like several zoos around the world, the Atlanta Zoo is hoping its panda couple will try for another baby.

But mating season or not, pandas tend to have a lot more on their mind than getting lucky. They love to sleep, munch[5] on bamboo and lounge[6] blissfully[7]; but mating, not so much.

The Atlanta Zoo is hoping its panda couple, Lun Lun and Yang Yang, will try for a third cub, but it has no illusions[8] about how tough it's going to be. Females can conceive only once a year for three days. Miss that window and you have to wait another year.

Rebecca Snyder, Curator of Animals, Atlanta Zoo

I think part of it is they aren't very stimulated[9] by each other, these two, anymore. They've known each other since they were young cubs, like a year old, and I think they're just not very interested in each other, frankly, anymore.

CNN 主播 卡蘿・寇斯特洛

牠們很可愛，而且牠們是全世界最受到威脅的動物——貓熊。牠們的交配季節對全球動物愛好人士而言是件大事。亞特蘭大動物園希望該園的兩頭貓熊能利用這短暫的時間成功受孕。羅莉莎・瓦希利娃的進一步報導。

CNN 特派員 羅莉莎・瓦希利娃

貓熊的存續是世界人類追求的目標。目前在中國境內的野生貓熊僅剩下數百頭，這也就是為何貓熊的交配季節對全球貓熊愛好者來說是一件大事。孕育貓熊寶寶的短暫季節才剛展開，一如世界許多其他動物園，亞特蘭大動物園希望他們的貓熊夫妻能夠試著再生一個寶寶。

但無論是否處於交配季節，貓熊們腦子裡想的往往不只是生寶寶而已。牠們喜歡睡覺，喜歡嚼食竹子和無憂無慮地撲來撲去，但對交配這檔事就不那麼熱中了。

亞特蘭大動物園希望他們的貓熊夫妻倫倫和洋洋能夠嘗試生出第三隻寶寶，但園方非常清楚這件事有多困難。母貓熊一年只有三天能夠受孕，錯過這段時間就得再等一年。

亞特蘭大動物園園長 雷貝卡・史奈德

我想部分原因是在於這兩頭貓熊已經不太能夠挑起對方的情慾了。牠們從還是一歲左右的幼熊時就認識對方了。我想坦白說，牠們已經不再對彼此感興趣了。

Notes & Vocabulary

have (sth) on one's mind
惦記著某事物

have sth on one's mind 是指「惦記著某事物」，而另一個易混淆片語 have sth in mind 則是指「心中有某種想法」，即「想著；打算；考量」之意。

- I had you on my mind all day, so I had to call you.
  我整天惦記著你，所以我必須打電話給你。
- What do you have in mind for your class paper?
  你課堂報告想好要寫什麼了嗎？

1. **reluctant** [rɪˋlʌktənt] *adj.* 不情願的
2. **mate** [met] *v.* 交配；成配偶
3. **window** [ˋwɪndo] *n.* 一絲機會；短暫時機
4. **cub** [kʌb] *n.*（熊、獅等的）幼獸
5. **munch** [mʌntʃ] *v.* 用力咀嚼（脆的食物）
6. **lounge** [laʊndʒ] *v.* 懶洋洋地站（或坐、躺）著
7. **blissfully** [ˋblɪsfəlɪ] *adv.* 幸福地；快樂地
8. **illusion** [ɪˋluʒən] *n.* 錯覺；幻想
9. **stimulate** [ˋstɪmjəˏlet] *v.* 刺激；使興奮

Ralitsa Vassileva, CNN Correspondent

And so far, the two babies that they've had were all in vitro.

Rebecca Snyder, Curator of Animals, Atlanta Zoo

Uh huh, yes, they were artificial[10] inseminations.[11]

Ralitsa Vassileva, CNN Correspondent

So, what are your hopes?

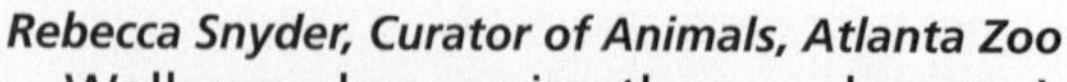

Rebecca Snyder, Curator of Animals, Atlanta Zoo

Well, we always give them a chance. I can say I'm a little less hopeful than I used to be in the past, but hopefully they'll surprise me. We have done things like bring in urine from males at other zoos and put that around in the enclosure.[12] You know in the wild, pandas, males, come together in a group around a female who's cycling, they fight for access to each other. It's a different situation than you have in captivity,[13] and it's not something we can really replicate,[14] especially with just two pandas.

We try other things like bring in urine from another male. See if that stimulates the male more, and the female too, like maybe there's some competition around, that kind of thing. It didn't do anything for our pandas, but you know, maybe for another pair it would help a little bit. But really, I think the key is the breeding centers that have more individuals are doing much better in terms of captive breeding.

Ralitsa Vassileva, CNN Correspondent

Even though it's easier for pandas to mate outside of captivity, only about 1,000 remain in the wild. Pandas could once be found in eastern and southern China, as well as north

CNN 特派員　羅莉莎．瓦希利娃

目前為止，牠們的兩隻熊寶寶都是試管寶寶。

亞特蘭大動物園園長　雷貝卡．史奈德

嗯，對，牠們都是用人工授精的方式產下的。

CNN 特派員　羅莉莎．瓦希利娃

所以你們抱著什麼樣的希望呢？

亞特蘭大動物園園長　雷貝卡．史奈德

我們一直會給牠們機會。我可以說我不像以前那樣充滿希望，但希望牠們能讓我有意外驚喜。我們有試過將其他動物園的公貓熊的尿液放到圍欄裡。在野外，公貓熊會成群圍繞著正值發情期的母貓熊，公貓熊們會為了親近母貓熊而打架。這點和圈養的情形不同，這是我們沒辦法複製的部分，尤其是只有兩隻貓熊的時候。

我們嘗試其他方法，像是把其他公貓熊的尿液帶進來，看看會不會給我們的公貓熊和母貓熊帶來更多刺激，就像是四周有某種競爭之類的。這對我們的貓熊來說完全沒用，但也許對其他對貓熊夫妻會多少有點幫助。但我認為問題的關鍵在於，從圈養繁殖的角度來看，貓熊數量較多的繁殖所成果會比較好。

CNN 特派員　羅莉莎．瓦希利娃

雖然貓熊在野外比較容易進行交配，目前野外也只剩下約一千頭貓熊。中國的東部和南部一度能見到貓熊的足跡，還有越南的北部和緬

Notes & Vocabulary

in vitro　在生物體外進行的

字首 vitro- 可表「玻璃；玻璃狀的」，而 in vitro 指的便是「在生物體外進行的」或「在科學儀器中進行的」。

- Susan conceived through in vitro fertilization.
  蘇珊藉由植入胚胎而受孕。

bring in　引入

bring in 可指「帶入；引入」，亦可指「（政府、公司等）引進或採用（新法律、新系統等）」。另一個相似片語 bring about 則是「使發生；導致；引起」的意思。

- The company brought in a corporate trainer to improve management skills.
  公司延攬了一位企業訓練人員來改善管理技巧。

in terms of　依據；從……方面而言

term 這個字可以解釋為「看待某事的一種方式」，也就是「視角」、「觀點」之意。in terms of 是英語中很常用的介系詞片語，意指「在……方面」或「從……的角度來說」。

- In terms of overall sales, we are doing quite well.
  就整體銷售量而言，我們的表現很不錯。

10. artificial [͵ɑrtə`fɪʃl] *adj.* 人工的
11. insemination [ɪn͵sɛmə`neʃən] *n.* 懷孕；受精
12. enclosure [ɪn`kloʒɚ] *n.* 圍欄；圍場
13. captivity [kæp`tɪvətɪ] *n.* 監禁；圈養
14. replicate [`rɛplɪ͵ket] *v.* 複製

Vietnam and Myanmar. Today, wild pandas are limited to 30 wilderness reserves,[15] mostly within China's Sichuan province. The reason is mostly habitat loss and human encroachment;[16] and the deadly 2008 Sichuan earthquake made giant pandas even more endangered because it badly damaged their diminished[17] habitat. With their natural habitat shrinking, scientists are making every effort to increase the birthrate in captivity and keep every baby panda alive.

甸。目前，只有三十個野生保留區內有野生貓熊，其中大多數位於中國四川省境內，原因多半是因為棲息地消失以及人類的侵犯。二〇〇八年傷亡慘重的四川地震使得大貓熊瀕危的情況更形嚴重，因為地震嚴重破壞牠們日益縮減的棲息地。隨著貓熊的天然棲息地逐漸縮小，科學家們正傾全力提高圈養貓熊的出生率，並確保每一頭貓熊寶寶都能存活下來。

Notes & Vocabulary

15. **reserve** [rɪ`zɝv] *n.*（動植物）自然保護區
16. **encroachment** [ɪn`krotʃmənt] *n.* 侵入；侵佔
17. **diminished** [də`mɪnɪʃt] *adj.* 減少的；縮減的

Think Globally, Eat Locally

Bringing Eco-Friendly Cuisine to Hong Kong

環保就從選擇食材做起

Step 1 如果你是使用 MP3 ，請聽 MP3 Track 93；如果你使用電腦互動光碟，請點選 DVD-ROM【實戰應用篇—Part I：Unit 16】，試試看是否聽懂新聞內容。

Step 2 請瀏覽下列關鍵字彙，再仔細聽一次。

-friendly 對……友善的	deliberate 蓄意的
cuisine 菜餚；料理	organic 有機的
exploit 利用；剝削	gorgeous 美麗的；極好的
advertise 為……做廣告	

Step 3 如果你還不是聽的很懂的話，請參考下列發音提示，再仔細聽一次。

連音	it's certainly、year round、top priority、best-tasting
同化音	we can say
省略音	just now、restaurant、about 90

試著作答下列聽力測驗題目。

True or False 是非題

____ 1. Shipping tomatoes from far away means a smaller carbon footprint.

____ 2. All of the food at the restaurant is grown on local farms.

____ 3. The restaurant owners tell their customers that it is an organic restaurant.

____ 4. The most important thing for the restaurant is taste.

____ 5. The people who run the restaurant say that eating is like voting.

Multiple Choice 選擇題

____ 1. What kind of products does the restaurant offer?
a. low-cost products
b. premium products
c. strange and exotic products
d. dirty products

____ 2. What kind of mozzarella do they use in the restaurant?
a. gorgeous
b. simple
c. seasonal
d. homemade

____ 3. What are they in the business of doing?
a. creating occasions for people
b. cooking new dishes
c. making more money each year
d. reducing their carbon footprint

Step 5 試著用較慢的速度，再仔細聽一遍（MP3 Track 94），檢查答案是否正確。

Step 6 對答案、驗收成果，並詳讀原文，若仍有不懂的地方，可反覆多聽幾次。

（答案請見 p. 313）

Kristie Lu Stout, CNN Anchor

Sustainable dining can mean a lot of things. As you saw just now, it's certainly about being careful, about avoiding the foods that are over-exploited.[3] It's also about eating seasonally and locally. For example, tomatoes. Now many of us eat tomatoes all year round, and for a lot of us that means tomatoes that were shipped from very far away, and that means a big carbon footprint. So, how do we eat more sustainably? According to one restaurant, it's about getting back to basics.

And you don't advertise[4] your restaurant as being sustainable. Is that a deliberate[5] move?

Robert Spina, Co-Owner, Posto Pubblico

It is deliberate. We don't call ourselves an organic[6] restaurant. We have . . . we offer premium products. We have . . . we are clean. Ninty-five percent of our ingredients are clean, and we use it as a talking point. So when a guest enters the restaurant, it's something that we can say, hey, by the way, you know, 95 percent of our produce[7] is local, clean, organic. It's a conversation starter.

Kristie Lu Stout, CNN Anchor

And do you think it would take away from the dining experience here if you pushed that sustainable angle more?

Robert Spina, Co-Owner, Posto Pubblico

I do. I do, because we really believe that it should be a way of life. You know, we're not eco-warriors,[8] but we do feel that it should be a way of life. It's socially conscious, it's responsible.

CNN 主播　克莉絲蒂．陸．史道

永續飲食可能指很多種做法。正如各位剛剛看到的，永續飲食確實必須謹慎小心，避免食用遭到過度剝削的食物，也可以選用當季當地的食物。以番茄為例，現在許多人一年四季都吃番茄，而我們大部分都是食用從很遠的地方運來的番茄，這表示會造成很多碳足跡。所以，我們該怎麼吃才能比較合乎永續的理念？根據一家餐廳的說法，方法就是回歸基本。

你們並沒有以永續的名義宣傳你們的餐廳。這是故意的嗎？

帕布里克義式餐廳合夥人　羅伯．史賓納

是故意的。我們不自稱為有機餐廳。我們……我們供應頂級的食材，我們……我們很乾淨，我們的食材有百分之九十五都很乾淨，我們就以這一點做為話題。顧客走進餐廳時我們就可以這麼說：嘿，順帶一提，我們的蔬果有百分之九十五都是在地生產，是無污染的有機產品。這是一種和顧客打開對話的話題。

CNN 主播　克莉絲蒂．陸．史道

你覺得你們如果太強調永續飲食的概念，會剝奪顧客的用餐樂趣嗎？

帕布里克義式餐廳合夥人　羅伯．史賓納

的確，的確，因為我們真心認為這種飲食應該是一種生活方式。我們不是生態戰士，但我們確實覺得這應該是一種生活方式。這是一種具有社會意識的做法，也是負責任的做法。

Notes & Vocabulary

think globally, eat locally
環保思維，在地飲食

本課標題 think globally, eat locally 其實是取用於 think globally, act locally，這個用語最早起源於鄉鎮規劃，後來也被廣為應用在環保或商業領域中，主要是力勸人類能在自己的社群或城市裡有所付出、作為時也要同時思考整個地球。

take away from　剝奪；拿走

take away from 原本字面上的意思就是「從……拿走」，因此有「剝奪」之意。

- The poor weather took away from everyone's enjoyment of the outdoor concert.
  糟糕的天氣將大家享受戶外演唱會的興致一掃而空。

1. -friendly [ˋfrɛndlɪ] *adj.* 對……友善的；便於……使用的
2. cuisine [kwɪˋzin] *n.* 菜餚；料理
3. exploit [ɪkˋsplɔɪt] *v.* 利用；剝削；開發
4. advertise [ˋædvɚˏtaɪz] *v.* 為……做廣告、宣傳
5. deliberate [dɪˋlɪbərət] *adj.* 蓄意的；故意的
6. organic [ɔrˋgænɪk] *adj.* 有機的
7. produce [ˋprodjus] *n.*（蔬、果等）農產品
8. warrior [ˋwɔrɪɚ] *n.* 鬥士；戰士

Kristie Lu Stout, CNN Anchor

And these, I can't get my eyes off them. These are absolutely gorgeous.[9]

Robert Spina, Co-Owner, Posto Pubblico

These are the best, you know. These are really incredible.[10] And so these are definitely seasonal. These will only be available for about 90 days starting in the beginning of April. You know, we like to use wedges[11] of tomatoes with our homemade fresh mozzarella[12] on the plate, or we serve it with a burrata,[13] you know, and that's all great ingredients need. You know, it's very simple.

Kristie Lu Stout, CNN Anchor

Now all this is grown locally, and when you talk to localvores, they say eating locally usually comes down to three things: taste, price and saving the planet. What's the top priority for you?

Robert Spina, Co-Owner, Posto Pubblico

Taste.

Kristie Lu Stout, CNN Anchor

Taste?

Robert Spina, Co-Owner, Posto Pubblico

Taste. You know, I think at the end of the day, we're a restaurant, you know, and so, you know, we're in the business of creating an occasion for people, and you know having the tastiest product is obviously one of the best things to us. But, you know, I think it's important that, you know, restaurants also provide us with an opportunity to make decisions, either as the

CNN 主播　克莉絲蒂・陸・史道
看看這些番茄，我都看呆了。真是太美了。

帕布里克義式餐廳合夥人　羅伯・史賓納
這些是最好的番茄，品質真的非常好，也絕對是當令的時材。這些番茄四月初起才買得到，只會供應九十天左右。我們喜歡在盤子上放些蕃茄切塊，搭配我們自製的新鮮莫札瑞拉乳酪，或者配上黃油乳酪，好的食材就這些就夠了。非常簡單。

CNN 主播　克莉絲蒂・陸・史道
這些蔬果全都是當地種植的。如果你問在地食家，他們都會說，支持在地飲食主要有三項重點：口味、價格和拯救地球。對你而言，哪一點是最重要的？

帕布里克義式餐廳合夥人　羅伯・史賓納
口味。

CNN 主播　克莉絲蒂・陸・史道
口味？

帕布里克義式餐廳合夥人　羅伯・史賓納
口味。我想我們畢竟是一家餐廳，我們的工作就是為顧客創造情境。所以，供應最美味的產品，對我們來說顯然是最棒的事情。不過，我認為重要的是，餐廳給大家機會去做決定，不論是餐廳老闆還是顧客，因為吃飯有點像是投票。我們常說吃東西就像投票，你選擇是否

Notes & Vocabulary

come down to　終歸於；取決於

come down to 的意思可從字面上來推敲，就是指經過計算、縮減之後，可總結出一個精要的結果，即中文說的「終歸於……；取決於…… 」的意思。

- This business' success or failure comes down to whether we can turn a profit in the next quarter.
  這樁生意的成敗與否取決於下一季是否能有獲利。

at the end of the day　終歸

at the end of the day 字面意思是「一天的終了」，但其實是指某件事的總結，意義與 when all is said and done 相近，相當於中文的「終歸；總之」之意。

- At the end of the day, if you are healthy and happy, you have much to be thankful for.
  總之，如果你健康又快樂，你得要滿懷感恩的心。

9. **gorgeous** [ˋgɔrdʒəs] *adj.* 美麗的；極好的
10. **incredible** [ɪnˋkrɛdəbəl] *adj.* 驚人的；難以置信的
11. **wedge** [wɛdʒ] *n.* 楔形物；用作楔子的東西
12. **mozzarella** [ˏmɑtsəˋrɛlɑ] *n.* 莫札瑞拉乳酪（白色味淡的義大利乾酪）
13. **burrata** [bəˋrɑtə] *n.* 義大利黃油乳酪

business owner or as the customer, you know, to . . . you know, eating is sort of like voting. You know, we always say, right, eating is like voting, and you sort of either choose to support your local organic farmers and your sort of local community, you know, reducing[14] your carbon footprint and all those sort of feel-good ideas. And, you know, but it all comes around at the end of the day to having the best-tasting product.

支持本地的有機農民和本地社群來減少自己的碳足跡，還有各種令人感覺正面的觀念。但說到底，我們還是必須供應最美味的產品。

Notes & Vocabulary

14. **reduce** [rɪˋdjus] *v.* 減少；縮小

NOTES

實戰應用篇
Part II

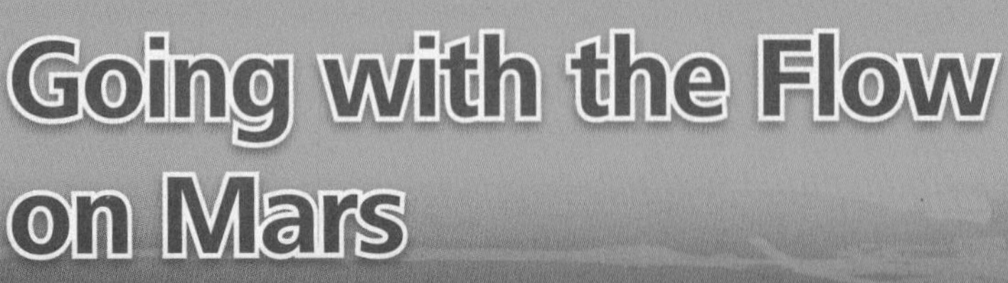

Going with the Flow on Mars

NASA Probe Discovers What Looks Like Water on the Red Planet

天文大發現 火星・生命・水

Step 1 如果你是使用 MP3 ，請聽 MP3 Track 95；如果你使用電腦互動光碟，請點選 DVD-ROM【實戰應用篇—Part II：Unit 1】，試試看是否聽懂新聞內容。

Step 2 請瀏覽下列關鍵字彙，再仔細聽一次。

probe 太空探測器	building block 基本條件
Martian 火星的	crater 火山口
a smoking gun 確切的證據	briny 鹽水的
sediment 沉積物	

Step 3 如果你還不是聽的很懂的話，請參考下列發音提示，再仔細聽一次。

連音	crucial element、look again、life forms、crater's slope、Mars scientists
弱化音	intrigued by
同化音	British scientist、evidence yet

試著作答下列聽力測驗題目。

True or False 是非題

____ 1. Water is a crucial element in the search for life on other planets.

____ 2. The Mars Global Surveyor sends back sounds from Mars.

____ 3. Scientists don't believe the gullies carry water.

____ 4. The flow appears as a light-colored material.

____ 5. Scientists also saw smoke, which they think is from a gun.

____ 6. The Mars Global Surveyor has been sending images for 10 years.

Multiple Choice 選擇題

____ 1. What do scientists believe the flow might be composed of?

a. slushy water
b. water and sediment
c. acidic water
d. all of the above

____ 2. Where do scientists think the water could be coming from?

a. rain clouds
b. from inside the Martian surface
c. from three billion years ago
d. from some sort of animal

____ 3. How many gullies have scientists found on Mars?

a. tens of thousands
b. thousands
c. hundreds
d. millions

____ 4. What is the consensus on what is flowing through the gullies?

a. icy water
b. liquid water
c. sand
d. mud

試著用較慢的速度，再仔細聽一遍（MP3 Track 96），檢查答案是否正確。

對答案、驗收成果，並詳讀原文，若仍有不懂的地方，可反覆多聽幾次。

（答案請見 p. 314）

CNN Anchor

Well, water. Many scientists consider it a crucial[2] element in the search for life forms on other planets. For decades, scientists have studied Mars to see if it had or has the necessary building block[3] for life. Now, some stunning[4] new images, well they could hold crucial clues. Lawrence McGinty reports.

Lawrence McGinty, ITV News Correspondent

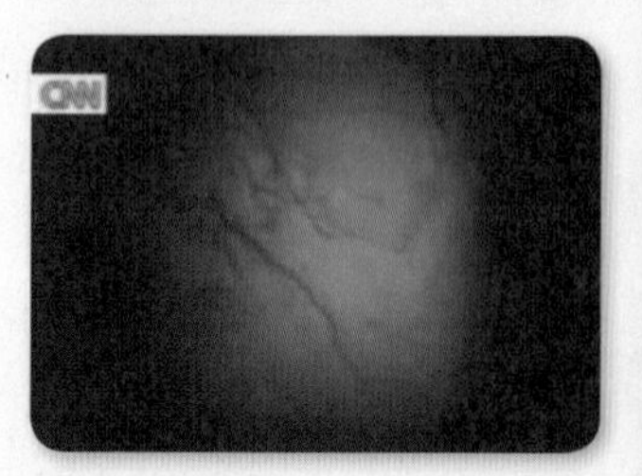

For almost a decade, a NASA probe called Mars Global Surveyor[5] has been sending back amazing images of the Martian[6] surface. Scientists are intrigued[7] by the discovery of tens of thousands of gullies.[8] Could they have been caused by flowing water?

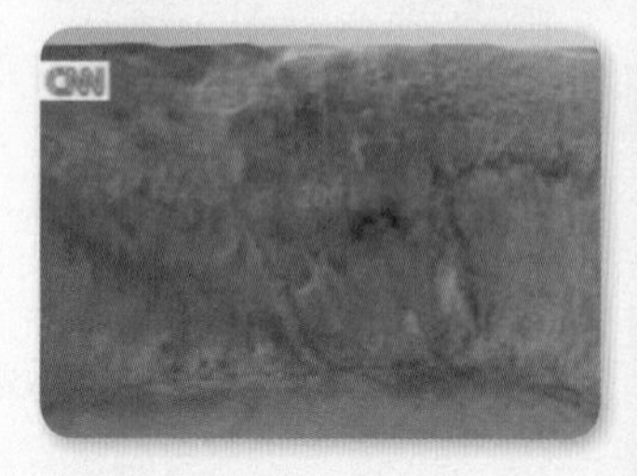

This is a crater[9] in Terra[10] Sirenum photographed in 2001, and this is one of those gullies. Look again, the same crater photographed last year. The gully has light-colored material in it stretching for over 300 kilometers. Scientists believe this is a new flow of water welling up[11] from inside the Martian surface carrying ice and rubble[12] down the crater's slope.[13] Today, NASA said this was not a smoking gun, but a squirting gun.

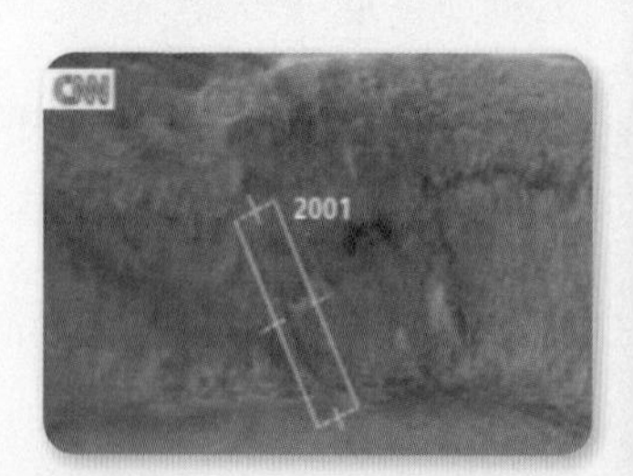

CNN 主播

水，許多科學家都認為水是其他行星上是否有生命存在的關鍵要素。數十年來，科學家不斷研究火星，想知道火星上是否曾經有過或者現在仍然具有生命存在的必要條件。現在有一些讓人嘆為觀止的影像，其中可能帶有關鍵性的線索。以下是勞倫斯．麥金提的報導。

ITV 新聞台特派員 勞倫斯．麥金提

將近十年的時間，美國航太總署一艘名為火星環球探測者號的探測器不斷傳回火星表面驚人的影像。科學家對火星地表上數以萬計的峽谷感到好奇。這些峽谷有沒有可能是流水侵蝕而成的呢？

這是在二〇〇一年所拍攝薩瑞南台地上的火山口，這是其中一個溝渠。再看看去年同一個火山口所拍的照片。溝渠裡有長達三百公里的淺色物質。科學家認為這是火星地底的水溢出地表，挾帶著冰塊與石礫流下火山口旁的斜坡。航太總署表示，這不只是證據確鑿，根本就是逮個正著。

Notes & Vocabulary

go with the flow 順其自然

go with the flow 字面上解釋是「順著水流」，因為水是生命的必要元素，科學家若想知道火星上到底有沒有生物，也必須先找到水流。亦可引申為「順從趨勢；隨遇而安」的意思。

- I wish Paul would stop arguing all the time and just learn to go with the flow.
  我希望保羅不要總是愛爭論，就從善如流吧。

Red Planet 火星

從地球觀看火星是紅色的，故有此別名。而地球（Earth）從太空中看起來是藍色的，故又稱為 Blue Planet。

a smoking gun 確切的證據

此語源自於犯罪偵查時找到確切證據時所用，因為槍剛發射過會冒出煙硝，可證明持槍者剛開過槍，應用在本文是指火星照片證明火星上有水。至於後面的 squirting gun 是「水槍」，則是開玩笑說科學家這個證據不只會冒煙，還會冒水呢！

- Many people believed he was the murderer, but a smoking gun was never produced.
  許多人相信他是殺人犯，但是確切的證據始終沒有找到。

1. probe [prob] *n.* 太空探測器
2. crucial [ˋkruʃəl] *adj.* 決定性的；重要的
3. building block [ˋbɪldɪŋ] [blɑk] *n.* 基本條件
4. stunning [ˋstʌnɪŋ] *adj.* 令人震驚的
5. surveyor [sɚˋveɚ] *n.* 調查員；考察者
6. Martian [ˋmɑrʃən] *adj.* 火星的
7. intrigue [ɪnˋtrig] *v.* 激起……的好奇心（或興趣）
8. gully [ˋgʌlɪ] *n.* 小峽谷
9. crater [ˋkretɚ] *n.* 火山口；隕石坑
10. terra [ˋtɛrə] *n.* 地；土地
11. well up *v.* 湧溢；情緒逐漸高張
12. rubble [ˋrʌbl̩] *n.* 粗石；碎石
13. slope [slop] *n.* 坡；斜面

Dr. Kenneth Edgett, NASA

These are in gullies and people have been talking now for six and a half years about what could form gullies and what could flow through gullies. By and large[14] the consensus[15] is liquid water. It could be acidic[16] water, it could be briny[17] water, it could be water carrying all kinds of sediment,[18] it could be slushy,[19] but H_2O is involved.

Lawrence McGinty, ITV News Correspondent

British scientist Colin Pillinger has become one of the many Mars scientists.

Colin Pillinger, Mars Scientist

It's the culmination[20] of their search-for-water campaign.[21] They've brought water from sort of three billion years ago on Mars to three years ago on Mars.

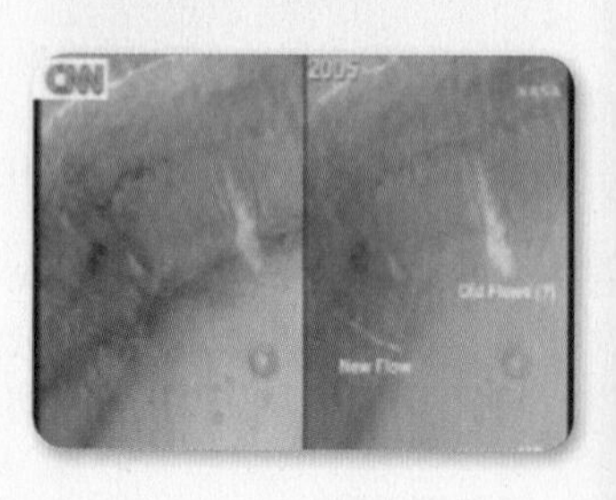

Lawrence McGinty, ITV News Correspondent

This is by far the most convincing[22] evidence yet of water on Mars. And if there's water, there could be life.

美國航太總署 肯尼斯．艾吉特博士

這些都是溝渠。過去六年半以來，大家都在談論溝渠的成因，以及哪些東西可能流過這些溝渠。大多數人的共識都是液態水。可能是酸性水，可能是鹽水，裡面可能帶有各種沉積物，也可能是冰雪融化而成的水，但是反正一定有水就對了。

ITV 新聞台特派員 勞倫斯．麥金提

英國科學家柯林．皮林傑已經成為許多火星科學家的其中一員。

火星科學家 柯林．皮林傑

這是他們多年來探水行動最重要的發現。由於他們的努力，火星上存在水的可能時間點從原本大約三十億年前變成了三年前。

ITV 新聞台特派員 勞倫斯．麥金提

要證明火星上有水，這是至今為止最具說服力的證據。只要有水，就可能有生物存在。

Notes & Vocabulary

by far 至今；截至目前為止

by far 用來修飾事情到目前為止，達到「極度」的狀態，不論此事為好或壞。

- That's by far the craziest thing I've heard in a long time.
  這是我長久以來聽過最瘋狂的事了。

其他與 far 相關的片語有：

go too far 太過分；太過火

- This time, you've gone too far!
  你這次太過分了！

as far as sth goes 就某事本身而言

- As far as that suit goes, it makes you look short and dumpy.
  就那件西裝來說，它讓你看起來又矮又笨拙。

14. **by and large** *phr.* 一般而言
15. **consensus** [kən`sɛnsəs] *n.* 共識
16. **acidic** [ə`sɪdɪk] *adj.* 酸的；酸性的
17. **briny** [`braɪnɪ] *adj.* 鹽水的；海水的
18. **sediment** [`sɛdəmənt] *n.* 沈積物
19. **slushy** [`slʌʃɪ] *adj.*（雪融後）泥濘的
20. **culmination** [ˏkʌlmə`neʃən] *n.* 頂點；高潮點
21. **campaign** [kæm`pen] *n.* 活動
22. **convincing** [kən`vɪnsɪŋ] *adj.* 令人信服的

Bent into Shape

Overworked Indians Rediscover Yoga

古老印度瑜珈 現代人的解壓良方

Step 1 如果你是使用 MP3 ，請聽 MP3 Track 97；如果你使用電腦互動光碟，請點選 DVD-ROM【實戰應用篇—Part II：Unit 2】，試試看是否聽懂新聞內容。

Step 2 請瀏覽下列關鍵字彙，再仔細聽一次。

overworked 工作過度的	purport 號稱
deskbound 長時間坐辦公室的	stress out 壓力過大
modernization 現代化	homegrown 本國產的

Step 3 如果你還不是聽的很懂的話，請參考下列發音提示，再仔細聽一次。

連音	tired out、deskbound in、sends so many
弱化音	overworked professionals
省略音	executive

試著作答下列聽力測驗題目。

True or False 是非題

____ 1. This report is part of a series called *I Love India*.

____ 2. Some people say yoga classes give them a new view on life.

____ 3. Because yoga is popular in the West, most Indians don't want to do it.

____ 4. More Indians are getting office jobs where they sit at desks all day.

____ 5. Yoga teachers in India are becoming as stressed out as Western workers.

____ 6. Yoga has always been popular in India.

Multiple Choice 選擇題

____ 1. According to the news, what sort of people practice yoga?

a. overworked professionals
b. celebrities
c. office workers
d. all of the above

____ 2. Where is the yoga institute in the story located?

a. Hong Kong　　b. Mumbai
c. London　　d. Dubai

____ 3. How long has the visitor from Hong Kong been taking yoga classes?

a. this is her first class　　b. one year
c. five years　　d. 30 years

____ 4. Why are more and more Indians taking yoga classes?

a. to better cope with stress
b. to compete with Americans
c. They don't want to modernize.
d. More people are coming to India.

試著用較慢的速度，再仔細聽一遍 (MP3 Track 98)，檢查答案是否正確。

對答案、驗收成果，並詳讀原文，若仍有不懂的地方，可反覆多聽幾次。

(答案請見 p. 314)

CNN Anchor

Do you know your asanas[4] from your elbows? I know you do. But if you don't, you might do some catching up as the popularity of yoga makes a big return.

CNN Anchor

As part of our *Eye on India* series, Veronica Pedrosa went to visit what purports[5] to be the oldest organized yoga center in the world.

Veronica Pedrosa, CNN Correspondent

Sun salutations[6] in London. Warrior poses in Hong Kong. Yoga's gone international. Tired out[7] celebrities and overworked professionals, in fact all manner[8] of people in Asia, Europe and the rest of the world have been turning to yoga as a way of strengthening their bodies and minds to cope with modern life. Its ancient birthplace is India, and now that yoga's big everywhere else, more Indians are rediscovering yoga's benefits.

Institutes like this one in Mumbai say they're enrolling[9] more and more students, including a visitor from Hong Kong.

I've been going to yoga classes on and off[10] for about five years, but always in Hong Kong or even London, never before in India itself. So, let's see how it goes.

I can honestly say the class gave me a whole different view on life, a view bank executive Usha's been practicing for 30 years.

CNN 主播

您曉得您正確的手肘瑜珈姿勢嗎？我知道你曉得。但您若不知道，那可能要惡補一下了，因為瑜珈又再度盛行了起來。

CNN 主播

在我們製播的《今日印度》系列中，薇若妮卡．佩卓莎探訪了自稱為全世界歷史最悠久的瑜珈組織中心。

CNN 特派員 薇若妮卡．佩卓莎

倫敦的人們做著拜日姿勢。香港的人們擺出了戰士式。瑜珈已經邁向國際化。不論是身心疲憊的名流還是工作過度的專業人士，其實全亞洲、歐洲及世界其他各地裡形形色色的人們，都藉由瑜珈來鍛鍊身心以應付現代生活。印度是瑜珈的誕生地，如今瑜珈已風靡各地，而越來越多印度人也開始重新發現它的益處。

像在孟買的這所瑜珈學校就表示，他們招收的學生越來越多，其中還包括我這位來自香港的訪客。

我上瑜珈課斷斷續續有五年了，但總是在香港，甚至是在倫敦，從沒在印度上過瑜珈課。我們這就去瞧瞧吧。

我可以坦白講，這門課讓我對人生有了全新的看法，銀行主管烏夏奉行這套哲學已有三十年之久。

Notes & Vocabulary

in shape 體能狀況良好

標題中的 shape 一字具有「健康情形；狀況」之意，接近 condition，例如要形容人的健康情形良好，或物品的狀況不錯，便可用 in good shape 來表示，相反的用法為 in bad/poor shape。若要強調人的體能狀況（fitness）好壞，可直接說 someone is in shape / out of shape。要「練出好體能」，可說 get into shape，而「保持體能狀況」則是 keep/stay in shape。須特別注意的是，本文標題的 bent into shape 就字面上而言是指「透過（瑜珈）彎曲身體的動作改善身體狀況，進而達到身心平衡」，不過卻也和英文中常用的片語 bent out of shape（火冒三丈；發怒）形成了對比，是一個有趣的雙關語。

- Robert is in good shape since he exercises regularly.
  羅伯特自從定期運動之後身體狀況就保持得很好。

1. **bend** [bɛnd] *v.* 彎腰；彎曲
2. **overworked** [ˋovɚˋwɝkt] *adj.* 工作過度的
3. **rediscover** [ˏridɪsˋkʌvɚ] *v.* 重新發現；再發現
4. **asana** [ˋɑsənə] *n.* 瑜珈體位法；瑜珈姿勢
5. **purport** [ˏpɚˋport] *v.* 號稱；聲稱
6. **salutation** [ˏsæljəˋteʃən] *n.* 行禮；致意；招呼
7. **tire out** *v.* 使十分疲累；累垮
8. **manner** [ˋmænɚ] *n.* 種類
9. **enroll** [ɪnˋrol] *v.* 招生
10. **on and off** *phr.* 斷斷續續地

Usha Thorat, Yoga Student

People are becoming more conscious, and I think the fact that the West and that the rest of world is recognizing yoga makes people realize that OK you have a good thing going.

Veronica Pedrosa, CNN Correspondent

As more Indians become deskbound in demanding office or outsourcing[11] jobs, the teachers here say they're getting as stressed out[12] as Western workers and turning to yoga.

Firooza Ali, Yoga Teacher

When you need something you go looking for it. If you don't need it, and even if it's there, you don't value it. You don't even see it.

Veronica Pedrosa, CNN Correspondent

Ironically,[13] it's India's modernization[14] that sends so many Indians back to an ancient, homegrown[15] tradition.

瑜珈學員 烏夏・索羅特

人們越來越有覺察力，我認為西方和世界各地對瑜珈的認同，讓人們了解到「不錯，你在從事一件有益的事」。

CNN 特派員 薇若妮卡・佩卓莎

越來越多的印度人因為操勞的辦公室事務或外包工作而久坐辦公桌。這裡的老師表示，這些印度人逐漸和西方世界的上班族一樣感到壓力過大，而求助於瑜珈。

瑜珈老師 費魯沙・阿里

當你需要某種東西時，就會去尋求。如果你不需要的話，即使它就在那兒，你也不會重視它，甚至會對它視而不見。

CNN 特派員 薇若妮卡・佩卓莎

耐人尋味的是，讓這麼多印度人重回古老且本土的傳統懷抱中的，正是印度現代化的趨勢。

Notes & Vocabulary

deskbound

長時間坐辦公桌的；離不開辦公桌的

bound 是 bind 的過去分詞，bind 是指「綁；約束；使連結」的意思。deskbound 可還原為 be bound to the desk，意思是忙得彷彿跟辦公桌綁在一起了。

其他類似的字還有：

- spellbound 入迷的；被符咒鎖位的
- stormbound 被暴風雨困住的

另外，bound 也可以與方向副詞合成形容詞，如：inbound（向內的）、outbound（向外的）、southbound（向南行的）等。

11. **outsource** [ˋaut͵sɔrs] *v.* 工作外包
12. **stress out** *v.* 緊張；使承受壓力；壓力過大
13. **ironically** [͵aɪˋrɑnɪklɪ] *adv.* 諷刺地
14. **modernization** [͵mɑdɚnəˋzeʃən] *n.* 現代化
15. **homegrown** [ˋhomˋgron] *adj.* 來自本國的；本國產的

A Hard Blow for the Big Easy

New Orleans Devastated as Hurricane Katrina Ravages Gulf Coast

颶風狂掃 爵士城一夕變色

Step 1 如果你是使用 MP3 ，請聽 MP3 Track 99；如果你使用電腦互動光碟，請點選 DVD-ROM【實戰應用篇—Part II：Unit 3】，試試看是否聽懂新聞內容。

Step 2 請瀏覽下列關鍵字彙，再仔細聽一次。

the Big Easy 悠閒城（紐奧良的別稱）	unleash 釋放出
brace for 做好準備去面對	debris 碎片；瓦礫
torrential 湍急的	inundate （大水）淹沒
loot 掠奪	deploy 調派（物資）

Step 3 如果你還不是聽的很懂的話，請參考下列發音提示，再仔細聽一次。

連音	wind gusts up to、further east、local authorities、coastal areas、widespread damage、Katrina's storm、has suffered
省略音	wind gusts up to
同化音	had sought shelter、Interstate

試著作答下列聽力測驗題目。

True or False 是非題

____ 1. New Orleans was hit directly by Hurricane Katrina.

____ 2. The wind damaged many buildings in New Orleans.

____ 3. There were many people in the streets of New Orleans when the hurricane struck.

____ 4. Louisiana was the only state affected by Hurricane Katrina.

____ 5. There was a lot of damage caused by flooding along the coast.

____ 6. President Bush encouraged Gulf Coast residents to be careful and wait for help.

Multiple Choice 選擇題

____ 1. How fast was the wind blowing during the hurricane?

a. 200 miles an hour
b. 120 kilometers an hour
c. 100 kilometers an hour
d. 120 miles an hour

____ 2. What building did 10,000 people use for shelter during the storm?

a. a supermarket
b. the Superdome
c. city hall
d. a hospital

____ 3. Where was President Bush when he gave his speech?

a. Arizona
b. Mississippi
c. New Orleans
d. Alabama

____ 4. After the storm had passed, what new problem began to occur?

a. residents letting their guard down
b. drowning in a foot of rain
c. looting of New Orleans stores
d. city streets were deserted

Step 5 試著用較慢的速度，再仔細聽一遍 (MP3 Track 100)，檢查答案是否正確。

對答案、驗收成果，並詳讀原文，若仍有不懂的地方，可反覆多聽幾次。

(答案請見 p. 314)

CNN Anchor

Well, Hurricane Katrina has weakened to a Category 1 storm this Monday after unleashing[3] major flooding and devastation on the U.S. Gulf Coast. CNN's Wolf Blitzer has more now on the widespread[4] damage left by one of the most powerful storms ever to hit the U.S.

Wolf Blitzer, CNN Correspondent

With each passing hour, new images of devastation. New Orleans, bracing for[5] catastrophe[6] was spared[7] a direct hit by Hurricane Katrina, but even with the storm passing to the east, the effects on the Big Easy are nothing short of devastating. Wind gusts[8] up to 120 miles an hour shattered[9] windows on downtown high-rises,[10] and sent potentially deadly debris[11] rocketing through the city's deserted streets. They were powerful enough to shred[12] part of the roof covering the Superdome,[13] where some 10,000 people had sought shelter.

CNN 主播

摧殘美國灣岸地區並引發嚴重水患的颶風卡崔娜，已在本週一減弱為一級風暴（註）。對於這場美國史上罕見的強烈風暴所造成的大規模災情，本台記者沃夫·布里策有進一步的報導。

CNN 特派員 沃夫·布里策

每一個小時，都有新的災情畫面出爐。對天災嚴陣以待的紐奧良市雖然沒有正面迎上卡崔娜，但即使颶風路徑已向東偏移，這個素有「悠閒城」之稱的地區仍然災情慘重。時速高達一百二十英里的強風擊碎了市區高樓的外窗玻璃，空盪的街道上到處飛竄著可能致命的玻璃碎片。強風的威力也將巨蛋體育館部分屋頂給吹掀了，而館內正聚集著上萬名前來避難的民眾。

註 :Category 1 指的是颶風的分級。美國的颶風強度分級基本上是根據一九六九年所研發的薩菲爾一辛普森颶風等級表（Saffir-Simpson Hurricane Scale）來劃分，依近中心最大風速共分五級，以第五級為最強，卡崔娜颶風在登陸前就曾達到此一量級。就氣象學而言，颶風和颱風都是由熱帶氣旋（tropical cyclone）發展而成。除了因生成地區不同而有不同名稱之外，本質上並無顯著差別。一般而言，形成於北太平洋西部和南中國海一帶的稱為颱風，而形成於大西洋、加勒比海、墨西哥灣及北太平洋國際換日線以東的則稱為颶風。

Notes & Vocabulary

the Big Easy 悠閒城（紐奧良的別稱）

（取自標題）以爵士樂和嘉年華聞名的紐奧良市，素來標榜著輕鬆悠閒（easygoing）的生活步調與無憂無慮（carefree）的人生態度，因此有 the Big Easy（悠閒城）和 the City That Care Forgot（被憂慮遺忘的城市）之稱。本篇報導以 a hard blow for the Big Easy 為標題，除了表達「對悠閒城的重大打擊」這層字面意思之外，也透過 hard/easy 的對比，暗指紐奧良的「輕鬆」時光已逝，「艱苦」歲月才要開始。

Gulf Coast 灣岸地區

（取自標題）Gulf Coast 一詞指的是美國南部墨西哥灣（Gulf of Mexico）沿岸各州，由西至東分別為：德州（Texas）、路易斯安那州（Louisiana）、密西西比州（Mississippi）、阿拉巴馬州（Alabama）和佛羅里達州（Florida）。這個地區有時也被稱為美國在東西兩岸之外的「第三海岸」（Third Coast）。

1. **devastate** [ˋdɛvəˏstet] *v.* 破壞；摧殘
2. **ravage** [ˋrævɪdʒ] *v.* 蹂躪
3. **unleash** [ʌnˋliʃ] *v.* 放出
4. **widespread** [ˋwaɪdˋsprɛd] *adj.* 廣泛的
5. **brace for** [bres] *v.* 做好準備去面對
6. **catastrophe** [kəˋtæstrəfɪ] *n.* 災難
7. **spare** [spɛr] *v.* 免除；免去；赦免
8. **gust** [gʌst] *n.* 一陣強風
9. **shatter** [ˋʃætɚ] *v.* 將……擊碎
10. **high-rise** [ˋhaɪˏraɪz] *n.* 設有電梯多層樓房；高樓
11. **debris** [dəˋbri] *n.* 碎片；瓦礫
12. **shred** [ʃrɛd] *v.* 將……撕成一片片的
13. **Superdome** [ˋsupɚˏdom] *n.* 奧良市的巨蛋體育館

Flooding was widespread across the low-lying[14] region, Katrina's storm surge[15] combining with torrential[16] rain to inundate[17] some neighborhoods. And in the storm's wake, a new problem, looting[18] seen in at least one New Orleans store. Devastating floods also swamping[19] coastal areas of neighboring Mississippi, some areas drowning under more than a foot of rain. State officials underscored[20] the scope[21] of what they're facing.

Haley Barbour, Mississippi Governor

The state today has suffered a grievous[22] blow on the coast. And we're not through. It's a major disaster, and there's much left to happen.

Wolf Blitzer, CNN Correspondent

Further east in Alabama, Katrina pushed waters of Mobile Bay into downtown streets, and left parts of Interstate 10 underwater. President Bush, traveling in Arizona, urged Gulf Coast residents not to let their guard down.

George W. Bush, U.S. President

Don't abandon[23] your shelters until you're given clearance[24] by the local authorities. Take precautions[25] because this is a dangerous storm. When the storm passes the federal government has got assets[26] and resources that we'll be deploying[27] to help you.

這片地勢低窪的區域淹水的現象十分普遍。卡崔娜颶風所造成的風暴潮，再加上豪雨肆虐，使得鄰近一些地區都成了水鄉澤國。但在風暴過去後，又有新的問題，紐奧良市至少有一家商店遭人趁亂打劫。而在鄰近的密西西比州，大洪水也淹沒了沿海地區，有些地方水深甚至超過一英尺。州政府官員在發言時特別強調了這場災難的慘重。

密西西比州州長 哈里・巴柏爾

本州沿岸地區今天遭受了沉痛的打擊，但是事情還沒有結束。這是一場重大災難，後續還會有更多的災情傳出。

CNN 特派員 沃夫・布里策

而在位置更偏東的阿拉巴馬州，卡崔娜颶風不但讓莫比爾灣的水倒灌商業區，還造成十號州際公路的部分路段遭洪水淹沒。正巡訪亞歷桑那州的布希總統，呼籲灣岸地區的居民不可掉以輕心。

美國總統 喬治・布希

在地方當局宣佈狀況解除之前，別離開避難地點。這次的風暴來勢洶洶，大家要做好預防工作。等風暴過去之後，聯邦政府會調派物資幫助大家。

Notes & Vocabulary

in the wake of 尾隨而至

wake 在此作名詞，指的是「（船的）尾波；航跡」。當船隻向前航行必定會引起漣漪，in the wake of sth 便是用來表示伴隨的現象。若 sth 是一個字的話，也可以寫成 in the sth's wake，如文中的 in the storm's wake。

- In the fire's wake, hundreds of people were left homeless.
  火災後，數百位民眾無家可歸。

let one's guard down 放鬆戒備

guard 作名詞時除了指「守衛；衛兵」外，也可以指「警戒心」。let one's guard down 即指「掉以輕心」，和 off guard（未加防備）意思接近。相反詞為 to be on guard 或 to be on alert（留神戒備）。

- The soldiers can't let their guard down or the enemy will attack.
  士兵們不可鬆懈戒備，否則敵人會藉機進攻。

14. **low-lying** [ˋloˋlaɪɪŋ] *adj.* 位於低處的
15. **storm surge** [stɔrm] [sɝdʒ] *n. phr.* 風暴潮（強大風雨造成的海潮水位暴漲）
16. **torrential** [tɔˋrɛnʃəl] *adj.* （形容水勢）湍急、猛烈的
17. **inundate** [ˋɪnən͵det] *v.* （大水）淹沒；漫過……
18. **loot** [lut] *v.* 劫掠；掠奪
19. **swamp** [swɑmp] *v.* 使……淹水
20. **underscore** [ˋʌndɚ͵skɔr] *v.* 強調；突顯
21. **scope** [skop] *n.* 規模；視野；格局
22. **grievous** [ˋgrivəs] *adj.* 悲傷的；沉痛的
23. **abandon** [əˋbændən] *v.* 放棄；拋棄
24. **precaution** [prɪˋkɔʃən] *n.* 預防措施
25. **clearance** [ˋklɪrəns] *n.* （狀況）清除；解除
26. **asset** [ˋæ͵sɛt] *n.* 資產；物資
27. **deploy** [dɪˋplɔɪ] *v.* 調派（物資）；部署（軍隊）

Cheetahs Race for Survival

Habitat Loss and Competition Closing In on World's Fastest Land Animal

與絕種命運賽跑的獵豹

Step 1 如果你是使用 MP3 ，請聽 MP3 Track 101；如果你使用電腦互動光碟，請點選 DVD-ROM【實戰應用篇—Part II：Unit 4】，試試看是否聽懂新聞內容。

Step 2 請瀏覽下列關鍵字彙，再仔細聽一次。

cheetah 獵豹；印度豹	extinction 滅絕
wage 進行；展開	predator 掠食者
livestock 家畜	conservation 保育
decline 減少	

Step 3 如果你還不是聽的很懂的話，請參考下列發音提示，再仔細聽一次。

連音	land animal、novel idea、scientists say、guard dog
省略音	birth defects、conservationists

Step 4 試著作答下列聽力測驗題目。

True or False 是非題

____ 1. In the last 50 years, cheetahs have disappeared from 16 countries.

____ 2. On private reserves, cheetahs don't have any competition for food.

____ 3. Cheetahs can easily fight off larger predators.

____ 4. Namibia has the world's smallest population of cheetahs.

____ 5. The number of cheetahs in Namibia has gone up in recent years.

____ 6. Ranchers shoot and poison cheetahs because cheetahs often attack them.

Multiple Choice 選擇題

____ 1. Up to what speed can a cheetah run?

a. 50 miles an hour　　b. 70 miles an hour
c. 40 miles an hour　　d. 60 miles an hour

____ 2. How many cheetahs survive in the wilds of Iran and Africa?

a. 2,000　　b. 5,000
c. 12,000　　d. 7,000

____ 3. Why are cheetahs suffering from birth defects?

a. They're competing with lions and hyenas.
b. Their body is built for speed.
c. They are poisoned by ranchers.
d. They lack genetic diversity.

____ 4. What is the Cheetah Conservation Fund providing farmers with to protect their livestock from cheetahs?

a. guard dogs　　b. poison
c. traps　　d. guns

Step 5 試著用較慢的速度，再仔細聽一遍（MP3 Track 102），檢查答案是否正確。

Step 6 對答案、驗收成果，並詳讀原文，若仍有不懂的地方，可反覆多聽幾次。

（答案請見 p. 314）

Daniel Sieberg, NEXT@CNN

And there's another battle for survival being waged,[3] this time for the survival of a species.[4] Cheetahs are some of the fastest animals on earth, and now they are trying to run away from extinction.[5] Gary Strieker follows the story.

Gary Strieker, CNN Correspondent

Nature built this cat for speed. Scientists say there's never been a land animal as fast as the cheetah. But even at 70 miles per hour, it's losing its race for survival.

Laurie Marker, Cheetah Conservation Fund

In the last 50 years, we have had cheetahs go extinct in 16 countries. Today, the populations[6] in many—throughout 28 countries—many of them are just holding on by a thread.[7]

Gary Strieker, CNN Correspondent

Altogether, fewer than 12,000 cheetahs are believed to be holding out in the wilds[8] of Africa and Iran. They suffer from birth defects[9] because they lack genetic diversity.[10] They're losing habitat and they don't do well in protected reserves, in confined[11] spaces competing with lions and hyenas.[12]

《科技新世代》丹尼爾．席柏格

又有一場生存戰爭點燃了戰火，這次是為了一個物種的存續而戰。獵豹是地球上速度最快的動物之一，現在牠們卻要努力讓自己免於絕種。記者蓋瑞．史崔克的報導。

CNN 特派員 蓋瑞．史崔克

大自然讓獵豹擁有與生俱來的速度。科學家說，陸地上從未有任何動物的速度快過獵豹。但即便時速高達七十英里，獵豹卻仍在生存的競賽上漸居下風。

獵豹保育基金會 羅瑞．馬克

五十年來，獵豹在十六個國家中絕跡。如今，在二十八個擁有獵豹的國家中，有許多國家的獵豹數量所剩無幾。

CNN 特派員 蓋瑞．史崔克

據信目前在非洲和伊朗野外存活的獵豹總共不到一萬兩千隻。由於這些獵豹的基因多元性不足，因此先天便有缺陷。牠們逐漸失去棲息地，在保護區裡的狀況也不好，得在有限空間裡與獅子、土狼競爭。

Notes & Vocabulary

hold out 繼續生存；堅持；捱著

hold out 用來表示處於逆境或艱險情況時，有繼續「堅持」、「撐下去」的意思，中文可譯為「維持、支撐、捱住、抵抗、堅持、不退讓、拒絕妥協」等意思。hold out 後接不同介系詞，形成不同的用法及意義：

hold out against 堅決抵抗……

- We held out against the strong wind and big waves for three days and nights.
  我們與大風大浪搏鬥了三天三夜。

hold out for sth 拒絕妥協而堅決要求某事

- Cindy held out for a better offer.
  辛蒂不願退讓，堅持等待更好的條件。

hold out on sb 拒絕／不願給予某人

- Janet felt her employer was holding out on her when she didn't get a raise.
  珍娜發現自己沒有加薪，覺得是她的雇主刻意不給她調薪。

1. **cheetah** [ˋtʃitə] *n.* 獵豹
2. **close in on** *v.* 逼近……；包圍……
3. **wage** [wedʒ] *v.* 進行；展開
4. **species** [ˋspiʃiz] *n.*（生物的）物種
5. **extinction** [ɪkˋstɪŋkʃən] *n.* 滅絕；消滅
6. **population** [ˏpɑpjəˋleʃən] *n.* 族群；（生物）總數
7. **hold on by a thread** [θrɛd] *v. phr.* 岌岌可危
8. **wild** [waɪld] *n.* 野地；荒地；未開發的地區
9. **defect** [dɪˋfɛkt] *n.* 缺陷；缺點；不足之處
10. **diversity** [daɪˋvɝsətɪ] *n.* 多樣性
11. **confined** [kənˋfaɪnd] *adj.* 受限的；狹窄的；受侷限的
12. **hyena** [haɪˋinə] *n.* 鬣狗；土狼

Laurie Marker, Cheetah Conservation Fund

Every part of their body is built for speed versus aggression,[13] so they can't fight for their food against these other large predators.[14]

Gary Strieker, CNN Correspondent

That forces cheetahs to move outside protected areas, where they prey on[15] domestic[16] livestock[17] and are often poisoned or shot by ranchers.[18] But this cat's future looks brighter in Namibia, which has the world's largest population of cheetahs, more than 90 percent of them on private ranches.[19] After 14 years of work supported by donations, the Cheetah Conservation Fund is now credited with reversing[20] the animal's decline[21] in Namibia with research studies, educational programs, capturing and removing problem cheetahs to other areas and the novel[22] idea of providing farmers with hundreds of special guard dogs for protecting livestock. These conservationists[23] are showing how humans and cheetahs can coexist.

Laurie Marker, Cheetah Conservation Fund

For the cheetah we have to look at a mixed management, and how to find a way that they can live outside of reserves as well as inside of reserves.

Gary Strieker, CNN Correspondent

They're now taking there methods to other countries where cheetahs face extinction, in what many wildlife experts believe is the last best chance to save this vanishing[24] species.

獵豹保育基金會 羅瑞．馬克
牠們身上的每一部分都是為了速度而建構，而非用來抵禦攻擊，因此牠們無法和其他大型掠食者爭食。

CNN 特派員 蓋瑞．史崔克
獵豹因而被迫離開保護區，牠們在保護區外獵食家畜，因此常遭到毒害或被牧場人員射殺。不過在納米比亞，獵豹的前途較為光明，這裡有全世界數量最多的獵豹，其中超過百分之九十生活在私人牧場中。在捐款的支持下，獵豹保育基金會歷經十四年的努力，如今透過研究、教育計畫、將不健康的獵豹捕捉並遷至其他地區、以及提供農家數百隻保護家畜的特殊看門犬的新點子，成功逆轉了納米比亞境內獵豹數量減少的趨勢。這些保育人士讓大家看到人類和獵豹可以共存。

獵豹保育基金會 羅瑞．馬克
就獵豹而言，我們必須採取混合管理的方式，並且設法找到一個讓牠們可以在保護區內外都可以生存的方式。

CNN 特派員 蓋瑞．史崔克
現在他們正將他們的方法推廣到其他獵豹面臨絕種的國家，許多野生動物專家相信，這是拯救這種消失中的物種最後、也是最好的機會。

Notes & Vocabulary

be credited with
歸功；被認為有……

credit sb with sth 意思是「將某事歸功於某人」(= credit sth to sb)，常見用法為 all credit to sb（歸功於）。

- All credit to Jack for taking the lead during the crisis.
  這場危機中多虧有傑克的領導。

credit 作名詞時有「信用；功勞」的意思。另外，credit 亦可指「增光的人（事、物）」，用法是 a credit to sb/sth。

- A lawyer who helps the poor is a credit to his profession.
  幫助窮人的律師是律師界的光榮。

13. **aggression** [əˋgrɛʃən] *n.* 侵略；侵略性；侵略行動
14. **predator** [ˋprɛdətɚ] *n.* 食肉動物；掠食者
15. **prey on** [pre] *v.* 捕……為食；獵食
16. **domestic** [dəˋmɛstɪk] *adj.* 馴服的；家庭的；國內的
17. **livestock** [ˋlaɪv͵stɑk] *n.* 家畜；牲口
18. **rancher** [ˋræntʃɚ] *n.* 農、牧場主人；農牧場工人
19. **ranch** [ræntʃ] *n.* 大牧場；大農場
20. **reverse** [rɪˋvɝs] *v.* 逆轉
21. **decline** [dɪˋklaɪn] *n.* 減少；衰退
22. **novel** [ˋnɑvl̩] *adj.* 新的；新穎的；新奇的
23. **conservationist** [͵kɑnsɚˋveʃənɪst] *n.* 保育人士
24. **vanishing** [ˋvænɪʃɪŋ] *adj.* 消逝中的

Hack-Off!

Convention Showcases the Light and Dark Sides of Computer Insecurity

網路犯罪的新剋星——網路駭客

Step 1 如果你是使用 MP3 ，請聽 MP3 Track 103；如果你使用電腦互動光碟，請點選 DVD-ROM【實戰應用篇—Part II: Unit 5】，試試看是否聽懂新聞內容。

Step 2 請瀏覽下列關鍵字彙，再仔細聽一次。

recruit 徵募新成員	do-gooder 做好事的人
arguably 有理由地	incarcerate 監禁
talent pool 人才庫	tap into 開發

Step 3 如果你還不是聽的很懂的話，請參考下列發音提示，再仔細聽一次。

連音	works as a
省略音	who explained、who would

 試著作答下列聽力測驗題目。

True or False 是非題

____ 1. The U.S. government is hoping to arrest former hackers in Las Vegas.

____ 2. All the hackers at the convention are there to cause trouble.

____ 3. Robert Imhoff-Dousharm believes credit cards are not very secure.

____ 4. Imhoff-Dousharm's hacker name is Jar-Jar.

____ 5. Kevin Mitnick is a famous hacker.

____ 6. Hackers often have cheap cars like Honda Civics.

Multiple Choice 選擇題

____ 1. What do most people think hackers want to steal?

a. information　　b. computers
c. credit cards　　d. video games

____ 2. What type of work is Mitnick currently doing?

a. He is a hacker.
b. He is a security consultant.
c. He is a celebrity.
d. He owns several major corporations.

____ 3. What does Mitnick compare hacking to?

a. bungee jumping　　b. sky diving
c. big game hunting　　d. biting the forbidden fruit

____ 4. Why do many hackers hack into their own devices?

a. to fix them
b. to see how they work and what's under the hood
c. to sell the parts
d. to ruin them

 試著用較慢的速度，再仔細聽一遍（MP3 Track 104），檢查答案是否正確。

 對答案、驗收成果，並詳讀原文，若仍有不懂的地方，可反覆多聽幾次。

（答案請見 p. 314）

Daniel Sieberg, NEXT@CNN

The U.S. government is looking for a few good men and women who happen to[3] be computer hackers, not to arrest them but to recruit[4] them in the fight against computer crime. And what better place to do recruiting than in Las Vegas?

It's easy to think all computer hackers are the same: shadowy figures hunched[5] over a keyboard, plotting[6] ways to steal your information, breaking into banks and government agencies. From the darkness to the light—these guys are attending the annual hacker convention in Las Vegas, but they're not all here to cause trouble.

Robert Imhoff-Dousharm, Hacker

I've been trying for three years now to really show all the insecurities in the credit card industry, to show the credit card industry that they need to make sure my credit cards are secure.

Daniel Sieberg, NEXT@CNN

Imhoff-Dousharm, who prefers the handle "Hackajar," also shows how a thief could buy a card reader online, read the data from a stolen credit card and use another machine to create a new card with your information. We encountered[7] several hackers at the convention who explained the difference between the do-gooders[8] and the criminals.

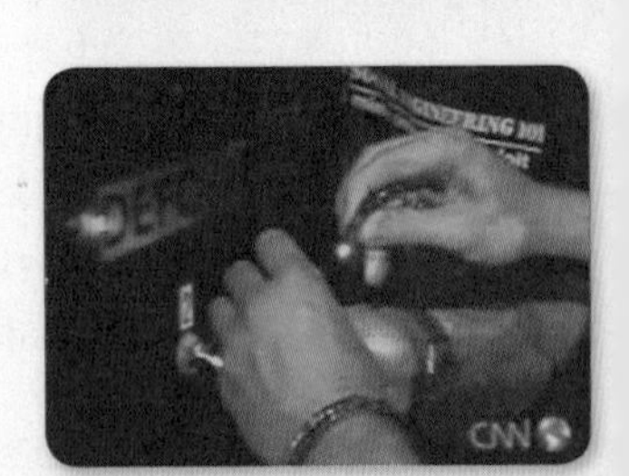

《科技新世代》丹尼爾．席柏格

美國政府正在找尋剛好是駭客的好人，目的不是要逮捕他們，而是要徵召他們一同對抗電腦犯罪。要找這樣的人才，還有哪裡會比賭城拉斯維加斯更合適呢？

我們總以為電腦駭客都是一個模樣：埋首在鍵盤上的陰暗身影，滿腦子只想竊取別人的資料，侵入銀行與政府機關。如今這些傢伙從黑暗走入光明，齊聚賭城參加年度駭客大會（註），但他們到這裡並非都是來製造麻煩的。

駭客 羅伯特．因默夫－朵商姆

我這三年來一直努力揭露信用卡產業中的各種安全漏洞，以便讓信用卡業界了解他們必須設法確保我手上這些信用卡的安全。

《科技新世代》丹尼爾．席柏格

比較喜歡別人以代號「駭客家」稱呼他的駭客因默夫－朵商姆同時也示範了一種竊盜手法。竊賊可以上網購買讀卡機，讀取偷來的信用卡上的資料，再以這些資料用另外一台機器複製一張新卡。我們在大會上遇到了幾位駭客，向我們說明正派人士與犯罪份子的不同。

註：指 DEF CON，為世界規模最大的駭客年會，自一九九三年起每年於拉斯維加斯舉行。

Notes & Vocabulary

handle 暱稱；頭銜

handle 在這裡作名詞用，意思是「暱稱」，與 nickname 類似，不同的是 handle 是用在別人不知道真實身份的情況，為口語用法。

- On the Internet, Tom used the handle CoolBoy23.
  湯姆在網路上用的暱稱是「酷男孩二三」。

你知道 Hackajar 這個暱稱怎麼來的嗎？原來是一九九四年時，Imhoff-Dousharm 的朋友自稱是很厲害的 hacker，他便吐嘈說 you couldn't hack your way out of a jar，喻他朋友其實一點能耐也沒有。Imhoff-Dousharm 便自創了 Hackajar 這個字來開他朋友的玩笑。

1. showcase [ˋʃoˏkes] *v.* 使展現；使亮相
2. insecurity [ˏɪnsɪˋkjʊrətɪ] *n.* 不安全；危險
3. happen to *v.* 正好；碰巧
4. recruit [rɪˋkrut] *v.* 徵募新成員；雇用
5. hunch [hʌntʃ] *v.* 弓起背
6. plot [plɑt] *v.* 密謀；策劃
7. encounter [ɪnˋkaʊntɚ] *v.* 遇到；遭遇
8. do-gooder [ˋduˏgʊdɚ] *n.* 做好事的人

Kevin Mitnick is arguably[9] the most famous former hacker. At the hacker gathering in Las Vegas, where he now lives and works as a security consultant,[10] he's treated like a celebrity. He served nearly five years in federal prison for breaking into systems at several major corporations. He was released in January 2000.

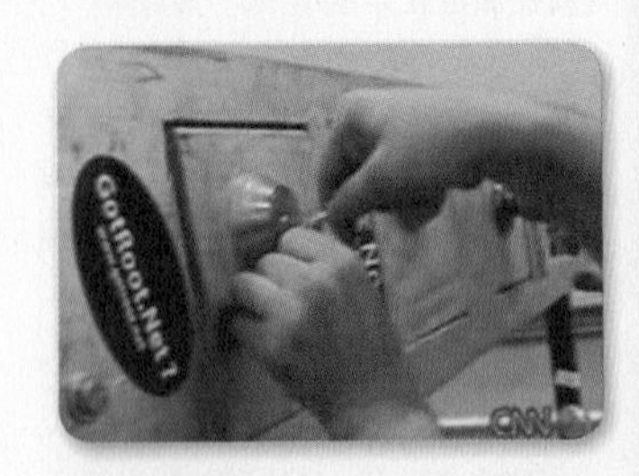

Kevin Mitnick, Former Hacker

It's like the bite of the forbidden fruit. It's all about knowledge and information and sharing, and it's [up] to each individual's own morals and ethics[11] of how they're going to use that information. Is it going to be for good or is it going to be for bad.

Daniel Sieberg, NEXT@CNN

Many hack into their own devices, like video game machines. Some simply want to see what's under the hood.

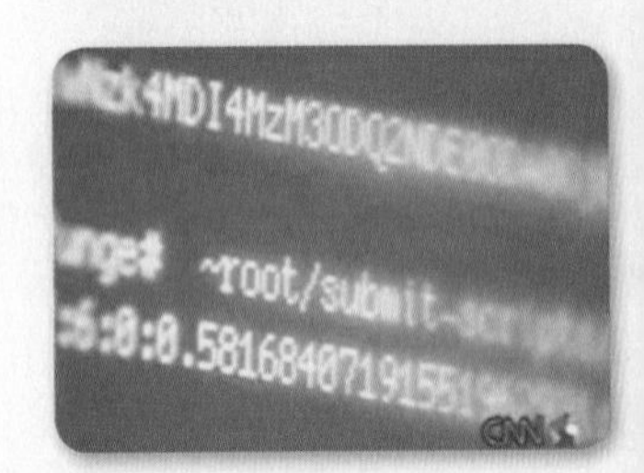

Bunnie, Hacker

Guys who really like cars will buy a cheap car like a Honda Civic or something, and they'll put all these fins[12] on it and new wheels and they'll just do everything. By the time they're through with it, it's like a completely different car. Hackers are exactly the same sort of thing. They're just really into the network or they're really into their video games or something like that.

凱文·米特尼克大概可算是最有名的前駭客。他目前居住在賭城，擔任安全顧問，他在駭客大會上受到明星般的待遇，他先前因為入侵若干大公司的系統而在聯邦監獄裡服了近五年的刑期，在二〇〇〇年一月獲釋。

前駭客 凱文·米特尼克

這就像是偷嚐禁果一樣。在駭客的世界裡，一切就是知識、資訊以及分享交換知識與資訊；至於要怎麼運用這些資訊，則完全仰賴個人的道德觀所決定。他們可以決定用來為善，也可以用來為惡。

《科技新世代》丹尼爾·席柏格

有許多人會拆開自己的機器，例如電玩遊戲機。有些人則只是對裡面的東西感到好奇。

駭客 邦尼

愛車人會買一輛像喜美這種便宜的車，然後加裝整流板，換輪胎，用各種方式加以改裝。完工之後，這輛車就完全變了一個模樣。駭客也和愛車人一樣。他們要不是熱愛網路，就是熱愛電腦遊戲，或者諸如此類東西。

Notes & Vocabulary

forbidden fruit 禁果

舊約聖經《創世紀》章中記載，上帝將亞當（Adam）和夏娃（Eve）安置在伊甸園（Eden），告訴他們園中所有的果子都可以隨意食用，唯有「分別善惡樹」上的果子絕不可以碰，然而兩人受到蛇的蠱惑而偷吃了禁果，開始知道善惡羞恥，上帝震怒之下將他們逐出了伊甸園。後來西方文化中便以 forbidden fruit（禁果）比喻為法律或道德所不容的歡愉。

- Melissa thought reading banned literature was like eating forbidden fruit.
  梅莉莎覺得讀禁書彷彿就像偷嚐禁果一般。

what's under the hood 葫蘆裡賣的是什麼藥

hood 可指「引擎蓋」，而引擎蓋底下便是引擎以及其他相關機械，然而，汽車的運轉除了引擎蓋下的硬體設備之外，還包括許多機械動力學的理論，因此 what's under the hood 便有表示對某個產品內含有什麼軟、硬體感到好奇之意。

- The car doesn't look fast, but it has a powerful engine under the hood.
  那輛車看起來跑不快，但它其實有很有力的引擎。

9. **arguably** [ˋɑrgjuəblɪ] *adv.* 可以認為；有理由地
10. **consultant** [kənˋsʌltənt] *n.* 顧問；參謀
11. **ethic** [ˋɛθɪk] *n.* 道德；規律（常作複數）
12. **fin** [fɪn] *n.*（汽車等的）整流板

Daniel Sieberg, NEXT@CNN

In a few cases they're exactly who the government is looking for. Not to incarcerate,[13] but to hire. At this hacker gathering, the feds are part of the program.

Linton Wells, U.S. Dept. of Defense

We don't have all the answers. We seek talent wherever we can find it, and so here there's a significant[14] talent pool[15] that's worthwhile[16] tapping into.[17] At the same time, there's a line that we cannot cross. If people have engaged[18] in illegal behavior, then we're not interested in having them work for us.

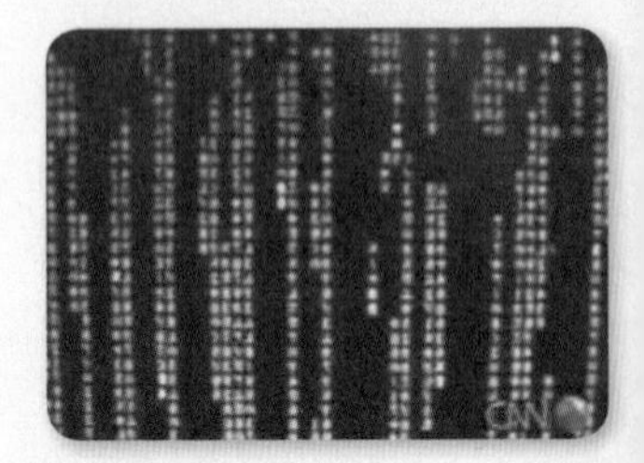

Daniel Sieberg, NEXT@CNN

Like any field of expertise,[19] there are those who would enhance[20] it and those who would exploit[21] it. The hacking world is no different.

《科技新世代》丹尼爾．席柏格

他們之中有些人正是政府所要找的對象。不是要抓去關起來，而是要予以雇用。在這場駭客聚會當中，聯邦調查人員也參與了這項計劃。

美國國防部 林頓．威爾斯

我們並非無所不知，我們只是隨時隨地在找尋傑出人才，而這裡正好有個重要的人才庫，值得來挖掘。同時，我們也有一條不能跨越的界線。如果有人涉及犯罪行為，我們就不會找他來效力。

《科技新世代》丹尼爾．席柏格

在每個專業領域當中，都可能有促進該領域發展的人才，也會有濫用專業技術的壞蛋。駭客的世界也是一樣。

Notes & Vocabulary

the feds 聯邦調查局人員

fed 是 federal 的簡稱，fed 在此可指 federal agent、federal official（聯邦調查局人員，即 FBI），通常會用複數 the feds 來表示，而用 the feds 來稱 FBI 為口語用法，大約是從一九一六年開始的。

13. incarcerate [ɪn`kɑrsə͵ret] *v.* 監禁
14. significant [sɪg`nɪfɪkənt] *adj.* 具重大意義的
15. talent pool [`tælənt] [pul] *n. phr.* 人才庫
16. worthwhile [`wɝθ`waɪl] *adj.* 值得的
17. tap into *v.* 利用；採用；開發
18. engage [ɪn`gedʒ] *v.* 從事
19. expertise [͵ɛkspɚ`tiz] *n.* 專門知識；專門技術
20. enhance [ɪn`hæns] *v.* 提高；改進；增強
21. exploit [ɪk`splɔɪt] *v.* 利用；剝削

Staying Alive in the Triangle of Death

我要活著回去——駐伊美軍每日面對的死亡威脅

Step 1 如果你是使用 MP3 ，請聽 MP3 Track 105；如果你使用電腦互動光碟，請點選 DVD-ROM【實戰應用篇—Part II：Unit 6】，試試看是否聽懂新聞內容。

Step 2 請瀏覽下列關鍵字彙，再仔細聽一次。

reassure 使放心	improvise 臨時湊成
suit up 全副武裝	impending 即將發生的
insurgency 暴力突襲	accomplice 共犯

Step 3 如果你還不是聽的很懂的話，請參考下列發音提示，再仔細聽一次。

連音	stall owners、insurgent attack、turns civilians、next task
省略音	worst stretch

試著作答下列聽力測驗題目。

True or False 是非題

____ 1. The soldiers know they could run into a bomb any time they go out.

____ 2. The safest road in the Triangle of Death is called Route Tampa.

____ 3. Finding friends is very easy for the American soldiers.

____ 4. The soldiers think the Iraqis they questioned are telling the truth.

____ 5. The Iraqi commander on duty wasn't wearing his uniform.

____ 6. One of the soldiers interviewed knew a soldier killed by a bomb.

Multiple Choice 選擇題

____ 1. What do soldiers in Iraq have to do every day?

a. train the Iraq army
b. reassure local civilians
c. suit up to go on patrol
d. all of the above

____ 2. What is another name for roadside bombs?

a. LTD　　b. IED
c. ITC　　d. LED

____ 3. What do the soldiers not want to do when asking for information?

a. create new enemies
b. look at people in the eye
c. turn accomplices into civilians
d. walk a fine line

____ 4. What does the American officer think of the Iraqi soldiers?

a. They're improving every day.
b. They're scared to death.
c. They won't survive an attack.
d. They work hard.

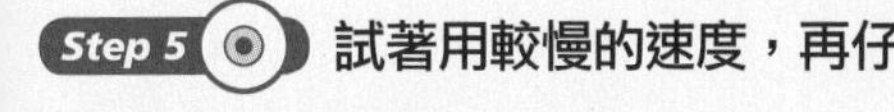

試著用較慢的速度，再仔細聽一遍（MP3 Track 106），檢查答案是否正確。

對答案、驗收成果，並詳讀原文，若仍有不懂的地方，可反覆多聽幾次。

（答案請見 p. 314）

CNN Anchor

Every day in Iraq U.S. soldiers work very hard to reassure[1] local civilians,[2] train the Iraqi army and stay alive. But with the increasing power of improvised[3] explosive devices, IEDs, staying alive takes a lot of training and time. Aneesh Raman is embedded[4] with American soldiers in Northern Babil province.[5]

Aneesh Raman, CNN Correspondent

Like the soldiers he commands,[6] Lieutenant Colonel[7] Ross Brown suits up[8] daily, trying to rid his area of[9] roadside bombs.

Lt. Col. Ross Brown

Whenever you roll out[10] of the gate and you're out there operating, you don't know if you're going to hit one of these or not.

Aneesh Raman, CNN Correspondent

The first stop today is Route Tampa, some of the worst stretch[11] of highway in what's called the "Triangle of Death," where these stall[12] owners, Brown's told, are aware of impending[13] attack.

Lt. Col. Ross Brown

Did you know in advance that the IED was going to go off?[14]

U.S. Soldier (Translator)

No.

Lt. Col. Ross Brown

Tell him to look me in the eye and tell me that again. He's lying.

CNN 主播

駐紮在伊拉克的美軍每天都得努力安定當地民心，訓練伊拉克軍隊，並設法保住自己的性命。但隨著即造爆炸裝置 IED 的威脅力逐漸增強，美軍也必須耗費大量時間、接受許多訓練才能保命。以下是阿尼許．拉曼跟隨美軍在北巴比爾省的報導。

CNN 特派員 阿尼許．拉曼

羅斯．布朗中校和他麾下的士兵一樣，每天都會全副武裝，設法除去設置在轄區內的土製炸彈。

羅斯．布朗中校

每次出了營區大門開始在外作業，你就不知道自己會不會碰上一枚這樣的炸彈。

CNN 特派員 阿尼許．拉曼

今天的第一站是坦帕路，這段被稱為「死亡三角」的路程，是最危險的快速道路路段之一。布朗聽說，這些攤販對於何時會有攻擊發生都很清楚。

羅斯．布朗中校

你事先就知道那顆 IED 炸彈會爆炸了嗎？

美軍（翻譯員）

不知道。

羅斯．布朗中校

叫他看著我的眼睛再說一次。他在說謊。

Notes & Vocabulary

improvised explosive device, IED
即造爆炸裝置

這個名詞是用來稱呼游擊隊、恐怖份子、突擊部隊等所製造的非正統爆裂性裝置，亦稱作 roadside bomb，就是中文所謂的「土製炸彈」。這類爆裂物的設計千變萬化，製造水準不一，但當製造者具足夠資源和技巧，便可使成品精密穩定，恐怖組織尤其擅長此道。他們通常從經由特殊管道得來的正統軍火武器中，取出火藥等爆裂物質，再以容易取得的電鈴或手機等電子裝置改裝成引爆器，造出致爆率和殺傷力都很高的炸彈。這種從正宗軍火的火藥改製成的 IED 則可稱為 homemade bomb。

1. **reassure** [ˏriəˋʃʊr] *v.* 使放心；使消除疑慮
2. **civilian** [səˋvɪljən] *n.* 平民百姓
3. **improvise** [ˋɪmprəˏvaɪz] *v.* 臨時湊成；就地製作
4. **embed** [ɪmˋbɛd] *v.* 嵌入；使…… 附在……內
5. **province** [ˋprɑvəns] *n.* 省份
6. **command** [kəˋmænd] *v.* 指揮；控制；命令
7. **lieutenant colonel** [luˋtɛnənt] [ˋkɝnl̩] *n.* 美國陸軍、空軍或海軍陸戰隊中校
8. **suit up** *v.* 穿戴齊全（為特定任務或活動）；全副武裝
9. **rid . . . of** [rɪd] *v.* 消滅；清除；除去；擺脫
10. **roll out** *v.* 離開
11. **stretch** [strɛtʃ] *n.*（土地、時間的）延亙；連綿
12. **stall** [stɔl] *n.* 攤位；攤子；貨攤
13. **impending** [ɪmˋpɛndɪŋ] *adj.* 即將發生的；逼近的
14. **go off** *v.* 爆炸

Aneesh Raman, CNN Correspondent

It is a fine line to walk. Routing out information without creating new enemies, battling an insurgency[15] that kills at will[16]—that turns civilians into accomplices.[17] Finding friends locally seems the toughest part of Brown's strategy, but his next task proves just as difficult.

Here the Lieutenant Colonel has stopped at one of the firm bases, one of the areas that Iraqis are manning[18] their own position. The commander on duty emerges[19] out of uniform and the lieutenant colonel struggles[20] to find progress.

Lt. Col. Ross Brown

They didn't do too much work yesterday; they didn't do too much work the day before; they haven't done too much work since they've been here.

Aneesh Raman, CNN Correspondent

Brown is unsure if this unit can survive an insurgent[21] attack, uncertainties shared by the U.S. forces as well, each soldier with his own way to cope.

U.S. Soldiers

I carry my wedding ring, a bracelet my wife sent me.
Carry a Bible, Psalms 91.
Picture of an angel. Archangel.

Aneesh Raman, CNN Correspondent

Overhead helicopters are responding to an IED attack that moments ago killed Colonel William Wood, the highest-ranking U.S. officer to die in combat[22] in Iraq. A personal friend of Brown's, an added personal reason why tomorrow he'll be suiting up again.

CNN 特派員 阿尼許．拉曼

分寸很難拿捏。在對抗這些肆意殺戮的突擊過程中，一面要取得情報，一面還要小心避免樹立新敵人，而這些殺戮攻擊也將平民百姓變成共犯。布朗所採取的策略中，最難的部分就是在當地找到盟友，而他的下一項任務也同樣棘手。

布朗中校的部隊在一座駐紮基地停下腳步，這裡是伊拉克人派兵駐守的陣地之一。當地的值星官未著軍裝就現身，布朗中校很努力想看到他們的訓練是否有任何一點進展。

羅斯．布朗中校

他們昨天沒做什麼事，前一天也沒做什麼事。他們自從來到這裡以後，根本沒怎麼在幹活兒。

CNN 特派員 阿尼許．拉曼

布朗不太確定這支部隊如果遇到突襲有沒有辦法存活。這樣的不確定感在美軍間瀰漫，每名士兵都有自己的適應方法。

美軍

我手上戴著婚戒，和一條我太太寄給我的手鍊。
我帶著聖經詩篇 91 篇。
一張天使的照片，大天使。

CNN 特派員 阿尼許．拉曼

在我頭頂上，直昇機正在對剛才發生的一次 IED 炸彈攻擊進行反擊，威廉．伍德上校在這次炸彈攻擊中身亡，他是目前在伊拉克戰役中死亡的美軍軍階最高的軍官。他也是布朗中校的一個好友，這又多給了布朗一項私人理由，讓他明天再次全副武裝上陣去。

Notes & Vocabulary

rout out 搜出；挖掘出

rout 作動詞用，可以用來形容豬或其他動物用鼻子在地上翻翻找找的覓食動作，進而引申為「搜索；探尋」之意。rout out 代表「搜出；挖掘到」，通常含有「費了一番工夫；付出不少心血」的意味，也可以說 root out。

- Police routed out several terrorist cells.
  警方搜到了幾個恐怖份子的巢穴。

on duty 值勤中

duty 在此指的是「職務」，on duty 的相反詞為 off duty。

- The city pool had two lifeguards on duty.
  市立游泳池有兩名救生員值勤。
- The thief was caught by an off-duty cop.
  這名竊賊被一位非勤務中的警察抓到。

duty 也可以指「稅；關稅」，如免稅則可說 duty-free。

- Sam bought some chocolate at the duty-free shop in the airport.
  山姆在機場免稅商店買了些巧克力。

duty 也可指「責任；義務」，相關的用法有 duty bound to do sth，指「有責任去做某事」。

- Jack felt duty bound to go to the police with information about the kidnapping.
  傑克知道那樁綁架案相關消息，他覺得有責任去報案。

15. **insurgency** [ɪnˋsɜdʒənsɪ] *n.* 暴力突擊；暴動
16. **at will** *phr.* 任意；隨心所欲地
17. **accomplice** [əˋkɑmpləs] *n.* 共犯；共謀
18. **man** [mæn] *v.* 部署人員；就位
19. **emerge** [ɪˋmɜdʒ] *v.* 出現；現身；浮現
20. **struggle** [ˋstrʌgəl] *v.* 費力、困難重重地前進
21. **insurgent** [ɪnˋsɜdʒənt] *adj.* 叛亂的；暴動的
22. **combat** [ˋkɑmˏbæt] *n.* 戰役；戰鬥

Design Acrobatics

Adobe Tries to Outmaneuver Software Rival Microsoft

Adobe 卯上微軟　軟體大戰開打

Step 1 如果你是使用 MP3 ，請聽 MP3 Track 107；如果你使用電腦互動光碟，請點選 DVD-ROM【實戰應用篇—Part II：Unit 7】，試試看是否聽懂新聞內容。

Step 2 請瀏覽下列關鍵字彙，再仔細聽一次。

building blocks 基礎要件	ubiquitous 普遍存在的
clip 削減	assault 襲擊
copycat 模仿者	bring . . . into the fold 將……納入旗下

Step 3 如果你還不是聽的很懂的話，請參考下列發音提示，再仔細聽一次。

連音	all-out assault、sets its sight on something
省略音	software

試著作答下列聽力測驗題目。

True or False 是非題

____ 1. Adobe says its programs are on more computers than Microsoft's Windows.

____ 2. Photoshop, Illustrator and Acrobat are all Microsoft products.

____ 3. Almost all computers can read Adobe PDFs.

____ 4. Microsoft is planning on buying Adobe very soon.

____ 5. Experts think the economic slowdown will help Acrobat's business.

____ 6. There is a new version of Adobe that can show blueprints in 3-D.

Multiple Choice 選擇題

____ 1. What was the expected growth of Adobe in the year of the report?

a. 1.9 percent b. 3.4 percent
c. 15 percent d. 29 percent

____ 2. What company is Adobe going to pay $3.4 billion to take over?

a. Microsoft b. Macromedia
c. Acrobat d. Coke

____ 3. Which company is known as the "beast from Redmond?"

a. Adobe b. Macromedia
c. Acrobat d. Microsoft

____ 4. How will most Indians and Chinese likely be accessing the Internet?

a. on a mobile device b. at home
c. on a PC d. by going to America

試著用較慢的速度，再仔細聽一遍 (MP3 Track 108)，檢查答案是否正確。

Step 6 對答案、驗收成果，並詳讀原文，若仍有不懂的地方，可反覆多聽幾次。

(答案請見 p. 314)

Christie Lu Stout, SPARK

While we're all familiar with Microsoft, one of its rivals is steadily becoming a major player in helping media outlets[3] to realize[4] their visions. When I was in California for last month's show, I entered the world of Adobe.

A pop video, a can of Coke, a magazine layout[5]—no matter where you look, Adobe is probably there.

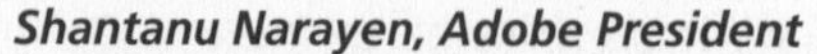

Shantanu Narayen, Adobe President

If you look at the different ways in which people are communicating—through print, through Web, through video, through wireless—as well as, you know, the different devices on which people are consuming information—if you want it to be good, chances are it's Adobe software that's helping you do that.

Christie Lu Stout, SPARK

Photoshop, Illustrator, Acrobat—these are the building blocks of almost everything you see in print and on the Web. And just when you thought Microsoft ruled the world, Adobe says its technology sits on[6] more computers than Windows. Give it up for the humble PDF, Adobe's format for viewing digital documents.

Shantanu Narayen, Adobe President

We think it's virtually ubiquitous.[7] I don't know of a single PC which doesn't have the ability to read the Adobe PDF file format.

《科技新火花》克莉絲蒂．陸．史道

大家都熟知微軟公司，微軟的其中一個對手正穩健地成為協助媒體事業實現遠景的重要業者。上個月我在加州做節目時，進入了奧多比（Adobe）的殿堂。

一支流行音樂錄影帶，一罐可樂，或一本雜誌的版面設計，舉目所及，都可能有奧多比的蹤影。

奧多比總裁 山塔努．納拉言

你只要看看人們彼此不同的溝通方式，透過平面印刷、網路、影像、無線傳輸等、種種人們使用資訊的工具，如果你希望它夠好用的話，很可能幫你達成目標的都是奧多比研發的軟體。

《科技新火花》克莉絲蒂．陸．史道

Photoshop、Illustrator、Acrobat，這些都是建構平面印刷和網路上一切文字與圖像的基礎元素。就在你以為微軟稱霸天下時，奧多比卻說該公司研發的軟體，安裝於電腦中的比例比微軟視窗多。不露鋒芒的數位文件檔案閱讀格式 PDF，即為奧多比的產品。

奧多比總裁 山塔努．納拉言

我們覺得它幾乎無所不在。我不知道有哪台個人電腦無法讀取奧多比的 PDF 檔案格式。

Notes & Vocabulary

building blocks 基礎要件

block 意思是「塊狀物、積木」。building blocks 原指建築工程中一塊塊可堆疊在一起，以小單位集合起來形成大型構造體的「砌塊」，後引申為事物的「基礎材料」、「基本要素」。

- A healthy diet and exercise are the building blocks of good health.
  良好的飲食習慣和運動是保持身體健康的基本要素。

give it up for 為……掌聲鼓勵

此為口語上的說法，即中文的「讓我們為……拍拍手、鼓鼓掌」之意，常在節目或活動中主持人帶領觀眾歡迎某人、物出場時使用，等同於 to applaud for、(let's) give a big hand to 或 have a round of applause for。

- The emcee told the audience to give it up for the show's star.
  主持人請觀眾為參加節目的明星鼓掌。

1. **acrobatics** [ˏækrəˋbætɪks] *n.* 巧妙手法；技巧
2. **outmaneuver** [ˏaʊtməˋnuvɚ] *v.* 運用策略擊敗；以計謀勝過
3. **outlet** [ˋaʊtˏlɛt] *n.* 商店；暢貨中心
4. **realize** [ˋriəˏlaɪz] *v.* 實現
5. **layout** [ˋleˏaʊt] *n.* （書籍、廣告等）版面設計；佈局
6. **sit on** *v.* 裝置在……中；存在於
7. **ubiquitous** [juˋbɪkwətəs] *adj.* 到處都是的；普遍存在的

Christie Lu Stout, SPARK

The company's Acrobat software writes the files. Sales of Acrobat along with Adobe's other titles are fueling the company's 15-percent growth forecast this year to a revenue target of $1.9 billion. And yet, Adobe is facing a rough patch.[8] There's an economic slowdown[9] that could clip[10] media budgets and hurt one of its core clients—creative professionals. And then, there's Microsoft. The software giant is planning an all-out[11] assault[12] with an Acrobat copycat.[13]

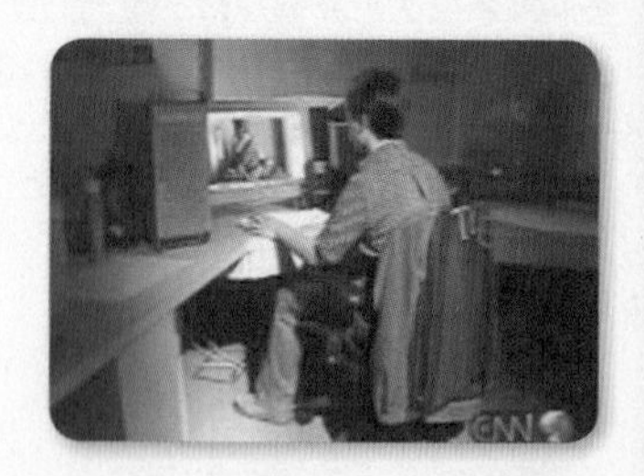

Michael Gartenberg, Jupiter Research

When Microsoft sets its sights on something, you want to take that seriously. They can't ignore the threat, but they're well poised[14] right now to defend against it.

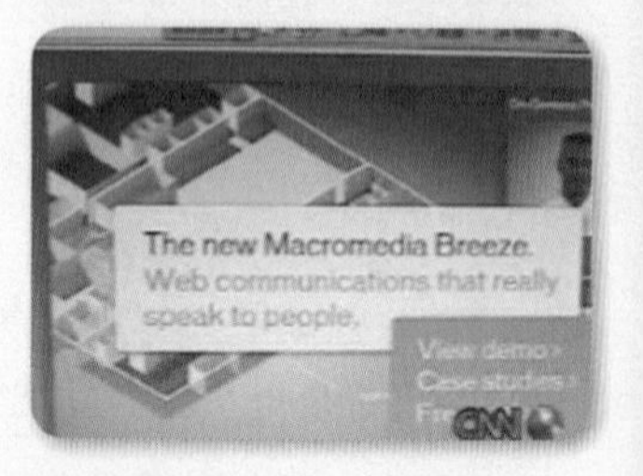

Christie Lu Stout, SPARK

Adobe stands a better chance[15] of fighting off[16] the beast from Redmond thanks to a $3.4 billion takeover[17] deal. The target—Macromedia, a software house known for its Web design tools, as well as Flash, the popular Web animation[18] technology. By bringing Macromedia into the fold, Narayen believes his company can better serve an emerging digital audience.

《科技新火花》克莉絲蒂．陸．史道

該公司的 Acrobat 軟體負責編寫 PDF 檔案。Acrobat 搭配奧多比其他軟體的銷售成績，將該公司今年的獲利預測推升了百分之十五，年營收目標為十九億美元。但奧多比卻面臨一道難題。經濟成長減緩可能使該公司縮減媒體預算，進而傷害到該公司的一部分核心客戶：創意專業人士。另外還有微軟。這家軟體巨擘正計畫推出一種與 Acrobat 雷同的軟體，打算對奧多比發動全面攻擊。

朱比特研究 麥可．卡頓柏格

一旦微軟將目光鎖定某樣東西時，你就要小心了。他們不能忽視這項威脅，但他們現在在市場上站得夠穩，足以對抗微軟的攻勢。

《科技新火花》克莉絲蒂．陸．史道

拜一筆價值三十四億美元的併購案之賜，如今奧多比有更大的勝算能擊退微軟這隻巨獸（註）。奧多比的併購目標 Macromedia，這是一家以網頁設計工具聞名的軟體公司，其中包括廣受好評的網路動畫科技 Flash。在將 Macromedia 納入旗下後，納拉言相信奧多比將能為越來越多的數位用戶提供更好的服務。

註：Redmond 位於美國華盛頓州西雅圖附近，是微軟公司總部的所在地。

Notes & Vocabulary

set one's sights on 將……作為目標

sight 原指「視力；目光」，在這裡則是「目標；志向」。set one's sights on 就相當於「將其眼光放在……、將目光鎖定在……」，引申表示「將目標設定在……」之意。

- Marcus set his sights on a management position.
  馬可斯將目標設定在管理職。

bring . . . into the fold 將……帶入（群體、集團）；將……納入旗下

fold 作名詞可表示「羊群」。此語原意是牧人將落單的羊隻帶進羊群中，引申為將某個對象納入群體中，使其加入某一特定團體之意。如本文的奧多比公司收購 Macromedia 公司，使其成了奧多比家族的一員。

- The company brought several new sales executives into the fold.
  這家公司為自己的工作團隊帶進了幾位新的業務主管。

8. **patch** [pætʃ] *n.* 期間；一段時間
9. **slowdown** [ˋslo͵daʊn] *n.* 減緩；減速
10. **clip** [klɪp] *v.* 削減；減少；刪去
11. **all-out** [ˋɔlˋaʊt] *adj.* 全力以赴的
12. **assault** [əˋsɔlt] *n.* 襲擊；攻擊
13. **copycat** [ˋkɑpɪ͵kæt] *n.* 模仿品；抄襲者
14. **poised** [pɔɪzd] *adj.* 泰然自若的；不慌不忙的；準備好的
15. **stand a chance** *v. phr.* 有可能；有希望（成功、獲勝等）
16. **fight off** *v.* 擊退
17. **takeover** [ˋtek͵ovɚ] *n.* 併購
18. **animation** [͵ænəˋmeʃən] *n.* 動畫

Shantanu Narayen, Adobe President

Mobility[19] is a huge area. I mean, when you think about countries in Asia, countries like India and China, where people will likely access the Internet through a mobile device rather than a PC, we want to be the company that enables people to offer content for those devices.

Christie Lu Stout, SPARK

But more immediate returns are expected from the latest version[20] of PDF, a version that supports 3-D animated blueprints[21] for engineers and architects. Now this is a full-throttle digital file and it's coming soon to a desktop near you.

奧多比總裁 山塔努・納拉言

移動性是極大的商機所在。像在亞洲的印度、中國這些國家，人們可能會想要透過行動工具而非個人電腦來上網。我們想成為一家公司，而這家公司是能幫助那些為行動工具提供內容的人。

《科技新火花》克莉絲蒂・陸・史道

奧多比預計近期將有更多的獲利來自新推出的最新版 PDF 格式，新版本將可支援工程師和建築師使用的 3-D 立體動畫藍圖軟體。不久後您將可以在生活周遭的電腦中看到這種功能強大的數位檔案。

Notes & Vocabulary

full-throttle 強力的

throttle 是機件中控制燃料進量的節流閥（如汽車的油門），決定機件運轉動力的強弱或轉速的高低。如果運轉的情況是油門全開、全速運轉或前進，英文就是用 at full throttle 來表示，這個用法可引申表示「為……盡全力、全速進行（某事）」。文中的 full throttle 是加上連字號轉為形容詞來表示「功能最強的、強力的」。

- He's working at full throttle to get the job finished.
  他正傾全力來完成這份工作。

19. **mobility** [mo`bɪlətɪ] *n.*
    行動力；移動性（**mobile** 為形容詞）
20. **version** [`vɝʒən] *n.* 版本
21. **blueprint** [`bluˏprɪnt] *n.* 藍圖

That Sinking Feeling

Reversing the Effects of Time and Tide in Venice

水都威尼斯的水患之苦

Step 1 如果你是使用 MP3 ，請聽 MP3 Track 109；如果你使用電腦互動光碟，請點選 DVD-ROM【實戰應用篇—Part II：Unit 8】，試試看是否聽懂新聞內容。

Step 2 請瀏覽下列關鍵字彙，再仔細聽一次。

astonishing 驚人的	embark on 從事
under way 在進行中地	hinged 裝有鉸鏈的
barrier 水閘；柵欄	lagoon 潟湖
inlet 入口；小水灣	

Step 3 如果你還不是聽的很懂的話，請參考下列發音提示，再仔細聽一次。

連音	has strong opinions、flood defense systems
去捲舌音	owner、bookstore、personal、portico、river

試著作答下列聽力測驗題目。

True or False 是非題

____ 1. Businesses in Venice close for 70 to 90 days each year because of flooding.

____ 2. The barriers will come up when the water level is too high.

____ 3. The authorities say flooding is part of Venice's culture and must be accepted.

____ 4. Alberto Scotti says that it will be extremely difficult to stop the flooding.

____ 5. The Thames Barrier has caused a lot of environmental problems.

____ 6. The Mose project will be completed by 2007.

Multiple Choice 選擇題

____ 1. Why has the Venetian government decided to build the Mose project?

a. to attract tourists
b. to compete with other countries
c. to protect the English capital
d. the flooding was no longer acceptable

____ 2. Where will the barriers for the flood defense system be located?

a. on the portico outside the shop
b. at the inlets of the lagoons near the city
c. at the city gates
d. across the river at Woolwich Reach

____ 3. In which other European countries have similar flood defense systems been built?

a. England and France
b. Germany and France
c. England and Holland
d. Holland and Spain

____ 4. How much will it cost to build the Mose project?

a. $50 million
b. $2 billion
c. $4.5 billion
d. $20 billion

試著用較慢的速度，再仔細聽一遍（MP3 Track 110），檢查答案是否正確。

對答案、驗收成果，並詳讀原文，若仍有不懂的地方，可反覆多聽幾次。

（答案請見 p. 314）

Shantelle Stein, CNN Correspondent

Like most of his fellow Venetians,[2] Cesare Zanini has strong opinions on what should be done to save his city from flooding. As the owner of a bookstore, his interests are both personal and professional.

Cesare Zanini, Owner, Libreria Sansovino

The problem is that we just can't work. On average, we lose from 70 to 90 working days a year just because of the flooding. Just outside the shop on that portico,[3] when the water level rises to 85 centimeters above sea level, it spills over.[4] And when that happens, there's 20 centimeters of water on the ground itself, and that means people don't walk by, so our business dries up.[5]

Shantelle Stein, CNN Correspondent

Every year the city attracts up to 50 million tourists, drawn to one of the world's most beautiful and astonishing[6] places. But while it is undoubtedly the water that brings the visitors, it is also in danger of killing the city. Every year businesses lose millions of dollars because of the flooding, a situation that the authorities realize is no longer financially or culturally acceptable. To that end,[7] the city has embarked on[8] one of the most ambitious building projects currently under way[9] in the world, namely[10] the construction of a set of massive underground gates designed to protect the city.

CNN 特派員 珊泰兒・史坦

西薩・札尼尼和大多數威尼斯人一樣，對於當地水患的防治之道胸有定見。他是一間書店的老闆，水患的問題不僅影響到他個人，也影響到他的生意。

桑索維諾書店老闆 西薩・札尼尼

問題在於我們沒辦法工作。我們每年光是因為水災，就平均損失七十到九十個工作天。就在店門外門廊那邊，每當水位上升到高過海平面八十五公分的時候，水就會淹進來。這時候地面積水足足有二十公分高，那就表示一般人不會走經這裡，我們的生意就乏人問津了。

CNN 特派員 珊泰兒・史坦

每年威尼斯都會吸引五千萬觀光客來到這個堪稱世上最美、最令人讚嘆的地方。毫無疑問的，水是吸引眾多訪客來此一遊的原因，但水同時也威脅了這座城市的生命。每年威尼斯都因水災損失數百萬美元的生意，政府當局知道這種情況無論在財務面或文化面，都已經到了讓人忍無可忍的地步。為了解決這個問題，威尼斯市已展開目前全球最具雄心的建築計畫，即興建一組保護這座城市的巨型水底閘門。

Notes & Vocabulary

that sinking feeling
事情不妙的感覺；懊喪、擔憂的心情

標題中的 sinking 表示「向下沈、被淹沒」，同時也有「沮喪」的意思。sinking feeling 是指見到事情有惡化的徵兆或趨勢，知道將會出問題而感到憂慮、無奈或懊喪。

- When the stock price slipped, investors began to get that sinking feeling.
  當股價下滑，投資人開始覺得事情不妙而憂心忡忡。

time and tide 時間；光陰

標題中的 time and tide 出自英文諺語：Time and tide wait for no man.，意為「歲月不居，光陰易逝」，提醒人應把握時間，也可用來強調歲月的無情易逝。

tide 和 time 在此都指「時間、光陰」，在古英文中，tide 是指「一段特定的時間或時令季節」，如 Christmastime 與 Christmastide 均表示「聖誕節期」。此外，time and tide 有時也用來借喻大自然中無可避免，一定會隨時間推移而發生的事。比如本文副標題就以 the effect of time and tide 點出隨著時間過去，威尼斯水位不斷上升，當地總免不了水患之苦，同時還以 tide 字的現代字義「潮浪」玩弄了一個雙關。

- In the end, nature has the final word. As the proverb says, "Time and tide wait for no man."
  最後作主的還是大自然。正如俗語所說，歲月不居，該發生的一定會發生。

1. **reverse** [rɪˋvɝs] *v.* 徹底改變；使逆轉
2. **Venetian** [vəˋniʃən] *n.* 威尼斯人
3. **portico** [ˋpɔrtɪˏko] *n.* 柱廊；門廊
4. **spill over** [spɪl] *v.* 滿出；溢出
5. **dry up** *v.* 枯竭；乾涸
6. **astonishing** [əˋstɑnɪʃɪŋ] *adj.* 驚人的
7. **end** [ɛnd] *n.* 目標；目的
8. **embark on** [ɪmˋbɑrk] *v.* 從事；開始做
9. **under way** *adv.* 在進行中地
10. **namely** [ˋnemlɪ] *adv.* 即是；也就是

The Mose project involves 79 hinged[11] barriers[12] located at the lagoon's[13] three inlets.[14] They will rise from the seabed when high tides threaten the city. The system was designed by Alberto Scotti, who is convinced he has come up with a plan that can help man win his age-old[15] battle with the sea.

Alberto Scotti, Designer, Mose Project

I mean it's not so difficult to stop the sea. After studying [it for] 20 years, I can tell you that it can be done.

Shantelle Stein, CNN Correspondent

Other European countries, namely England and Holland, have already completed flood defense systems. In London, the Thames Barrier, which spans[16] 520 meters across the river here at Woolwich Reach,[17] took eight years and around $2 billion to build. Compact[18] and environmentally friendly, it protects the English capital from surge tides.[19]

In Rotterdam, giant swinging gates[20] meet in the middle of the river leading into the city. Again, the plan is to save the city from storm surges. Back in Venice, the $4.5 billion Mose project is due to be completed by 2011.

Over the years, several concerns have been raised about the gates, ranging from environmental to economic, but what everyone seems to agree on is that come hell or high water, Venice must be saved.

這項名為「摩西」的計畫要在連接潟湖的三個主要灣口設置七十九座鉸鏈樞紐控制的屏障。當漲潮威脅到威尼斯市時，這些屏障便會自海底升起。這套系統是由艾伯特．史考提設計，他相信自己已經想出了方法，來幫助人類打贏這場與海洋之間亙古的戰爭。

摩西計畫設計師 艾伯特．史考提

要阻擋海水並沒有那麼難。這個我研究了二十年，可以告訴你這是做得到的。

CNN 特派員 珊泰兒．史坦

其他歐洲國家，例如英國與荷蘭，都已經完成了水災防禦系統。位於倫敦沃爾威治河段，橫跨河面五百二十公尺的泰晤士水閘，前後共耗費八年時間，斥資二十億美元才興建完成。這道堅固又環保的閘門，保護英國首都免於洪水侵襲。

在鹿特丹，巨型的活動式防洪閘門位於流往市區的河川中央。這項計畫也是為了使鹿特丹市不致遭受暴風雨引發的水災侵襲。回到威尼斯，耗資四十五億美元的摩西計畫預定在二〇一一年竣工。

過去幾年來，興建防洪閘門一事引發了一些憂慮，從環保到經濟方面的問題都有，但大家似乎都有一個共識：不管有多困難，威尼斯都非救不可。

Notes & Vocabulary

come hell or high water
哪怕艱難險阻；無論如何

西洋文化中的 hell（地獄）是個烈焰永不熄的地方（例如英文中常用 not until hell freezes over「除非地獄結冰」來表達「絕不可能」之意），因此將 hell 與 high water 並列，不但構成了「水、火」兩種意象的對比，而且兼具押頭韻（alliteration）的效果。come hell or high water 在字義上代表「哪怕碰上烈火與洪水」，即「無論如何、不怕任何困難」之意，和成語「赴湯蹈火，在所不辭」頗有異曲同工之妙。

- Come hell or high water, Jim always returns home for the holidays.
  吉姆無論如何都一定會回家過節。

與此片語類似的用法還包括：

in spite of all obstacles

come what may

no matter what happens

11. **hinged** [hɪndʒd] *adj.* 裝有鉸鏈的；有鏈的
12. **barrier** [ˋbɛrɪɚ] *n.* 水閘；柵欄；阻障
13. **lagoon** [ləˋgun] *n.* 潟湖
14. **inlet** [ˋɪnˏlɛt] *n.* 入口；小水灣
15. **age-old** [ˋedʒˋold] *adj.* 古老的；由來已久的
16. **span** [spæn] *v.* 橫跨；延伸；持續
17. **reach** [ritʃ] *n.* （江、湖、河的）流域；大片地區
18. **compact** [ˋkɑmˏpækt] *adj.* 結實的；緊密的
19. **surge tide** [sɝdʒ] [taɪd] *n. phr.* 湧上的潮浪；潮浪的波濤（**surge** *n.* 波濤引起的水位上升；波濤的湧入；忽起的強潮）
20. **swinging gate** [ˋswɪŋɪŋ] [get] *n. phr.* 活動閘門；活動門

French Thumb Their Noses at Apple

iPod Maker Refuses to Sell Music Playable on Rival Products

iPod 的市場壟斷策略

Step 1 如果你是使用 MP3 ，請聽 MP3 Track 111；如果你使用電腦互動光碟，請點選 DVD-ROM【實戰應用篇—Part II：Unit 9】，試試看是否聽懂新聞內容。

Step 2 請瀏覽下列關鍵字彙，再仔細聽一次。

bill 法案	revenues 收益
parliamentary 國會的；議會的	copyright 版權
access 使用權	pricing 定價
libertarian 自由派的	

Step 3 如果你還不是聽的很懂的話，請參考下列發音提示，再仔細聽一次。

連音	approval in、played on、its opposite
去捲舌音	software、lawmaker

試著作答下列聽力測驗題目。

True or False 是非題

____ 1. French lawmakers are discussing a bill that will make Apple and Microsoft happy.

____ 2. Music purchased from Apple can only be played on Apple devices.

____ 3. Apple will not lose money if it closes down in the French market.

____ 4. The leaders in the music download market are Apple and Microsoft.

____ 5. Some people say that Apple had a good idea in the beginning.

____ 6. Apple does not make a lot of money from the iPod.

Multiple Choice 選擇題

____ 1. How much do songs bought from Apple's iTunes cost?

a. 99 cents　　b. 99 euros
c. 99 dollars　　d. 99 marks

____ 2. How will Apple probably respond to this new law?

a. Apple will raise prices on iPods.
b. Apple will share their copy protection systems with competitors.
c. Apple will face trouble in other markets.
d. Apple will pull out of the French market.

____ 3. How many songs are downloaded from iTunes every day?

a. less than one million　　b. more than three million
c. more than five million　　d. more than seven million

____ 4. Why do people love the iPod?

a. They can buy songs online.
b. It's the biggest source of revenue for Apple.
c. It's very libertarian.
d. It's a cool device.

試著用較慢的速度，再仔細聽一遍（MP3 Track 112），檢查答案是否正確。

對答案、驗收成果，並詳讀原文，若仍有不懂的地方，可反覆多聽幾次。

（答案請見 p. 314）

CNN Anchor

A bill[2] that's on its way to parliamentary[3] approval in France threatens to strike a sour note for Apple and Microsoft. The two are market leaders in the business of selling music for download, but to listen to your downloads, you have to have been using the company's own software. But lawmakers in France's lower house, the National Assembly,[4] have now voted to force the companies to make their online content available to users with rival software. Mallika Kapur reports.

Mallika Kapur, CNN Correspondent

It offers everything from Arctic Monkeys to Frank Zappa. One click and 99 cents later, the song is yours, to be played on your iPod and only on an iPod. That's because all the songs sold in Apple's iTunes store are electronically[5] locked and can only play on an iPod and no other MP3 player. But now French lawmakers want to change that, voting for a draft[6] of an online copyright[7] bill, which would force companies like Apple to share their copy protection systems with competitors. Apple may have to allow consumers in France to download music from iTunes to any device they want, not just the iPod, and iPod users, [to be] able to buy their tunes from any online store, or pull out of[8] France. How will Apple respond?

CNN 主播

法國國會即將通過的一項法案，對於蘋果與微軟來說可能是壞消息。這兩家公司是音樂下載市場的領導廠商，但是下載來的音樂必須使用該公司的軟體才能播放。法國下議院的國民議會已表決通過，要求廠商必須開放讓消費者在不同廠牌的軟體上播放線上下載的音樂檔案。瑪莉卡．卡波帶來以下的報導。

CNN 特派員 瑪莉卡．卡波

這個網站販售各種音樂，不論是北極潑猴還是法蘭克．查帕的歌曲。只要滑鼠一點，支付九十九分美元，就可以買到你要的歌曲，放在 iPod 上面播放，而且只能在 iPod 上播放，原因是蘋果 iTunes 網路商店所販售的歌曲都已電子鎖碼，只能用 iPod 播放，其他 MP3 播放器都不行。不過，法國議員打算改變這種狀況，目前已經表決通過線上版權草案，以迫使蘋果這樣的公司和其他競爭廠商分享版權保護系統。蘋果可能必須開放讓法國的消費者能把 iTunes 的音樂下載到任何播放器上，不只限於 iPod，同時也開放讓 iPod 的使用者能夠到任何網路商店去購買音樂。否則就得退出法國市場。蘋果公司會如何因應呢？

Notes & Vocabulary

thumb one's nose at
向……提出反抗；對……表示輕蔑

西方文化中有個類似作鬼臉的肢體語言，將大拇指頂在鼻子下面，然後擺動其他四隻手指，向人表現輕視不屑或抵抗不從的意思。thumb one's nose at 直接描述這個動作，意同於：make a gesture of contempt/defiance/ridicule/scorn。

- The artist thumbed his nose at the critics.
  這位藝術家對藝評人表現出輕視不屑的態度。

strike a sour note for/with
令……不愉快

note 在這裡指「音符」。a sour note 原是指演奏時因為走音而破壞整首音樂美感，形成樂曲效果不暢的音符，引申為「令人不快的事物」。所以 strike a sour note for 就是對……採取某種不利的行動，導致對方不愉快或不順利之意。

- Management struck a sour note with workers when it announced pay cuts.
  管理階層宣佈減薪，令員工相當不快。

1. rival [ˋraɪvl̩] *adj.* 競爭對手的
2. bill [bɪl] *n.* 法案
3. parliamentary [ˏpɑrləˋmɛntərɪ] *adj.* 國會的；議會的
4. assembly [əˋsɛmblɪ] *n.* 議會
5. electronically [ɪˏlɛkˋtrɑnɪklɪ] *adv.* 電子地
6. draft [dræft] *n.* 草案
7. copyright [ˋkɑpɪˏraɪt] *n.* 版權
8. pull out of *v.* 從……撤出

Jonathan Arbur, Ovum

France is not a major source of revenues[9] for Apple, and its business model[10] for iTunes and the iPod is built upon the fact that it's a very . . . kind of closed model. I think it will choose to just take a hit on its revenues and perhaps close down[11] in the French market, rather than be forced to break this, and then possibly, you know, face troubles in other markets.

Mallika Kapur, CNN Correspondent

One online music executive hopes the move will loosen Apple's grip[12] on the online music market.

Rudy Tambala, Virgin Digital

I think that Apple's initial[13] impulse[14] to create a service of excellence[15] was the right impulse. It's kind of turned into its opposite now that it's starting to restrict[16] the consumers' access[17] and its consumers' flexibility.[18] A consumer should have the ability to make a choice of different stores. They should make the choice of different pricing[19] models that they go for. But with the Apple model, you have only one choice. And it's kind of . . . not very libertarian.[20]

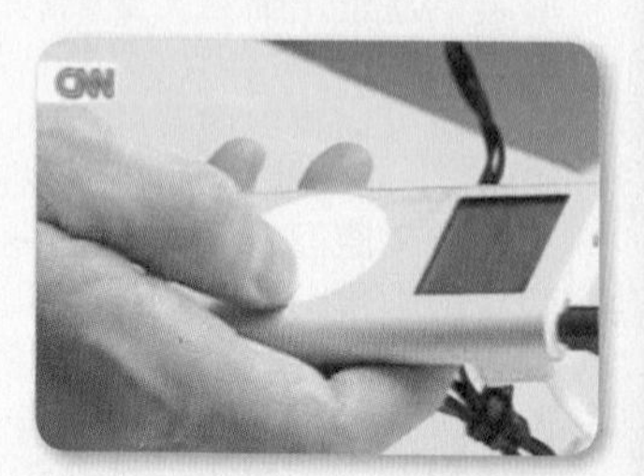

Mallika Kapur, CNN Correspondent

But it's popular. Apple says more than three million songs a day are downloaded off iTunes.

Jonathan Arbur, Ovum

People love iPods chiefly[21] because the iPod is a cool device.

Mallika Kapur, CNN Correspondent

So cool, it's the single biggest source of revenue for Apple.

歐馮市調公司 強納森．亞伯

法國不是蘋果公司主要的收入來源，而且 iTunes 與 iPod 的經營模式是一種封閉模式。我認為蘋果會選擇承受營收損失，甚至退出法國市場，而不會同意開放版權保護系統，以免其他市場出現問題。

CNN 特派員 瑪莉卡．卡波

一家線上音樂公司主管希望此舉能鬆動蘋果對線上音樂市場的箝制。

維京數位 魯迪．唐巴拉

我認為蘋果原本想要創造優質服務的動機是正確的。不過，現在已經呈現相反的發展狀況，反而限制了消費者的選擇彈性。消費者應該能夠自由選擇不同的商店，自由選擇不同的定價模式。不過，在蘋果提供的模式之下，消費者只能有一種選擇，這實在不太符合自由主義的概念（註）。

CNN 特派員 瑪莉卡．卡波

但是卻很熱門。蘋果表示，每天從 iTunes 下載的歌曲多達三百萬首。

歐馮市調公司 強納森．亞伯

大眾喜歡 iPod，主要是因為 iPod 很炫。

CNN 特派員 瑪莉卡．卡波

炫到什麼程度呢？iPod 可是蘋果最大的營收來源。

註：蘋果一向以標榜自由、不受體制侷限的精神作為行銷策略來吸引客群。

Notes & Vocabulary

take a hit 承擔損失

hit 作名詞時雖然有「安打」、「暢銷作品（例如電影、歌曲或書籍）」等較為正面的意義，但在此片語中則表示「打擊、挫折或損失」，可代換為 beating、blow、know。

- Steve took a hit on his taxes this year.
  史帝夫今年繳稅付了不少錢。

若將此片語中的 a 換成 the，則往往有「代人受過；一肩扛下所有責任」的意味。

- The star took the hit for the failure of her latest film, even though most critics believe it was the director's fault.
  儘管多數影評認為這部新片的問題出在導演身上，但失敗的責任還是由這名女星來扛。

9. **revenue** [ˋrɛvə͵nu] *n.* 收益；收入
10. **business model** [ˋbɪznəs] [ˋmadḷ] *n. phr.* 經營模式
11. **close down** *v.* 歇業；關閉
12. **grip** [grɪp] *n.* 控制；箝制；掌握
13. **initial** [ɪˋnɪʃəl] *adj.* 最初的；開頭的
14. **impulse** [ˋɪmpʌls] *n.* 念頭；推動力；衝動
15. **excellence** [ˋɛksləns] *n.* 優秀；卓越
16. **restrict** [rɪˋstrɪkt] *v.* 限制；約束
17. **access** [ˋæk͵sɛs] *n.* 使用；使用權；門路
18. **flexibility** [͵flɛksəˋbɪlətɪ] *n.* 彈性；靈活性
19. **pricing** [ˋpraɪsɪŋ] *n.* 定價；價格制定
20. **libertarian** [͵lɪbɚˋtɛrɪən] *adj.* 自由派的；自由意志主義的；講究個人（思想、行為）自由的
21. **chiefly** [ˋtʃiflɪ] *adv.* 主要地；大部分地；首要地

Musical Man

Exclusive Interview with Stage Composer Andrew Lloyd Webber

打造劇院魔力——
安德魯．洛伊．韋伯談音樂劇

Step 1 如果你是使用 MP3 ，請聽 MP3 Track 113；如果你使用電腦互動光碟，請點選 DVD-ROM【實戰應用篇—Part II：Unit 10】，試試看是否聽懂新聞內容。

Step 2 請瀏覽下列關鍵字彙，再仔細聽一次。

musical 音樂劇	spectacular 壯觀的
surpass 勝過	production（戲劇）演出
bite the bullet 咬緊牙關	venture 冒險
frisson 興奮感	

Step 3 如果你還不是聽的很懂的話，請參考下列發音提示，再仔細聽一次。

連音	had earned、performer on、sums up
去捲舌音	spectacular、hear、performances、compared、theater、certain、performer、working

試著作答下列聽力測驗題目。

True or False 是非題

____ 1. Andrew Lloyd Webber sings in the musical *The Phantom of the Opera*.

____ 2. Webber doesn't think his next musical will be as big as *The Phantom of the Opera*.

____ 3. *Phantom* has earned more money than any other entertainment venture ever.

____ 4. Michael Jackson has performed in *Phantom*.

____ 5. The only place you can see *Phantom* is at the London Palladium.

____ 6. The popularity of *Phantom* is dying down.

Multiple Choice 選擇題

____ 1. How many years has *The Phantom of the Opera* been running?

a. seven years b. eight years
c. 18 years d. 80 years

____ 2. How many performances of *Phantom* have been there?

a. less than 700 b. more than 7,000
c. more than 17,000 d. more than 70,000

____ 3. What is the problem with a major hit like *Phantom*?

a. It gives people goose bumps.
b. Everything else gets compared to it.
c. You have to bite a bullet.
d. No one knows how it will do in the theater.

____ 4. What made Webber realize that *Phantom* was going to be a hit?

a. Michael Jackson was thrilled with it.
b. It dwarfed the competition.
c. He saw a magazine created by a fan.
d. He saw the show in London.

試著用較慢的速度，再聽一遍（MP3 Track 114），檢查答案是否正確。

對答案、驗收成果，並詳讀原文，若仍有不懂的地方，可反覆多聽幾次。

（答案請見 p. 314）

Richard Quest, CNN Correspondent

When people talk about the bold, the spectacular,[2] the all-conquering[3] musical, Andrew Lloyd Webber is usually the name you hear. The week we met in New York, he surpassed[4] even himself in Broadway's books. After 18 years and more than 7,000 performances, his gothic[5] epic[6] *The Phantom of the Opera* had earned itself a new title—the longest-running show in Broadway history. *Phantom* outlasted[7] Webber's own *Cats*.

The problem, of course, with a major production[8] like this is that everything that you do subsequently[9] is compared back to it, isn't it?

Andrew Lloyd Webber, Composer

Of course. And one has to just bite the bullet on that one and know that it's not going to happen again. I mean, I don't think I've ever known anything in the theater which has done what *Phantom* did. And it's not dying down.[10] I mean, the extraordinary[11] thing is that it's got a production coming up[12] in Vegas. If that works, there will be productions of it then in places like Dubai and in Singapore and Macau and all these sort of places. But I don't think anybody thought that it would necessarily go on longer than *Cats*. One thing I can be certain [of] is that it's not going to happen again.

Richard Quest, CNN Correspondent

But at what point did you realize that there was, if you like, a *Phantom* phenomenon?[13]

CNN 特派員 理查・奎斯特

提到大膽、壯觀、所向披靡的音樂劇，你通常會聽到安德魯・洛伊・韋伯的大名。我們在紐約見面的那個禮拜，他甚至超越了自己在百老匯寫下的紀錄。在歷經十八年、七千多場的演出後，他的哥德式史詩鉅作《歌劇魅影》贏得了一個新頭銜，也就是百老匯史上演出最久的一齣戲。《魅》劇的演出壽命比韋伯的另一部作品《貓》還久。

當然，像這樣一齣大製作的問題就是，你之後的作品都會被拿來和它作比較，不是嗎？

作曲家 安德魯・洛伊・韋伯

那是當然的。你只能硬著頭皮接受事實，心裡清楚這樣的盛況不會再有。我認為沒有一齣劇作的成就超越《歌劇魅影》，而且它還沒退燒。特別的是，這齣戲即將在賭城拉斯維加斯製作推出，如果能成功，接下來就能在杜拜、新加坡、澳門演出。但我認為大家沒有料到《歌劇魅影》的壽命竟然會比《貓》劇還長。我能肯定的，這種盛況不會再現。

CNN 特派員 理查・奎斯特

你是從什麼時候開始意會到所謂的「魅影現象」？

Notes & Vocabulary

bite the bullet 咬緊牙關

此成語源於十九世紀，當時有效的麻醉技術（anesthetics）尚未出現，在戰場上施行外科手術時，醫護人員往往會給傷患一顆彈頭讓他咬住，以減輕手術的疼痛（當時的子彈頭為鉛製，咬下去略有彈性，不會因用力過度而傷到牙齒）。此後便以 bite (on) the bullet 表示「忍耐不愉快的事」或「鼓起勇氣面對困難」，與中文成語「咬緊牙關」類似。

- Sylvia bit the bullet and paid her parking tickets.
  席薇亞牙一咬，忍痛付了停車費。

1. **musical** [ˋmjuzɪkl̩] *adj., n.* 喜愛音樂的、擅長音樂的；音樂劇、歌舞劇
2. **spectacular** [spɛkˋtækjələ] *adj.* 壯觀的；豪華的
3. **all-conquering** [ˋɔlˋkɑŋkərɪŋ] *adj.* 戰無不克的；全勝的
4. **surpass** [sɚˋpæs] *v.* 勝過；優於
5. **gothic** [ˋgɑθɪk] *adj.* 哥德式的
6. **epic** [ˋɛpɪk] *n.* 史詩般的作品
7. **outlast** [ˋaut͵læst] *v.* 較……持久；比……命長
8. **subsequently** [ˋsʌbsɪ͵kwəntlɪ] *adv.* 接著；隨後
9. **production** [prəˋdʌkʃən] *n.* （戲劇）演出；（電影）攝製
10. **die down** *v.* 減弱；平息
11. **extraordinary** [ɪkˋstrɔrdə͵nɛrɪ] *adj.* 不凡的；特別的
12. **come up** *v.* 即將出現；即將到來
13. **phenomenon** [fɪˋnɑmə͵nɑn] *n.* 現象

Andrew Lloyd Webber, Composer

Really, it was about sort of two, three years into the run when we realized that there were things going on that were most unusual. I mean, like, there was a fan magazine, which was edited by a girl who changed her name to Christine Daaé, and it had branches[14] in, like, every major country in the world. And then, when we realized how the album was selling, it was doing sort of Michael Jackson *Thriller*-type quantities[15] at one time and it was extraordinary.

Richard Quest, CNN Correspondent

When it comes to making money, *The Phantom* is very real. With six productions currently running, *Phantom* has become the most valuable entertainment venture[16] of all time. Its worldwide box office draw of more than $3 billion dwarfs[17] the competition.

The love of the theater. What ~~it~~ is [it] about the theater that makes it unique?[18]

Andrew Lloyd Webber, Composer

If you walk into the London Palladium, I think everybody gets a sort of frisson[19] of some kind. I mean there is something so extraordinary about the relationship between that building and the performer on stage that I think that the Palladium for me sums up[20] the great magic of the theater.

作曲家 安德魯．洛伊．韋伯

大約在《歌劇魅影》推出兩、三年後，我們才察覺到有些事非常不尋常。有一本劇迷辦的雜誌，雜誌編輯是個女孩，她將自己的名字改成克莉絲汀．黛耶（註1），這家雜誌社在世界主要大國都有分社。當我們知道這張專輯的銷售成績，一度和麥可．傑克森的《顫慄》專輯（註2）的發行量不相上下時，那種感覺很特別。

CNN 特派員 理查．奎斯特

說到賺錢，《魅》劇可就非常真實了。目前有六組人馬在各地同時演出的《魅》劇，已成為史上最有價值的娛樂事業。該劇在全球的三十億美元票房，遙遙領先競爭對手。

這是一股對劇場的熱愛。是什麼特質讓劇場如此獨特？

作曲家 安德魯．洛伊．韋伯

當你走進倫敦的帕里底亞劇場（註3）時，我想每個人都或多或少會產生某種顫慄感。那棟建築和舞台上的表演者之間存在一種極為玄妙的關係，而我認為，帕里底亞代表了劇場的偉大魔力。

註1：《歌劇魅影》女主角之名。

註2：一九八二年發行，為史上最暢銷的專輯，迄今約賣出五千一百萬張。

註3：位於倫敦西區的著名大劇院。

Notes & Vocabulary

when it comes to
提及；談起；就……而言

when it comes to 是慣用語，後面要接名詞或動名詞。意思類似的用語還有：with/in regard to、in reference to。

- When it comes to wine, I prefer a nice French red.
  說到喝酒呢，我比較想來一杯好喝的法國紅酒。

14. **branch** [bræntʃ] *n.* 分部；分公司
15. **quantity** [ˋkwɑntətɪ] *n.* 數量
16. **venture** [ˋvɛntʃɚ] *n.* 冒險；賭注
17. **dwarf** [dwɔrf] *v.* 使……相形見絀
18. **unique** [juˋnik] *adj.* 獨特的
19. **frisson** [friˋson] *n.*（突然的）興奮感；恐懼；震顫
20. **sum up** *v.* 總結

Richard Quest, CNN Correspondent

And that really is a truism[21] across the theater?

Andrew Lloyd Webber, Composer

I think it is. I think there is a certain magic when you see a performer, or maybe an unknown performer in an audition[22] and it's just a piano and maybe some unknown girl comes up and gives you goose bumps. And I mean I happen to love live performers and I love working with them.

CNN 特派員 理查・奎斯特

真的是所有劇場都如此嗎？

作曲家 安德魯・洛伊・韋伯

我想是的。我認為真的有某種魔力。當你看到一個表演者，或甚至是在試鏡時看到一個沒沒無名的表演者，現場只有一架鋼琴，也許某個不知名的女孩上台來表演後讓你感動到渾身起雞皮疙瘩。我剛巧喜歡現場表演者，而且我熱愛和他們一起工作。

Notes & Vocabulary

goose bumps 雞皮疙瘩

當我們覺得寒冷或是看到可怕的東西而感到恐懼時，皮膚上往往會泛起許多突出的小粒，另外有些人在興奮激動時也會出現這樣的生理反應；在中文裡我們稱之為「雞皮疙瘩」，英文則把它叫作 goose bumps（鵝皮疙瘩），兩者可謂異曲同工。常見用法為 get goose bumps「起雞皮疙瘩」、give sb goose bumps「讓某人起雞皮疙瘩」。

- The horror movie gave Sharon goose bumps.
  那部恐怖片讓雪倫嚇到渾身起雞皮疙瘩。

21. **truism** [ˋtru͵ɪzəm] *n.* 自明之理；不言而喻的話
22. **audition** [ɔˋdɪʃən] *n.* 試鏡；試聽

Pistol-Packing Pilots Fly the Not-So-Safe Skies

捍衛駕駛艙 民航機師帶槍飛行

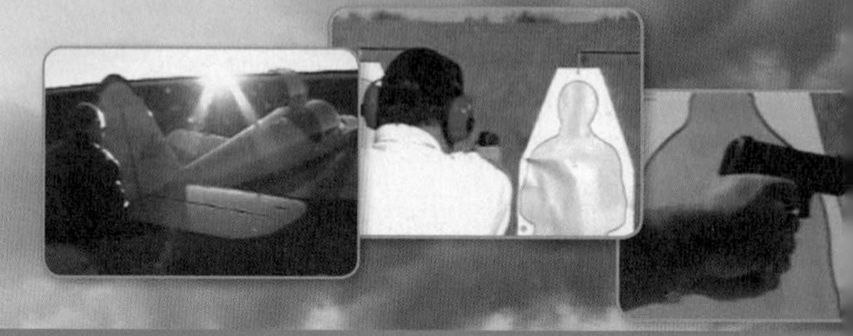

Step 1 如果你是使用 MP3 ，請聽 MP3 Track 115；如果你使用電腦互動光碟，請點選 DVD-ROM【實戰應用篇—Part II：Unit 11】，試試看是否聽懂新聞內容。

Step 2 請瀏覽下列關鍵字彙，再仔細聽一次。

eventuality 可能性	cockpit 駕駛艙
drill 訓練	jurisdiction 轄區
boot camp 新兵訓練營	in close quarters 在狹小空間裡
deterrence 嚇阻	tactic 戰術

Step 3 如果你還不是聽的很懂的話，請參考下列發音提示，再仔細聽一次。

連音	aviation emergency、federal agents

試著作答下列聽力測驗題目。

True or False 是非題

____ 1. Pilots who have gone through this training become federal officers.

____ 2. The Federal Law Enforcement Training Center is located in New York City.

____ 3. Most pilots already know how to fight.

____ 4. The pilots pay for the training themselves.

____ 5. John Wiley says pilots often have to deal with engine failures.

____ 6. The government said that over 3000 pilots have gone through the training.

Multiple Choice 選擇題

____ 1. How long have pilots been allowed to take these gun combat training courses?

a. six months　　b. one year
c. two years　　d. six years

____ 2. What is another name for a federal flight deck officer?

a. DIDO　　b. FIDO
c. FLIDO　　d. FFDO

____ 3. How long is the training course that trains pilots to fight?

a. one week　　b. one month
c. three months　　d. six months

____ 4. The trainer says the pilots are trained to be aggressive, like which animal?

a. a dog　　b. a tiger
c. a gorilla　　d. a hyena

試著用較慢的速度，再聽一遍（MP3 Track 116），檢查答案是否正確。

對答案、驗收成果，並詳讀原文，若仍有不懂的地方，可反覆多聽幾次。

（答案請見 p. 314）

CNN Correspondent

When it comes to flight safety, airline pilots want to be prepared for every eventuality,[2] including the chance that an armed terrorist will storm[3] the cockpit.[4] Miles O'Brien tells us how today's captains are learning how to defend the flight deck.

Miles O'Brien, CNN Correspondent

Airline pilots are used to spending endless hours drilling[5] in simulators[6] for unlikely problems. But this is not your average simulation, or your traditional aviation[7] emergency. They are training to be pistol-packing pilots, sworn federal officers with perhaps the smallest jurisdiction[8] in the world—an airliner[9] cockpit.

Captain for a Major Airline

People have to realize, hijackers,[10] they're professionals. They've been through training also.

Miles O'Brien, CNN Correspondent

He is a captain for a major airline, and for security reasons, we agreed to leave it at that. We met at the Federal Law Enforcement Training Center in remote Artesia, New Mexico, a veritable[11] boot camp[12] for federal agents of all stripes, including, for the past two years, federal flight deck officers, or FIDOs.

Captain for a Major Airline

If you look at the personality of pilots, a lot of us have never been into a fight, some of us, well maybe in the second grade on the sandbox. But most of us are so naive[13] in this area that we wouldn't have a clue what to do.

CNN 特派員

提到飛行安全，客機飛行員總會想為各種可能發生的事件做好預備，其中包括了武裝恐怖份子侵入駕駛艙這一項。邁爾斯．歐布萊恩將告訴我們今日的機長如何來學習保衛駕駛艙。

CNN 特派員 邁爾斯．歐布萊恩

客機飛行員早就習慣在模擬器裡無止盡地演練各種不太可能發生的狀況。不過，這可不是一般的模擬演練，也不是傳統的飛行意外。他們現在必須受訓成為佩槍機師，且是經過宣誓的聯邦執法人員，而他們管的可能是全世界最小的轄區：客機駕駛艙。

某大航空公司機長

大家要知道，劫機犯是專業罪犯。他們也是受過訓練的。

CNN 特派員 邁爾斯．歐布萊恩

他是一家著名航空公司的機長。為了安全考量，我們答應不曝露他的身分。我們約在聯邦執法訓練中心見面，這個機構位於新墨西哥州偏遠的阿蒂西亞，十足是各種聯邦人員的新兵訓練營。過去兩年來，這裡的受訓人員還包括聯邦駕駛艙飛行官，簡稱 FIDO。

某大航空公司機長

如果你去看一下飛行員的性格，就會發現我們很多人根本從來沒打過架，頂多是小學二年級的時候在沙坑上打過。大多數的飛行員在這方面都毫無經驗，一旦碰上狀況就完全不知道該怎麼辦。

Notes & Vocabulary

of all stripes 各種背景的……(人)

(one's) stripe 在十九世紀用來指一個人的政治立場或宗教信仰，而 of all stripes 則指各種政治或宗教背景的人，現在則引申泛指各種各類的人，尤指各種不同背景（政治、種族、宗教、信念）的人。

- People of all stripes backed the candidate.
  這位候選人受到各類型選民的支持。

1. **pistol** [ˋpɪstl̩] *n.* 手搶
2. **eventuality** [ɪˏvɛntʃuˋælətɪ] *n.* 可能發生的事件；可能性
3. **storm** [stɔrm] *v.* 強擊；猛攻
4. **cockpit** [ˋkɑkˏpɪt] *n.* 駕駛艙
5. **drill** [drɪl] *v.* 訓練
6. **simulator** [ˋsɪmjəˏletɚ] *n.* 模擬訓練裝置
7. **aviation** [ˏeviˋeʃən] *n.* 飛行；航空
8. **jurisdiction** [ˏdʒʊrəsˋdɪkʃən] *n.* 轄區；管轄範圍
9. **airliner** [ˋɛrˏlaɪnɚ] *n.* 大型客機；班機
10. **hijacker** [ˋhaɪˏdʒækɚ] *n.* 劫機犯
11. **veritable** [ˋvɛrətəbl̩] *adj.* 十足的；名符其實的
12. **boot camp** [but] [kæmp] *n.* 新兵訓練營
13. **naive** [nɑˋiv] *adj.* 單純的；天真的

Miles O'Brien, CNN Correspondent

They are here on their own time, their own dime,[14] to get a clue. You could call it "Hijack Defense 101," a weeklong course in the basics. Hand-to-hand combat?

George Barrett, Trainer

We're fighting in a phone booth-type cockpit, so not a whole lot of room, so everything we do is designed for fighting in close quarters.[15]

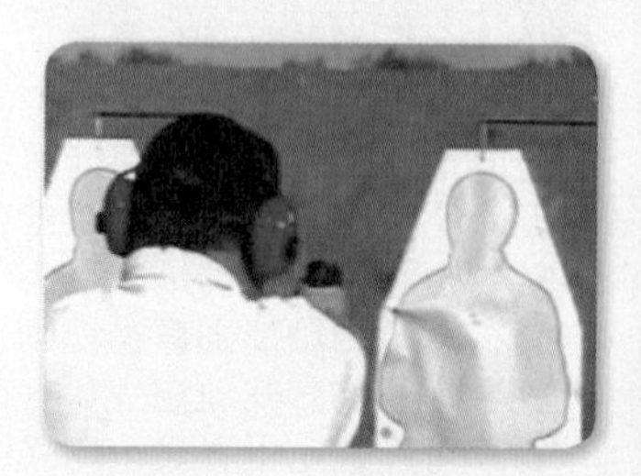

Miles O'Brien, CNN Correspondent

Marksmanship.[16] And shoot, don't shoot scenarios.[17]

George Barrett, Trainer

You need to do it very aggressively,[18] and getting into the "swing all the way through" concept, somewhat acting as though the pack of hyenas do when they take the animal down in some of those African shows as they have their teeth sunk into that flesh and are shaking their heads back and forth[19] and delivering as much pain as they can.

John Wiley, CNN Aviation Consultant

I realize that I've gone through training all my life for situations—engine failures, hydraulic[20] failures and stuff.

Miles O'Brien, CNN Correspondent

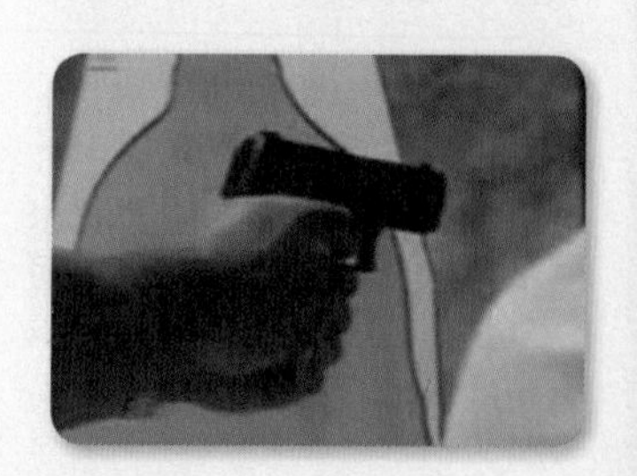

Retired US Airways Captain John Wiley carried a gun to work for the last seven months of his 25-year career.

CNN 特派員 邁爾斯．歐布萊恩

他們利用自己的休假時間，而且自掏腰包到這裡來學點概念。你可以把這個為期一週的基本課程稱為「劫機自衛入門」。徒手搏鬥？

訓練師 喬治．巴列特

我們必須在電話亭般大小的駕駛艙內打鬥，空間有限，所以我們設計的動作都適用於近距離搏鬥。

CNN 特派員 邁爾斯．歐布萊恩

訓練槍法，還有何時射擊，何時不該射擊的狀況演練。

訓練師 喬治．巴列特

你必須毫不留情，而且要完全投入這種情境概念。就像那種非洲生態節目裡成群的土狼，將他們的牙齒深咬進肉裡面然後不斷甩頭，使盡全力令對方痛苦。

CNN 航空顧問 約翰．韋利

我發現我這輩子都在接受因應各種狀況的訓練，像是引擎失效、液壓系統故障等等。

CNN 特派員 邁爾斯．歐布萊恩

美國航空公司退休機長約翰．韋利二十五年工作生涯的最後七個月，每天都帶著槍去上班。

Notes & Vocabulary

swing all the way through
揮到底；完全投入

在一些揮棒、揮拍或揮桿的運動中，揮的動作必須做得徹底、揮到底才能達到最大效用，英文就是用 swing all the way through 來表示，引申表示「完全投入」。而 get into the swing 則是表示對某事的了解漸入佳境，也逐漸融入其中的意思。

- Golfers hit the ball farther when they swing all the way through.
  打高爾夫球時，一桿揮到底球就會飛得比較遠。
- It took Frank a couple of weeks to get into the swing of working with the new program.
  法蘭克花了幾星期才逐漸熟悉新案子的工作。

sink one's teeth into
深入、陷入、完全投入某事

這個用法字面上的意思是獸類將牙齒深咬入獵物的肉中。本文中亦表示某人主動陷入或將自己深深投入某事的情況。

- Margo was hoping for a job she could really sink her teeth into.
  瑪歌想要找一份能讓她真正盡情發揮的工作。

14. **dime** [daɪm] *n.* 一角硬幣
15. **in close quarters** *phr.* 在狹小、擁擠的空間裡
16. **marksmanship** [ˋmɑrksmən͵ʃɪp] *n.* 槍法；射擊術
17. **scenario** [səˋnɛrɪ͵o] *n.* 情態；局面
18. **aggressively** [əˋgrɛsɪvlɪ] *adv.* 具侵略性地
19. **back and forth** *phr.* 前後來回地
20. **hydraulic** [haɪˋdrəlɪk] *adj.* 液壓的

John Wiley, CNN Aviation Consultant

I have to prepare myself. Although engine failures are remote, the likelihood[21] that I would incur[22] an attack, that's remote too, but you prepare for the worst.

Miles O'Brien, CNN Correspondent

The Transportation Security Administration won't say just how many pilots have gone through this training program so far, [there are] security reasons for that. But this program is about deterrence,[23] as much as anything else. Simply the perception[24] that a pilot might be armed forces a would-be hijacker to change tactics.[25]

CNN 航空顧問 約翰・韋利

我必須預先做好準備。儘管引擎失效和遭攻擊的可能性都微乎其微，但你總得未雨綢繆，學著應付最壞的狀況。

CNN 特派員 邁爾斯・歐布萊恩

美國交通運輸管理局不願透露目前有多少飛行員已受過這種訓練，這也是為了安全考量。不過，這項課程和其他措施一樣，都是以嚇阻為目的。光是察覺到飛行員可能配備武器，就足以讓有意劫機的人士改弦易轍了。

Notes & Vocabulary

prepare for the worst

做最壞的打算；為最糟狀況做好準備

這裡的「準備」意義視情形而定，有時是指對某種情況實質上的應對方法或策略：

- Residents didn't know how bad the storm would be, so they prepared for the worst.
  居民不知道這場暴風雨會有多強，因此他們為最糟的狀況做好了準備。

另一種用法的意義較偏向心理準備的層面：

- The doctor told the patient's family to hope for the best and prepare for the worst.
  醫生要病人的家屬抱持最大的盼望，同時做最壞的打算。

21. **likelihood** [ˋlaɪklɪˏhʊd] *n.* 可能、可能性
22. **incur** [ɪnˋkɝ] *v.* 招致；惹起
23. **deterrence** [dɪˋtɝəns] *n.* 嚇阻；威懾
24. **perception** [pɚˋsɛpʃən] *n.* 察覺；感知；認識
25. **tactic** [ˋtæktɪk] *n.* 戰術；策略

To Never Forget

Remembering History's "Greatest Crime"

歷史上難以抹滅的一頁——納粹集中營解放六十週年

Step 1 如果你是使用 MP3 ，請聽 MP3 Track 117；如果你使用電腦互動光碟，請點選 DVD-ROM【實戰應用篇—Part II: Unit 12】，試試看是否聽懂新聞內容。

Step 2 請瀏覽下列關鍵字彙，再仔細聽一次。

Holocaust 納粹大屠殺	anniversary 週年紀念日
tattoo 刺青	commemoration 紀念活動
testify 證明	validation 憑據
deportee 遭流放、驅逐出境者	distort 曲解

Step 3 如果你還不是聽的很懂的話，請參考下列發音提示，再仔細聽一次。

連音	60th anniversary、rail road、shipped off
省略音	he annonced

試著作答下列聽力測驗題目。

True or False 是非題

____ 1. Germans are not responsible for the Holocaust.

____ 2. French students go to Germany every week to learn about the Holocaust.

____ 3. During World War II, the French rounded up 70,000 Nazis and sent them to Germany.

____ 4. Jules Fainzaing thinks it's important to tell people what happened to him.

____ 5. Former deportees help people try to forget or distort the past.

____ 6. Teachers says students don't understand the Holocaust before this trip.

Multiple Choice 選擇題

____ 1. What did the Nazis tattoo on Jules Fainzaing's arm?

a. his name
b. an identification number
c. the word "Holocaust"
d. a history lesson

____ 2. What did a French political candidate say wasn't that bad?

a. the war years
b. the warriors of France
c. the Nazis
d. Auschwitz

____ 3. Out of the 1,000 people on Jules Fainzaing's train, how many survived?

a. 8
b. 80
c. 18
d. 972

____ 4. The mayor of Paris said that a DVD about the Holocaust would be given to whom?

a. death camp survivors
b. French teachers
c. all Frenchmen
d. every school student in Paris

Step 5 試著用較慢的速度，再聽一遍（MP3 Track 118），檢查答案是否正確。

對答案、驗收成果，並詳讀原文，若仍有不懂的地方，可反覆多聽幾次。

（答案請見 p. 314）

CNN Anchor

In Berlin today Chancellor Gerhard Schroeder tells Germans that most living today do not bear guilt for the Holocaust, but that they do continue to bear a special responsibility. In Paris, on the 60th anniversary[1] of the liberation[2] of the death camps, correspondent Jim Bittermann also assesses[3] history's lessons for Germany's neighbors.

Jim Bittermann, CNN Correspondent

On a grey day, French high school kids [are] learning about a dark heritage.[4] Several times a week young people are brought here to the drab[5] suburbs of Paris to visit Drancy, the World War II transit camp where 70,000 French Jews, rounded up[6] by their own countrymen, were stuffed[7] into railroad boxcars[8] and shipped off to the Nazi concentration camps.

A thousand people were in Jules Fainzaing's train load. He is one of only eight who survived. If the young visitors ask, he shows them the identification number the Nazis tattooed[9] on his arm. Just part of his living history lesson that he believes is essential to properly educating a new generation of Europeans.

CNN 主播

德國總理施若德今天在柏林向全德人民指出，今日大多數德國人無需為納粹大屠殺擔罪，但他們仍需為此承擔一種特別的責任。時值死亡集中營獲得解放的六十週年紀念，特派員吉姆．比特曼要在巴黎探討歷史為德國諸鄰國帶來的教訓。

CNN 特派員 吉姆．比特曼

在這灰濛濛的一天，法國高中生正在學習一段黑暗的歷史。一星期中有好幾天，都會有年輕學生被帶往平淡無趣的巴黎郊區，參觀二次世界大戰期間的德蘭西中轉營，當年共有七萬名法國猶太人被自己的同胞拘禁於此，然後分別塞入火車貨櫃送往納粹集中營。

儒爾斯．方贊所搭乘的那班列車上載有一千人，後來只有八人倖存，他是其中之一。參觀的學生只要向他提出要求，他就會把納粹刺在他手臂上的識別碼露給他們看。他認為這樣的活歷史，是教育歐洲下一代所不可或缺的課程。

Notes & Vocabulary

Holocaust 納粹大屠殺

Holocaust 是指二次世界大戰期間納粹對於猶太人及其他弱勢團體（如政治異議者、同性戀等）有系統的大規模殺戮。此字源自希臘文，代表「奉獻給神、完全（holos）焚燒（kaustos）的祭物」。在許多猶太人眼中，用這種帶有「獻祭」意味的字眼來指稱民族悲劇相當不妥，因此他們多以源自希伯來文的 Shoah（災難、浩劫）取而代之。但對不諳此字原意的一般大眾而言，Holocaust 不但早已變成納粹屠殺的代名詞，其小寫形式也漸漸演化為 genocide 的同義字，用來泛指大規模的種族殺戮事件。

1. **anniversary** [ˌænəˋvɝsərɪ] *n.* 週年紀念日
2. **liberation** [ˌlɪbəˋreʃən] *n.* 解放
3. **assess** [əˋsɛs] *v.* 衡量；評估
4. **heritage** [ˋhɛrətɪdʒ] *n.* 遺產；繼承物
5. **drab** [dræb] *adj.* 平淡枯燥的；乏味的
6. **round up** [raʊnd] *v.* 召集；使……聚集；圍捕
7. **stuff** [stʌf] *v.* 將……擠入、塞進
8. **boxcar** [ˋbɑksˌkɑr] *n.* 鐵路運貨車廂
9. **tattoo** [tæˋtu] *v.* 刺青；刺字

__Jules Fainzaing, Concentration Camp Survivor__

That's what I told them. That is something that ~~was~~ happened to me, and that is more important than all that we can find in books.

__Jim Bittermann, CNN Correspondent__

Fainzaing is 82, but feels that it's so vital to bear witness about the war, that he's in a classroom lecturing nearly every other day. In a world where a British prince appears to think that parading[10] in a Nazi uniform is good fun . . . and a former French presidential candidate says the war years in France really were not all that bad, the teachers who lead the field trips[11] to Drancy worry how well their students will handle history when they no longer have the advantage of hearing from eyewitnesses.

__Estelle Mondine, High School Teacher__

It just remains pretty abstract to them and it's good for them to come to places and to see real people to realize that it just happened, that it was the truth.

集中營倖存者 儒爾斯．方贊

我跟他們述說我的經歷。那是我曾遭遇過的事，而這比我們在書上所能讀到的任何事情都還要重要。

CNN 特派員 吉姆．比特曼

方贊高齡八十二，但他覺得為那場戰爭留下見證是非常重要的事情，因此幾乎每隔一天就為學生講課。在今天這個時代裡，英國王子認為穿上納粹制服示人只是好玩……法國還曾有一名總統候選人聲稱該國在二次大戰期間的狀況其實沒那麼糟糕。帶領學生參觀德蘭西的老師不禁擔心：在目擊證人紛紛凋零，無法再為學生提供見證之後，未來的學生對這段歷史能夠理解多少。

高中教師 艾絲蝶爾．孟婷

這段歷史對他們來說其實很抽象。所以，讓他們到這類地方來看看真實的人物，讓他們知道這一切確實發生過，對他們是件好事。

Notes & Vocabulary

bear witness 為……做見證；證明

bear 在本文中出現三次，在第一段主播提到 bear guilt 和 bear responsibility 時，是「承擔；擔負」之意。而 bear witness 則是一固定片語。以人為主詞時，代表「為……做見證；宣稱……真實可信」之意，但若以事物為主詞，則可作「見證」或「證明」解釋。例如滿屋的獎座可以 bear witness to（證明）某人的傑出。一般而言，bear witness to 是習慣用法，本文以 about 取代 to 是為了強調其人所見證的是「戰爭的某一層面」，但這種說法較為少見。

- Africa has born witness to countless human tragedies.
  非洲見證了無數的人道悲劇。

10. **parade** [pə`red] *v.* 遊行；招搖而行
11. **field trip** [fild] [trɪp] *n.* 校外教學；實地考察

Jim Bittermann, CNN Correspondent

That need to solidify[12] the truth in European minds is behind a lot of activity as the 60th anniversary of the liberation of Auschwitz draws near. The Holocaust Memorial here in the Jewish Quarter of Paris has been refurbished[13] and expanded.

As commemorations[14] began here for the Auschwitz remembrances,[15] the mayor of Paris invited several hundred death camp survivors to a concert at city hall. A DVD testifying to[16] the horrors of World War II, he announced, will soon be given to every Paris school student; an additional tool for teachers, additional validation[17] for what he called the worst crime ever committed. The former deportees[18] remain the most powerful weapon against those who try to forget or distort[19] the past. But their dramatic and living history cannot go on much longer.

CNN 特派員 吉姆．比特曼

隨著奧許維茨集中營解放六十週年紀念日逐漸接近，許多活動的基本概念便是要讓歐洲人確切認知這段歷史的真實性。巴黎猶太區的納粹大屠殺紀念館，也已重新裝修以及擴建。

就在對於奧許維茨過往歷史的紀念活動展開之際，巴黎市長邀請了數百位死亡集中營倖存者到市政廳參加一場音樂會。他在會場上宣布，巴黎各級學生將在不久之後每人領到一片見證二次大戰慘況的 DVD，作為老師教學上的課外教材，也可進一步證實這項他所稱歷史上最殘酷的罪行。對於那些企圖遺忘或扭曲過往史實的人，這些曾經遭到驅逐的猶太人就是反駁他們最有力的武器。然而，這些人身上深富戲劇性而且活生生的歷史，卻也將在不久之後消逝。

Notes & Vocabulary

Auschwitz 奧許維茨集中營

Auschwitz 是二次世界大戰期間納粹在波蘭南部奧斯維辛鎮所設三大集中營的統稱。Auschwitz 一詞即波蘭 Oswiecim 的德文拼法。在一九四〇到一九四五年間，約有一百五十萬名囚犯（以猶太人居多）先後在此遭屠戮或折磨至死，Auschwitz 因此成為納粹暴行的具體表徵。一九七九年，聯合國教科文組織將奧許維茨集中營列為世界遺產保護區（World Heritage Site），讓歷史的慘痛教訓能世世代代長留人心。

12. **solidify** [səˋlɪdəˏfaɪ] *v.* 使……穩固、落實
13. **refurbish** [rɪˋfɝbɪʃ] *v.* 重新整修
14. **commemoration** [kəˏmɛməˋreʃən] *n.* 紀念活動
15. **remembrance** [rɪˋmɛmbrəns] *n.* 往事；紀念活動
16. **testify to** [ˋtɛstəˏfaɪ] *v.* 證明
17. **validation** [ˏvæləˋdeʃən] *n.* 憑據
18. **deportee** [ˏdɪpɔrˋti] *n.* 遭流放、驅逐出境者
19. **distort** [dɪˋstɔrt] *v.* 扭曲；曲解（真理、事實）

Almost Superhuman

An Iron Determination and a Body That Knows No Bounds Carry Armstrong to the Top

揭開阿姆斯壯過人體能的秘密

Step 1 如果你是使用 MP3 ，請聽 MP3 Track 119；如果你使用電腦互動光碟，請點選 DVD-ROM【實戰應用篇—Part II：Unit 13】，試試看是否聽懂新聞內容。

Step 2 請瀏覽下列關鍵字彙，再仔細聽一次。

athlete 運動員	oxygen 氧氣
altitude 海拔	substance 物質
lactic acid 乳酸	dedication 奉獻
inherent 與生俱來的	

Step 3 如果你還不是聽的很懂的話，請參考下列發音提示，再仔細聽一次。

連音	best endurance、maximum exertion
省略音	with his genes、large amounts、more efficiently、probably、20-year-old (twenty)、which spans

試著作答下列聽力測驗題目。

True or False 是非題

____ 1. Armstrong's excellence as an athlete begins with his genes.

____ 2. Armstrong's heart is smaller than most people's.

____ 3. Armstrong's lungs take in twice the amount of oxygen as an average healthy 20-year-old.

____ 4. Lance Armstrong's red blood cells make it more difficult to breath at high altitudes.

____ 5. Many people think that Armstrong is superhuman.

____ 6. Armstrong began training four weeks before the Tour de France.

Multiple Choice 選擇題

____ 1. What does Lance Armstrong's mother say made her son a success?

a. hard work　　b. sitting on a couch
c. potato chips　　d. performance enhancing drugs

____ 2. How long does Lance train for every day?

a. three hours　　b. five hours
c. six hours　　d. twelve hours

____ 3. What substance does Armstrong's muscles produce less of?

a. citric acid　　b. sweat
c. blood　　d. lactic acid

____ 4. When training, about how many miles per week does Armstrong pedal?

a. 40　　b. 40 or 50
c. 400　　d. 450

Step 5 試著用較慢的速度，再聽一遍（MP3 Track 120），檢查答案是否正確。

Step 6 對答案、驗收成果，並詳讀原文，若仍有不懂的地方，可反覆多聽幾次。

（答案請見 p. 314）

CNN Anchor

Well, how does Lance Armstrong really do it? CNN's Dr. Sanjay Gupta has this interesting look.

Sanjay Gupta, CNN Correspondent

He's possibly the best endurance[1] athlete[2] in the world. Most of us know Lance Armstrong's name, but few know how he does it. It all starts with his genes.[3]

Edward Coyle, Human Performance Lab

We found that even at a young age, because of his ~~tense~~ [intense] training, he had a big engine, a big heart, and was able to consume[4] large amounts of oxygen. Probably less than one percent of the population would have as much of a genetic head start[5] as Armstrong has.

Sanjay Gupta, CNN Correspondent

Lance Armstrong's physiology[6] characteristics are nothing short of astounding.[7] His heart, it can pump[8] nine gallons of blood per minute working at its hardest, compared to only five gallons per minute for the average person. In one minute of maximum exertion,[9] Armstrong's heart can beat twice that of a normal person. His lungs, he gets almost double the amount of oxygen out of every breath that a healthy 20-year-old would. Everyone takes in the same breath, but Armstrong uses his two times more efficiently.

He also has more red blood cells to deliver oxygen to his body, meaning he can breathe better at higher altitudes.[10] And that's a key in the treacherous[11] Pyrenees and Alps mountains along the route of the Tour de France.

CNN 主播

阿姆斯壯究竟是怎麼辦到的？CNN 的桑傑．古普塔醫師提出一個有趣的觀點。

CNN 特派員 桑傑．古普塔

他很可能是世界上耐力最強的運動員。我們都知道蘭斯．阿姆斯壯的大名，但是很少人知道他是怎麼辦到的。這一切須從他的基因談起。

人類行為實驗室 愛德華．科以耳

我們發現，由於他年紀輕輕就開始密集訓練，所以他有個很大的引擎，就是他的大心臟，能夠吸納大量的氧氣。全世界像他先天條件這麼好的人，大概還不到總人口的百分之一。

CNN 特派員 桑傑．古普塔

阿姆斯壯的生理特質極為驚人。他的心臟在跳動最激烈的時候，每分鐘可以送出九加侖的血液，相較於一般人則只有五加侖。在一分鐘竭力運作下，阿姆斯壯的心臟跳動是一般人的兩倍。至於他的肺，他每吸一口氣所獲得的氧氣，幾乎是二十歲健康年輕人的兩倍。大家都同樣吸一口氣，但阿姆斯壯對這口氣的使用效率卻比常人高出一倍。

他身上負責運送氧氣的紅血球數也比較多，意思就是說他在高海拔處的呼吸也會比一般人來得更為順暢。對於環法自由車賽裡艱難的庇里牛斯山與阿爾卑斯山路段來說，這是一大關鍵。

Notes & Vocabulary

know no bounds 無限地；極其地

標題中的 bounds 意思是「界限；範圍」，片語 know no bounds 常用來形容事物「非常……；無止盡地……」。本文標題中 a body that knows no bounds 是直接取其字面意思，表示「不知體能界限為何物的身體」，引申有「體能非常棒」的意思。注意 bounds 一定要用複數形。

- Martha's love for her family knows no bounds.
  瑪莎非常深愛她的家人。

nothing short of 不折不扣；簡直就是

short of 是指「短缺、不足」，故 nothing short of 的字面意思就是「不缺乏……」，也就是「不折不扣、少不了」的意思。這是英文中強調語氣時常用的表現方式之一，後面可以接上形容詞、名詞或子句。

- It is nothing short of a miracle that modern methods of instruction have not yet entirely strangled the holy curiosity of inquiry.
  現代的教育方式竟然還沒有完全扼殺掉神聖的好奇探索心，真可說是個奇蹟。

1. endurance [ɪn`djʊrəns] *n.* 耐久力；持久力
2. athlete [`æθ͵lit] *n.* 運動員；體育家
3. gene [dʒin] *n.* 基因；遺傳因子（形容詞為 genetic）
4. consume [kən`sum] *v.* 消耗；花費
5. head start [hɛd] [stɑrt] *n.* 搶先起步的優勢；有利的開端
6. physiology [͵fɪzɪ`ɑlədʒɪ] *n.* 生理；生理機能
7. astounding [ə`staʊndɪŋ] *adj.* 令人驚奇的；令人震驚的
8. pump [pʌmp] *v.*（唧筒般）抽出、注入氣體或液體
9. exertion [ɪg`zɝʃən] *n.* 努力；費力
10. altitude [`æltə͵tjud] *n.* 高度；海拔
11. treacherous [`trɛtʃərəs] *adj.* 危險的；變化莫測的

His muscles: Lance's muscles produce less lactic acid[12] than most people, which means his muscles can go longer and harder without major fatigue.[13]

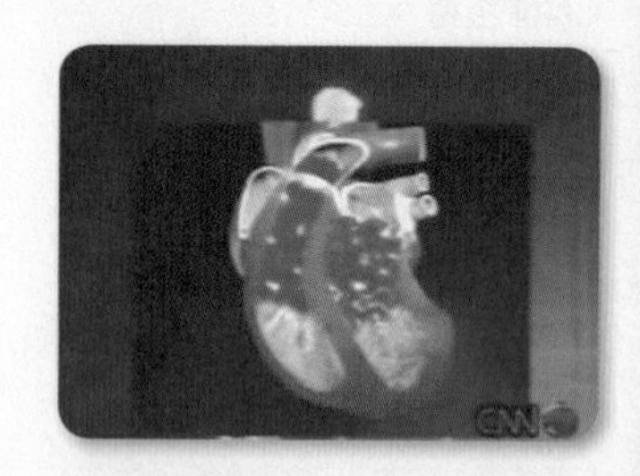

All of this can ultimately[14] make many people think Armstrong is superhuman.

Spectator

The guy's a superhero.

Sanjay Gupta, CNN Correspondent

And that's a question his mother has heard many times before.

Linda Armstrong Kelly, Lance's Mother

Is Lance superhuman? That's a question everyone has asked. He didn't get that way sitting on a couch, eating potato chips. So, lots of hard work. A lot of dedication.[15]

Sanjay Gupta, CNN Correspondent

In fact, Armstrong trains at least six hours a day. And for the Tour de France, which spans[16] less than four weeks, he begins training eight months before its July start date. That's an average of 450 miles per week. A distance of about halfway[17] around the globe pedaled[18] during a season of training. All that for what would be seven straight[19] Tour wins.

From every beat to every breath, Lance Armstrong has certainly had a genetic head start, but at 33 it's his training and his inherent[20] physiology that will carry him to this year's finishing line.

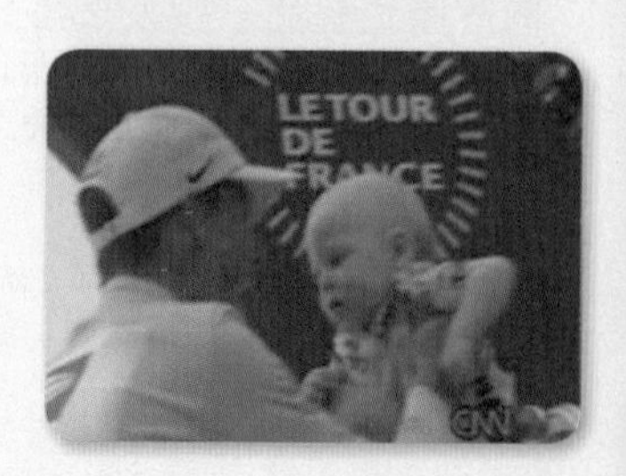

他的肌肉所產生的乳酸比大多數人要少，也就是說他的肌肉在長時間施力下也不容易疲勞。

這種種條件結合起來，便讓許多人認為阿姆斯壯是超人。

觀眾

這傢伙根本是個超級英雄。

CNN 特派員 桑傑．古普塔

阿姆斯壯的母親早就聽過這個問題不知多少次了。

阿姆斯壯之母 琳達．阿姆斯壯．凱莉

「阿姆斯壯是超人嗎？」大家都問過這個問題。他今天的成就不是坐在沙發上吃薯片就憑空得到的，而是需要投入許多的努力，還有很多的付出。

CNN 特派員 桑傑．古普塔

實際上，阿姆斯壯每天至少訓練六個小時。而為了賽程不到四個星期的環法大賽，他更是在七月開賽前的八個月就展開訓練。每個星期平均要騎四百五十哩。一季訓練所騎的距離就足以環繞地球半圈。這一切的訓練，造就的是環法大賽七連霸的紀錄。

從心臟的每一次跳動到吸入的每一口氣，阿姆斯壯確實擁有遺傳上的先天優勢。不過，今年三十三歲的他，仍必須仰賴訓練與本身的生理特質，才能邁向今年比賽的終點。

Notes & Vocabulary

Le Tour de France 環法自行車賽

環法自由車賽為多日賽，一般於每年七月初至七月底舉行，每天進行一站（stage），共二十一站，總賽程約三千兩百公里，為歐洲規模最大、水準最高的自行車賽。賽段中按比賽形式分為個人計時賽和團體計時賽，按比賽道路分平地賽段和山地賽段，海拔最高可達兩千兩百公尺。起點每年不同，多在法國北部城市，環繞法國一周後到達終點巴黎。

- 黃衫（maillot jaune / yellow jersey）：總成績領先者，即所有參賽選手中每站成績累積起來時間最短者。
- 綠衫（maillot vert / green jersey）：總積分領先者（每站前幾名均可獲積分）即「衝刺王」。
- 紅點衫（maillot à pois rouges / polka dot jersey）：「登山王」，為登山路段積分領先者。

12. **lactic acid** [ˋlæktɪk] [ˋæsəd] *n.* 乳酸
13. **fatigue** [fəˋtig] *n.* 疲勞；勞累
14. **ultimately** [ˋʌltəmətlɪ] *adv.* 最終；終極
15. **dedication** [͵dɛdɪˋkeʃən] *n.* 專心致力；奉獻；敬業
16. **span** [spæn] *v.*（時間）持續；延伸
17. **halfway** [ˋhæfˋwe] *adj.* 中間的；半途的
18. **pedal** [ˋpɛdḷ] *v.* 騎自行車
19. **straight** [stret] *adj.* 連續的；不間斷的
20. **inherent** [ɪnˋhɛrənt] *adj.* 內在的；與生俱來的

Pixar Perfect

A Look behind the Scenes of the Award-Winning Animation Studio

3-D 動畫武林盟主 皮克斯的成功之路

Step 1 如果你是使用 MP3 ，請聽 MP3 Track 121；如果你使用電腦互動光碟，請點選 DVD-ROM【實戰應用篇—Part II：Unit 14】，試試看是否聽懂新聞內容。

Step 2 請瀏覽下列關鍵字彙，再仔細聽一次。

insight 洞悉	critically 批判性地
acclaim 推崇	headquarters 總公司
harness 利用	merge 融合
precious little 鳳毛麟角	

Step 3 如果你還不是聽的很懂的話，請參考下列發音提示，再仔細聽一次。

連音	visit to
去捲舌音	working、animators、player、fair、perception、headquarters、workspaces、harness、merge、monster hits、market

試著作答下列聽力測驗題目。

True or False 是非題

____ 1. Pixar was founded by Steve Jobs.

____ 2. People at Pixar work well together because they're very similar.

____ 3. Pixar encourages workers to follow company traditions.

____ 4. Pixar's headquarters are located in San Francisco.

____ 5. The characters in Pixar's movies are made completely on computers.

____ 6. Workers at Pixar try to separate art, technology and business.

Multiple Choice 選擇題

____ 1. Which part of Pixar does Steve Jobs run?

a. the creative part
b. the business part
c. the technology part
d. the animation part

____ 2. What does the animator say should be avoided when making animation?

a. squishing and squashing things
b. easing in and out of poses
c. the principles of animation
d. mechanical movements

____ 3. What is the worst thing that happens when a company gets successful?

a. They start to get famous.
b. It happens again and again.
c. They don't pay attention to their problems.
d. It encourages creativity.

____ 4. How many hit movies has Pixar made?

a. one
b. four
c. six
d. ten

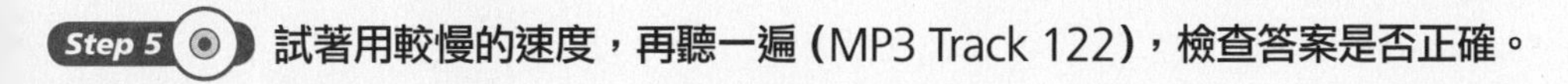
Step 5 試著用較慢的速度，再聽一遍 (MP3 Track 122)，檢查答案是否正確。

Step 6 對答案、驗收成果，並詳讀原文，若仍有不懂的地方，可反覆多聽幾次。

(答案請見 p. 314)

Christie Lu Stout, SPARK

We stay with the movies now, with an incredible visit to Pixar, the animation company that's helping to change the way movies are made. Now with a string of[2] hit films behind it, the Steve Jobs-led studio appears to have the same magic touch its characters are bringing to the screen. Liz George has the story.

Liz George, CNN Correspondent

Grainy[3] home video gives a unique insight[4] into the working methods used by the award-winning animators at Pixar studios. Here they are seen mapping out a scene from the critically[5] acclaimed[6] film, *The Incredibles*. It's the sixth in a series of films that has witnessed the company, founded by Ed Catmull, becoming a major player in the movie business.

Ed Catmull, Pixar President

We're extremely fortunate in that we have in the company three people who are very different from each other but also work very well together. So we've got John Lasseter who's leading the creative [side] for the company. There's Steve Jobs who really runs the business side, the dealing with Wall Street and the outside negotiations. And then I run things operationally inside.

Liz George, CNN Correspondent

You've been described as the geek's geek. Is that insulting,[7] flattering,[8] fair?

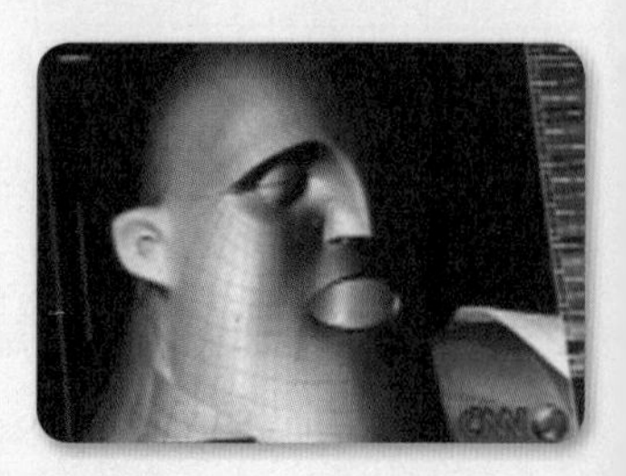

《科技新火花》克莉絲蒂・陸・史道

依然是有關電影的新聞，我們要到皮克斯來趟驚奇之旅。這家動畫公司改變了電影的製作方式。在接連推出了好幾部賣座片後，這家以史帝夫・賈伯斯為首的工作室，似乎像它創造出的電影角色一樣具有魔力。請看麗茲・喬治的報導。

CNN 特派員 麗茲・喬治

畫質粗糙的家庭錄影帶帶領我們深入皮克斯，一窺金獎動畫師們的工作方法。影片中的他們正在為大受好評的《超人特攻隊》安排一幕戲。《超人特攻隊》是該公司接連推出的第六部電影，而這家由艾德・卡穆所創立的公司，也成為電影界的巨擘。

皮克斯公司總裁 艾德・卡穆

公司裡三位主要人物差異極大，卻又能合作無間，這實在是件非常幸運的事。我們有約翰・拉賽特負責帶領公司的創意部分。史帝夫・賈伯斯負責公司的經營、和華爾街打交道，以及涉外的協商工作。公司內部的執行面則由我來負責。(註)

CNN 特派員 麗茲・喬治

你曾被人形容為是「技客中的技客」，你認為這算侮辱還是溢美，這樣的評價恰當嗎？

註：皮克斯動畫公司已經在二〇〇六年時與迪士尼公司（Walt Disney Company）合併。Ed Catmull 目前是擔任皮克斯和迪士尼總裁、John Lasseter 擔任創意總監，而 Steve Jobs 目前則是迪士尼公司的大股東及董事會成員。

Notes & Vocabulary

map out 安排

map 在這裡當動詞用，map sth out 是指「安排某事」，其他與 map 相關的片語還有：

put sb/sth on the map 讓某人／某事出名

- Windows is the product that put Microsoft on the map.
  讓微軟成名的產品就是視窗系統。

wipe sth off the map 徹底消滅某事

- Iran has threatened to wipe Israel off the map.
  伊朗威嚇要消滅以色列。

1. **behind the scenes** *phr.* 幕後；後臺
2. **a string of** *phr.* 一串；一列
3. **grainy** [ˋgrenɪ] *adj.* 粒狀的；(相片等)顆粒粗糙的
4. **insight** [ˋɪnˏsaɪt] *n.* 洞悉；深刻的理解
5. **critically** [ˋkrɪtɪklɪ] *adv.* 評論性地；關鍵性地；嚴重地
6. **acclaim** [əˋklem] *v.* 稱讚；推崇
7. **insulting** [ɪnˋsʌltɪŋ] *adj.* 侮辱的；無禮的
8. **flatter** [ˋflætɚ] *v.* 過譽（flattering 為形容詞）

Ed Catmull, Pixar President

I do know technology very well. But I also know the art side very well. And I'm privileged[9] to be able to see how much they have in common. And I enjoy setting up environments where those groups function well together.

Liz George, CNN Correspondent

The popular perception of animation is that these films are created purely on computer. But at Pixar's headquarters[10] in San Francisco, there's plenty of evidence to suggest that these characters have at least had some form of physical[11] life. But it's when they enter the computer and are put in the hands of the animators that they really become believable.

Andrew Gordon, Pixar Animator

You want to avoid mechanical movements, so I don't want it to be like ba-ba-ba-ba-ba-ba, you know? I want it to, like, feel like there's muscle, and if things are squishing and squashing and easing in of the poses and easing out, you know. These are all principles of animation.

Liz George, CNN Correspondent

At the studios, animators are encouraged to customize[12] their workspaces in the hope that it will encourage creativity. But they're keenly[13] aware of the need to harness[14] their talents with the existing technology. There's precious little that's conventional at Pixar, including its ability to merge[15] the seemingly disparate[16] disciplines of art, technology and business.

皮克斯公司總裁 艾德・卡穆

我對科技十分瞭解，但對藝術方面也相當嫻熟。我有幸能夠看出這兩者間有這麼多的交集，也很高興能建造出一個能夠統合兩者，並讓它順利運作的環境。

CNN 特派員 麗茲・喬治

一般人都認為動畫完全是靠電腦創造出來的，但是在皮克斯位於舊金山的總公司中，有許多證據顯示這些角色至少在某種程度上是以實體形式存在的。不過要等到將這些模型掃入電腦、交到動畫師手中後，它們才真正開始變得栩栩如生。

皮克斯動畫師 安德魯・戈登

要避免機械化的動作出現，我不要看到這麼硬梆梆的東西，我希望它看起來有肌肉的感覺，要利用擠壓技巧來表現，動作的速度變化要平順；這些都是動畫的基本原則。

CNN 特派員 麗茲・喬治

皮克斯工作室鼓勵動畫師建立個人化的工作環境，希望能藉此激發創意。但動畫師們都很清楚，必須利用既有科技來發揮他們的才華。在皮克斯，你幾乎找不到什麼尋常的事物，連他們將藝術、科技和事業三個不同領域成功整合的能力都很有一套。

Notes & Vocabulary

squishing and squashing 擠壓

squish, squash and stretch（擠壓和伸展）及後面提及的 ease in and ease out（緩入與緩出）都是動畫的基本原則之一。前者是指做動畫時要配合動作扭曲物體外型，而後者則是指要讓動作的加速、減速很平順。

precious little 鳳毛麟角；少得可憐

precious 是「珍貴」之意，用 precious 修飾 little 或 few（稀少），是一種不太正式但頗為常見的加強語氣用法，表示「非常少」（少到一旦發現了就會顯得很珍貴的程度），用於反諷的情況居多。

- There was precious little that made Steve stand out from the crowd.
  史蒂夫身上實在很難找到什麼出眾之處。

9. **privileged** [ˋprɪvlɪdʒd] *adj.* 有榮幸的
10. **headquarters** [ˋhɛdˏkwɔrtɚz] *n.* 總公司；總部
11. **physical** [ˋfɪzɪkḷ] *adj.* 物質的；有實體的；身體的
12. **customize** [ˋkʌstəˏmaɪz] *v.* 定製；自定
13. **keenly** [ˋkinlɪ] *adv.* 敏銳地
14. **harness** [ˋhɑrnəs] *v.* 利用；駕馭
15. **merge** [mɝdʒ] *v.* 融合；合併
16. **disparate** [ˋdɪsprət] *adj.* 不同的

Ed Catmull, Pixar President

The worst thing that happens to companies is that they are successful and they don't pay attention to the problems, because a success disguises[17] the problems. And I've seen this happen over and over again. You get all the attention, you get the fame[18], and all these things happen, and you don't pay attention to these little things that start to grow. And so our belief is, fix the problems while you can.

Liz George, CNN Correspondent

With six monster hits and a market cap of around four and a half billion dollars, it appears that challenging the norm[19] can be profitable.[20]

皮克斯公司總裁 艾德．卡穆

對一家公司來說最糟的情況，就是經營得很成功，卻不去注意問題所在，因為成功的光芒會將問題遮蔽。這種事我看多了，一旦功成名就，好運紛紛降臨的時候，一些開始浮現的小問題就會被忽略。所以我們的信念是，趁早解決問題。

CNN 特派員 麗茲．喬治

六部賣座鉅片再加上約四十五億美元的市值，看來挑戰傳統是件有利可圖的事。

Notes & Vocabulary

market cap 市值

cap 是 capitalization（資本額；資本化）的簡稱。market cap（市值；市場價值；資本市場）是一種投資專家用來衡量一間公司規模的指標，根據流通在外、公開發行股票的價值所計算出來的公司價值。

17. **disguise** [dɪs`gaɪz] *v.* 掩藏；隱瞞
18. **fame** [fem] *n.* 名聲；聲譽
19. **norm** [nɔrm] *n.* 規範
20. **profitable** [`prɑfətəbəl] *adj.* 有利的；有用的

United Front

British Politicians Put Aside Differences to Face Terror

英國朝野同心　面對反恐難題

Step 1 如果你是使用 MP3 ，請聽 MP3 Track 123; 如果你是使用電腦互動光碟，請點選 DVD-ROM【實戰應用篇—Part II: Unit 15】，試試看是否聽懂新聞內容。

Step 2 請瀏覽下列關鍵字彙，再仔細聽一次。

massacre 屠殺；殘殺	flinch 畏懼；退縮
counter 反擊	revulsion 嫌惡；強烈反感
resolute 堅定的	fanaticism 狂熱
undermine 暗中破壞	

Step 3 如果還不是很了解的話，請參考下列提示，再仔細聽一次。

連音	as resilient as those、let terrorists
去捲舌音	minister、lawmakers、still there、familiar、reasserting、adversity、leader、bombers、startlingly、years、worst、rarely、determined、finger、eagerness、heard

試著作答下列聽力測驗題目。

True or False 是非題

____ 1. After the bombings, people of different religions came together.

____ 2. Blair said terrorists can destroy the spirit of Londoners.

____ 3. The bombing happened just before the 60th anniversary of the end of World War I.

____ 4. London today is a mix of many religions, races and cultures.

____ 5. Blair promised he would not rest until the bombers were caught.

____ 6. Getting lawmakers from opposing parties to work together took a lot of planning.

Multiple Choice 選擇題

____ 1. What did Blair promise to counter future terror?

a. more troops in Iraq　b. military action
c. new laws　d. new taxes

____ 2. Who did Blair say could not be blamed for the attack?

a. terrorists　b. security services
c. Islamic extremists　d. suicide bombers

____ 3. What have opposition Conservatives called for?

a. revenge　b. a homeland security department
c. Blair's resignation　d. stricter immigration laws

____ 4. What did the opposition leader say the terrorist failed to do?

a. divide the people of Britain
b. get through London's security
c. communicate without political baggage
d. pay tribute to the Prime Minister

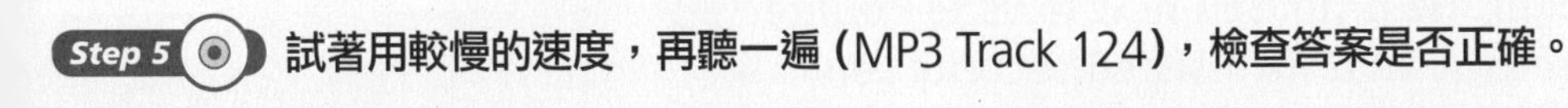
試著用較慢的速度，再聽一遍 (MP3 Track 124)，檢查答案是否正確。

對答案、驗收成果，並詳讀原文，若仍有不懂的地方，可反覆多聽幾次。

(答案請見 p. 314)

CNN Anchor

After the attacks, London residents from all faiths and walks of life[2] came together; even the lawmakers who sit on different sides of the House of Commons. European political editor Robin Oakley has this report.

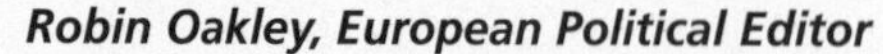

Robin Oakley, European Political Editor

Terrorists can massacre[3] innocent people, Britain's Prime Minister told the country's lawmakers, but they can't destroy the spirit of people as resilient[4] as those in London.

Sunday's 60th anniversary of the end of World War II, said Mr. Blair, had honored the civilian[5] heroes of the city's blitz.[6] And the steely[7] determination is still there.

Tony Blair, British Prime Minister

Today, what a different city London is—a city of many cultures, faiths and races, hardly recognizable from the London of 1945. So different, and yet in the face of[8] this attack, there is something wonderfully familiar in the confident spirit which moves throughout the city, enabling it to take the blow, but still not flinch[9] from reasserting[10] its will to triumph over adversity.[11]

Robin Oakley, European Political Editor

He pledged[12] no rest until the bombers were caught. He promised new laws to counter[13] terrorism. And he insisted security services couldn't be blamed for last Thursday's assault.[14]

CNN 主播

攻擊事件發生之後，倫敦居民不分信仰與職業，全都團結在一起；就連下議院分坐兩邊的議員也是一樣。歐洲政治新聞編輯羅賓．歐克萊帶來這則報導。

歐洲政治新聞編輯 羅賓．歐克萊

英國首相對國會議員指出，恐怖份子可以殘殺無辜民眾，但是像倫敦居民如此堅毅的精神，卻是他們無法摧毀的。

布萊爾先生表示，星期日的二次大戰結束六十週年紀念活動，表彰了倫敦遭受轟炸期間的平民英雄。而當年那種鋼鐵般的意志力，至今依然存在。

英國首相 東尼．布萊爾

今天，倫敦是個多麼不同的城市——是一個融合眾多文化、信仰與種族的城市，和一九四五年的倫敦已截然不同。雖然變化這麼大，但在這次攻擊事件裡，這個城市所散發出來的自信精神卻又如此熟悉，使其不但禁得起打擊，同時又不怯於再次展現其克服逆境的毅力。

歐洲政治新聞編輯 羅賓．歐克萊

他矢言不抓到炸彈客絕不罷休，也承諾訂定新法案對抗恐怖主義。另外，他還堅決表示上星期四的攻擊事件不能責怪軍警單位。

Notes & Vocabulary

united front 聯合陣線

標題中 united front 指「聯合陣線」，通常指數個立場、意見不同的團體或個人，因彼此擁有某種共通的利害關係，而暫時放下原本的歧異，結盟聯合對付共同的對手。政治上常可看到這個詞，像民初國共合作北伐打倒軍閥，之後又於中日戰爭（Sino-Japanese War）中聯手抗敵，史上分別稱為「第一次、第二次國共聯合陣線」（The First/Second United Front），就是典型的例子。

- Bill and Rita formed a united front when they approached their boss for a raise.
  比爾和麗塔組成聯合陣線，向老闆要求加薪。

take the blow 承擔打擊

blow 在這裡指的是「（用拳頭或武器等）一擊；毆打」，此語類似的用法有 take a hit、take one for the team。

- When Evan's store burned down, he took the blow and worked hard to start over.
  伊凡的店燒掉時，他接受了這個打擊、努力重新開始。

1. put aside [pʊt] [əˋsaɪd] *v.* 撇開；把⋯⋯放在一邊
2. walk of life *phr.* 行業
3. massacre [ˋmæsɪkɚ] *v.* 屠殺；殘殺
4. resilient [rɪˋzɪljənt] *adj.* 堅韌的；能迅速恢復的
5. civilian [səˋvɪljən] *adj.* 平民的；百姓的
6. blitz [blɪts] *n.* 閃電戰；全面攻擊
7. steely [ˋstilɪ] *adj.* 鋼鐵般的
8. in the face of *phr.* 面對；儘管
9. flinch [flɪntʃ] *v.* 畏懼；退縮
10. reassert [͵riəˋsɝt] *v.* 再斷言；重申
11. adversity [ədˋvɝsətɪ] *n.* 災禍；逆境
12. pledge [plɛdʒ] *v.* 許諾；使保證
13. counter [ˋkaʊntɚ] *v.* 反擊；還擊
14. assault [əˋsɔlt] *n.* 攻擊；襲擊

Dominic Armstrong, Aegis Security Expert

Britain in many ways is the envy[15] of a lot of countries because it has a system that analyses threat across all the different agencies and all those involved in this, called the Joint Terrorism Analysis Centre, JTAC, that is able to call on all the different intelligence agencies, the police, and others with a contribution to make. They communicate relatively seamlessly[16] and without any of the political baggage[17] that is sometimes associated with these sorts of entities.[18]

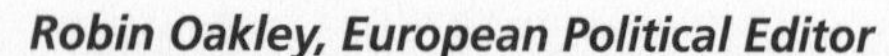

Robin Oakley, European Political Editor

Parliament was anxious for detail, but united in its revulsion[19] of the slaughter of the innocent. And the opposition leader who'd suggested an enquiry[20] into how the bombers had got through, insisted there was no question of blaming anyone. The terrorists, he said, had failed in their aim of dividing British society. He was startlingly[21] generous to an old foe.[22]

Michael Howard, Conservative Party Leader

And I want to begin by paying tribute to the Prime Minister for the calm, resolute[23] and statesmanlike[24] way in which the government responded to the attack last Thursday.

神盾保險公司專家 多明尼克．阿姆斯壯

英國在許多方面都是很多國家羨慕的對象，因為英國有一個研判威脅的體系，能夠跨越所有不同機構以及所有相關人員。這個體系叫作聯合恐怖活動分析中心，簡稱 JTAC。該中心能夠要求各個情報機構、警方、以及其他握有情報的機關提供資訊。他們之間的溝通相當順暢，而且也沒有這類機構所通常必須背負的政治包袱。

歐洲政治新聞編輯 羅賓．歐克萊

國會雖然急著想知道細節，但是所有議員對於殘害無辜的行為都同感憤慨。反對黨領袖儘管提議對炸彈客如何能夠進入大眾運輸工具展開調查，卻也堅稱沒有怪罪任何人的問題。他表示，恐怖份子企圖分裂英國社會的目的沒有得逞。他對老對手的寬容程度令人訝異。

保守黨領袖 麥可．霍爾德

首先，對於首相以冷靜、堅決而且具備政治家風範的態度因應上星期四的攻擊事件，我要表達敬意。

Notes & Vocabulary

pay tribute to 公開讚揚感謝

tribute 這個字原意指「貢品、貢金」，而 pay tribute to 自然是指「納貢」了。番邦向大國天朝進貢，多半是為了對其表示尊敬和感激（至少表面上是如此），因而發展出「致敬」、「歌功頌德」的意義。其同義詞為 pay homage to。

- Community leaders paid tribute to local soldiers serving overseas.
  社會領袖向在海外服役的本國軍人表示感謝。

15. **envy** [ˋɛnvɪ] *n.* 令人羨慕的對象
16. **seamlessly** [ˋsimləslɪ] *adv.* 無縫地
17. **political baggage** [pəˋlɪtɪkl̩] [ˋbægɪdʒ] *n. phr.* 政治包袱
18. **entity** [ˋɛntətɪ] *n.* 實體；本質
19. **revulsion** [rɪˋvʌlʃən] *n.* 嫌惡；強烈反感
20. **enquiry** [ɪnˋkwaɪrɪ] *n.* 調查；詢問
21. **startlingly** [ˋstɑrtlɪŋlɪ] *adv.* 驚人地；使人驚奇地
22. **foe** [fo] *n.* 敵人；仇敵
23. **resolute** [ˋrɛzəˏlut] *adj.* 堅定的；堅決的；不屈不撓的
24. **statesmanlike** [ˋstetsmənˏlaɪk] *adj.* 有政治家風範的

Robin Oakley, European Political Editor

Over 30 years, I've seen the British parliament at its best and at its worst. High drama and low politics. But rarely have I seen it so united. Lawmakers came together instinctively[25] in revulsion against fanaticism,[26] determined not to let terrorists undermine[27] British values or the British way of life. For once, government and opposition said no finger-pointing, no blame, and showed an eagerness to work together. It won't last, but they really meant it and those of us who heard them won't forget it.

歐洲政治新聞編輯 羅賓．歐克萊

過去三十年來，我看過英國國會最好與最壞的一面，有令人激昂的高潮和下流的政治操作。不過，我卻很少看到英國國會這麼團結。國會議員本能地共同譴責狂熱主義，堅決不讓恐怖份子破壞英國價值或者英國人的生活方式。這一次，政府與反對黨共同表示沒有責任追究及責怪，且展現出積極合作的意願。這種情況不會持久，但是他們確實真心誠意，而我們聽到這些發言之後，也不會忘記他們的表現。

Notes & Vocabulary

finger-pointing 指責；責怪

當我們在指責別人的時候，時常會伸出食指來，指著別人說話，英文的說法就是 point the finger at，文中的用法則是藉由連字號把這個動詞片語轉化成名詞。

- Newspaper reports pointed the finger at politicians who had accepted bribes.
  報紙報導指責那些收賄的政客。

25. **instinctively** [ɪn`stɪŋktɪvlɪ] *adv.* 本能地；憑直覺地
26. **fanaticism** [fə`nætəˏsɪzəm] *n.* 狂熱
27. **undermine** [ˏʌndɚ`maɪn] *v.* 暗中破壞；侵蝕……的基礎

Rotten Apples

Cheap iPad Rip-Offs Are Big Business in China's Tech Markets

到底誰抄誰？山寨平板電腦與 iPad 的羅生門

如果你是使用 MP3 ，請聽 MP3 Track 125；如果你是使用電腦互動光碟，請點選 DVD-ROM【實戰應用篇—Part II：Unit 16】，試試看是否聽懂新聞內容。

Step 2 請瀏覽下列關鍵字彙，再仔細聽一次。

incidentally 偶然；附帶地	lawsuit 訴訟
gizmo 小玩意兒；小裝置	run-down 破舊的；失修的
sensation 引起轟動的人（或事物）	devastating 破壞性極大的
sprawling 廣大的；蔓延的	decline 謝絕；委婉拒絕

如果還不是很了解的話，請參考下列提示，再仔細聽一次。

連音	first tablet、it's sold、tablet to hit、this small
同化音	want to know、ripped off
弱化音	cheaper、either、similar、consider this
省略音	locally made、about this、I don't think、factory、declined to comment

試著作答下列聽力測驗題目。

True or False 是非題

____ 1. Apple's iPad is the very first tablet computer to hit the market.

____ 2. The alternatives to the iPad in China are more expensive.

____ 3. The Apple iPad caused a sensation when it was released in China.

____ 4. Wu Yei-bin only needed 90 days to make the J10 tablet.

____ 5. One manufacturer says that his P88 tablet is for adults.

____ 6. Apple sold far less than 300,000 iPads on their first day.

Multiple Choice 選擇題

____ 1. Why can't people in China get an iPad?

a. There aren't enough of them.
b.It doesn't work there.
c. It is too expensive.
d. It isn't for sale there.

____ 2. What does Apple's iPad cause everywhere it is sold?

a. a rise in prices   b. a sensation
c. a parade   d. unhappy people

____ 3. What is TRUE about the electronic markets in Shenzhen?

a. They are empty.   b. They are big.
c. They are the holy grail.   d. They look like an iPad.

____ 4. How long does it take Mr. Wu to make 300,000 tablets?

a. one month   b. one week
c. one year   d. one day

試著用較慢的速度，再聽一遍（MP3 Track 126），檢查答案是否正確。

對答案、驗收成果，並詳讀原文，若仍有不懂的地方，可反覆多聽幾次。

（答案請見 p. 314）

Charles Hodson, CNN Anchor

Well, Apple's device is by no means the first tablet computer. In China, where incidentally[1] the iPad still hasn't been released, CNN's John Vause looks at the alternatives with a much cheaper price tag.

John Vause, CNN Int'l Correspondent

Can't get an iPad? No problem.

The iRobot. Oh, OK.

This is the iWeb?

Unidentified Male

Uh, iPad.

John Vause, CNN Int'l Correspondent

It's like an iPad.

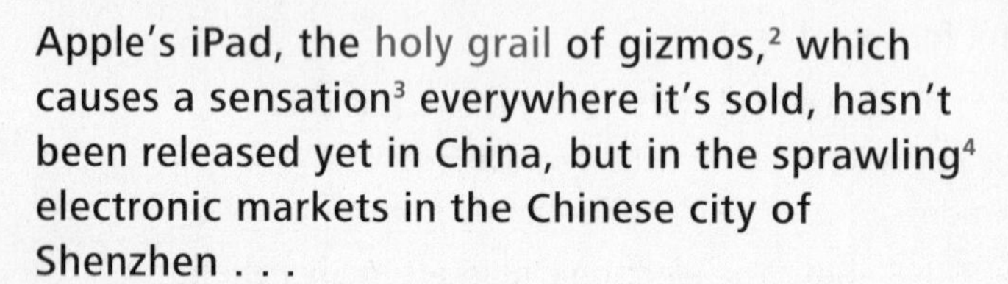

Apple's iPad, the holy grail of gizmos,[2] which causes a sensation[3] everywhere it's sold, hasn't been released yet in China, but in the sprawling[4] electronic markets in the Chinese city of Shenzhen . . .

It looks the same.

Unidentified Male

Yes.

John Vause, CNN Int'l Correspondent

There's no shortage of locally made wannabes.[5]

That's pretty good.

Does Apple know about this?

And they're cheap.

Best price.

CNN 主播　察爾斯．哈德遜

蘋果的裝備絕不是第一台平板電腦。iPad 仍未在中國上市，本台約翰．沃斯帶我們去中國看看價格更便宜的替代品。

CNN 國際特派員　約翰．沃斯

買不到一台 iPad 嗎？沒問題。

iRobot。嗯，好。

這是 iWeb 嗎？

不知名男士

嗯，iPad。

CNN 國際特派員　約翰．沃斯

這很像 iPad。

蘋果推出的 iPad 是大家夢寐以求的發明，在各銷售地點無不造成轟動。雖然 iPad 仍未在中國上市，但是在中國深圳市廣大的電子市場裡……

這看起來簡直是一模一樣。

不知名男士

是啊。

CNN 國際特派員　約翰．沃斯

這台中國製的仿製品幾乎沒有任何缺點。

這台真的不錯。

蘋果公司知道這件事嗎？

而且它們相當便宜。

最好的價格。

Notes & Vocabulary

by no means　絕不；一點也不

名詞 means 是「方法；手段」的意思，片語 by no means 則是「絕不；一點也不」的意思。其他與 means 連用的片語有 by all means「無論如何；沒問題」；beyond one's means「超出某人可以負擔的」。

- The team is good, but it is by no means the best in the league.
  這支隊伍很不錯，但絕不是全聯盟最棒的。

holy grail　渴望得到的東西

Holy Grail 是中世紀傳說中耶穌在最後晚餐（the Last Supper）中用的聖杯，具有可使人重生的神奇魔力，騎士紛紛追尋這只杯子，因此後來 holy grail 便被引申用來指「渴望得到或努力追尋的東西、目標或理想」。

- A universal cancer drug is considered the holy grail of medical research.
  萬用治癌藥被視為醫藥研究追求的目標。

1. **incidentally** [ˏɪnsəˋdɛntəlɪ] *adv.* 偶然；附帶地
2. **gizmo** [ˋgɪzmo] *n.* 小玩意兒；小裝置
3. **sensation** [sɛnˋseʃən] *n.* 引起轟動的人（或事物）
4. **sprawling** [ˋsprɔlɪŋ] *adj.* 廣大的；蔓延的
5. **wannabe** [ˋwɑnəˏbɪ] *n.* 崇拜模仿的對象

So, $140.

And how much is this? $175.

Seven hundred, 700 RMB.

Unidentified Male

Yeah. Very cheap, yeah.

John Vause, CNN Int'l Correspondent

This is $100?

All the tablet PCs we saw ran on either Android or Windows.

I don't think it's working. Some better than others.

It looks like a great big iPhone.

Wu Yei-bin boasts it took just three months for his J10 tablet to hit the market. Next month he hopes to sell a new generation more like an iPad, he says, but with enough differences to avoid an Apple lawsuit.[6]

So, some people might want to know if you have any moral[7] qualms,[8] any problems with what seems to be kind of a rip-off of an Apple product?

"I'm not copying from them," he says. "I'm only following them and producing something similar."

And at this small, run-down[9] factory complex in Southern China, the makers of a tablet PC say they, too, have been ripped off, only in this case, the accusations[10] are being leveled[11] at Apple.

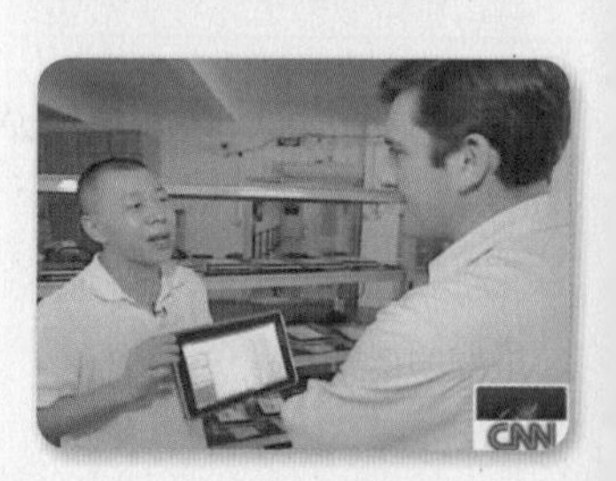

一百四十塊美金。

那這多少錢呢？一百七十五元美金。

七百元，七百塊人民幣。

不知名男子

是的，非常地便宜。

CNN 國際特派員 約翰．沃斯

這只要一百美金？

我們看到的所有平板電腦都可在 Android 或 Windows 的作業系統下運作。

我認為這不可行。有一些品質比較好。

這看起來就像是放大版的 iPhone。

吳業濱（音譯）誇口說他的 J10 平板電腦只需三個月便可上市。他表示希望下個月可以販售新一代更像 iPad 的產品，但卻有足夠差異以避開蘋果公司的訴訟。

所以，有些人可能會想知道你是否有任何道德上的疑慮，看起來有點像蘋果產品的仿製品會不會有問題呢？

「我並不是抄襲他們。」他表示：「我只是依循他們的模式，生產類似的產品。」

中國南方的這間小型破舊工廠是平板電腦製造工廠，他們表示他們也被仿冒，只不過在這個案例中，控訴卻是矛頭指向蘋果公司。

Notes & Vocabulary

rip-off 剝削；欺騙；偷竊；冒牌貨

rip-off 作名詞可指「（因剝削而造成的）物非所值的東西；偷竊；欺騙」等等，也可延伸表示「冒牌貨」。

動詞片語 rip off 的意思則因受詞而異，rip sb off 是指「剝削；欺騙某人」，而 rip sth off 則是指「偷竊；剽竊某物」。

- Some unscrupulous vendors will rip off their customers.
  有些不誠實的攤販會欺騙客人。
- Someone broke into my car and ripped off my GPS.
  有人破車而入偷走了我的全球定位系統。

6. **lawsuit** [ˋlɔ͵sut] *n.* 訴訟；官司
7. **moral** [ˋmɔrəl] *adj.* 道義上的；道德上的
8. **qualm** [kwɑlm] *n.* 顧慮；不安
9. **run-down** [ˋrʌn͵daʊn] *adj.* 破舊的；失修的
10. **accusation** [͵ækjəˋzeʃən] *n.* 指控；控告
11. **level** [ˋlɛvəl] *v.*（尤指用槍）瞄準；對準

Zan Wu says he's been selling his P88 for more than a year. "This is for grownups," he says. "iPads are for kids."

And Mr. Wu says he's gathering evidence for possible legal action.

"When Apple released its new product, everyone around the world started pointing fingers at us, saying we're the fake[12] version of the iPad. It was devastating,"[13] he says.

Apple declined[14] to comment on the accusation, but consider this: Mr. Wu can make about 300,000 tablet PCs a year. That's how many iPads were sold on their very first day, making a potential legal case a battle between a giga-Goliath and a nano-David.

吳展（音譯）表示他販售他的 P88 一年多了。他表示：「這是給大人用的，而 iPad 是給小朋友用的。」

吳先生表示他正在蒐集可能採取法律行動的相關證據。

他說：「當蘋果發行他們的新產品時，全世界的人都在指責我們，說我們的產品是 iPad 的仿冒品，此說法殺傷力相當大。」

蘋果拒絕回應這項指控，但是想想看：吳先生每年可製造出三十萬台平板電腦。這個數字可是 iPad 在上市日當天的銷售數字，這也形成潛在的一場小蝦米對上大鯨魚的法律訴訟案件。

Notes & Vocabulary

point fingers at 指責；責怪

字面意思是「把手指指向……」，常是罵人時指著對方的動作，因此引申表示「指責、責怪某人」，亦可寫成 point the/one's finger at。

- Some parents point their fingers at video games as a source of violence and anti-social behavior.
  有些家長指責電玩遊戲是暴力及反社會行為的源頭。

giga-Goliath and nano-David 小蝦米對上大鯨魚

在舊約聖經中，有一篇《大衛和歌利亞》（David and Goliath）的故事，講述一位名叫 David 的年青人，用彈弓（sling）和五顆石頭擊敗全副武裝的巨人 Goliath。後來 goliath 亦用來指「巨人；巨擘；巨亨」，而 David and Goliath 常被用來比喻「相差懸殊的對抗」，類似中文俚語所說的「小蝦米對上大鯨魚」。文中更運用了 giga（十億）與 nano（十億分之一）這兩種表示極大、極小的度量單位來強調懸殊對比。

12. **fake** [fek] *adj.* 冒充的；偽造的
13. **devastating** [ˋdɛvəˏstetɪŋ] *adj.* 破壞性極大的
14. **decline** [dɪˋklaɪn] *v.* 謝絕；委婉拒絕

NOTES

實戰應用篇 Part I

Unit 1
是非題：1.T 2.F 3.T 4.F 5.F
選擇題：1.b 2.c 3.d

Unit 2
是非題：1.T 2.T 3.F 4.T 5.T
選擇題：1.b 2.a 3.c

Unit 3
是非題：1.F 2.T 3.F 4.T 5.F
選擇題：1.c 2.b 3.c

Unit 4
是非題：1.F 2.T 3.T 4.F 5.T
選擇題：1.c 2. a 3.c

Unit 5
是非題：1.F 2.T 3.F 4.F 5.F
選擇題：1.d 2.c 3.d

Unit 6
是非題：1.F 2.T 3.F 4.T 5.F
選擇題：1.d 2.b 3.a

Unit 7
是非題：1.F 2.T 3.T 4.F 5.F
選擇題：1.b 2. c 3.a

Unit 8
是非題：1.T 2.F 3.F 4.F 5.F
選擇題：1.b 2.c 3.a

Unit 9
是非題：1.T 2.F 3.T 4.F 5.F
選擇題：1.d 2.b 3.b

Unit 10
是非題：1.T 2.F 3.F 4.F 5.T
選擇題：1.d 2.c 3.a

Unit 11
是非題：1.F 2.T 3.F 4.F 5.T
選擇題：1.c 2.b 3.d

Unit 12
是非題：1.F 2.T 3.F 4.F 5.F
選擇題：1.c 2.a 3.c

Unit 13
是非題：1.F 2.T 3.T 4.F 5.T
選擇題：1.c 2.b 3.d

Unit 14
是非題：1.F 2.T 3.F 4.T 5.F
選擇題：1.b 2.c 3.d

Unit 15
是非題：1.T 2.F 3.T 4.F 5.T
選擇題：1.c 2.d 3.a

Unit 16
是非題：1.F 2. F 3.F 4.T 5.T
選擇題：1.b 2. d 3.a

實戰應用篇 Part II

Unit 1
是非題： 1. T 2. F 3. F 4. T 5. F 6. T
選擇題： 1. d 2. b 3. a 4. b

Unit 2
是非題： 1. F 2. T 3. F 4. T 5. F 6. F
選擇題： 1. d 2. b 3. c 4. a

Unit 3
是非題： 1. F 2. T 3. F 4. F 5. T 6. T
選擇題： 1. d 2. b 3. a 4. c

Unit 4
是非題： 1. T 2. F 3. F 4. F 5. T 6. F
選擇題： 1. b 2. c 3. d 4. a

Unit 5
是非題： 1. F 2. F 3. T 4. F 5. T 6. F
選擇題： 1. a 2. b 3. d 4. b

Unit 6
是非題： 1. T 2. F 3. F 4. F 5. T 6. T
選擇題： 1. d 2. b 3. a 4. c

Unit 7
是非題： 1. T 2. F 3. T 4. F 5. F 6. T
選擇題： 1. c 2. b 3. d 4. a

Unit 8
是非題： 1. T 2. T 3. F 4. F 5. F 6. F
選擇題： 1. d 2. b 3. c 4. c

Unit 9
是非題： 1. F 2. T 3. F 4. T 5. T 6. F
選擇題： 1. a 2. d 3. b 4. d

Unit 10
是非題： 1. F 2. T 3. T 4. F 5. F 6. F
選擇題： 1. c 2. b 3. b 4. c

Unit 11
是非題： 1. T 2. F 3. F 4. T 5. F 6. F
選擇題： 1. c 2. b 3. a 4. d

Unit 12
是非題： 1. F 2. F 3. F 4. T 5. F 6. T
選擇題： 1. b 2. a 3. a 4. d

Unit 13
是非題： 1. T 2. F 3. T 4. F 5. T 6. F
選擇題： 1. a 2. c 3. d 4. d

Unit 14
是非題： 1. F 2. F 3. F 4. T 5. F 6. F
選擇題： 1. b 2. d 3. c 4. c

Unit 15
是非題： 1. T 2. F 3. F 4. T 5. T 6. F
選擇題： 1. c 2. b 3. b 4. a

Unit 16
是非題： 1. F 2. F 3. F 4. T 5. T 6. F
選擇題： 1. d 2. b 3. b 4. c

國家圖書館出版品預行編目資料

STEP BY STEP 聽懂 CNN / 陳豫弘, 王琳詔總編輯
--再版. --臺北市：希伯崙公司, 2011.05
面；　公分

ISBN 978-986-6406-95-9（平裝附光碟片）

1. 新聞英語 2. 讀本

805.18　　　　100007293

光碟黏貼處

《STEP BY STEP 一聽懂 CNN 全新增修版》讀者回函卡

謝謝您購買 LiveABC 互動英語系列產品

如果您願意，請您詳細填寫下列資料，免貼郵票寄回LiveABC即可獲贈《CNN互動英語》、《Live互動英語》、《每日一句週報》電子學習報3個月期（價值：900元）及LiveABC不定期提供的最新出版資訊。

姓名		性別	□男 □女
出生日期	年 月 日	聯絡電話	
住址	□□□		
E-mail			
學歷	□國中以下 □國中 □高中 □大專及大學 □研究所		
職業	□學生 □資訊業 □工 □商 □服務業 □軍警公教 □自由業及專業 □其他＿＿＿		

您從何處得知本書？
□書店 □網站 □電子型錄 □他人推薦 □雜誌 □其他＿＿＿

您以何種方式購得此書？
□一般書店 □連鎖書店 □網路 □郵局劃撥 □其他＿＿＿

您覺得本書的價格？ □偏低 □合理 □偏高

您對本書的評價

	書名	封面	內容	編排	紙張
很滿意	□	□	□	□	□
還不錯	□	□	□	□	□
普　通	□	□	□	□	□
不滿意	□	□	□	□	□
很後悔	□	□	□	□	□

您希望我們製作哪些學習主題？

您對我們的建議：

黏 貼 處

廣告回信
台北郵局登記證
台北廣字1194號

105

台北市松山區八德路三段32號12樓

希伯崙股份有限公司客戶服務部 收

縣市

市區
鄉鎮

村路
里街

段

鄰巷

弄

號

樓

室